Fate of the God Stones

JENNIFER ABRAHAMSEN

DEDICATION

This book is dedicated to all of us who have felt as if we don't belong, even if it was only for a short time. If you haven't already, I hope you find your tribe.

PROLOGUE

*T*he rulers of Skalve held their kingdom in a tenuous grip. Although their reign had lasted hundreds of years, the Larsen family could ensure the future of their people no longer. The weather was turning colder year by year and the growing season was becoming too short to produce enough crops to sustain life through the winters. Wildlife, once a staple of the people's diet in the colder months, was migratory now, following its food south once the snow started falling.

The old gods of this land were to blame for the kingdom's circumstances. Krieg Larsen landed boats on the shores of Skalve hundreds of years prior and immediately fell under the attack of the gods. From the land, the sea and the air, the gods struck down more than half of the explorers and soldiers in Krieg's scouting party. The remaining members managed to land their boats on the sandy shores and hide within the dense forests.

Over time, the pioneering community grew and commenced trade with local tribes who worshipped the gods of the land. The tribe members shared information about the serpent-like deities and their magic, and the Skalven people learned how to deter, and later how to kill, those deities. Sightings of the gods became scarce and the Skalven people grew in power. Land was cleared and cities were built. The native population was pushed north and disregarded, as their knowledge of the old gods and of the land was no longer needed.

Now, the old gods were seeking revenge. At least, that was what the counselors to the king and queen believed. Since the old gods had power over the weather and elements, the advisors decided the gods must have devised a plan to retake the land that they once roamed. If the advisors were correct, then the deities had no need to make their presence known. They were slowly casting the Skalven people out from afar, and no one knew where that far-away place was.

King Palden and his wife, Queen Brynn, called in their eldest subjects and questioned them meticulously about the old gods. Scholars consulted every text held in the royal library as they attempted to create a plan to end the attack wrought by the unseen forces. In the end, the collective investigation determined that the only way to fight off the deities was to lure them back to Skalve and engage in battle. A strategy was set in motion.

CHAPTER 1: LANDIS

The halls of Blackwell Palace were nearly silent in the predawn hours. Prince Landis Larsen, sole heir to the Skalven throne, tried to contain his excitement for the upcoming excursion. As commander of the Skalven army, his orders were to take a large contingent of troops south in search of precious artifacts. As he understood it, the purpose of the relics was to draw the old gods of the land back to the kingdom where they could be killed and Skalve would prosper once again.

Skalve was a kingdom of several cities, spread out over hundreds of square miles. The city of Broen was at the relative center of the domain, and home to Blackwell Palace. Primitive villages dotted the surrounding landscape, but the tribal people who occupied them kept to themselves. Those villages did not seem to experience the same lack of resources the Skalve were forced to endure.

Landis did not believe in the old gods, or any gods for that matter. Landis put his faith in himself and his desire to accomplish all tasks put before him. He did not believe in magical forces beyond his control. If Landis could not solve a problem, it was simply because he had yet to discover the solution. Nothing was out of his hands or left to fate. His parents viewed the world differently. They had decided the pitiful state of the kingdom was not within their control to change.

The soil in the kingdom had never offered a bounty of nutrients, but even the meager sustenance it had once offered eluded the local farmers. On top of the change in the soil, water had become an issue. In the months where the plants required rain, there was drought, and frequent deluges plagued the land when it should be dry. Between the farmers' accounts and historical texts in the library, Landis felt the answer to the kingdom's environmental plight could be found closer to home, but he would keep his mouth closed about it if it gave the king and queen a reason to send him out into the countryside.

King Palden had read a first-hand account in a diary of one of his ancestors describing the departure of the old gods all those years ago. In the diary, the forgotten relative shared the story of the old gods leaving precious dragon eggs behind when they fled Skalve. The eggs were supposed to maintain the gods' connection to the land.

Landis's mother and father felt the recent colder temperatures and climate issues were the wrath of these forgotten deities. When Palden shared the story of the dragon eggs with his wife, the pair irrationally concluded the connection established by the eggs gave the gods the ability to control the natural elements and the weather from afar. They decided that if Skalve were in possession of those priceless eggs, the gods that created them would rush back to claim the eggs so they could regain their hold over the Skalven people.

Once the deities arrived, the Skalven army would kill them all and restore the climate of the kingdom. At the suggestion of the kingdom's most trusted advisors, the king and queen of Skalve were directing their only child into lands populated by the primitive tribes to discover and retrieve the eggs of mythical serpents, hoping to save the Skalven people from starvation.

Landis did not care what idiocy had provoked his current directive. His focus was solely on mounting his horse and riding out from behind the walls of the kingdom and into the wilderness to explore. This was his chance to prove to his parents that he was capable of leading the army and could eventually be trusted to rule the kingdom. Landis took the reins from the stablehand and nodded his thanks. He mounted and turned his horse to face the troops amassed before the gate. There were over two hundred men at his command, and Landis could not help but feel empowered.

"Men," Landis called, and the troops quieted. "We have been tasked with a mission of great importance. The future of the kingdom rests upon our shoulders and we have no choice but to succeed for the good of our people."

Landis paused to allow the troops to let out a cheer that never came. He noticed two female soldiers whispering to each other, though. He continued his speech.

"It is you men… and women that shall be celebrated upon our return. We are tasked with retrieving jewel-encrusted artifacts crafted in the likeness of dragon eggs. It is said that these marvels are hidden throughout the tribal lands, but it is uncertain how many of them exist. The treasures are held in the temples of the primitive people to the south and guarded out of reverence by the foolish souls who think the artifacts belong to gods. We shall visit these villages and enter the temples. We will return with as many of these priceless and ancient relics as possible."

When the crowd failed to show excitement, Landis injected a little more candor into the conclusion of his speech.

"It is known that these temples are rich with additional treasure. Apart from the eggs, which must be returned to the palace safely, you may take all that you desire!"

At this, the soldiers let out a raucous cheer. A bout of queasiness overtook Landis as he realized the sole motivation for the soldiers under his command was treasure. He had not been aware of how little sense of duty and honor the army had retained. He was confident he could leverage the soldiers' greed into a successful command, but a weight settled upon him at this reminder of how far from greatness his kingdom had fallen.

Landis turned his horse and nodded to a guard to raise the gate. As soon as the bottom of the massive wooden structure rose higher than his animal's ears, Landis led his army out from behind the walls of the city of Broen and along the dirt road towards the tree line.

Over the years, the forest that once surrounded Broen had been systematically cut down to provide building material and fuel for fires. The result was a two-mile trek over a dusty plain before the army would reach the edge of the forest. At the front of the long line of soldiers, Landis was not concerned that his pressed blue uniform would become covered in dust. This concern was for others. Moving at a canter, the stallion carrying Landis kicked up clouds of dust and forced the soldiers behind him to cover their faces with bandanas.

Oblivious and confident, in a way that only a prince in his twenties could be, Landis slowed his horse to a walk when he entered the forest a short time later. Second Commander Samuel Torrence rode up beside Landis when the prince slowed. Torrence pulled his bandana from his face. The cloth emitted a cloud of dust as the commander shook it out before tucking it away. Sam Torrence had led the Skalven army until Landis was appointed to its head for the purpose of the current mission. Landis was reminded the man likely took the demotion personally when he saw the expression on Torrence's face.

"Sir, we can make it to the Serpent River by lunch if we keep a steady pace. It would be an ideal spot to break for food and water."

Landis turned to his second, confusion written on his face. "We are soldiers. Surely the expectation of the men is not one of three meals a day?"

"Sir? This is not a time of war, nor are there any rationing laws in place. The men and women of this army may be soldiers, but they are also people and will require nourishment."

Landis clenched his jaw. His journey toward greatness had barely begun, and he was already being forced to contemplate stalling its forward progress. Still, Torrence was speaking some sense. If the soldiers were expected to complete their task, they could not be weakened by lack of food. Landis nodded his agreement and resigned himself to a break for lunch in just over five hours.

Despite the lack of haste, Landis found pleasure in the ride. It was good traveling weather and Landis felt his lungs open up and welcome air that was not choked with wood smoke. Instead, it held a light, but invigorating, scent of pine.

When the army stopped to rest for the night, tents were erected with practiced speed and the soldiers set about dinner preparations with little direction. Landis's concerns only crept in once the forest was in complete darkness. The prince did not remember packing so many casks of ale. It was the first night away from the palace, though, and Landis expected the troops might need an evening to unwind before getting more serious about the journey.

The following evening, Landis tossed pebbles into the fire burning outside the entrance to his tent. As much as the time to enjoy the scent of wood smoke and lack of courtiers was relaxing, the delay frustrated him. He had not anticipated the amount of time it would take to move an army of this size only fifteen miles. Had Landis been alone, he could have reached this point the day before and been poised to enter the first of the tribal villages when the sun crested the horizon the following day. Instead, he was digesting the fact that it would be afternoon before his fighters saw more than the inside of their eyelids.

The soldiers within the camp were treating the mission as if they were on holiday. After setting up camp on the first night, casks of ale had been tapped, and the camp became filled with the sounds of laughter, as well as the occasional disagreement. Landis had been appalled at the unregimented, disorderly behavior of his men. He had retreated into his tent in disgust and awoke the following morning to find sleeping bodies strewn throughout the camp. The loud snoring from many of the figures dashed Landis's hopes for an early start.

The march had been slow and tedious once it had finally commenced. A foot soldier near the back of the convoy twisted an ankle before the troop had even stopped for lunch. Of course, lunch had been eaten around three because the journey had not started until just before eleven that morning. Once it was evident to Landis that the man with the damaged ankle would be useless, he sent him home on horseback.

Disheartened by his men's lack of honor and less than enthusiastic need to complete the mission, Landis watched the general debauchery unfold in his camp for the second consecutive evening. Commander Torrence appeared from the darkness outside the firelight and sat on one of the rocks beside Landis. The prince was happy to see the commander did not have a cup of ale in his hands, nor did the man smell as if he had recently enjoyed one.

"This is not how this journey was supposed to progress,"

lamented Landis. "I expected to lead the royal army on a gallant mission. Instead, I am barely steering a band of mercenaries on nothing more than a treasure hunt. None of them are taking their duty seriously. I feel as if I could accomplish the task better on my own. I have no need for the greedy lot of them."

Torrence let out a small laugh, but did not comment. He stared into the fire until the prince spoke again several minutes later.

"Seriously, Sam, how did you let these noble men become so undisciplined?"

Torrence sat straighter at the sound of the accusatory tone Landis used. The prince did not notice the offense he caused and continued on.

"I know I am young, but I have been to the training grounds the same as all the men here. I have seen the skillful fighting arts these men possess, and the disciplined response each has displayed when orders are received. Why did you let all that training fall apart?"

Landis watched his second in command take a deep breath and let it out between his barely parted lips. Landis assumed Sam Torrence had no response for his dereliction of responsibility, but Torrence finally replied and the calmness of his answer put Landis further on edge.

"I'm sure the troops are simply excited to be away from the daily demands of the kingdom. Give them time."

"Give them time?" Landis replied exasperatedly. "We'll be entering the Yahkanah village tomorrow. My original plan was to circle around to the far side of the island and approach the temple from the south, unnoticed. The entrance is on the beach, outside of the village. A small band of us could go in and remove the egg kept there without being noticed. Can you imagine anyone in this camp doing anything while remaining undetected? I've known you my whole life, and you are regarded as an excellent commander. I never imagined you would let the army fall apart like this."

Torrence's reply was less calm than his first, but he still kept from raising his voice. "Prince Landis, what do you believe makes an army great?"

"Training, obviously," replied the prince.

"Do you feel this army has had sufficient training?" asked Torrence.

"As I said, I have trained with these men for most of my life. There is no comparison to the quality and breadth of training imparted to these men."

Torrence said, "So, if I understand correctly, you are implying that these men have received the best training available and were turned over to me as top-notch soldiers. You believe that they have grown slack under my leadership and are no longer the elite fighters they once were?"

Landis was arrogant, but he was not stupid. He knew his second in command was baiting him into making an official accusation. Though Landis fully believed that Commander Torrence had allowed the men to become undisciplined and their days unstructured, Landis was not about to say so and give the muscular commander an excuse to become as untamed as the rest of the soldiers. Landis chose his words carefully.

"I am struggling to understand how soldiers I know to be disciplined and capable can lose all sense of duty once out from under the watchful eyes of those who have trained them."

Torrence matched the caution of Landis's words with care of his own. "What is it about those that train our soldiers that makes you feel they are so capable?"

Landis replied quickly and easily. "Leadership! The kingdom ensures that those responsible for training the soldiers have strong leadership qualities. Many of the men who trained me had a way about them that just made you feel as if you had to obey them. The strangest part was that you didn't even resent them for it! I remember feeling as if I *wanted* to do what they told me to do, and I longed for their approval."

Landis stared into the fire, waiting for Torrence to reply. When no reply came, Landis felt the satisfaction of having won the argument. He'd also been able to put the difficulties of his army into words. The Skalven soldiers lacked leadership. Having identified the source of the problem, Landis was more able to tune out the distractions around him and enjoy his small fire.

His pride in identifying the problem ebbed from him. Torrence was not the commander of the army spread out among this camp. True, the man was second in command and was expected to advise Landis, but he would be overstepping his bounds if Torrence took control of the entire army. That was a task reserved for the first commander. It was the task allotted to Landis. Landis felt his heart grow heavy as he realized it was he who lacked the ability to lead successfully. Landis had expected the army to do as they were trained to do. He had tried to *command* the army, as his title implied he should, instead of inspiring the men and women of the army to follow him.

A ceramic jug smashed to the ground off to the left, and Landis looked up to see one of his men stagger and trip over a woman sitting by the fire. His soldiers were drunk again. He was now sure it was his own lack of leadership skills that had allowed his camp to become this disorganized, but he had no idea how to fix the problem. Landis got up from his log and trudged to his tent. Though he would be up around dawn, he knew he would have until close to noon to decide how the army would approach the village.

CHAPTER 2: MEARA

*T*he sun beat down on Meara's mottled skin and she wished, not for the first time, that she looked like the other tribe members. The deep reddish-hued skin tone, unique to the Yahkanah people, must have developed from a need for protection from the sun's rays. Meara's skin only had some of that protection. She was unsure if her skin was deep brown with bright patches, or pink with dark brown patches. Either way, it was only half-decent at protecting itself from being burned by the sun. Right now, the lighter skin patches were turning red as she sat on the beach drying from her swim.

Meara quickly finger-combed her thick hair so that it fell in long, tangle-free clumps down her back. This would be the only time today that her hair behaved. Once her hair dried, it would have a mind of its own, showing off the two-inch wide lock of bright white, where her hair lacked pigment. Once dry, her hair would need to be braided back or she would contemplate cutting it all off to keep it out of her face. Other than when it was damp, Meara only wore her hair loose when she attended village meetings or ceremonies. The untamed locks helped hide the mottled skin on her face and enabled Meara to draw less unwanted attention.

She donned her deerskin dress, struggling to pull it past the places on her skin that were still wet. To hide more of her unique skin, Meara wore her dresses down to her ankles, longer than the other women of the tribe, and took the time to sew sleeves for all of her garments. The extra material often caused Meara to overheat, and she found respite by stripping off her clothes at the beach for a swim at the hottest point in the day if no one else was around. The battle between cool water and the tropical sun on her skin would then begin. Meara found the trick was to know exactly when the breeze evaporating the moisture from her skin began to lose the fight to the sun's rays trying to scorch off her epidermis.

Meara held her slippers in her left hand as she used her right to hold the trunks of the trees she passed while picking her way back to the outskirts of her village from the beach. The relaxing sound of the waves rolling in gave way to the sounds of civilization. With those fresh sounds, tension crept back into her body. Meara walked the outskirts of the small village until she reached the grass hut where she lived with Mamma Jade. As Meara drew near, she heard voices from within.

Mamma Jade said, "How long have you known of this?"

A male voice replied, "At least a day. Our scouts have seen evidence of the bush being disturbed outside of our hunting grounds. We thought it might be a nomadic tribe passing through the area. I'm only bringing it to your attention now because the remnants of a camp were found. The tools and detritus left behind were not tribal. They were Skalven."

Meara sat near the side of the hut, trying not to make a sound. This was a conversation she did not want to interrupt, nor did she want to miss it.

"Skalven?" Mamma Jade sounded surprised. "How could you know the camp was of their people?"

"No tribe in harmony with the land would leave evidence of

a camp at all. They especially would not leave behind broken utensils or tools."

Mamma Jade was pensive for a moment and then agreed. "It sounds like Skalven people from the north. The reckless treatment of the land would not stem from a tribal people. If they are not Skalven, then it would mean another group of people has invaded our land. I do not wish to think that is the case, though. You and your hunting party must be careful, but it would be helpful to know the intentions of the people who are moving among us on our lands. Collect reports from those arriving with off-island scouting and hunting parties."

Abruptly, the man exited the tent and turned around to the side of the hut where Meara was sitting. She startled when the man nearly stepped on her. He stood eyeing her face for a moment, his lip pulled back in disgust, then stepped around Meara and continued on.

"You can stop listening to whispers now, child," Mamma Jade called from within the hut.

Meara stood and entered the hut, keeping her eyes lowered to show respect, she was engulfed in the home's familiar scent of herbs. As the tribal elder, Mamma Jade held a position of honor, but even more so as a female. The Yahkanah people believed females were closer to nature than males because of their ability to bring life into the world. Meara was unsure how she felt about that. She had never known a woman to usher in life without a man doing his part as well, but she was in no position to argue with tradition.

Mamma Jade was both mother and grandmother to Meara. The elder had discovered Meara's swaddled form on the beach of the island community twenty-five years ago. At that point in Mamma Jade's life, the woman had been better able to make the short trek to the ocean. Lately, it was a struggle for her to exit their hut.

Mamma Jade had never married. Dedication to a man would be unbefitting of a priestess such as herself. It was Mamma Jade's calling to commune with nature and protect the tribe's link to the deities. Since Mamma Jade could no longer walk to the temple, those wishing to ask for guidance came to the hut. It was left to Meara, as an extension of Mamma Jade's connection to the gods and goddesses, to visit the temple and see to its upkeep.

"Sit, child," said Mamma Jade. "Let us speak plainly. I know you heard the young man's report. Do you have any thoughts on the matter?"

As wise as Mamma Jade was, she always included Meara in her ruminations. Meara's only source of pride was the trust Mamma Jade put into her opinions. It made her feel as if she mattered. This was made even more meaningful to Meara because the rest of the village ignored her. Well, most ignored her. Some of the more vocal tribe members called her names and threw curses of banishment her way when Meara walked by. Mamma Jade had tried to instill the understanding that people feared those who were different. The support had helped over the years, but only a little.

"I think it's a scouting party," said Meara. "The Skalven are probably moving to take more land."

"Truly, you don't believe that is the reason for their incursion? We inhabit a small island. What could the Skalven want with it?"

"The island of Innut is where we dwell, but our hunting lands stretch to the south and west. If the Skalven need food, they may desire our hunting lands for themselves."

"True enough," said Mamma Jade. "One would think the warmer hunting ground to the west of the Skalven city of Broen would be a more desirable acquisition, though. Our lands grow sparse in the winter months. I cannot support your argument that they are here for the land. I fear there is another cause driving their movements."

The two women sat in silence. Mamma Jade motioned for Meara to turn her back to her and the elderly woman began weaving braids into Meara's drying hair. As usual, Mamma Jade separated the white lock of hair into its own braid. Once she had created multiple braids from Meara's dark hair, Mamma Jade used the white braid to tie them back, wrapping it around the others, and then tucking it back under itself. Meara turned to face Mamma Jade and the old woman smiled.

"I wish I could see your full beauty, child. These eyes have seen better days, but I can still see your radiance shining through."

It was Meara's turn to smile. The woman before her was the only reason she had for continuing life here among the tribe members. She was unsure what she had done to earn Mamma Jade's love, but Meara was grateful to the gods for every ounce of it. The deep sound of a throat clearing at the entrance to the hut startled Meara, and she twisted toward the doorway.

"Mamma Jade, may I have a word?"

The man looking for Mamma Jade's attention was Lokar. He was five years older than Meara and the grandson of Saff, the tribe's male elder. If Saff had been born female, he would be the one advising the people of the village and getting visits from the tribal scouts. Meara thought of Saff's kin as the second most powerful family within the village, though there was no tradition that recognized them as such.

Lokar sat cross-legged, facing Mamma Jade, but his eyes remained on Meara. Feeling the weight of his stare, Meara excused herself and began to get to her feet. On her way up, her foot caught something and Meara sprawled face first, facing the doorway. She rolled over onto her back and saw her foot was snared by the strap of Lokar's hunting pouch. Meara was sure the bag had not been near her moments ago. Lokar barely stifled his laugh as Meara climbed to her feet and exited the hut.

Meara wound her way through the trails to the temple of the gods. The Yahkanah people had worshiped the gods since the time gods used to roam among humans. The inhabitants of Innut Island respected the natural world around them above all else, and their gods controlled all things in nature. No resources were taken from the environment without a thankful prayer thrown out to the gods, and those resources were never squandered.

The stories passed down through the generations of all tribal people living in the southeastern territory depicted the gods as living among their people on the land. Temples, similar to the one Meara was approaching now, were not just places for people to worship the gods, but also places for the gods to live. The tale differed from tribe to tribe as to why the gods abandoned the people, but the reality was the same. There were no gods in any of the temples across the territory and had been none in hundreds of years.

The temple on Innut Island looked just like an ordinary cave from the outside. The space was carved out of the rock face that made up the cliffs north of the beach, where Meara liked to cool herself during the day. Pounding waves had worn the rock away over time and created an entrance to several tunnels that each led to a chamber hidden within the rock. The entrance to the temple was tricky to access at high tide, but at low tide, one could enter the temple without even getting wet.

Meara made her way through ankle-deep water to enter the temple. Sound from the outside world did not permeate the interior of the cave. Her footsteps echoed on the stone floor as she passed the first passageway. Meara knew the layout of this temple better than that of her village. She spent more time here, enjoying the solitude, than anywhere else on the island. The main cavern was plain and offered no evidence that the space was anything other than a sea cave in a cliff face, but Meara knew that almost all the passages ended in chambers filled with precious metals and jewels. If the Skalven people knew the contents of the temple, there would be no doubt why the invaders were camped in the area.

The treasure was worthless to the Yahkanah. Occasionally, someone might twist some silver to adorn a beautiful shell or stone pendant, but the focus of Yahkanah jewelry was never metal. Metal was cold and held little feeling of life. It was this sentiment that carried Meara past each entrance to the treasure chambers. Instead, she took the passage to the only chamber that mattered to her and to the people of the island.

Meara ran her hands over the carvings on the walls of the passage. Torches, kept lit by Meara as part of her duties to care for the temple, illuminated the story of the gods. Meara stopped before one of her favorite scenes. Smok, god of smoke and flame, rained fire on men in boats. There was enough detail in the carving to show the metal helmets on the heads of the terrified men as they tried to paddle away from the giant serpent in the sky. Smok was merciless. His rampage across the territory had left only ash and embers, cleansing the land of more than half the human population.

There was no depiction on the walls of the temple describing what humans had done to enrage the deities. Meara had spent hours analyzing the carvings in her quest to uncover the truth. Mamma Jade, who had been responsible for the upkeep of the temple before Meara, felt the gods and goddesses had simply grown bored with humans and wanted to start over with clean territory, free from the humans' disregard for the land's majesty. It was just as likely a reason for their wrath as any other. They were divine beings, after all. They could act however they wanted.

Further down the passage, Meara leaned against the wall as if to embrace it. The carving beneath her skin was of the Goddess Tala. She controlled the very breath of life. Meara liked to think Tala had created her with a magnificent purpose in mind. She thought of the goddess as the mother she never had. Meara let a little laugh squeeze from her lungs. The story had been comforting when Meara was a child, but now that she was a young woman she believed her life had been a mistake, as opposed to the grand creation of an absent goddess. Still, the memories of her comforting childhood fabrication provided some security to Meara each time she viewed the carving of Tala.

Winding her way to the end of the passage, Meara came to the nest. It was not like any nest created by birds or insects, but a simple stone pillar measuring two square feet. Upon the pillar was the reason this was called the nest; a dragon egg. It held a rock in the shape of a dragon egg, anyway. The stone was about a foot tall and half as wide, with patterned carvings decorating the whole thing. The slightest flat area on the bottom of the God Stone allowed it to sit on its end, but it was impossible to see. To any observer, it looked as if the egg balanced impossibly on the pillar.

The symbolism was obvious to Meara. The carved dragon egg represented rebirth for the gods. They may have left the lands of the humans, but there were new gods waiting to be born. Meara ran her hand over the surface of the rock, letting her fingers fall into the crevices of the carvings. The stone of the egg felt warmer, somehow, than the rock walls of the cave. The edges were smooth, worn down by so many people doing as she had just done. Since there were no gods in the temples anymore, people came to pray and ask for guidance from the gods' children who sat waiting to hatch and take their place as the center of life.

Meara could see why the temple received fewer and fewer visitors. It was damp and dark here. The stone was cold and didn't make one feel hopeful that a pilgrimage to a carved rock might enact any genuine change. Meara *wanted* to believe, but it was hard when she knew she spent more time praying in this temple than anyone and her own tribe still did not accept her.

Meara lifted the rock from its place on the stone pillar and started the walk back up the passageway. The daily trip to bathe the stone in the waters of the land was one aspect of her temple duties. Once she reached the ocean, the rock would need to be submerged in its waters and a prayer said over it. The walk back down the passage holding the rock would be even more arduous than this. At that point, the rock would be wet and a little slippery.

Meara sighed. At least she got to spend time alone when she was performing her duties. The God Stone provided all the companionship she desired. She hadn't seen another human near the temple in years.

CHAPTER 3: LANDIS

*I*n the end, Landis had opted to take a party of only ten soldiers across the waters to the island. There was much grumbling from those soldiers who were not picked for the excursion. Everyone wanted the chance to pillage and grab riches from the island's temple. One man imparted solace to a disgruntled comrade by proclaiming that the prince's inexperience would likely get the raiding party killed, anyhow.

Landis assured the army that all the treasures would be recovered from the temple and brought to the camp on the mainland to be shared. Begrudgingly, those staying behind ceased complaining and returned to sit by fires and fill their bellies, or returned to tents to catch some sleep while they waited for Prince Landis to return with his party.

Once Landis reached the water's edge, it occurred to him that he and his soldiers had no way to cross the water. The prince turned and faced his chosen raiders.

"Well, gentlemen, it seems we shall need to swim."

Without waiting for replies, Prince Landis dropped his weapon belt on the sandy shore, and stripped off his mail. He removed everything but his sword and scabbard from his belt and placed the items in his pack. He strapped the bag to his back and his belt to his waist; making sure the sword would stay in place.

He waded out into the water, lifting his knees to push through the surf as quickly as possible, while considering his own poor planning. He had known they were journeying to an island. In his excitement at taking command of the Skalven army, he had forgone much of what he was taught at the kingdom's war academy. Only now, as the water reached his chest, did Landis admit to himself that the phrase, 'planning wins battles and battles win wars', took on meaning for him. Once he was forced to swim, because the water became too deep for walking, Landis wished he'd realized the mantra had been a warning.

Because he was a prince, Landis had received instruction in swimming since before he toddled around on two feet. He was tired when he reached the shore, but he was not breathing much heavier than usual. Landis removed his belt again and upended his scabbard to be sure no water remained in its depths. He looked around as he replaced his belt around his waist.

To the unknowing eye, there was nothing special about the island. It looked like the shore of the mainland had looked, but it felt different. The air seemed dull in some way. Landis did not feel the energy that should be flowing through him now that he was one step closer to his prize. Instead, he was tempted to find a nice place to sit for a while and collect his thoughts. Was it possible the tranquility of island life had ensnared his spirit so quickly?

Landis turned back to the water to watch his small band of soldiers make its way onto the beach. A wiry warrior named Grundar was the first to drag himself up onto the beach. He did not get to his feet. Instead, he lay face down in the sand with his head turned to the side so he could breathe. Grundar took in large gulps of air each time the waves ran back out toward the sea, and then held his breath when the water ran back in.

Pria was the next to emerge from the water. Having paced herself better than Grundar during the swim, she was able to walk to where Landis stood and sit down beside him. She glared at Landis as she struggled to pull air into her lungs. Landis placed a hand on her shoulder, as if to welcome her to the shore of the island.

"You know," she said as she panted, "I am a woman, right?"

"Of course," said Landis. "What kind of fool do you think I am?"

"The kind that refers to his crew as 'gentlemen' before swimming off without them," Pria said.

Before he could think of an appropriate response to her truculent comment, Landis glanced down the beach and saw that his soldiers were landing in the open. He turned and retreated off the beach and into the safety of the tree line, beckoning for his soldiers to follow. With a small groan, Pria dragged herself to her feet and trailed the prince.

One by one, and with varying degrees of exhaustion, Landis's raiding party joined him among the trees. Landis took the time to get his bearings. The island appeared to be void of other people. The silence outside of the land's civilized areas felt eerie.

Once the soldiers' breathing quieted, Landis laid out the plan for securing the dragon egg from the temple. Considering there were no Skalven people who had ever seen the temple on the island of the Yahkanah people, Landis did his best to sound as if he commanded an understanding of the temple, as well as the island.

"We're going to split our force. The primitives inhabiting this island will be gathered around their small village. Half of us will enter the village as if we intended to pillage there. You may take what you want, though I doubt you will find much of value. The rest of us will travel down the beach to the temple. I assume you know our mission once we are there."

Grundar, recovered from his swim, said, "I noticed your words imply you will be leading the raiding party to the temple. How will you be deciding those of us who will also have first crack at the gold and gems?"

Landis suppressed his urge to lash out at Grundar and tell him he had no right to question a prince. Instead, he took a breath and recalled the conversation he had shared with Torrence about leadership. Drawing on the little patience he possessed, he answered through an only slightly clenched jaw.

"Since there are only eleven of us —"

Grundar cut Landis off. "Nine. There are only nine of us."

"I beg to differ, Grundar. I had the finest tutors in Skalve, and I assure you that the ten soldiers I hand-picked plus myself give us a band of eleven soldiers for our assault."

"I am not arguing with your mathematics, sir," replied Grundar. "I only mean to explain that only nine of us washed up on the beach."

Landis counted the surrounding soldiers. There were indeed only eight others standing within the protection of the trees.

"What happened to the others?" Landis asked.

Pria answered, "Pritchet never made it off the mainland. He doesn't know how to swim. Apparently, Torkel's swimming prowess was not much better. He entered the water, but he never came back out."

"Why would you choose not to inform me before we made the swim? We could have picked two other men for the raid."

Pria stared at Landis disapprovingly. Landis sighed.

"If you had told me we had members of the party who were unable to swim, we could have selected two other men or women."

24

"Maybe, sir, we could have told you about Pritchet, but by the time he said he couldn't swim, you were way out in the water," said Pria. "None of us knew Torkel wouldn't make it."

Landis sighed. He was aware he had been doing that a lot. Her words made sense. He had rushed off into the water without a thought. Impulsivity; that was something else he needed to work on.

"True enough," Landis said. "Since there are only nine of us, you are welcome to draw straws or otherwise determine which of you will travel to the temple. I will need three soldiers with me. I'd prefer if some of the stronger among you pulled the longer straws. Be mindful of the treasure we will be carrying."

Ignoring Landis's request, Pria gathered eight twigs. She left three long and broke the others into shorter lengths. She turned her back and when she faced the soldiers once again, she was holding all eight sticks in her fist so that they all stuck up the same amount. Pria went to each soldier and allowed them to pull a twig from her hand. When Pria opened her fist to check the stick left for her, she found it to be one of the longer ones. The two other long sticks went to Grundar and a muscular soldier named Solvis.

Solvis had almost twenty years on Landis, but was still in better fighting shape than the prince. The prince had never been able to best Solvis during training. Though Solvis had not outright taunted Landis about it, the prince had felt the sentiment emanating from the large man. Landis knew Solvis would be invaluable on the raid, but he had hoped the soldier would have been attacking the village instead of accompanying him to the temple.

As the other group headed deeper into the trees toward the village, Landis led Pria, Grundar and Solvis back out onto the beach. They walked along the tree line, within its shadows, toward the temple on the other side of the island. The hope was that the soldiers attacking the village would keep the tribe occupied, allowing Landis's party to make their way to the far side of the island without being noticed. After several hundred yards, Landis held his hand up to halt those behind him. Solvis, ignoring the command, continued on to step up beside Landis.

Landis ignored Solvis and watched a group of men dressed in deer skins spear-fishing along the water's edge. Each man held a sturdy, slim tree limb, sharpened to a point, and watched the water intently. One of the men stabbed down into the water with his spear and pulled it back to reveal a silver fish, as long as Landis's forearm, wriggling on the point. Landis could not help but be impressed with the skill and wondered if it would translate well to battle. The man turned to bring his catch back to the beach and Landis held his breath, hoping the fisherman did not look in the direction of the soldiers.

Landis need not have worried. Screams came from the center of the island, and Landis knew the other half of his raiding party had arrived at the village. The tribesmen turned when they heard the sound and ran off toward it with their spears gripped in their hands. Landis would need to ask the others how well the primitives wielded those spears while fighting.

Solvis raised his hand in the air and motioned for the group to continue on. Landis stared incredulously in Solvis's direction, but the big warrior gave no indication that he noticed the affront. Landis took a few quick steps to ensure he was at the head of the group.

They continued toward the temple that Landis knew was farther down the beach. There was no way to tell it was a temple just by inspection. A cliff face blocked any progress along the beach at the location. One would need to enter the water to continue around the island. Landis simply felt he had found what he was looking for.

"That's our destination," Landis told the soldiers behind him. "It looks like we will be getting our feet wet. The treasure we seek is within that mass of rock."

"Do we climb it, or is there an entrance?" asked Pria.

"I'm not entirely sure," Landis admitted. "It would be illogical to hide treasure in the open, so I would think there is an entrance to a cave or underground tunnel."

"If you don't even know how we get in, how do you know that is where the treasure is?" asked Solvis.

"I just do," Landis said, in a voice just above a whisper.

As Landis neared the start of the cliff, movement in the water caught his eye and he brought the group to a halt. There was a young woman standing among the rocks, up to her knees and within the waves. She appeared to be scrubbing something heavy. The woman, clad in a deerskin dress that reached below the surface of the water, was struggling to keep hold of a slippery rock. She had the round stone resting atop another flatter rock. She dipped a cloth into the water and then scrubbed one side of the rounded boulder. Each time she attempted to maneuver the stone so she could clean another side, the rock threatened to tumble into the shallows of the sea.

Landis pondered his next course of action. He did not want to kill the woman, but his raiders did not have the luxury of waiting for her to finish her chore. Sounds of battle were still coming from the village, but that would not continue indefinitely. Landis had no way to know if the conclusion of that encounter would provide more time, or require a quick departure from the island.

Pria tapped Landis on the shoulder and interrupted his thoughts. She stared off towards the horizon. Landis followed her line of sight and his eyes widened as he witnessed the sea reaching for the sky. Rolling toward the island was a wave taller than any tower Landis had seen. When that wave hit the beach, it would eradicate anything in its path. Landis broke into a run. If there was an entrance into the temple, it would be close by and the temple might provide the only possible shelter from the wave's destruction.

When Landis splashed into the water where the cliff met the sea, the woman looked up from her task. The rock she had been cleaning tumbled into the water and she bent to retrieve it. Pria saw the entrance to the temple first and shouted to alert the others. Solvis and Grundar changed course and ran for the safety of the cave opening, splashing through the ankle-deep water and slipping on the algae-covered rocks.

Landis entered the cave soon after the rest of his raiders. He saw the tunnel snaked upward. Relief rolled through him as he concluded they would be able to access higher ground. He turned back to check the progress of the wave. It was no longer looming in the far distance. Its proximity had Landis marveling at the speed with which it traveled. The woman, still trying to secure a grip on her stone, had not run for cover. Landis yelled to her and pointed at the rapidly approaching wave. The woman could not hear him.

Landis started running. He was inches from the water when it started retreating from him. With a similar swiftness to the wave, the sea began to flow away from the temple as if to escape back out into the depths. Just before Landis reached the woman, the water pulled back from her and she was able to grab her stone from the ground. She struggled to keep hold of it as she stumbled over the exposed rocks of the shoreline toward the island. Landis made a decision.

He grabbed the woman's arm as he ran by her toward the wave. She cried out when her fingers fumbled with her stone, but she regained her grip on it. With no time to argue about a rock, Landis took the stone from her and dumped it into his sack. It was not as heavy as he had expected. The size of the stone had implied that its weight was the reason the woman had been struggling to carry it, but the rock had simply been slippery. Landis tugged the woman farther from the island until they were back in the water and encouraged her to swim. The wave would have crushed them before they entered the temple. The only way they might survive was to get beyond the wave before it crashed onto land. Thankfully, she swam, and Landis joined her, using powerful, fear-driven strokes to move away from the shore like a deer trying to outrun a mountain cat.

Landis was now swimming up-hill. He lost sight of the woman and could only hope she would be able to save herself. He carved through the water with all the strength he had, trying to get up and over the wave. The feeling he was being pulled back toward the island contended with the distance Landis covered with each stroke. When the pull felt as if it would win, and Landis feared he was about to be smashed into the shoreline as the wave crashed, he took a deep breath and dove deep beneath the surface of the water. He swam almost straight down, trying to escape the currents created by the wave.

To Landis's surprise, the pull on his body subsided, and it was easier to swim. He turned his body in the direction of the surface, still heading away from the island. He swam with all the energy his exhausted body could muster, but he never found the surface. Was he even moving in the correct direction? Landis needed air. His muscles screamed and his throat burned. Landis gave in and took a breath. His lungs filled with water and his vision faded. The only things moving his body were the ocean's currents.

CHAPTER 4: MEARA

*M*eara coughed water into the sand. She was lying on her stomach and barely holding her face away from the ground as she expelled the water from her lungs. Her head hurt, but there was nothing she could do about it at the moment. Her body instinctively made it a priority to make breathing possible, even though each splutter and wretch made her head pound harder. At last, Meara was able to take a breath that did not make her choke. She rolled over onto her side and collapsed into the sand, concentrating on pulling in as much air as possible.

Meara put her hand to the back of her head. There was a lump and her scalp was tender, but when she held her hand before her eyes, she saw no blood. Slowly, Meara sat up and checked the function of her limbs. There was blood leaking from other parts of her body, but none of the wounds seemed serious. She climbed to her feet with effort and swayed. Making her way to the water's edge, Meara sat in the wet sand and scooped water in her hands to wash out her cuts. The salt water burned.

As Meara's senses gradually returned, she contemplated the recent events. She looked around for the blond man who had charged at her and thrown her into the water. She didn't see him. Meara had seen the wave as she plunged into the water. It was too big. There would be little left of the island. Meara looked up into the cloudless blue of the sky. There had not been a storm. There had been no cause for a wave that size. She tried to push concern for Mamma Jade's wellbeing aside and took comfort that she had at least saved the island's most precious item. Her gut turned. Meara climbed to her feet. She had not saved anything. The blond man had the dragon egg in his satchel, and the blond man was not here on the beach.

Meara chose a direction and started walking. Dead or alive, it was likely the man had washed up on the beach as well. Meara needed to find him and hoped the stone was still in the bag he wore across his body. The sun was strong, and the skins of Meara's dress dried as she walked. She kept wringing out parts of the dress with her hands, attempting to keep the leather material from becoming stiff. She was losing the battle when she stopped and sat back down in the sand. Meara tore at the shoulder seams of the dress. Covering her mottled skin was not her highest priority. She needed to be able to move. With the sleeves of the dress removed, Meara started cutting at the skirt of her dress with a broken shell. It was not pretty, but she was able to shorten its length to her knees. On her feet again, Meara found she could cover more ground without the dress hindering her progress. The stiffness of the bodice was still uncomfortable on her skin, but that problem was outweighed by the throbbing in her head.

Miles from where Meara had landed on the beach, she came upon a tangle of driftwood. Buried in the pile was the body of the blond man she was searching for. Meara stood and stared at him for a time, trying to decide if he was breathing. She could not see his chest rising and falling, and she was unable to convince herself to touch him. A broken branch from the wood pile protruded through his chest, just below his right shoulder. If the man had not drowned, he had likely died of his wound. She circled the body and the pile of wood, looking for the man's satchel. She saw a corner of the bag sticking out from beneath the man. Meara was going to need to touch the body if she hoped to discover if the bag still contained the dragon egg.

Meara filled her lungs, hoping to draw fortitude and make her mind calm. She took hold of the man's hand and pulled with all of her strength. The man's body ripped from the wood on which it had been impaled and the man screamed. Meara screamed as well. She had been convinced the man was no longer alive and the horrible sound coming from between his lips as she pried him from his cage of branches took her completely off guard. She changed her tactic and dropped his hand. Meara picked her way over the driftwood to squat beside the man. She pulled up on the man's tunic, balled it over the wound, and pressed down on it. The man screamed again. The string of curses that followed took a moment to fade.

Meara spoke to the man. "You had a stick through your chest. I pulled you off of it."

"So your plan was to save me by removing the tree and causing me to bleed to death?" the man spluttered.

Meara decided not to tell the man she had not considered that he might bleed to death because she had thought he was already dead. Instead, she adjusted his tunic to apply pressure to the back of his shoulder while simultaneously staunching the flow of blood from his chest. As she did so, she scanned the grassy areas nearby with her eyes.

"I'll be right back," she said to the man.

Meara sprinted off and began pulling yarrow plants and flowers from the ground. She ran to the water and soaked a handful of the plant, then carried it back to the man. Blood was now soaking through the areas of his tunic that covered his wound. Meara tore off the man's shirt and put globs of the soaked yarrow on the entrance and exit punctures, then tied the remnants of the tunic's material around the man to pin the poultice in place. It was not a perfect solution, but the yarrow would act as a coagulant and at least the man wouldn't bleed to death before her eyes.

"My name is Meara," she said to the man. "Thank you for saving me from that wave."

The man's demeanor changed. He sat a little straighter and seemed to forget that he had been in the middle of complaining about his own unfortunate circumstances.

"You're quite welcome. I could not have a defenseless woman swept away by the scourge of nature if there was something to be done about it."

Meara decided she preferred it when the man was whining about his wounds. She did not like being described as a 'defenseless woman.'

The man continued. "I am Prince Landis Larsen, of the kingdom of Skalve. I was raised in the court of Blackwell Palace, and I am forever bound by the rules of chivalry."

Meara did her best not to snort a laugh. Now the fool was portraying himself as a savior of all those in need. He was a prince of Skalve. All he understood was the destruction of nature and the conquering of tribal people. He may see himself as some form of gallant knight, but Meara was looking at a sniveling boy with a hole through his shoulder. Prince Landis was about Meara's age, maybe older by a few years, but his demeanor was that of a child.

Meara suppressed her urge to call Landis out on his opinion of himself and asked, "So, what do we do now?"

Landis looked at her as if she had sprouted wings. "We? We go our separate ways! I will find my raiders and retrieve the artifact for which I came, and you will continue your tribal chores. The danger has passed."

"That might be more difficult to accomplish than you think," Meara replied. "We are no longer on Innut. I'm not even sure the island survived that wave. You need to consider that your friends are lost."

"Nonsense," the prince replied. "I watched my soldiers enter the temple and climb the path to high ground."

Meara hummed as she chose her words. "That path does climb at its start, but once you travel a short distance into the cave, the path falls off and leads into the depths of the rock. The passages of the temple are primarily below the water level. Your people will have been swept down into those corridors and drowned."

Landis was silent. Meara took a moment to study him while his mouth ceased to spew ignorance. He was attractive when he wasn't speaking. Though his skin was fair, he had a large birthmark where his skin looked tanned. The mark ran from his left collarbone, onto his shoulder and tapered off below his rib cage. The mark, though not as dramatic, reminded Meara of the markings on her own skin. Prince Landis's eyes were blue, but one portion of his right eye was brown. The defect was small enough that it would go unnoticed unless one was inches from the prince's face. Meara checked herself. She was far too close to Landis. She sat back in the sand and turned her gaze from the prince.

Landis spoke at last. "I failed. It was going to be easy. I just had to grab the dragon egg and bring it back to Blackwell. It should have been the first of my many successes as the commander of the Skalven army."

Meara, realizing the prince was back to feeling sorry for himself, listened absently while she consciously kept her eyes from straying toward the satchel that was tangled within the driftwood. The prince had been on Innut to steal the dragon egg. He was unaware he had accomplished his task. How had he not realized it when he placed the stone in his bag?

Meara interrupted Landis's rambling. "What does this dragon egg look like?"

"Oh," Landis took a moment to switch the direction of his thoughts. "It's beautiful. It's about the size of a loaf of bread and entirely made of gold. The jewels that decorate its surface are worth an incomprehensible amount. The old gods loved treasure and the dragon eggs are the show-piece of every dragon's collection. Temples, like the one on your island, were built as vaults to protect the treasures collected by the dragons. Most of the temples have been destroyed, but the more remote temples remain. Each contains a priceless egg."

"Why is an additional shiny item so important to a kingdom that already has tons of gold and jewels?" Meara asked.

The prince looked as if he were about to speak, but then closed his mouth and shook his head. He dropped his gaze for a moment before looking up at Meara again.

"I honestly don't care. I only know that the acquisition of these artifacts was my chance to prove myself as a leader. It is a way for me to earn the respect of my people and my parents' approval."

Landis's honesty surprised Meara. The prince did not believe in the power of the eggs, and through misinformation or through his own disconnection from the gods, he was convinced he was hunting treasure. Meara understood the truth. The prince was on a mission to claim the power of the eggs for the Skalven people. These were the exact people she was entrusted to protect the Innut Egg from.

"Listen," Meara said. "I can tend to your wound and help you find your army. I'm trained in tracking, and I expect a war party of considerable size would be easy to locate as long as we continue to follow the coast."

Landis looked confused. "My dear girl, what would make you think I can't do that on my own? I intend to walk along the water's edge until I reach the area where I entered the sea with my party. It was only several hours ago. With luck, Commander Torrence will have sent a second raiding party to the island to retrieve the egg. He would have had no issue finding men ready to explore the island after the wave passed."

Meara took a moment to untangle the line of thinking the prince's words revealed. He was unfamiliar with the workings of the sea and the surrounding land. He also did not like to be told he was mistaken, so she needed to choose her words with care.

"Prince Landis, I'm scared for the men of your army. Some may have been injured when the wave swept past the island and crashed onto the shore of the mainland. I'd like the chance to repay you for saving my life. If I accompany you when you return to your forces, I can help tend the wounds of those who survived."

Landis sat soundlessly for a moment. He was not slow in the mind, and Meara could see understanding dawning on his face. The prince suffered from arrogance to the extent that his mind refused to allow him to see any outcomes that were unfavorable. It took time, but he at last recognized that the rogue wave would have had consequences for his men on shore as well. Once Landis had a more realistic grasp of the situation, his demeanor changed.

"Right. It just occurred to me that my force may have needed to disperse into the woodlands to find higher ground. It is likely that my entire army has been scattered and is working to regroup. Some of my men may have been injured. I require you to accompany me. You've done a fine job with my shoulder wound and could prove useful in tending to my men. I shall retrieve my satchel and we shall be on our way."

Meara jumped to her feet and ran to pull the satchel from within the driftwood. She slung it over her shoulder, grateful to feel the weight of the God Rock within.

"I'll carry your bag. There is no sense aggravating your injury," Meara said.

Landis climbed to his feet, fumbling at first to rise with the use of only one arm. He headed off down the beach.

"Come now. We should not waste time," Landis said over his shoulder.

Meara hastened to catch up to the prince. The pack was heavy, but she would suffer its weight to keep it in her possession. It was unlikely Landis would find his army. The landlocked Skalven people would have stood on the beach and stared as death came for them in the form of the giant wave.

Meara was not sure what motivated her to follow the prince. She had the stone she was entrusted to guard, and she should turn on her heel and disappear into the woods. The prince would either attempt to pursue her and be thwarted by his injury and ignorance of the surrounding land, or continue on without her.

She had nothing right now. No one on Innut would have survived. The only trace of her people might be scouts that were on the mainland when the wave had come. The Yahkanah had never accepted her, though. Mamma Jade had been the only person Meara considered as family or friend. The old woman had served as both. Meara allowed her mind to envision Mamma Jade being swept from her hut. The woman would have likely sat in repose with her legs crossed, as the water poured into the village, removing all evidence that a tribe had once dwelled there.

"It's just me and the stone now," Meara mumbled under her breath.

"What did you say?" The prince's voice called from several

feet in front of Meara.

"Nothing. I was just thinking out loud."

CHAPTER 5: LANDIS

*L*andis clenched his teeth to prevent himself from grunting every time he took a step. It felt like the tribal girl had never taken the branch out. He glanced down again to be sure it was really gone. He remembered her yanking it out and cleaning his wound. She had then stuffed it full of crushed plants. How could that be sanitary?

Once Landis found the rest of his men, he would have one of the medics clean all the plant goop out of the wound and bandage it properly. The girl was falling behind. She insisted on keeping that rock with her. Tribal superstitions were odd. At least it meant that she was willing to carry his pack. It was not very chivalrous of Landis, but his shoulder really was in bad shape. He made a mental note to be sure to get the bag back from the girl before he returned to the island to collect the dragon egg.

Landis turned to check on the girl's progress. She had stopped. His bag was at her feet and she was looking into the woods that ran along the beach.

"What's the issue?" Landis called to Meara.

She scooped up the bag and caught up to Landis. He turned to continue walking, but she stopped him.

"Wait!" Meara closed the distance between them. "I think someone is spying on us from the trees."

"Someone or something?" Landis asked.

"I'm not sure. I just feel like we're being watched."

"I'm not in my best form at the moment, so we should make our way a little more quickly. I think I recognize this area. We likely have just a little more walking to do before we are back at my camp."

Landis turned to continue up the beach, but the girl didn't follow. Instead, she dropped his bag in the sand and headed off decisively toward the tree line. Landis hesitated and then followed her. They broke through the trees together. It was darker here in the shade, and several degrees cooler. Why weren't they walking in the shade instead of along the sunny beach?

Something whistled past Landis's ear, followed by the sound of something hitting wood. Landis turned to see an arrow sticking out of the tree just over his wounded shoulder. He looked back in the direction from which the arrow had come in time to see two men, wearing the royal blue of the Skalven Army, step from the bushes.

"Well met!" Landis called to the soldiers.

One soldier raised his bow.

"Good sirs," Landis called. "I forgive you for not recognizing me. I am not wearing my cloak. It is I, your prince, and commanding officer!"

"He does not even know our names," said the soldier with the bow.

"This is our chance," said the other. "We can rid ourselves of him and claim he was taken by the wave."

"Taken by the... what are you saying? Come now. Escort us back to Torrence and the rest of the men."

The soldier with the bow lowered it an inch and said,

"Torrence is dead. Almost everyone was washed away. We're out here to find any survivors that might have been on patrol when the wave hit. Only those of us far from the water had a chance."

Landis laughed. "What was the plan? Re-group and run back to Blackwell Palace?"

"Don't be ridiculous. We're putting together another party to travel to the island and raid the Temple. If the egg is still there, we'll bring that back to the king and queen. We'll be heroes."

"That's the spirit!" said Landis. It made him proud to see the dedication of his men. "We can still complete our mission."

Landis took a step toward the soldiers. The archer drew his bow back up and pulled back the string in a single swift motion. Something barreled into him and the arrow released, flying into the air above Landis's head.

Landis watched as the girl, whose name he could not remember at the moment, grappled with the soldier. The girl was absolutely feral. Landis was concerned about his soldiers' safety. Her wild attack had nearly caused the archer to send an arrow into his own commanding officer. The girl pulled an arrow from the quiver on the soldier's back and thrust it into the other soldier's thigh as he approached to join the fray.

Landis started toward the scuffle on the forest floor. His hesitancy vanished when the soldier with the arrow in his thigh pulled his hunting knife from the sheath on his belt. Landis quickened his pace and closed the distance to the soldier. He caught the man's wrist as he swiped at the tribal girl. Landis released the soldier's wrist and held his hands up to show he didn't want to fight.

The man did not share the prince's desire for a peaceful resolution. With the speed of a rattlesnake, the soldier stabbed toward his commander. Landis kicked the knife from the man's hand and caught hold of it. The soldier scooted backward to move from Landis's reach. His eyes grew wide and Landis followed his gaze to see the cause of the man's distress.

The girl was holding the shaft of an arrow. The point of the arrow protruded from the back of the archer's throat. The man's body slumped to the ground, lifeless. The tribal girl pulled another arrow from the dead man's quiver and rose to her feet. She strode toward Landis and the second soldier.

Landis put himself between the girl and the man under his command. He held his hands up before his body as if he was trying to calm a wild animal.

"What are you doing, girl? These are my men."

"These men intended to kill you, Landis! I should think you would thank me for defending you in your diminished state."

"Diminished state? You mean my wound? These men weren't going to kill me."

Only some of Landis's thoughts escaped his lips. The thoughts were coming so quickly and in such quantity that most of them just rolled by before he could voice them. The soldier behind him groaned as he worked to rise to his feet.

"You need to open your eyes, princeling. With Captain Torrence gone, all restrictions on our behavior towards you are forfeit."

The soldier laughed. At first, it was just a chuckle, but as the realization of his current situation broke on him, the laughter grew into hysterics.

"Who would have thought? A simple trip to an island filled with primitive people, and you failed. Instead of easily crushing a small band of woodmen with pointed sticks, the Prince was defeated by a wall of water called down by the gods themselves. I can't wait to hear what your mum and dad have to say about this disaster!"

With lightning speed, Landis lashed out with the hunting

knife and cut the soldier's throat. Gurgling sounds came from the man for several seconds before he passed into silence.

Landis sank into the leaves of the forest floor and put his head in his hands. He knew he had not earned the respect of his men, but the attempt to kill him was startling. His face flushed and his body grew warm until he felt almost feverish. His own men had tried to kill him. The treasonous bastards deserved to die.

For several moments, Landis listened to the sounds of the forest. He breathed in the scent of pine mixed with dead leaves and soil. Were there more of his men out here in the forest? Did they all want to kill him? Landis was unsure if he should continue looking for the remnants of his army, or if he should be running from them.

When Landis lifted his head, the girl was gone. It would be safer for her to be away from him anyhow if his own army was hunting him. He really wanted to go back to the beach and follow it until he reached more familiar surroundings, but if his soldiers wanted him dead, he would be an easy target out in the open. The soldiers in the forest had to be an exception, but Landis decided to stay hidden in the trees as a precaution. If he could find a horse, he could head back home. Landis felt confident about the plan. First, though, he needed to retrieve his pack from the beach.

Landis was surprised to find this was no simple task. His wound had reopened in the fight and the pain it caused seemed to have redoubled. His movements were slow now that the adrenalin from the fight was wearing off. When he stepped onto the sand, the pack was gone and a trail of small footprints headed off toward the tree line in the direction from which he and the girl had come earlier. His eyes caught a flash of light skin as it passed through a thinner place in the brush.

"Girl! My pack! You forgot to return my pack!"

Was she moving faster? Landis picked up his pace, taking an angle suited to intercepting the girl's trajectory. Just before he reached the edge of the forest, the tribal girl burst back out onto the beach.

"I have a name, you know! I can understand why your soldiers show you such contempt. You show no respect for them. You didn't know their names either."

Landis was within a few feet of the girl now. "I don't believe you told me your name, girl. I'm sure I would have remembered it if such a lovely lady had shared such an important thing."

Landis was happy to see his use of flattery did not fail him. The prince prided himself on his skills with diplomacy. The girl's face softened. She glanced at his shoulder.

"You were in a great deal of pain at the time, Prince Landis. I'm sorry for not providing my name again as we walked down the beach and you were feeling better."

Landis relaxed. The girl had realized she had been mistaken. He waited for her to continue.

"I'm sure your soldiers were sorry they did not re-introduce themselves to you when we all met in the clearing. It is strange that they did not do that several times on the journey from the Skalven lands. I would imagine they should have understood how hard it is for the commander of an army to remember the name of each and every soldier. Besides being a commander, you are a prince, and they should not have expected you to ask for their names if you did not remember them."

It started to feel as if the girl was laying it on a little thick. Worse, she still had not restated her name.

Landis said, "Ok. I concede your point. I'm sorry, my lady, I do not recall your name. Would you be so kind as to share it again?"

The girl smiled. "That wasn't so bad, was it? My name is Meara. Now, I think it will be best for both of us if we change direction and head away from what might remain of your army."

Meara turned and headed back into the trees. Landis looked longingly down the beach toward where his camp had been. There was still a chance he could send someone to the island. There might be some soldiers who were still loyal to him. In the end, he followed Meara. When he caught up to her, she placed his bag on the floor and pointed at his shoulder.

"You should let me take a quick look at that. Our fight back there might have disturbed the poultice."

Landis found a relatively smooth rock and sat so Meara could unwind the bandage from his wound. She hummed disapprovingly, prodded at him a few times, and then went about re-wrapping the bandage. While Meara worked, Landis stared at the island, distant but visible, protruding from the water.

"I don't suppose I can convince you to swim back out there and grab that dragon egg from the temple for me?" Landis asked.

Meara made a sound somewhere between a scoff and a giggle. Landis considered trying to make the swim on his back, or using his side-stroke skills. If Meara was still on the beach when he returned, she could always re-wrap his wound for him. It was also possible that he would drown. His shoulder throbbed with his arm wrapped and pinned, motionless against his body. The pain might be unbearable once the water had its way with his arm. He could give it a try. He should know right away if he would be able to handle the swim.

Landis stood and started walking back toward the beach. With his eyes fixed on the water, he built himself up for the challenge. He had not even been short of breath after making the swim the first time. This would be slightly more challenging, but he could still swim with the use of only one arm. He heard

Meara calling him, faintly, but continued walking. Landis felt confident she would wait for him. She had already saved his life. Technically, Landis supposed, she had saved his life twice. Meara was invested in his survival and she would wait on the beach to be sure he made it back.

As Landis's toes touched the water, he heard something hit the sand beside him. The fletching of an arrow stuck up into the air. Landis looked up the beach. Several soldiers were running along the water's edge toward him. Of all the survivors, it made sense that many of them would be archers. They were accustomed to staying back behind the bulk of the forces and out of harm's way. Still, Landis wasted no time. He turned and ran back toward the cover of the trees.

Meara was there waiting for him. Landis felt a small surge of satisfaction, knowing she had not moved on without him. Some of that left, though, as he realized she had moved a little farther down the beach and he remembered he had only been away from her for a minute or two. As he grew closer, he saw she was smiling at him. That was a comfort.

CHAPTER 6: MEARA

*M*eara laughed to herself as Landis hurried back and she couldn't hide the smile on her face. She had seen the arrow land at his feet, but she hadn't seen the archer. She knew Landis had seen him, though, and he was displaying speed on his way back to the tree line. As the prince approached, Meara turned and started off again, angling away from the beach. The archer would have little chance of a clear shot if they were deeper in the forest.

"Come on now! We'll need to move a little faster if we want to lose him," Meara said.

"Them," Landis corrected. "It seems the number of remaining disgruntled soldiers is higher than one might expect after escaping a rogue wave."

Meara did not reply. She hopped over a fallen log and made her way around a large tree. She had never been off the island and found herself fascinated by the forest here. On her island, the forest consisted of a swath of trees and brush about ten feet wide between the beach and the village. Here, there seemed to be no end to the greenery. The canopy above kept the air cool, and Meara enjoyed the knowledge that the sun was not roasting her skin. The air still smelled of the ocean, but it felt less dense.

She could hear the Prince stumbling through the brush behind her.

"Don't they teach you how to tiptoe through the woods in training?" Meara asked, noticing she was a little breathless.

"It's not… One does not really have a need… Large armies march on roads."

Landis was much more out of breath than she was. He did also have a hole in his shoulder and the run through the forest was likely painful.

"There's a rise ahead. When we get to the top, we will stop and rest," Meara said.

"I would… be happy… to let you… rest," the Prince panted.

Just before heading up the hill, Meara felt as if a weight lifted from her shoulders and she put on an extra burst of energy to clamber to the top. She allowed her body to drop to the ground, and she breathed in deeply. The air smelled different. There was the expected scent of damp earth from the forest floor, but this was more. Meara felt as if she could smell each individual flower in the field beyond the hill where she and Landis perched. She smelled the birds above her, nesting among the branches of the trees, and she could smell the trace of a deer that had come through the area earlier.

The sights were crisper, as well. As Landis sat beside her, taking in breath more leisurely than he had been moments before, she felt as if she saw more shades of green and brown than she'd known existed. Maybe it was just a result of her being in a new place that caused her to notice more than green leaves and brown bark, but she felt as if a veil had been lifted from her senses. The rocks seemed to sparkle in the light that filtered through the canopy and the land seemed almost magical.

"Well," said Landis. "This brief respite has been surprisingly helpful. I'm shocked at how much better I feel already."

Meara was not sure if she was more surprised that Landis had admitted he needed the rest, or at how true his words rang. They had only been sitting for a brief time, but it felt as if they had rested for over an hour. She felt rejuvenated and was ready to continue on with a strength she had not felt since before the wave washed her away. It was as if the air and earth around her were feeding her energy.

"It's the gods," Meara said aloud. "Tala is sending us breath and Vigilia is sending us energy."

Landis laughed. "The old gods are long gone and are likely dead. My ancestors scourged the land of…"

Landis trailed off when he saw the reproachful look on Meara's face. The prince stirred the dirt on the ground with a stick.

"I suppose you don't believe in the gods. It is no matter. They hold power over all, even those who do not recognize them," Meara said softly.

The prince looked up at her. "I loved the stories of the old gods when I was a child. I suspect I heard them differently than you did, though."

"Why do you refer to them as the 'old gods'? They are still in control and they will return to this place. It's one of the reasons we are entrusted with the temple."

Meara looked back in the direction of the beach. There would be no one left to care for the temple now. She sighed and got to her feet. It was an enormous loss, but she was comforted by the knowledge that she had the temple's most precious treasure in the pack on her back.

Landis climbed to his feet as well. His shoulder did not appear to be as much of a hindrance as it had been earlier. As the two of them started down the hill, moving farther from the familiarity of the beach, and farther from the threat of the remains of the prince's army, Meara felt her back warming. It was causing sweat to soak her shirt, and she slid the pack so that it hung on only one shoulder. The heat from the bag seemed to increase. After several more steps, Meara was unable to hold the bag near her skin and she dropped it to the ground and stared at it.

Landis stooped to grab the bag, but tendrils of smoke were now emanating from the material and he pulled his hand back. Meara pounced on the bag and upended it, dumping the stone into the dirt of the forest floor. She stomped on the material of the bag to stop it from smoldering and stood watching the rock begin to glow with orange light. Landis took a step back, but Meara crouched down to get a better look. There was a large crack in the rock now, and the edges of the fissure blazed as red as lava. The crack melted into a wider split as Meara watched, and light shone through the opening. The light grew in brightness until Meara had to shield her eyes and then turn away. A loud crack echoed through the air as the rock must have split open, and then Meara heard a sound somewhere between the purr of a mountain cat and the chirp of a bird.

Meara spun around so quickly that she lost her balance and ended up sitting on the ground. Huge golden eyes, covered by long lashes, stared back at her from inches away. The eyes belonged to a creature about the size of a raccoon. It had no fur, but was covered in iridescent purple scales. The creature took a few tentative steps toward Meara. Meara didn't know what to do. She had no desire to touch the animal. She threw her hands above her head and sat as still as possible while the creature stepped into her lap. It turned several times and then curled up, making a nest of her legs.

"Meara," Landis said softly. "I think you have a baby dragon in your lap."

Suddenly afraid the prince might try to kill the creature,

Meara brought her arms down around it protectively. The little dragon nuzzled Meara's hand and emitted the same chirping purr it had voiced moments ago.

Meara tentatively stroked the creature's head with the tip of her index finger and it pressed up into her like a cat, causing her finger to run down the back of its neck. The creature gave Meara a gentle swat when her finger trailed down its rib cage toward its stomach.

"Does that tickle?" Meara asked in a soft voice.

Meara experienced the affirmative response as a warm sensation within her mind. The little dragon dipped its head so that Meara's fingers would continue scratching its head.

"Demanding little thing, aren't you?" Meara mumbled.

Landis's voice severed the moment. "You're going to need to feed that thing. It might seem sweet right now, but it is as likely to eat your fingers as allow you to use them to pet it."

"He wouldn't do that," Meara replied.

Her response had been automatic. In truth, she had no idea what the little dragon might do next, but she felt the need to protect him.

"I am not a he!" the dragon said into Meara's mind. "Can't you see my ear fins?"

The affronted voice pushing into her mind caught Meara off-guard, but she relayed the information to Landis without indicating anything was amiss.

"Forgive me," Meara said. "*She* wouldn't do that. We will need to find her some food, though."

"Is that thing communicating with you?" Landis asked. "What made you decide it was a girl?"

"See these little flaps here?" Meara stroked the scaled appendages that swept back from the little dragon's cheeks, partially covering her ears. "Only female dragons have these."

Landis's shoulders dropped as tension left his body. "Oh.

51

For a moment there, I thought she could talk!"

Landis laughed, as if his question had been ridiculous, and started walking down the hill. He looked back over his shoulder after taking a few steps, eyebrows raised questioningly.

"Yes, we're coming."

Meara opened the slightly charred pack beside her and encouraged the little dragon to climb inside. She was going to need to give this creature a name.

"I already have a name," said the voice in her mind. "I will be called Dabwey."

"Dabwey," Meara repeated.

She liked the name. Meara knew this word and had seen it inscribed on the temple walls. In the ancient tribal language, it roughly translated to the word 'truth'.

A few yards ahead, Landis slammed his sword down into the earth. When he raised the tip back up, he turned and brandished the corpse of a vole hanging limply from the steel.

"For your new pet," Landis said.

"How do you know what Dabwey eats?" Meara asked.

"So, you've already named her?"

"Yes, and she is not my pet."

"Whatever she is, I'd rather be her friend than her foe. She is a dragon, and dragons eat meat. At least, that's what all the stories say. I figure presenting her with food will keep her from eating me while I sleep," said Landis.

As if smelling the meal, Dabwey popped her head out of the pack and looked over Meara's shoulder. Landis reached the sword tip toward the dragon's head. Dabwey struck like a snake, pulling the small carcass from the blade. She tossed it into the air and opened her mouth wide. The vole disappeared down the dragon's throat.

Meara's stomach rolled. She was slightly nauseated by the sounds in proximity to her ear as Dabwey swallowed her first meal and licked her teeth clean.

"Next time, let me put her down before you feed her," Meara said to Landis.

The prince let out a chuckle and then continued down the hill. Meara could tell Landis was intrigued by Dabwey. Who wouldn't be interested in a baby dragon? It was as if he was giving Meara and Dabwey space. He was likely dying to poke, prod and otherwise investigate the incredible animal, but he was showing far more reserve than Meara would have thought him capable. Then again, they were fleeing his army and there was not much time to do much of anything but walk.

"Of course he's interested in me," Dabwey spoke into Meara's mind. "It's in his blood. You need not worry about him hurting me."

"What do you mean?" Meara forgot to speak only in her mind.

This time, Landis came to a full stop and turned around. "I knew it! She is talking to you! Ask her where the other temples are."

"I will do no such thing!" said Meara. "Even if she knows, and decided to share the locations with me, what makes you think I would tell you? You were raiding the temple on Innut! All you care about are jewels and riches."

"That's not so bad," Meara heard Dabwey saying. "I particularly like the amethyst stones. They match my scales."

Meara ignored the little dragon. At least she tried to ignore her. She was amused by the comparison Dabwey had just drawn between herself and Landis. Dragons were just as greedy when it came to shiny objects as Landis and his soldiers.

The prince peppered Dabwey with questions. He asked about the temples. He asked about other dragon eggs. At last, Landis threw his hands up and trudged on ahead of Meara.

As Landis emerged into the field at the bottom of the hill

and started walking through the flowers, Meara realized she did not know where they were going. She was not sure Landis was certain where he was leading them, either. Were they going back to his home, or was the prince just putting distance between himself and his men?

"I failed you," Meara said to Dabwey. This time, she was careful to keep from speaking out loud. "It was my job to protect the temple."

Sleepily, Dabwey replied, "It was your job to protect me, not to protect the temple."

Meara thought about that. Mamma Jade had entrusted her with the care of the temple and all its riches. Had Mamma Jade known the dragon egg was not just a stone? Had she known there was a genuine dragon inside the temple, just waiting to hatch? Why had Dabwey decided to hatch, anyhow? The egg had been in the temple for hundreds of years, and there had been no sign of life within it.

"I can hear you, you know," Dabwey said mentally.

"Are you listening to everything in my head? Can you read my mind? Do you see my memories?"

"Yes, yes, and only if I look for them. Honestly, the only thing that happens automatically is hearing your current thoughts."

Meara thought about the implications of her mental connection to this newborn creature. She might never have another secret.

"Is there any way to turn that off?" Meara asked.

"No, but we'll both get better at quieting it and distancing ourselves from the other's thoughts. We should also be able to suppress some of what we are thinking to keep it from distracting the other person in our shared mind. Until then, stop thinking. I'm sleepy."

"You really are a demanding little thing," Meara thought

back.

"Yes. I am a dragon."

Meara shifted her attention to the prince, taking long strides and several paces in front of her. He walked purposefully, moving quickly, but watching where he placed his feet. Meara wondered if they should be running. It was unwise to be out in the open like this. She glanced back over her shoulder and walked directly into the prince's back.

"Sorry! I wasn't looking where I was going."

"A woman of the obvious... I am not surprised," said Landis.

Meara was unsure if the prince meant the comment to be an insult, or if his internal thoughts had simply escaped his lips. Either way, she ignored the statement and stepped up beside Landis to see why he had stopped so suddenly.

CHAPTER 7: LANDIS

"*W*hy are we stopping? Those soldiers could be right behind us."

Landis found he was not sure how to answer the question. He did not know much at the moment. He was in the middle of a field, far from home, with the enemy. Landis had failed to retrieve the dragon egg for his kingdom, and now his nemesis had an actual dragon. It was a small dragon, but still, it was a dragon.

"Hello? Landis? Are you well?"

"I am well," Landis replied. "I'm just thinking."

"After all that has happened, it is understandable you would need some time to think," said Meara. "I'm just not confident this is the right time or place for that."

Landis started walking again, but he had changed his direction. Instead of walking straight across the open field, he was now angling himself in a more southern direction. He was not going home yet.

"Where are we headed, anyway?" Meara asked.

"South," replied Landis.

"I can see that," said Meara. "What is our destination?"

Landis had to make a choice. Until recently, he had been telling himself he was only making sure the tribal girl was out of danger and then he would leave her and return home to regroup and report on the wave and the treasonous behavior of his soldiers. Now, though, the girl had an actual dragon.

"We're going to the Swamp Lands, south of the Dark Forest," Landis replied at last.

The look on Meara's face was all Landis needed to understand that Meara knew nothing about those places. The girl must have been terribly sheltered. He allowed an air of superiority to return to his voice when he explained.

"The Swamp Lands are controlled by the Dinnen. I'm surprised you don't know them. They are primitive, like your people. There is a temple there —"

Meara interrupted. "Dabwey said I don't need to listen to you. She'll tell me anything I want to know."

"I didn't hear her say anything. She didn't even poke her head out of the bag. I think you're making that up," said Landis.

Meara cocked her head, as if she were listening to something far off. A smile spread across her face, but she said nothing. Landis's heart quickened and his muscles tensed. He quickened his pace to release the tension and put distance between himself and the maddening girl.

"The Dinnen are dangerous," said Meara as they walked. "They kill any who emerge from the Dark Forest and enter their lands. How do you expect to get to their temple without meeting that fate?"

Landis looked at the bag on Meara's back and raised his eyebrows.

"Oh! I see! You think that Dabwey is your ticket in?" Meara asked.

Landis took a deep breath and pushed it out slowly between his lips.

"The stories say that the tribes are charged with protecting the riches of the old gods until the time they return. Over the years, many of the old god temples were destroyed, the treasures stolen. Only the better protected of the temples have survived all this time. I find it hard to believe that I am the one saying this to you. One would think it would be the tribal girl giving history lessons on the old gods to the prince from the progressive kingdom!"

Meara was quiet. Landis continued his march. They were nearing another tree-line and he would feel much better once they were within the copse of pine.

"I know the stories of the gods," Meara said. "I never thought of them as much more than that. The gods were just stories to me, and I protected the temple because I was given that duty. It was an expectation from the woman who raised me that I would not fail in that task, and so I did it. I guess now I understand why it was so important to keep the God Stone clean, anyway."

"Because it wasn't a stone at all," Landis finished as they pushed through blueberry bushes to get out of the open field.

Landis watched Meara filling the small pockets of her tattered dress with the berries and did the same with his own pockets. If there had not been a baby dragon in his pack, which Meara was carrying, he would have filled that instead. He caught sight of the bag as Meara stepped out of the bushes and sat on the soft pine needles in the shade of a tree. There was an actual dragon in there.

Landis joined Meara, dumping the berries he had collected onto a flat rock, not wanting to risk squishing them in his pocket by leaving them any longer than necessary. The two of them sat quietly, popping berries into their mouths.

The little purple dragon crawled out of Landis's pack and started playing with a blueberry. She rolled it back and forth between her front feet. Landis felt himself relax. The dragon was quite cute. The berry rolled from Dabwey's grasp and the little dragon pounced on it. The berry spit its juice onto the dragon's face and Landis laughed loudly.

The dragon was not amused. She pulled her lips back and showed the razor-sharp teeth ornamenting her mouth. Landis stiffened and was about to move back a few feet when Dabwey let out a delightfully cute roar. Landis laughed again, and this only made the dragon angrier. The creature began throwing the most adorable tantrum possible. Landis could not stop the enormous grin that spread across his face.

"She said to remind you she can kill you by severing an artery with just one talon," Meara said.

The grin fell from Landis's face. It would be wise to remember that no matter how cute Dabwey was, she was a killer. A small killer, but a killer none the less.

"I don't understand why she only talks to you," said Landis to Meara.

Meara sat still, listening. She smiled, then frowned, then shook her head slowly. She then sat up straight and turned her attention to Landis.

"She's still pretty mad, and there was a lot of name-calling, but basically she said to remind you she is a goddess and she will speak to whomever she pleases."

Landis felt his face heat. It was as if Meara and Dabwey were ganging up on him. Females could be infuriating. Landis grabbed his pack and pulled some wire from the front pocket. He dropped the bag back to the ground and stalked off into the brush.

Out of Meara's sight, the first thing Landis did was relieve himself. Had he still been traveling with his army, this would not have been something he felt he needed to do privately, but Meara was different. There was some irony to this. Meara was from a primitive group of people. It was likely the people of her tribe often tended to their bodily needs in each other's presence. Landis was not sure that comfort with the natural phenomena of the body would translate into Meara not using Landis's call from nature as the source of a joke, though.

Landis buttoned his britches and moved off to an area in the blueberry bushes that looked well worn by small animals. He created a loop out of the wire from his pack and attached it to the bush, so the opening of the loop covered most of the worn path. He repeated the process in a few more places along the length of the bushes. With luck, there would be some breakfast hanging in at least one of the traps by the morning.

"I do not think we should risk a fire tonight," Landis said when he returned to camp. "There is little chill in the air, so we should sleep well enough. I'd rather not call attention to ourselves if we are still quarry."

Meara laughed. "How does it feel to be hunted by your own men?"

Landis considered answering truthfully. Having seen, firsthand, the disorganization and drunken debauchery in his camp during the evening, he did not truly feel as if there was any danger. Then again, up until today, he had thought his men had respect for him and existed to do his bidding. Landis chose not to answer Meara's question.

"We enter The Swamp Lands tomorrow. It is then that we shall know what it feels like to be in true danger," Landis said.

The little dragon struck the ground with a single, knife-like talon. She raised its sharp point to show off the beetle she had skewered before sticking it into her mouth and pulling the bug from her talon with her teeth. Landis shook his head. If there was nothing in the traps the next morning, he and Meara might need to eat a few bugs as well.

Landis stretched out on the ground and stared up at the

darkening sky. The moon had been out for some time, but now the brightest of the stars were also beginning to twinkle into view. He wished Torrence were here. In hindsight, Landis knew the man had humored him in much the same way as the soldiers had, but at least Torrence had tried to help him. If he had listened more closely to what Torrence had been saying between his spoken words, it was less likely Landis would be alone in a forest right now. Well, alone, aside from a tribal girl and her dragon.

He was the prince of Skalve, and the sole heir to the kingdom's throne. What would his parents think if they knew he was lying in the dirt, hiding from the remains of the Skalven army? His future depended on getting the second dragon egg from the Dinnen. If he could return to Blackwell Palace with that egg, then his failure at Innut Island could be overlooked.

"Hey, Meara. Do you think the Dinnen Temple has a stone like the one Dabwey came from?"

"It's likely," Meara answered.

She sat up from where she had been curled on her side and Dabwey crawled sleepily into Meara's lap.

Meara continued. "I've been thinking about the purpose of the temples. I always assumed they were there to protect the gold and jewels until the gods returned for them. I suspect my interpretation of 'precious' led to some misunderstanding. Mama Jade told me our job was to care for the temple and the precious items within it. I viewed 'valuable' and 'precious' to be synonymous with gold and riches. I fell into a trap more akin to one set for the Skalve."

"What do you mean by that?" Landis asked.

"I didn't mean to offend you, Sir Prince." Meara smiled to let him know she was joking. "It's just that the Skalven people are well known for their desire for riches. The stories tell of how you landed on our shores as a result of a failed plundering mission."

"Neither of us was around at the time. There is no way for us to know exactly why my ancestors arrived in this land."

Meara just stared back at Landis for a moment. Finally, he smiled and dipped his head, acknowledging that she was correct.

"It is true. I am embarrassed to say that my ancestor, Krieg Larsen, was never supposed to land on these shores. He was leading a fleet of ships that should have made landfall thousands of leagues to the south of here. He had heard gold had been found and intended to take that gold from the people who discovered it."

Landis reached a finger out toward Dabwey's purple scales as he spoke. She swatted him and crawled out of reach before curling up again. Landis had seen Meara smile, but she said nothing, allowing him to continue speaking.

"Before any course corrections could be made, they were attacked by serpents from both the air and the sea. Several of the boats made landfall safely and other sailors washed up on shore after escaping the ships that were sunk into the depths of the water. Once on land, the people continued to be attacked from the air, and then they were also attacked by land serpents. It was the native people who called to the survivors and guided them to safety."

"It sounds like there are some holes in your story," said Meara.

Landis looked at her, confused. He had always taken the story he had heard since birth as fact. It was simply the explanation of how his ancestors had arrived in this land and founded Skalve. Meara had stoked his curiosity, though.

"Would you care to elaborate? Of what holes do you speak?"

"Have you ever considered how it was possible for the tribal people to hold off the enormous dragons that attacked the Skalven people when they landed on shore? Then, by what means were they able to outrun the land serpents? If they could outrun them, then how were they able to hide from them?"

Landis digested Meara's questions. They were good questions; questions a young boy would never have thought up, but it was disturbing to Landis that none of them had occurred to him as he grew older.

"As a child, I always just envisioned the survivors running into a copse of trees when the native people waved them over. I figured they ran to a cave with a small opening and the land serpents could not follow."

"So, the tribal people and the survivors just stayed in the cave until the danger passed and then they all lived happily until one day the survivors kicked the tribal people out of the cave and formed their own country?" Meara asked.

"Well, yes," said Landis. "Though, now that you are forcing me to analyze it from the perspective of a man who has come of age, it seems less likely that it would have been so simple."

"Agreed," said Meara. "As I said, there are quite a few holes in the story you were raised hearing."

Meara curled up on the ground, pulling Dabwey against her chest. She wore a smug smile on her face, even as her breaths slowed over the next several minutes. Landis watched her as she drifted off to sleep. In moments, the girl had made him question the origin of his entire people in this land. The histories he had heard were likely just generalizations, but the details must have been recorded somewhere. Landis made a note to visit the palace library when he returned home.

CHAPTER 8: MEARA

*M*eara's arms hurt, but she kept running the bow back and forth. Landis had declared it was safe to start a fire and then traipsed off into the woods to see if breakfast was ensnared in his traps. Meara had bored a hole into a piece of wood and then tied some twine from Landis's pack around each end of a stick to create a bow. She made a loop in the middle of the bowstring and threaded a second stick through it. She placed the end of the added stick into the hole she had dug in the wood. That had been the straightforward part, and Meara had completed the task in less than five minutes.

For almost twice that time, Meara ran the bow back and forth to spin the stick held in the hole with a flat rock pushing on the top. The wood in the hole finally gave off some smoke and Meara fed dried grass onto the super-heated area and blew on it gently. Thankfully, a small flame jumped to life. She didn't think her arms could work the bow anymore. Meara treated the small fire like a newborn baby in the hope she would not need to find out how tired her arms actually were. As the spark grew, she relaxed and added small twigs to the flames.

By the time Landis arrived, proudly holding a large hare,

Meara had a strong cook fire going. Meara glanced up at the prince's kill and noted that he had already gutted the animal. At least she wouldn't need to worry about him having let the meat be poisoned. It was a small comfort to know Landis was a capable trapper. His snares had produced breakfast, and he knew how to properly care for game. Landis placed his kill on a rock near the fire and turned to walk away.

"Are you serious?" Meara called after him. "My arms are killing me. The least you could do is to skin the thing!"

Landis turned to face her. "The least I could do was done. I caught breakfast. I then went a step farther and removed its entrails. Am I hearing you suggest you would prefer I also skin this hare?"

"I just don't think I can move my arms right now," said Meara.

Meara was pretty sure she saw the corner of the prince's mouth turn up. He was enjoying this. Meara suspected he wanted to feel needed right now. After experiencing his own men turning on him, it was probably a slight boost to his ego.

"Landis, I really don't think I have the strength. I would be grateful if you would skin our breakfast."

The prince snatched the hare off the rock. He peeled the skin back from the animal's skull with his blade. In a display of power and skill Meara had not expected, Landis used strength and fluid motion to pull the skin from the rest of the animal in one piece. He skewered it on a large stick and held the end out to Meara.

"Your wish is fulfilled," said Landis. "You can rest your elbows in your lap while you hold this over the fire."

Meara shook her head and sighed. This man was frustrating, to say the least. In one sentence he was kind, even sweet, but in the next sentence he was back to treating her like one of his servants. She found herself excusing Landis's behavior based on his station and stopped herself. Royal blood was not an excuse to treat people poorly.

"You know, it might behoove you to remember I am not one of your servants. I know you find my ways primitive, but I am still a woman and one would think your chivalrous upbringing would have you treat me as such. If that isn't enough for you, I remind you I do have a dragon in my company."

Though Meara was proud of her response to the prince's behavior, Landis did not seem impressed. He shrugged and sat down on the other side of the fire. A moment later, he was making a swirling motion in the air with his index finger to remind Meara to turn the meat she was holding over the flames.

Either the hare was exceptionally juicy or Meara was hungrier than she had thought. She tore a few slivers of meat off for Dabwey, but ate almost all of her share herself. She threw her bones to the dragon, who sat happily cracking them with her sharp teeth to get at the marrow within. The creature seemed to be enjoying the snack much more than the bugs she had been catching for herself.

Meara watched Dabwey in wonder. She was having a difficult time thinking of the creature as a god. She was only about the size of a small dog, but there was no denying that she was, at least, a child of the gods. Her ancestors had been the serpents that chased Krieg Larsen and his men inland after thrashing their boats from the water. Meara supposed it shouldn't be a surprise that Dabwey innately shunned Landis. A part of her felt a little sad about that, though. Communicating with a dragon was an amazing feeling, and there were no words to describe it to Landis. Meara wished that he could hear Dabwey, even once, so he would understand how amazing the creature truly was.

"You're overthinking things," Dabwey said into Meara's

mind.

Meara startled. She had completely forgotten that the little dragon was not only capable of communicating with her, but that she was present in her thoughts as well.

"Sorry," Meara thought back. "Why don't you say something to him?"

"It is very rare for a dragon to speak to someone other than their vincule," answered Dabwey.

"I don't know what that is. Is that like a family member? Am I your mother?"

"Right now, I think of you as such," said Dabwey. "That will change as I grow. A vincule is much more than that, though. It is a shared consciousness and state of being between a dragon and its human rider."

"Rider?" Meara was surprised enough to forget to speak within her mind.

Landis jumped to his feet. "You hear hoof beats approaching?" he asked. His eyes were wide.

Meara made a show of tilting her head as if she were listening to something in the distance.

"I'm sorry," she said to Landis. "I must have been mistaken. I am getting a little jumpy just sitting here. Maybe we should be on our way?"

There was no way Meara was going to share with Landis that Dabwey expected to have Meara ride her at some point in the future. As she considered the implication of the revelation, a tinkling sound echoed in her head. It took Meara a moment, but then she realized it was Dabwey's laughter. The dragon was laughing at her!

"See," Dabwey said. "You don't want to talk to him either. If I even said a word to him, there would be nothing but questions about my magic, our bond, and if I plan to eat him."

"You have magic?" Meara asked mentally.

The tinkling came to Meara in her head again and the little dragon scampered off, probably in search of more bugs. All Dabwey seemed to do was eat and sleep.

Before departing, Meara insisted on checking the prince's wound. She sat Landis down on a rock and unwound the tattered strips of his tunic from his shoulder. There was a scab, such as one would have if they had sustained a deep cut, but there was no evidence that the prince had been impaled on a large piece of driftwood less than a day before.

"Well, that is interesting," Meara said under her breath.

"What is the matter?" Landis asked.

"Nothing is wrong," replied Meara. "It is just that your wound is healing at an unnatural speed."

"Oh, that!" Landis laughed. "To the chagrin of many of my nannies, I've always healed very quickly. Reflecting on the acrobatics I attempted as a child, I suspect I'd have been dead several times over if not for that gift."

"Gift?" Meara asked. "Healing like that is not some skill, like being adept with a bow. This is more like magic."

"It might be," Landis said. "My mother used to tell me my father's family had magic in their blood. I doubt it, though. There is absolutely nothing magical about my father."

Landis rolled his shoulder to test the extent of his healing. He picked up his sack and tossed it to Meara. Meara felt a familiar irritation heating her skin when Landis raised his eyebrows at Dabwey and then looked back at the sack in Meara's hands.

"You could try using your words," she said to Landis. "It is more polite."

Meara scooped Dabwey up and helped her into the sack. She felt heavier than she had yesterday, or maybe Meara was just feeling more tired. She followed Landis deeper into the forest.

Dabwey's sleepy voice entered Meara's mind. "Why do you

do everything he tells you to do?"

"I do not," Meara thought back. "I refused to skin our breakfast."

"That was only because you were physically unable to do it. Otherwise, you argue with him, point out that he is being rude, and then proceed to do whatever he wanted you to do in the first place."

Meara wanted to rebuke the dragon, but as she considered her own actions since she had met Landis, she had to admit to herself that Dabwey had a point. Even now, she was following Landis to a place neither of them had ever been. She deferred to him as if he knew better, when in reality, he was more likely to get them lost or killed than she was. She had grown up with the land as her home and her provider. She was much better suited to leading this journey than any prince, raised behind the walls of a fortress.

Meara lengthened her strides and caught up to Landis. She quickened her pace a little more and overtook him. Landis matched her steps and walked beside her for a moment before pulling ahead of her. It only took a few moments before the two of them were racing through the trees. Meara, having Dabwey on her back, was at a disadvantage, but the little dragon seemed to sense the imbalance and crawled out of the pack. She launched from Meara's shoulder and took flight, faltering at first, and almost hitting the ground, but then gaining confidence and keeping pace beside her vincule.

When Meara next surpassed Landis, the prince came to a dead-stop. Meara slowed and turned to see why Landis was no longer running. The prince stood frozen, with his mouth hanging open.

"She can fly!" Landis said.

"She is a dragon," Meara replied, slightly breathless from the run.

Landis shook his head as if to clear it. "I know she is a dragon, but it really hadn't occurred to me what that entailed. She can fly. I bet she can breathe fire. She probably has magical powers too! Ask her what magic she has, Meara."

"How about we save that for another time? We're nearing the edge of the Dark Forest," Meara replied.

There was light shining through the hanging branches ahead, hinting at the open field that lay beyond. Meara and Landis walked the remaining steps to the place where the trees ceased to grow. It was not a field they faced. It was an open area, but instead of flowers and grass, the two were looking at a seemingly endless swamp.

"It seems our feet are going to get a little wet," Landis said.

Meara did not like the sound of that. She wasn't concerned about wet feet. There were more concerning things about the swamp before her. She couldn't see into the murky water, but she was sure there were things living in its depths that would not be fun to share space with. As if to emphasize her point, Dabwey swooped down and grabbed a small snake in her talons. She tossed the slithering animal into the air and flew at it with her mouth wide, swallowing it in one gulp.

Landis was already tromping through the water. It only came up to his knees, but that did not make Meara feel any better about joining him. Instead, she stepped out onto a rock and hopped from there onto a fallen log. She balanced along its length and climbed onto another rock when she reached the end. Landis looked over his shoulder and groaned loudly when he saw what she was doing.

"Do you plan to do that for the entire distance across the swamp? At the rate you're moving, you will reach the other side sometime tomorrow afternoon."

Meara considered this. If she just jumped down into the water, she could move a lot faster and in a straight line. It would definitely get her out of the swamp a lot faster. She looked to Dabwey for a second opinion, but the dragon was happily swooping in and out of the water, fishing several hundred yards ahead.

With a disgruntled growl, Meara stepped down into the water. The bottom of the swamp was silty, and it made standing still difficult as the ground slid away beneath her moccasins. She took a few steps and found she kept her balance better if she kept moving, but it was still not easy.

Landis saw Meara struggling and pushed toward her to take her hand. They used each other for balance as they walked through the water. Meara struggled more than Landis due to her shorter legs, but neither of them looked very graceful as they made their way over logs and jumped periodically when something swam by and grazed their skin.

Meara focused on keeping her balance and watched Dabwey up ahead. The little dragon had eaten so much that Meara thought her stomach should be visibly swollen by now. Suddenly, something broke the surface of the water as Dabwey dove for her next morsel. Meara and Landis froze, watching a giant reptilian body propel itself from the water and leap into the air. There was something twisted about the thought of a dragon being eaten by an alligator. Meara held her breath, hoping she was not about to witness that exact event.

Dabwey threw out her wings, stopping her forward motion, and then flapped furiously to gain height. The alligator's teeth snapped and would have caught Dabwey's tail, but the little dragon gave it a swish at the perfect time and flew free of the big lizard's grasp. If Meara hadn't been knee deep in water, she would have sat for a moment to collect herself as relief washed through her.

"That was close," said Landis. "Come now, we need to keep moving."

Meara tried to move. Her foot wouldn't lift and she toppled forward. Landis kept her from entering the water face first.

"What is wrong? Are you hurt?" he asked.

"I'm not hurt. My foot got stuck."

Meara tried to lift her foot again, this time pulling straight up instead of attempting to step forward. The muddy bottom of the swamp held her foot firmly in its grasp. She tried lifting the other foot and found that it was stuck as well. She took a deep breath and attempted to remain calm. Landis would just have to pull her free. Meara turned to the prince to ask for help and saw his face was ashen.

"Meara, I do not wish to cause alarm, but I am stuck as well."

Meara was impressed with how calm Landis had managed to keep his voice; especially when one considered the alligator that had just jumped from the water and tried to eat Dabwey. *Dabwey!* Meara called to the dragon mentally. She was hovering at Meara's side seconds later.

"Dabwey, we are stuck. Is there any way you can pull us free?" Meara said aloud.

Was it possible she was sinking? Meara was almost positive the water had barely covered her knees a moment ago, and it was now midway up her thighs. Panic invaded her thoughts, but Meara struggled to listen to Dabwey's directions.

"Grab a foot," the little dragon said as she hovered close to Meara.

Meara did as she was told, but it was clear that Dabwey was nowhere near strong enough to pull Meara free. In the attempt, Dabwey crashed into the water. She jumped free of the swamp and shook herself to dry off while hovering once again in the air.

"She's not strong enough," Landis yelled. "And we are sinking!"

The prince was no longer pretending to be calm. It was doing nothing to help Meara keep her own composure. She needed to think of something quickly. The water was now at the top of her legs.

"Grab this," Dabwey said into Meara's mind.

The dragon pulled a large branch over to Meara and Landis. Meara reached for it and pulled it close. With her weight on it, the branch sunk beneath the water. It was not going to do anything to hold her up.

Dabwey hovered in front of Meara. She looked as panicked as Meara felt. It made sense; Dabwey was present in Meara's mind. Meara watched a tear roll down the little dragon's face. What did that mean?

"No, Dabwey. We will not die. Go find some help," Meara said mentally.

The dragon looked uncertain, but turned and flew off. Meara did not know how far the Dinnen Village was, but they would be the only people in the area. With luck, Dabwey might find one of their scouting parties and help would arrive in a short time.

CHAPTER 9: LANDIS

"Great," said Landis. "Even the dragon is abandoning us. That cannot be a positive sign. Now might be a good time for me to reconsider my belief in the old gods."

Meara just stared at Landis. Her eyes were wide. If she was still scared, Landis thought, then she probably hadn't realized yet that there was nothing to be done. Instead of wasting her energy on fear, the girl should prepare her soul for the afterlife. Did tribal people even believe in the afterlife? Maybe Meara was scared because she thought she might be reincarnated as a leech after dying in a swamp.

Landis watched as the water touched Meara's chin. The liquid had not yet reached his shoulders, but Meara was a good deal shorter than he was. Not only was Landis going to die in a few moments, but he would first have to watch Meara drown. Landis closed his eyes so he wouldn't have to watch.

"Are you kidding me?" Meara yelled. "I'm still here, alive, and right in front of you! You're just going to close your eyes and pretend I'm not dying?"

"Not at all! I am saying a prayer for your soul."

Meara was unable to reply. She had her head tilted back and was working hard to keep her nose above the water. She was a fighter. In the end, Landis did not close his eyes. He felt as if he owed Meara more than that for her bravery as she faced death.

She slipped below the surface without a sound. One moment the tip of her sunburned nose was visible, and the next it was gone. By the time the bubbles stopped reaching the surface of the water, Landis was confronting his own demise. As he took his last breath, before the murky water claimed him, he caught a flash of purple scales.

⊢━━━━━━━━━━━━━━━━━━━━━━━━━━━

Landis woke and tried to draw breath. He felt hands roll him onto his side, and he vomited immediately. He took in a large gulp of air and then continued gasping and coughing. He felt as if he couldn't get enough air into his lungs. He was alive. He had not died in the swamp. *Meara!*

Landis sat up, and his vision blurred. Hands eased him back down onto his side and rubbed soothing circles on his back.

A woman's voice said, "The girl is alive. She is breathing. You need to rest a moment."

Landis relaxed, but only slightly. "The dragon?"

"We would never harm a god. You have her to thank for the air you now breathe. No one has ever survived the grip of the swamp lands before. The gods themselves left that land to protect us from outsiders."

"Dabwey convinced you to save us? Aren't you supposed to kill anyone who enters your lands?"

"So it is said," the woman sighed. "It is hard to refuse the demands of a god, though; especially one as insistent as the goddess you call Dabwey."

Landis laughed. It felt inappropriate, given the circumstances, but he could only imagine the look on the faces of the Dinnen people when Dabwey approached them and demanded they drop everything and save two people from the swamp. It was likely he would have done whatever she wanted if it had been him.

"She spoke to you?"

Landis was surprised at the irritation he felt, even though the circumstances had been dire.

"Not in words," said the woman. "She drove us into motion through our minds. She may be small, but she is a powerful being."

The woman was making it sound more like mind control than communication. Maybe it was, and the little dragon had not actually deigned to speak to these people either. Mind control would have been a lot faster than trying to convince someone to run off into danger and save a couple of complete strangers.

If it was mind control, then Landis hoped Dabwey had the sense to continue its use. That was likely what was keeping the Dinnen from killing Landis and Meara, even though they had just saved them. Landis sat up, more slowly this time, and stared at his would-be murderer, turned savior. The woman looked to be on the far side of forty. She had gray streaks in her dark hair and creases in her forehead and around her eyes, but her body was youthful, with well-defined muscles.

"The dragon and the girl are in the hut over there."

The woman pointed to the largest hut of many. The structures sat in a semi-circle around a giant fire pit. No fire was burning, but the charred remains of large logs hinted at a bonfire-sized blaze. There were many people about the village, but all avoided Landis's gaze and pretended to go about their business.

Landis stood and walked over to the hut the woman had identified. He stopped and drew a breath before he pushed aside the dried palm fronds that served as a privacy curtain and entered the shelter. Meara was on the bed, sleeping and covered in fur pelts. It was quite warm in the hut, so Landis took the presence of the furs as an ominous sign. Things seemed even less promising when Dabwey, curled at the foot of the bed, did not lift her head as Landis stepped closer. It would be nice to have a dragon of his own. No one would sit at the foot of his bed if he were in Meara's position.

"She has yet to wake," said a female voice from behind him.

Landis was startled to find the woman had followed him in from outside. He had not heard her steps. He turned and saw she had two other people with her. They were both men, likely in their twenties, and carrying sharp spears.

"Do not be alarmed," said the woman. "These are my sons, Tinen and Brond. They helped pull you and your friend from the bog. My name is Alaria. Come, sit. I'd like to speak about how you came to be in the company of a god."

Alaria took a seat on a log against the wall of the hut. Tinen, or maybe it was Brond, remained standing to her right. The other son sat on the floor before his mother. Landis was not enthralled by the idea of sitting on the floor. In his world, one's physical placement within a room reinforced his or her station at court. It was the primary reason the king and queen had thrones upon a dais. This kept them elevated among the masses even as they sat.

Landis decided he would sit, but first he would be sure this woman and her sons understood he was no common traveler.

"My name is Landis Larsen. I am Crown Prince of Skalve."

It was not unnoticed by Landis that the sound of his title caused both of Alaria's sons to tighten their grips on their spears, though neither of them pointed the weapons in his direction. After noting that Alaria gave a slight dip of her head in recognition of the presence of royalty, Landis sat down across from her.

"Please, Your Highness, enlighten me on how your party found yourselves attempting to forge through a bog in Dinnen territory."

"It is a rather long story, but it seems I have some time on my hands while I wait for Meara to wake."

"Ah," said Alaria. "The girl is called Meara. Is she a friend, or your prisoner?"

"She's not my prisoner. I barely know her."

"Then this shall be an interesting story indeed!" said Alaria. "A Skalven Prince traveling with a tribal girl who is not his prisoner... I am going to enjoy this."

Landis did something he had never intended to do. He told the truth. Most of the truth, anyway. Landis decided to leave out the part about being on the island of Innut to steal the jewel-encrusted dragon's egg rumored to be housed within its temple. He hadn't been able to get the artifact anyway, so it didn't matter if he omitted that detail. Landis had every intention of getting the twin to that egg from the Dinnen Temple and he did not want to put any of the tribe members on alert before he even determined if a Dinnen egg existed.

Alaria was quiet when Landis finished his story. He couldn't read her emotions, but she looked pensive. He gave her time to collect her thoughts. Tinen and Brond were not as willing to be patient. The one sitting beside Alaria stood and walked toward the doorway. His brother made no move to stop him, but knuckles were a shade whiter where his hand gripped the shaft of his spear. Landis turned to watch Meara. She looked peaceful in her slumber, though her brow seemed furrowed. Maybe it was always like that, and Landis had not noticed.

Dabwey was curled between Meara's legs at the foot of the bed. Her head was down, but she was not sleeping. The little dragon's eyes tracked every movement in the room, guarding her mistress while she healed, and seeming to preside over relations between Landis and the Dinnen. Landis wanted to ask her if she trusted these people, but he had no way of getting an answer from her. There was probably no one Dabwey trusted, so she wouldn't be the best judge of character.

Landis was startled from his thoughts when Alaria stood. He spun to face her and moved to stand as well, but she put her hand out to indicate he should remain seated. Alaria strode to the bed and stared into Dabwey's eyes. Landis felt a twinge of jealousy when he realized the dragon and the tribeswoman were conversing. Dabwey's golden eyes appeared to brighten for a moment and then Alaria dipped her head in deference to the young creature and turned back to address Landis.

"The Goddess wishes to check on her sibling. She feels it would be prudent for you to accompany us to the temple. She said to tell you Meara is safe here."

A wave of uncertainty washed over Landis when he realized Dabwey might not be communicating with him, but it was possible she was able to read his mind. Maybe he was just easier to read than he had thought? Still, it was comforting to know Dabwey felt Meara was safe if left in the hut. It was also a relief that Dabwey had requested access to the very place within the community that Landis wished to visit. Once they were inside the temple, he could keep his eyes open for signs of the dragon egg.

"I beg your pardon, Alaria. What does Dabwey mean by wanting to visit her sibling? Is there another dragon in this village?"

"Each of the tribal villages was entrusted with a child of the gods. Dabwey knows this village has remained safe from outsiders and rightfully assumes that we still protect our God Stone within our temple. She would like to see ours."

Landis stood, also anxious to see the temple. Dabwey unfolded her wings and crawled down from the bed. She stepped out of the hut, followed by Landis and Alaria. The tribal woman continued past Dabwey and led Landis and the little dragon down a path marked with flat stones laid into the earth. The foliage was particularly dense in this area, and Landis was amazed when the trio stood before the opening to a cave. He had not noticed that they were approaching the temple. Landis eyed the gold statues on either side of the dark entrance.

Dabwey's voice pushed into his mind. "It's a fallacy, you know. Dragons don't really have an attraction to riches. Humans once hid the riches of their kingdoms in the temples of the gods as a way to protect them from other humans."

Landis whipped his head in the goddess's direction. He narrowed his eyes at her.

"You choose to speak to me now?"

"I have amusing and pertinent information," Dabwey said simply. "Anyway, over the millennia, the people came to think of the riches as part of the temple, and therefore as belonging to the gods. It's actually pretty funny how silly humans are. You put your own wealth in a cave to protect it, and then you forgot it belonged to you."

Landis was affronted on behalf of his species. It was nice to know that when he took the artifact from this temple, he wouldn't be stealing it from the gods, nonetheless. Though not previously a believer, traveling with Dabwey was muddying Landis's feelings on higher powers. It would probably behoove him to avoid angering a deity, just in case.

Alaria led Landis and Dabwey through the temple entrance and into the darkness. Her sons took up the rear of the short procession. Alaria took a torch from the wall and lit it. She used her flame to ignite several other torches and the cave was bathed in a soft glow. It was just enough light to see the carvings that lined the walls. Landis reached out and brushed his fingers over the nearest carving, depicting a creature shaped like Dabwey, but massively larger. In the mural, it towered over a regiment of soldiers carved with enough detail to show little emblems on their breastplates. The design was remarkably similar to the Larsen family crest.

Noticing the group was moving deeper into the temple, Landis pulled his gaze from the carving and lengthened his strides to catch up. Dabwey and Alaria disappeared down a passage, and Landis found the twins blocking him.

"Fine warriors, permit me to pass. I do not wish to cause either of you harm."

The brothers shared a glance. Tinen, or maybe Brond, wore a little smirk on his face. The other brother gripped his spear more tightly. Unbelievably, these two thought they could stop him. Landis took a step back. This would be the time to draw his sword if it had not been back in the hut with Meara's sleeping form. Landis contemplated raising his fists and telling the brothers to throw down their weapons and fight like men, but the pair did not seem the type to take the bait.

Frustrated, Landis began pacing the chamber instead. He found himself drawn to more of the rock carvings. He switched from pacing back and forth to a leisurely stroll around the perimeter where he was able to see the history of man unfold on the walls of the cave. The story was not so different from the one he was told as a child. There were gods, and then there were gods and men. Later, more men came, and the gods disappeared. In between, there was quite a bit of blood and death. There was no indication of why the gods had left, though. In each scene, the gods were clearly dominant, having their way with the tiny humans carved into the wall. Landis had lived his life believing his ancestors had defeated the gods, but that was not the impression these carvings presented. Here, it seemed to Landis, the belief was that the gods simply picked up and left the humans to fight things out on their own.

Landis stole a glance at Tinen and Brond. The two were engaged in a casual conversation, oblivious to Landis. A low growl came from somewhere down the passage, and the brothers turned toward the sound. Landis sprinted toward the warriors. As they turned to face him, Landis crouched, while moving at a run, and kicked his feet out before his body. The move saw him successfully sliding between the brothers, who were not fast enough to react to a moving body that was close to the ground.

Just beyond the passage entrance, Landis's slide ceased, but he used his momentum to pop back to his feet, similar to a sackle player stealing the next acquisition point. Landis noted with satisfaction that the days playing the childhood game proved helpful when it came to combat. When he returned to the palace, he would need to ensure the young boys were still playing sackle in the schoolyard each day.

The impressive slide put Landis only feet from another chamber and he quickly covered the ground to its opening. Stepping inside, Landis had to consciously keep his jaw from hanging agape. Even the palace vault did not have the abundance of treasure piled in this room. There was barely room to walk as Landis made his way through the gold and jewels that seemed to have been dumped in the chamber by the cartful. As Landis passed a table laden with gemstones, he stepped close enough to palm a diamond the size of his sword pommel.

In the center of the chamber, Dabwey and Alaria stood beside a pedestal with an egg-shaped stone balanced upon it. Landis recognized it as another God Stone. He also recognized Dabwey's narrowed eyes as a particularly menacing glare. Landis dropped the diamond onto the nearest pile of treasure. Dabwey dipped her head in approval.

Alaria looked beyond Landis and held up her hand. Her sons

had followed Landis into the chamber, but the tribeswoman did not want them to continue any farther. Landis also stopped moving. Alaria's gaze was serene when she addressed the prince.

"After some discussion, Dabwey has convinced me that she should be permitted to take the dragon stone with her."

Landis, recalling the growl that had distracted the brothers and permitted Landis to gain access to this chamber, wondered how loosely Alaria was using the word 'discussion.' Landis looked at Dabwey, expecting instruction, but the small dragon just sat back on her hind legs and examined a front claw.

"Right," said Landis. "I suppose you'll need me to carry that for you."

Landis carefully removed the rock from the pedestal and turned to leave the chamber. He eyed the riches all around him as he stalked toward the exit, painfully aware that everyone's eyes were on him. He had expected the dragon egg to be displayed prominently somewhere. There was no sign of it. Tinen and Brond hadn't missed the objects of Landis's attention either. They closed in directly behind him and followed closely until Landis was out of reach of the treasure. Alaria and Dabwey exited after them and were the last to pass through the larger chamber and back outside.

CHAPTER 10: MEARA

*T*he light was much brighter than it should be. Meara was in a hut, protected from the sun, but even the light cascading through the reeds over the entrance made her head throb. She felt better with her eyes closed, but that made it impossible to evaluate her surroundings. She succumbed to the pain and closed her eyes again. Moments later, she heard feet pounding at a gallop. The sound stopped abruptly as they approached and when Meara squinted through her eyelids, Dabwey was careening toward her and the sound of feet was replaced with that of wing beats. The small dragon collided with Meara, pushing her out of the seated position she had only just established.

"Meara! You're awake!"

Thankfully, Dabwey yelling into her head was less painful for Meara than holding her eyes open. Meara just sat back and permitted the little dragon to inspect her for unseen injuries and chatter on about finding her sibling. The little creature could be a major source of confusion. One moment, Dabwey was proclaiming her godliness and practically requiring humans to bow before her, and the next moment, she was acting as if she were an infant in need of coddling. Meara considered that this was not dissimilar to the behavior of any young girl, switching from demanding the respect and freedom of someone twice her age to looking for her favorite blanket so she could curl up in an elder's lap and hear a story.

As Meara's head cleared further, she became fixated on the subject of Dabwey's story. The dragon was in possession of a God Stone. Well, Landis had one. Alaria had relinquished the prize to Dabwey, but the little dragon had needed Landis to carry it. This made Meara smile, despite the pain in her head. She wished she had been in the nest to see the look on the prince's face when Dabwey required him to act as a simple beast of burden.

Meara held up her hand to slow the stream of thoughts flooding from Dabwey. The dragon acquiesced and paused with her head tilted in expectation. Meara took a measured breath as she fought through the lightning striking through her brain when she opened her eyes. She managed a smile at the tiny goddess.

"So, you found a sister? I can see you are thrilled. Did Landis tell you what the plan is now?"

Dabwey drew her head back in indignation. The glare from her golden eyes attempted to burn holes through Meara's flesh.

"Your assumption that Landis has a plan at all is laughable! Even if the prince thought more than minutes ahead, do you think I would trust him with the future of my kin? Speaking of which, you also made the assumption the egg bears my sister. We cannot know such things."

Meara held up her hand again. "I'm sorry. You are correct. I am making far too many assumptions. Let's do this one thought at a time. My head is pounding."

"I imagine it would pain you. It was starved of oxygen and it is working hard to repair itself. I expect you will be well soon, though. There seems to be no permanent damage to your important parts."

"Thank you, Dabwey, for the analysis. I'm sure your years of training with the healers have made you an expert."

"Rude!" Dabwey screeched in Meara's head. "Also, slightly amusing and almost funny. I shall not roast you for your comment."

"I appreciate that," said Meara. "Now, tell me how you convinced the Dinnen to give you the God Stone."

It took nearly an hour, but Dabwey recounted every event since she had flown off to demand aid from the Dinnen people. Meara was careful not to push too hard or contradict any of Dabwey's obvious bias as the dragon told her story. The pounding in Meara's head couldn't contend with a fresh tirade from an indignant dragon, so Meara concentrated on listening instead of trying to hold a conversation and risk upsetting the creature. Dabwey's emotions were proving to be quite volatile.

Dabwey ended her tale with her own arrival here in the hut to find Meara awake. The dragon nuzzled Meara's chin with the top of her head and released a soothing sound that was similar to a forest cat's purr. Meara stroked the top of Dabwey's head absently for a moment as the two sat in silence.

"So," Meara spoke at last. "Where is our illustrious prince?"

"Landis? How should I know? He's probably sitting on a rock somewhere trying to figure out how to steal some of the treasure from the temple. The buffoon went all wide-eyed as soon as he saw it. I caught him trying to take some, but I discouraged him from doing so. It's only metal and stone. I don't see what the excitement is about."

Meara raised an eyebrow. Mamma Jade had been correct. The Skalven soldiers were not interested in hunting lands. They were driven by the prospect of wealth. That described the priority of the race. Almost immediately, a darkness swept through Meara over the assumption that there were more people with the same ill intent as the one Skalve she was traveling with. Landis coveted jewels and gold. It niggled at her that a man born into unimaginable wealth would be fixated on acquiring more. Meara's driving force for most of her life had been to try to be a part of her community and to serve Mamma Jade and the gods well. She supposed Landis would find that trivial and unbefitting as a life goal.

"Call the Prince," Meara said. "We need to decide on our next steps."

"There's no need to consult him. I know what we need to do."

"You only just hatched days ago, but you've got all the answers?"

"Meara, you are an amazing person, but I fear you may have forgotten I am a goddess. Of course I have the answers."

Meara couldn't help but smile. Dabwey was revealing herself to be more like a teenager each time she spoke. Meara chose not to refute the dragon's most recent comment.

"I think it is best we at least give the impression he has a say in the matter."

"You make a fine point there. The prince is much more likely to be compliant if we permit him to feel as if he is in charge."

"Yes, Dabwey. Those are my thoughts, exactly."

Meara shook her head at the irony and barely had time to register that the motion caused less pain than earlier, before Landis peered into the hut. Sunlight spilled in from behind the prince, and Meara closed her eyes against it. The pain bright light caused her did not seem to have lessened. The sound of Landis's steps neared Meara's bed, and she reopened her eyes to see genuine concern etched on the prince's face.

He spoke tentatively. "Are you… are you fully ok?"

"My head hurts, but other than that, I am fine."

The prince relaxed. "I was concerned. The tribal leader warned that your brain might not function properly after an ordeal such as yours. I was worried you might not be yourself. Does this mean you are able to travel?"

"I don't think I have many options. Dabwey insists we have a journey to take and I need to go with her."

"Need?" Landis asked. "That's a strong word."

Meara considered for a moment. "Even if I didn't feel so connected to Dabwey, I don't think I would want to stay in an unfamiliar village. My people always warned the Dinnen were ruthless. They have shown us kindness, but I suspect that is Dabwey's influence. If she leaves, I don't think we'll be offered the courtesies we currently have."

"Let me get this straight," said Landis. "Dabwey wants to leave and you want to go with her. Is there room for me on this upcoming journey?"

"I have no village to return to and a new connection to a dragon driving me to embark on the trip. To what do you owe your desire to accompany us?"

"I am troubled by the thought of leaving you on your own, especially in your weakened condition."

Meara's expression remained impassive as she stared at the prince. She waited to see if he would say more. After a moment, Landis released a large puff of air.

"Ok, honestly?" he asked.

"That is precisely what I am waiting for," replied Meara.

"I fear our situations are more alike than you realize. My own army tried to kill me. I knew they were an unruly bunch, but I didn't know the extent of it. Some part of that might be due to my inexperience leading them, but I don't think I did so poor a job that it should have driven them to hunt me down as they did. There is more to the story and I fear it is connected to unrest back home."

"If you fear trouble in the kingdom of Skalve, then shouldn't you be concerned about the safety of your parents?"

Landis was quiet. Meara couldn't read his expression, but the look did not appear to be one of concern. When Landis finally spoke, his voice was nearly too quiet for Meara to hear him.

"I'm scared. I worry my parents might be partially to blame for the soldiers' attempts on my life. I failed to acquire the one item I was sent to retrieve. My death might be the only way my parents can save face with our people. Someone must take responsibility and be held accountable for the failure."

"You think your own parents sent the soldiers to kill you?" Meara was unable to hide her horror at the thought.

"Not exactly," Landis replied. "I suspect the soldiers already had the orders when we left the palace grounds. They were likely instructed to kill me if I failed to steal the dragon egg artifact."

Landis appeared as if he was waiting for Meara to berate him, and she nearly did. Her first instinct was to lash out at him for attacking her people and attempting to plunder the temple. She held herself in check and allowed her brain time to process his words instead. Her head still hurt, and this did not help her feel any better.

Meara already knew the prince had been leading a force to steal the treasure from the temple. She had already been aware he was in search of the dragon egg, and she had established that Landis was under the misguided impression that the artifact he was seeking was some kind of jewel-encrusted fabrication. No additional affronts had been committed toward Meara or her people, and there was no reason to reignite her previous rage. Meara's initial anger disappeared when it occurred to her that the prince was unaware that he had unwittingly succeeded in his mission.

"Landis, there is something you should know. I think the legends your people know of the dragon eggs are embellished."

"I am not a fool, Meara. I do not believe the eggs are

anywhere near as large or as priceless as my people believe. It only makes sense that the stories would make the eggs out to be irresistible in an attempt to encourage more people to hunt for them."

Meara winced. "I fear you misunderstand me. The dragons' eggs that the tribes have protected for generations are nothing like those you describe. There are no jewels and none is made of gold. They are simply stone."

"I do understand," said Landis. "That is what I was saying. I expected the stories of the gold and jewels were hyperbole. It would be logical that the dragons' eggs were simply carved from precious stone."

Meara sighed. Her head was throbbing again. Her people had been so careful to keep the secret of the God Stones, it had never occurred to her that outsiders wouldn't believe the truth if they chanced upon it. She took a more direct approach.

"You did not fail in your mission to steal the dragon egg from the Innut Temple. We left the island with the egg when we escaped the crash of the wave. We carried the egg from the beach where we washed up and brought it with us as we fled into the forest. The egg hatched, Landis. We are traveling in the company of a young goddess."

CHAPTER 11: LANDIS

*T*he truth crashed through the prince's mind. Landis tried to close his gaping mouth. How had he not made this connection?

He had been so focused on the stories of the priceless artifacts the tribal people were charged with guarding that it had never occurred to him to wonder what made them so invaluable. His people really were as materialistic as others thought. There had been no question in Landis's mind that the egg he sought was covered in glittery gold or a giant sparkling jewel.

It seemed so obvious to Landis now. Of course, the dragon eggs were real eggs. That would make them more valuable than any other item known to man. When he and Dabwey entered the Dinnen Temple earlier, the dragon had mentioned that her kind was not attracted to treasure in the way humans assumed. A golden or bejeweled egg would never be enough to draw the old gods back to this land. On the other hand, holding their children hostage would have them flying to Skalve as fast as their wings would carry them.

Landis watched Dabwey as she sat sentry at the foot of Meara's bed. Her tail swished occasionally like that of a cat. She was the child of gods. Better than that, she was a god herself. Indeed, the dragon egg was priceless.

"I'm sorry, Landis," said Meara. "I was afraid you would take the God Stone and disappear if I explained it to you earlier. Once Dabwey hatched, I didn't think telling you that your dragon egg and the God Stone were the same mattered anymore."

Landis wanted to be angry at Meara for withholding information, but he couldn't bring the emotion to the surface. There was something in the way. Landis had trouble identifying the feeling crawling just under his skin. He didn't like it. It was chasing his assuredness away and causing his confidence to seek a hiding place deep within him.

"Please don't ignore me, Landis. It was not my intention to make you feel foolish."

Landis held up his hand to stop Meara from continuing. She had identified the feeling by name. Landis did not enjoy this new emotion. It wasn't her fault, though. It was he who had not been open-minded enough to realize he and his people had misinterpreted the old stories.

"No, Meara. It is I who should apologize. My own stereotypes and preconceptions led me to my understanding of the dragon eggs. If I hadn't been so sure of myself..."

Landis trailed off as another thought invaded his mind. He slid his pack from his back and brought it around to rest on the edge of the bed. He stared at it for a moment, waiting for the idea to fully form.

Suddenly, Meara sat up straight in bed. Her eyes grew wide, and she whipped her head toward Landis.

"Dabwey said to tell you not to be foolish."

"But, Meara. This is the answer to my problem. I was sent to your village to get the dragon egg and bring it back to my parents. The king and queen need the egg as leverage to use against the old gods."

"Think about what you are saying, Landis! More importantly, think about the company in which you are saying it."

Landis shook his head to clear his thoughts and glanced

from Meara to the dragon at her feet. Dabwey's eyes were narrowed to slits again and Landis thought he saw a little puff of smoke come from her nostrils. He immediately wished he had not voiced the words outside of his own mind.

The prince pulled the dragon egg from his pack, running his hands over its etched surface. He imagined the pride on his father's face when he returned to Broen with a real dragon egg. Dabwey huffed. The purple goddess before him was a potent reminder that the egg was more than just a symbol. He put the rock away.

With the pack closed and the stone out of view, Dabwey stopped scrutinizing Landis. The scaled creature resumed vigil over Meara. Based on Meara's side of the conversation, Landis gathered Meara was getting stronger and attempting to convince the dragon they should leave soon. When Meara pulled the covers back to leave the bed, Landis spun away. He had noticed the girl's deerskin frock folded on the chair beside him, but the blankets had kept Meara covered.

Red-faced, Landis mumbled an apology, grabbed his sheathed sword from where it leaned on the wall of the hut, and bumbled outside. Once in the sunlight, he was unsure what to do. The contents of his pack weighed on his mind and spurred him to walk. He did not stop. He walked south, in the opposite direction from the bog that had tried to end his life. At first, he checked over his shoulder often to see if anyone had watched him leave and decided to follow him. Only when Landis was satisfied he had made his escape did he slow.

He was unsure of his destination. 'Away' was not exactly a place. At some point, he was going to need to make his way back to Skalve. He needed to deliver the dragon egg to his parents if there was to be any hope for the future of the Skalven people. The king and queen had been sure in their beliefs that without the egg, there would be no way to lure the old gods from hiding. The deities couldn't be killed until they returned. Killing them was the only way to return the weather to its predictable patterns and allow life to continue for those in Skalve.

Unless, well...the Skalven people could move south and leave the increasingly uninhabitable lands behind. There was more to this land than the area claimed by Landis's ancestors hundreds of years earlier. Moving an entire people through the tribal lands and into the southlands would be a feat, but it was a possibility. Pride would be a hindrance to that solution, though. It was unlikely King Palden and Queen Brynn would contemplate abandoning their ancestral home. They would consider the move a defeat and that was unacceptable to the egotism of the Skalven people.

Landis stopped walking. A familiar sensation had come over him. It was the same feeling he had experienced when Meara and he had crested the hill as they fled from his treacherous soldiers. It was an invigorating lightness that made him feel as if he could walk forever without tiring. He felt stronger, and he breathed more easily. His senses seemed heightened. Was he smelling the dampened fur of an animal that passed through the area earlier, or was it just a trick of his mind? The scent of pine was heavy in his nostrils, yet there were no pine trees to be seen.

The first time energy had revived him like this, he had attributed it to adrenalin and the realization that he and Meara had outrun their pursuers. This time, there was no discernible cause for the feeling. Landis had determined he was not being followed some time ago. He backtracked a few yards, and the air pressed into his skin. It weighed on him and the pleasant scents of the surrounding forest dulled. Landis spun and walked in the direction he was heading previously. After a moment, the lightness returned, as if he had passed through an invisible barrier.

Landis removed his pack and sat down on a tree that had fallen across the game trail he was following. He placed his pack between his feet and removed his water skin from his belt. He had not filled it before leaving the village of the Dinnen, and it was empty before Landis felt he had properly quenched his thirst. Meara would not have let them set off from the village without properly resupplying. She may have come from a primitive civilization, but she was far better than him at surviving in the wilderness. Landis was accustomed to striking out with an entourage hand-picked for the purpose of serving his needs. It was their job to be sure he had all the supplies he might need on his journey.

The deep inhalation that was meant to precede a sigh brought the smell of something burning. Landis looked through the surrounding trees for the source of the smoke. It wasn't until his ankles warmed that he realized the pack between his feet was smoldering. He grabbed it and dumped the dragon egg onto the forest floor. The pack stopped smoking when Landis smacked it against the log a few times, but the stone before him started glowing with heat. He knew what was about to happen. There would be no way to bring the dragon egg to his parents now.

Landis stood and retreated to the far side of the log on which he had been sitting. He remained close enough to see a crack forming on the surface of the egg. Light emanating from the egg blinded him in spite of the distance he had gained. With his arm shielding his eyes, Landis still needed to turn away to keep them from burning. The voice in his head a moment later did not come as a surprise to the prince.

"Oh! Lucky me! I found a prince for a father. At least I can expect the food to be delicious. What delicacies have you procured for me?"

"I'm sorry to disappoint you so early in your life. Unless you enjoy tree bark, I am ill prepared to provide for you."

"This is outrageous! You bring a god into this world and have no offerings upon my arrival?"

"It was not my plan to hatch you. I expected to continue my travels with a rock, not with a creature requiring sustenance."

Landis took in the newly hatched dragon, making comparisons to Dabwey. The animal before him had shimmering blue scales, but the same golden eyes as Meara's hatchling. There were no cheek flaps on the sides of the dragon's face, so Landis deduced the creature was male.

"Young master," Landis said. "Now that we are to be traveling companions —"

The dragon interrupted. "You shall address me as Lord, or use my proper name. Please remember, I am a god."

To Landis, the tiny scaled creature was anything but a god. At the time, Landis only saw the creature as another mouth to feed. He was still trying to work out how a live dragon might change his plans to return to Skalve.

"Sure. May I know your proper name, lord?"

"My name is Ronvost, god of justice and equality."

"Ronvost. A strong name! How fitting that a prince should have a god of justice as his vincule," Landis said proudly.

"I see you have some knowledge of our ancient ways. Unfortunately, you are confused. You are my vincule, not the other way around."

"Whatever. It is one and the same."

Ronvost narrowed his snake-like eyes at Landis. "It is entirely different. I am a god. I am no one's vincule."

"It did not sound like being a vincule was such a terrible thing when Dabwey explained it to Meara."

"Becoming a vincule elevates a human to a place of honor. It is an extraordinary thing for your kind. A vincule has a connection to his dragon and a duty to serve him."

Landis was starting to understand. In the eyes of a dragon, a vincule was a servant. Ronvost felt Landis was beneath him. Well, that was not new information. Dabwey's attitude had been the same without her needing to spell it out. The little scaled gods would certainly make an arrogant pair. Landis decided it was best not to challenge his position with the blue dragon.

"I see, Ronvost. Forgive me. In which direction shall we proceed?"

The little dragon sniffed the air and turned. He sniffed again and paused. After a moment, he turned back to Landis.

"I don't know. I'm hungry and I'm tired. Hatching is quite an ordeal. I sense a pull to the south-east. I'll nap in your pack while you travel in that direction. With hope, the respite will keep me from deciding you are no better than a meal."

Landis sighed. He grabbed his pack from the ground and held it open so the tiny dragon could crawl inside. He wiggled into the straps so the bag pressed on his back. The feeling of Ronvost turning to find comfort was unnerving, but the dragon settled quickly and Landis started walking.

Landis had no food and no water. His ears were tuned to discover the first sound of a stream or river, but food was going to be an issue. The sword on Landis's hip was not a weapon for hunting. He wouldn't be able to throw the heavy blade at a deer. If he stopped to camp, he could set some small traps for rabbits as he had done when traveling with Meara, but if he caught nothing, he would be adding hours to his travels with nothing to show for the extra time.

Landis waded through a large stream an hour later. He stopped on the far side and filled his skin from a fast moving section a few yards upriver. A large rock on the river's edge provided a place for the prince to rest. The respite only lasted a moment.

"Have we stopped so I might eat?" Ronvost's voice asked weakly in Landis's mind.

"As I've informed you, I have no food."

"You must find some soon or I will perish. It is imperative that a dragon eat within hours of hatching."

Landis straightened at the words. He had believed Ronvost to be complaining when he shared his displeasure at the lack of food when he entered the world. The prince had brushed off the demand as unimportant. The dragon must not die. Landis needed him to bargain for forgiveness when he returned to Skalve. Without a dragon egg, the dragon itself would need to be the bargaining chip between the king and queen and the old gods.

A large fish leaped into the air, mere feet from Landis, taunting the prince. There was no way to catch it. Landis removed the snare wire from his pack and set some traps near the brush nearby. It didn't promise to be a suitable location for trapping, but Landis was running low on options. He moved a distance from the area and sat beneath a tree.

Ronvost crawled from Landis's pack and walked on unsteady feet to sprawl beside the prince, placing his head on Landis's lap. Both the dragon and the prince started to doze while Landis gently ran his fingers over the scales between the dragon's eyes. The tender moment was shattered when the earth shook.

Landis opened his eyes and stared straight at a giant scaled foreleg. A green dragon, nearly the height of a tall man at the shoulders, lowered its head before the prince and released a small puff of heated air. Ronvost lifted his tiny head from Landis's lap and opened his mouth. The green dragon opened his as well and dropped a lump of furry meat from his jaws. The smaller dragon swiped the torn carcass from the air and chewed ravenously.

CHAPTER 12: MEARA

*D*abwey was on fire. Not literally, but from within. The air around the scaled creature felt several degrees warmer as Meara approached the fuming goddess. The sounds Dabwey pushed into Meara's head vacillated between grumbles and terrifying roars, but the young dragon appeared placid. If not for the heat that seeped from her skin, one would think the dragon was passively awaiting her next meal to be served.

Meara tied her locks back with a strip of leather. Alaria herself had brushed out Meara's dark hair and re-braided it. Meara had asked her to make a single white braid from the bleached strands to mimic the look Mamma Jade had always provided.

"I checked the entire village. He is not here. Alaria has checked in with her scouts and none saw Landis leave," Meara said.

"He left alright. He has moved beyond the suppression boundary. I can no longer smell him."

Dabwey's words smoldered in Meara's mind. She knew the dragon wasn't angry with her, but Dabwey was having difficulty separating her anger from the conversation at hand. Meara's head throbbed.

"Suppression boundary?" Meara asked.

"Yes. When the old gods placed their children in the care of the land's tribal people, they ensured lasting protection for them by surrounding the temples in a magical boundary. Those who entered the area surrounding any temple would find their magic limited and therefore the tribal people would more easily be able to defend against any who came to do harm. Within this village, even my magic is limited."

Meara considered this information. "Is that why your egg didn't hatch?"

"Yes. A substantial quantity of magic is drawn from nature when a dragon egg hatches. Limiting that source of power keeps our eggs dormant and can protect us for millennia within our shell."

"So the only reason you hatched is because I brought you outside of the Yahkanah Temple's magical barrier?"

"Indeed, and now my sibling has left the Dinnen barrier with that idiot prince."

So many thoughts invaded Meara's mind. She wasn't sure which one to address first. Landis was not so terrible. Meara's sibling would hatch. Had other dragons hatched? That last thought sprung to the top of the list of important questions on Meara's mind.

"For years, our people have spoken of the destruction of God Stones across the tribal lands. Temples were desecrated and the God Stones were stolen or destroyed. Why have I never heard of a God Stone hatching? Wouldn't that occur as soon as someone brought the dragon egg across the magical boundary line?"

Dabwey's voice became calmer. "When I hatched and saw you for the first time, I knew you were worthy of elevation to the station of vincule. If not for that, I would have immediately destroyed you and all those around you. It would have protected me, but sentenced me to a solitary life. A dragon bonds a vincule at the time of hatching. If that bond doesn't form immediately, there will never be such a connection."

Meara paled. Landis had many faults, not least of which was

his open disbelief in the gods. There was no way a hatching dragon would find him worthy of becoming its vincule. The newly hatched deity would surely incinerate the prince.

"We need to leave before it is too late," said Meara.

Heat pushed from Dabwey once again. "It is already too late. The prince is outside of the boundary. My sibling has hatched."

Pushing aside thoughts of Landis dying, Meara asked, "What happens to a young dragon that does not form an immediate bond?"

"A hatchling needs to eat immediately or it will die. The new god will devour the human that carried the egg outside of the boundary and anyone else in the area. After that, the young dragon will have the strength to hunt on its own and will grow quickly. The god will thrive physically, but will not have the emotional balance provided by a vincule. It will be rash and destructive; unpredictable."

Landis was likely dead. Meara could not imagine a newly hatched god finding the prince worthy of anything but a meal. Meara was having a difficult time believing Dabwey had found her acceptable, and she was a temple keeper for the gods. She had been responsible for tending Dabwey's temple. The prince's mission was to steal the dragon eggs and bring them back to Skalve. He was exactly the type of person from whom the gods were looking to protect their children. This meant Landis was dead and there was a feral baby dragon on the loose in the land.

Meara grabbed her few belongings from the hut where she had convalesced and nodded her thanks to Alaria as she walked back out into the sunlight. The woman's frantic attempts to convince the pair to stay were alarming. At least, Meara was hoping the impending departure was the cause of her agitation. Dabwey had forced Alaria to turn over the Dinnen egg and now the prince had made off with it. There was every possibility that the desire to kill Meara causing the woman's agitation. She was Dinnen, after all.

Dabwey's golden eyes glowed as she caught Alaria's gaze and the tribal leader calmed at once. Alaria gave a peaceful wave as Meara struck out to find the newly hatched god within the grand expanse of the forest.

Someone from the tribe had washed and oiled her skins and then allowed them to dry in the sun. The clothing that had been neatly folded near Meara's bed was far more comfortable than when she had worn it last. It made walking easier, even if the dull thud in her head did not.

"At least we needn't worry that my sibling has perished," Dabwey spoke into Meara's mind. "If there were a chance the newly hatched god actually found the prince worthy, then we would need to be concerned that Landis did not know the god would need to feed."

"I hate that you have no faith in Landis's worth."

Even as Meara thought the words toward her dragon, she knew Dabwey was stating the obvious. If the hatchling found Landis worthy, the likelihood of Landis having the forethought to bring food for himself, let alone a baby dragon, was almost none. As a highborn male, this would not be a chore he would ever have been expected to perform for himself.

Meara contemplated the possibility that a new dragon might see Landis's demeanor and shortcomings the way she did. It was possible the dragon could forgive his transgressions and attribute them to the circumstances in which he was raised. If that were the case, might the dragon find Landis worthy after all?

Dabwey replied to Meara's musings. "I hadn't considered that. We might want to pick up the pace. Only a hatchling can determine a future vincule's assets. I find it difficult to express the process in words. When I broke through the shell of my stone, I met your eyes and immediately took you to be mine. It was not something I needed to consider, and I was not even aware the prince was also in the vicinity. Once I accepted you, that innate part of me fell away and I find I am already forgetting the feeling that initially drew me to you."

Meara never asked her next question. She felt something clamp onto her shoulders and her feet lifted from the ground. She closed her eyes to stop the vertigo caused by watching the forest floor retreat. The sight above her when she tilted her head and re-opened her eyes caused the hair on her skin to stand on end. Meara was in the grasp of a green dragon. She couldn't see past the creature's belly except for the tips of its wings each time they beat against the air, but she could tell this dragon was several times larger than Dabwey. How was it possible that the new dragon could already be so large? Dabwey was not even big enough to lift Meara, and she had been out of her stone for days.

Though Dabwey shared no words, her anxiety was palpable. Meara felt it grow as the purple dragon launched from the ground to chase behind the green monster. When her captor circled before landing, Meara glimpsed Dabwey, already many lengths behind, preparing to land as well. It occurred to Meara that Dabwey, outmatched in size by the green dragon, would be killed easily if it came to a fight.

The green dragon dropped Meara as it neared the ground. Meara ran as soon as her feet touched the dirt. After only a few steps, her momentum got the best of her and she fell forward, with her arms stretched before her. When she lifted her face, Meara stared directly into the eyes of a tiny blue dragon with saliva dripping from his sharp teeth. Heavy footsteps on the ground behind her alerted Meara to her precarious position between the two dragons. How were there two dragons? There had only been one God Stone in the Dinnen temple.

Dabwey had yet to arrive when feet, clad in black boots, cut off Meara's view of the shimmering blue dragon.

A familiar voice cried, "Pardon! Please! Meara is not food! She is a friend of mine!"

Though the green dragon behind Meara only let out a loud huff, Meara's heart lifted at the sound of Landis's voice. Between the prince and Dabwey, there might be a chance they could fight their way out of this situation. Meara didn't like the idea of killing a dragon, but Landis could slay the blue one, and then the green one might leave if it felt outmatched.

Dabwey's voice came to Meara at last. "You and the prince are only human, and I am too small. No god would cower in our presence. I need to try to speak with the green god."

"Well, get down here and start talking," thought Meara.

Meara's eyes grew wide as Landis stretched out to touch the blue dragon. The fool was going to have his hand removed by the little god's teeth! To Meara's surprise, the prince reached back and stroked the dragon's head. The tiny dragon looked up into the prince's eyes when Landis turned his head to look over his shoulder at the small, yet terrifying, animal. The miniature god sat back on its hind legs and closed its mouth.

Warm breath blew across the back of Meara's neck before she could enjoy the relief she should have felt with the loss of the minor threat before her. Behind her, Dabwey's words had not swayed the opinion of the larger threat. Meara still felt the purple dragon's presence in her mind. They were not out of danger, but at least Dabwey was still alive after her conversation with the green beast. As Meara prepared to turn toward the dragon with the emerald scales, a sharp whistle pierced the air.

All heads whipped toward the direction of the sound. A burly human, clad in Skalven trousers paired with a tribal vest made from animal skins, stood among the trees. The man's dark blonde hair was pulled back, but a single wisp fell over his forehead. He brushed it aside with the back of his hand.

"Brock, leave the innocent people alone!"

The green dragon snorted its displeasure toward its vincule. Meara chanced a glance at the terrifying creature behind her. She couldn't suppress a giggle when she saw the ear flaps at the sides of the dragon's face. She debated the merits of mentioning this to the man who called the dragon Brock when it occurred to her that this man couldn't be the dragon's vincule. If he were, he would already know his dragon was female.

Dabwey stepped up next to the green dragon. Her head was cocked so she could look up at the green dragon with her left eye. To Meara, it looked as if Dabwey was communicating with the larger female. The enormity of her situation washed over Meara as she watched the silent conversation between the two creatures. Landis was alive, a strange male was approaching, and she was in the presence of three gods. Meara turned her attention to Landis first.

"Did you feed him yet?"

"Hello, Meara! You are welcome. Balder and I accept your thanks and assure you we are glad to have been of service."

"Yes! Of course, thank you," said Meara. "You and… Balder, was it? I owe you both my life. Now, did you feed the hatchling?"

Several seconds passed before Landis answered, "Ronvost wants me to share that he is happy to see I, at least, keep the company of intelligent friends. He is still angry that I had no food offering for him when he hatched."

"So, you haven't fed him? Take food from my pack. He'll die if he doesn't eat within hours of hatching."

"So he said," said Landis. "Fortunately, Brock took care of feeding Ronvost before death came for him. Poor girl… I tried to tell Balder that Brock is a female, but he refused to believe me."

"I don't understand. Why didn't Brock inform Balder of her gender, as Dabwey did for me? Is Brock even the dragon's real name?"

"Balder has yet to answer those questions," said Landis. "He and I only had a moment together while Brock was off hunting in which we were able to speak. I have yet to learn how Brock and Balder found each other."

"Brock was hunting?" asked Meara. "That must mean I truly was meant to be Ronvost's next meal."

"You're rather large," replied Landis. "I suspect you were intended as a meal for Brock with the thought that you could be shared with Ronvost."

The corner of the prince's mouth turned up and some of the tension left Meara's body. Dabwey pushed into her mind.

"Our emerald friend is called Saldo. She is the goddess of balance and objectivity. We are fortunate a rogue like her is blessed with the responsibility of such serene characteristics."

"A world with balance only sounds serene," thought Meara. "If things are too pleasant, balance will require shifting events in the negative direction."

"You make a fair point," Dabwey admitted. "I suppose we should be grateful that things are looking rather unfavorable at this moment."

"Why doesn't Saldo's vincule know her real name?" Meara asked.

"It felt rude to ask," said Dabwey.

CHAPTER 13: BALDER

Thankfully, Brock stopped his advance on the tribal girl, but the situation had turned strange after that. None of the participants were speaking. After the prince and the girl exchanged a few words, all conversation had ceased. The girl glanced at the purple dragon, and then the dragon looked at Brock. The purple dragon turned to look back at the girl, and at last the girl spoke to Landis.

Balder was surprised to hear the tribal girl tell the prince Brock's name was Saldo. The prince had introduced Brock by name, so Balder did not understand why the girl was trying to change it. He approached the group with long, purposeful strides.

"Excuse me, Meara. The prince told you the dragon's name is Brock. What makes you think you can re-name him?"

"How did you know to call me Meara?"

"I heard Prince Landis scream it out loud when he commanded his baby dragon to keep from eating you."

The girl actually rolled her eyes. It had been almost a year since Balder had been in Skalve, but a man does not forget the eye-roll of a girl in her teens. The female before him looked older than that, though, old enough to no longer roll her eyes, anyway. Also, based on her attire, she was of the local tribes. Balder had never seen a tribal woman of any age meet his words with an eye-roll.

Meara said, "As evidenced by your belief that Landis

commanded a dragon to do anything, you don't really understand much about dragons, do you?"

"I expect I know more than the two of you. I've been traveling with Brock for nearly a year. By the looks of him, your dragon is barely a week old, and I already know Ronvost is newly hatched."

Meara gestured to Dabwey. "I am Dabwey's vincule. She and I share a bond that allows us to access each other's thoughts. I expect I've learned quite a lot from what she has shared. Also, Brock is a girl and her real name is Saldo."

"How do you know that?"

"Though I cannot communicate with the emerald goddess, Dabwey can. My dragon has shared this information with me through our mental bond."

Balder considered the new knowledge. He turned to look into Brock's eyes. The green dragon seemed to be imploring him to listen to Meara's words. Balder sighed.

"Ok, Saldo." The name felt funny on his tongue. "Forgive me if it takes me some time to start treating you like a lady."

The green dragon snorted and a puff of steam came from her nostrils. Over the months Balder had shared with the creature, he had come to understand this gesture as a laugh. Balder liked that the dragon appreciated his sense of humor. He shook his head in amazement, as he often did when he truly considered the green beast before him.

"I'm going to get a fire going. Brock —" Balder winced, then started again. "I'll start a fire and Saldo can hunt down some supper."

He removed his flint from his pocket and bent to look for kindling. After a moment, Balder noticed the green dragon hadn't moved.

"What gives, friend?" Balder asked the dragon.

Meara answered, "Dabwey took the liberty of informing

Saldo that she should not be taking commands from you. She tells me Saldo appreciates that you accept her name and gender, but now you will need to accept her elevated position as well."

Balder did not bother to ask what any of that meant. Now that he knew the dragon was female, it made sense. Like any woman, she didn't want to be told what to do. Balder turned his head up to Saldo.

"Dear Saldo, I beg of you, would you be so kind as to use your prowess to provide this evening's meal?"

"Laying it on a little thick, aren't you?" Meara asked.

Saldo beat her wings and took flight. Balder turned to Meara and smiled with satisfaction. He knew exactly how to speak to a lady.

The prince had used his own flint to get a small fire going, so Balder added the kindling from his arms to the flame, and then squatted to clear the leafy detritus from the area. Respect for nature was important to Balder, and he did not want to see it burn due to lack of care around a cook fire. Satisfied, he sat down beside the prince and beckoned for Meara to join the gathering. Though Balder was highly interested in learning how a tribal girl and a Skalven prince had met each other and then two dragons, he suspected he would need to share his own story first. He was outnumbered.

"I met Br — this is going to take some getting used to... I met Saldo almost a year ago. My company was sent from Skalve to retrieve her egg from the tribal village of Nahola. Of course, I didn't realize the damn thing was an actual egg at the time!"

Balder noticed the look of acknowledgement that crossed the prince's face. It was comforting to find the prince had also been unaware the dragon egg stories in Skalve were mostly fabricated. Balder's fears of being misled intentionally receded after months of uncertainty. He relaxed into his tale more easily.

"When we arrived in the village, it was hardly a fair fight. We

110

cut down the Nahola tribe without thought. I am ashamed to admit that I was no better than the others. To us, the tribal people were primitive and inconsequential."

Meara's face reddened. With no defense for his brutal treatment of the Nahola, Balder had to settle for a pleading look that he hoped conveyed to Meara that he knew it had been a reprehensible act. She had every right to be angry, but he was in no need of a lecture or tirade. He had learned much since that day. Meara remained silent, though her eyes smoldered. Balder continued his story.

"We entered the temple and easily found the treasure room. I'd never seen so many sparkling things in a single place. We all started filling our sacks with all the riches we could carry, even leaving clothing and other possessions behind to make more room in our bags. A few of the crew were content to leave after that. It was as if they had forgotten what our mission had been. They walked out of the temple as deserters. The rest of us eventually found a giant stone in a different chamber of the temple. It took us some time to come to terms with the idea that the dragon egg we were tasked with finding was a rock, and not some elegant piece of treasure."

Meara was unable to remain silent after that comment. "The stones are the greatest of treasures granted to us by the gods. It is both a duty and an honor to protect them and keep them safe from the wrath of time and those with evil intentions."

"Spoken like a true believer in the old gods," said Balder. "You'll need to remember I had no knowledge of these things at the time. I've since examined the carvings in the temple. I've seen a dragon born into this world. My view of the old ways has changed in the months since this story occurred."

Balder had battled within his own mind over the past several months trying to reconcile the beliefs he had been raised with among the Skalve and the knowledge he acquired while living among the ruins of the tribal village. Even with no one to share his feelings with, he had been embarrassed over his own ignorance. Since working through those emotions on his own, Balder found it easy to acknowledge his previous misconceptions now.

Meara took a breath and sat back. She still wore a daunting expression on her face, but she seemed content to allow Balder to speak without further interruption for the time being.

"We took the stone. We were unsure how we would explain the true nature of the dragon egg to the royalty back in Skalve, but we hoped the rock would provide some evidence of the reality we uncovered. We struck out from Nahola with a general understanding that we would not be greeted with fanfare when we returned home. Much of our conversation focused on speculating about the punishments we might need to endure for failing in our quest to obtain the coveted dragon egg the king and queen were expecting."

The prince let out a sound similar to a whimper. "I'm sorry, Your Highness. I meant no ill-will against your family, but —"

Prince Landis held up a hand to stop Balder from speaking. "It is not your ill words regarding my parents that have me distraught. I was sent on a mission, eerily similar to the one you are describing. Your story stirs undesirable thoughts. I'm sorry for the interruption. Please continue."

Balder considered the prince. He seemed deflated. It was as if his confidence had been physical support for his body. With Balder's words chiseling away at that sureness, the prince was collapsing in on himself. He considered ending his story before any other details could affect the prince, but a glance at Meara's expectant stare spurred him forward with his tale.

"About twenty of us remained. A small band of soldiers, about one fourth the size of our original force, were picking our way through the forest when Thomas screamed. The lad was barely sixteen, and the youngest among us by far. We had charged him with carrying the stone and he threw his pack to the ground as if it were burning through his back. As you might know, it was doing just that.

"The pack went up in flames and revealed the stone egg to be glowing a brilliant red, as if the fire of the earth were pushing out from within it. Thomas's clothing was blackened and stuck to the skin where the pack had rested moments before. I still don't understand why the boy didn't remove it earlier. He lay moaning on the ground when a loud crack echoed through the forest and my eyes were drawn back to the stone. A light, far too bright to be safe for one's vision, flashed, and I returned my eyes to Thomas, mostly to shield my eyes, though I tell myself it was also to check on his condition. The boy was unconscious. I crouched beside him and tried to get him to speak to me.

"When my ears ceased to greet sound from behind me, I turned to find a small green serpent in the place where the stone had been tossed to the ground. The other soldiers encircled it and were stealthily drawing near to the creature. The dragon opened his mouth and flame poured forth. I turned from the immense heat and ran."

The prince was unnaturally still when he said, "None of you returned. I suspect my parents sent many missions in search of the dragon eggs over the last few years. As far as I know, no one returned. The soldiers under my command were undisciplined. One, such as yourself, might even describe some of the men as dishonorable. I was thinking it may have been my lack of leadership that encouraged the undesirable behavior, but your story is bringing new considerations. I fear my parents knew of your ill-fated journey, as well as the others, and sent soldiers thought to be expendable on my mission. I was included in that group, essentially sent to slaughter."

"My Prince," said Balder. "You were not sent to be

slaughtered. You were their last hope. The evidence is there, but you are interpreting it incorrectly. The soldiers under your command were all that were left in the kingdom. It is evident to me that the king and queen were so desperate to procure a dragon egg that they had to risk the life of their only son. It doesn't make them undesirable people. They were trying to save an entire kingdom."

Prince Landis did not appear to be convinced. He stroked the top of the blue dragon's head absently, deep in thought. He was roused from his thoughts when Saldo returned with the carcass of a deer. The prince tore raw strips of meat from the bone and tossed them into his dragon's mouth as Balder and Meara prepared the meal for the humans over the fire. Balder kept his distance as he watched the blue dragon's jaws snap around the meat, imagining the creature's teeth doing that to one of his arms or legs. Once the venison was set to roasting over the flame, Balder tended to it as he told the part of the story where he returned to the gruesome scene.

"When I returned to the area later to check for survivors, the dragon was still there. He had consumed most of the soldiers I had once considered my equals. The green serpent was curled up next to the charred torso of a good friend of mine. I'd known the man since we ran wild in the planting fields outside of the palace walls as boys. I wanted to give the man a proper burial. The dragon slept so soundly I was able to drag the body of my friend away and back into the tribal village. I buried him and said words over his grave to speed him into the afterlife.

"I planned to spend the night in the village and strike out for Skalve in the morning. I needed to get back and inform the king and queen of the creature we released into the tribal forest lands. I was in my bedroll, beside a fire, when I was awakened by something prodding my shoulder. The blasted dragon was pushing at me with his muzzle. I thought he was investigating to see if I was edible. I was careful as I moved away from him. The last thing I wanted to do was startle him into an attack. I sat up and looked at him. The silly little thing tilted his head to the side like a puppy. It was cute in a way and caused great conflict within me. The dragon was dangerous and had killed all the soldiers I had been traveling with. He had feasted on them.

"I did not want to be this creature's next meal. I got to my feet and went to the pens where the tribal people kept livestock. I ran my knife across the throat of a goat and began cutting pieces of meat for the tiny killer. I tossed him slivers in much the same way the prince has done for his blue dragon. The green dragon and I became tentative friends. Soon, it was he who was providing food for me. We lived together in the village for months, and here I am, discovering *he* is actually *a she*, and there are more of her kind."

CHAPTER 14: MEARA

*T*he feelings roiling within Meara throughout Balder's story continuously threatened to bubble out of her mouth. If not for Dabwey keeping up a steady stream of rationalizations and calming thoughts in Meara's mind, Balder would never have finished his tale. She struggled with Balder's blatant disregard for the tribal people and how he and his fellow soldiers treated them as if they were little more than locusts to be exterminated from a farmer's fields. The man before her had no reverence for the god he had helped bring into the world. Dabwey continued to remind Meara it was Balder's ignorance, not a malicious nature, which drove his actions.

"Meara, what comes next is up to you. You can harbor ill-will and anger, or you can share the miracle of the God Stones with Balder. Tell him *your* story. Share the teachings of your people."

Meara wasn't sure she was capable of explaining the history of the gods without being overcome by anger. It had been different with Landis. Her anger had been tempered by his obvious inexperience with all things tribal. Balder was living among the teachings of tribal history. He claimed he had changed as he came to understand the carvings in the temple. If this man had changed, what must he have been like before? Meara was rescued from making an immediate decision about how she would proceed when Landis spoke.

"Oh, Balder. I fear we have both been lied to and raised

with beliefs that created prejudice against tribal people and the power they hold over this land. I, too, once felt they were primitive and naïve. It is true they lack understanding of Skalven society, but our people hold only a small part of this land. Most of the earth is populated by tribal people, raised with ancient stories about powerful beings you and I can only imagine."

"My Prince," replied Balder. "Those stories were shared with us as well. We know of the terrible beings that hunted our people. It took generations to drive them away from the great settlement your ancestors founded. Those same creatures continue to work against Skalve. They influence the weather, the water, and the very air we breathe as they continue to diminish our ability to thrive."

"I fear you have forgotten the role of the tribes in our valiant effort to drive the old gods from our lands," said Landis.

"True, but even they have left us to die. The old gods need not even make their presence known to destroy us."

Meara listened to the debate unfold and found she could not agree with either man. Raised among the Yahkanah people, she had a very different perspective to offer.

"You are both forgetting an important point. In the time before the Skalven people ventured to this land, the tribal folk lived in harmony with the gods. It is not all humans the gods set themselves against. They entrusted the care of the God Stones to humans before leaving these lands. You may wish to take a closer look at your supposed superior culture before proceeding with your shared musings."

Meara was impressed with the eloquence of her own speech. She watched the two men consider her words, hoping she had guided them in the correct direction without offending them.

"You did well," Dabwey's voice pushed into her mind.

"Good luck. I'm hungry."

The purple dragon gave a strong beat of her wings and lifted into the sky. Saldo joined her a moment later.

"Thanks for your continued support," Meara thought.

"Always," Dabwey replied.

Meara was uncertain if the young dragon was unaware of Meara's sarcastic undertone, or if it just didn't translate well when communicating telepathically. It hardly mattered. Landis pulled his eyes from his sleeping dragon and addressed Balder.

"Meara speaks truth," said Landis. "Even our tales tell of dragons terrorizing our people. There is no mention of them threatening the native population."

"What about the stories of the tribal people hiding with your ancestors in caves to seek protection from the wrath of the creatures dominating the land?" Balder asked.

"Take care with your words," Landis cautioned. "Telling of tribal people *helping* my ancestors hide is different from telling of the native people hiding with the invading Skalve."

Meara was encouraged by the prince's words. She was unsure if she should point out the use of certain words that showed Landis's turn against the traditional beliefs of his own people. She chose to keep those thoughts to herself.

"Tell me, Meara, why is it that you and Prince Landis are able to speak with your dragons, while I have no knowledge of Saldo's thoughts?"

Meara stopped herself from barreling into an explanation that might make Balder sound unworthy of a bond. She chose her words with care.

"When a dragon hatches, he or she takes the measure of the first human it sees. Within seconds, the young god will determine if the human has qualities considered desirable when forming a bond. The newly hatched dragon will either eat the human or bond with it. In the case of Saldo, she ate the human she saw upon hatching. This would normally create a solitary path in which a dragon will continue its life separate from humans. You fashioned a unique situation when you returned to reclaim the body of your friend. I am far from an expert, but I believe Saldo sensed something that she found compelling. Her bonding period had already passed, but she was still attracted to one or more qualities she saw in you."

Balder looked into the sky wistfully. It had to be difficult for the man to hear that things might have been different between him and the green dragon if he had simply been standing closer to the God Stone than the soldier next to him. He may have experienced some sadness at the thought, but Meara didn't think her choice of words had caused him pain.

Ronvost shifted position, and Landis cocked his head. The corner of his mouth quirked, but he didn't share what Meara knew were words from Ronvost. She stood, removed dinner from the fire and started slicing off chunks for her companions. Food preparation was not one of her favorite tasks and she had always avoided it in her village on Innut Island. Her lack of practice showed in the indelicate presentation of the venison.

Landis held the chunk of meat on a stick before his face and eyed it warily. This time, he spoke aloud when he answered Ronvost so Meara would get the gist of the conversation.

"I agree it is perfectly edible, and there is no need for you to test it. I'm just taking a moment to give thanks for this bounty provided by a god and prepared by Meara."

The prince's moment of thanks dragged on until Meara brought her own skewer to her mouth and took a bite of the meat. It tasted fine, and she continued to eat heartily. Only then did the prince taste his own portion.

"Interesting," Landis said after swallowing. "It tastes divine as long as I close my eyes. It seems it is only the appearance that leaves much to be desired."

Balder, showing no hesitation while he tore at his own dinner, laughed. His mirth stung Meara for a moment. Memories of Lokar tripping her and laughing as she fell flooded her mind. Meara had been tormented by him and others in the tribe for her entire life. She had nearly forgotten why she avoided the companionship of other people. Only Mama Jade had always treated her with respect.

Landis must have seen a change in her expression. "Hey, I didn't mean to hurt you. I'm not really criticizing your cooking. The meat tastes wonderful and I appreciate you cutting it up and serving it. It was just a little teasing between friends."

Meara's initial response was to label Landis's words as lies. She had heard similar excuses from tribal children when Mama Jade chastised them for mocking Meara. This felt different, though. The prince seemed genuinely upset over the change his words brought about in her. She felt her defenses fall.

"Forgive me. I'm not accustomed to having friends to tease me. Next time, I will permit you to demonstrate your slicing skills."

Landis quieted and looked away. Meara had truly meant that he could do the work because he would likely be better at cutting up meat, but as she considered the prince, she realized she had just inadvertently teased him. She supposed it wasn't in good fun if she hadn't meant to do it, though, and Landis did not appear to be laughing.

"I'm sorry," said Meara. "It was not my intention to make you feel bad. I should have considered that someone of your standing has had little occasion to cut your own meat from the bones of a fresh kill. As I said, I am not practiced with friendly joking."

"It seems I am not very good at it either," sighed the prince. "I am good at poking fun at others, but I've rarely had the occasion to be the brunt of the joke. Who in their right mind would tease a prince? I guess I'd have been better at it if I had a sibling."

Balder laughed aloud, reminding Meara that he was bearing witness to the entire scene. He shook his head as if he were disappointed in the two youths before him.

"Neither of you would have survived in my family. I am one of five children. I was forced to grow thick skin at an early age. I doubt there is much you could say to cause me anguish."

The man was laughing about his large family, but Meara knew he wasn't completely unfeeling. She had seen the look on his face when Balder realized he had missed his chance to bond with Saldo.

When Meara's stomach felt full, she tossed the bone to Ronvost. She had expected him to gnaw on it, similar to how a dog would. Instead, the blue dragon sat happily cracking into it and picking out the marrow. She had to remember a dragon had much sharper teeth than any pet.

Saldo and Dabwey returned. Curious, Meara asked her dragon if Saldo had shared her own story of how she came to be in the company of Balder.

"A bit. We mostly hunted and ate, but I get the impression she respects him. I'm sure she would have eaten him months ago if that were not the case. As I've explained, a god needs a vincule to temper his or her natural propensity toward destruction in the name of the essence for which the god is named."

"No, you really didn't explain it before. You only said a vincule provided emotional balance. I feel that may have been an understatement."

A tinkle Meara had not heard since the day Dabwey hatched fluttered through Meara's mind. Her dragon was laughing. The sound was sweet, even if it was caused by the thought of a god bringing destruction throughout the land. Dabwey's next words helped quash some of Meara's fear.

"It's a good thing, for all of us, that Saldo is driven by balance. She would not wish to cause trouble and risk upsetting the equilibrium we currently have. Just be careful you don't create any issues. If Saldo perceives an injustice, she may seek to right that wrong, even if it has nothing to do with her. It might be one of the reasons she has an affinity for Balder. A man returning to recover his friend's body without trying to avenge his death must have seemed proper. A kind of justice had been found in the thieves' deaths at the hands of a god, and Balder let it rest."

"I'm not sure he let it rest as much as he was too scared to engage in single combat with a dragon, even one that was recently hatched," Meara mused. "Wait, can Saldo hear us talking? I don't want to influence her feelings about Balder."

"Saldo and I do not share thoughts in the way you and I do. When dragons communicate, we must consciously direct our thoughts at them in much the way you are fond of doing with me. I probably should have told you that you don't need to try so hard to push your words into my mind. Your thoughts flow naturally in my head, similar to my own."

"Will I ever again have a secret from you, Dabwey?"

"There are ways to block your thoughts from me, but if you think I'm just going to tell you how to accomplish that, then it is you, not I, who was recently hatched."

The tinkling flowed through her mind, and Meara rolled her eyes. Just when the purple dragon had seemed to be speaking wise words, she reminded Meara that she was still a child.

Dabwey curled at Meara's feet when she stretched out to get some rest. Meara still wasn't fully recovered, and the day had been tough on her body. Her head no longer ached, but her energy was sapped and her full belly made her feel sleepy. She heard the others turning in as well. She wondered if they should quench the fire since no one would be awake to watch it.

"Sleep tight, Meara. You are in the company of three gods. There is no danger to you and there is certainly no chance we will permit a fire to ravage nature."

CHAPTER 15: LANDIS

*I*n the morning, Landis opened his eyes and saw only rippling blue scales. It took him a moment remember that he had been chosen as a vincule. To emphasize the point, Ronvost spoke sleepily into his mind.

"Yes, it is still true. Not a dream. I am in your head and here before you. Now, get up and scrounge some food for me. I find I'm grumpy when I wake."

Ronvost, it seemed, did not enjoy mornings. The prince was not the biggest fan of them either, especially when the sun had yet to burn the dew from the ground. Landis sat up and was immediately reminded that, unlike him, Meara was a morning person. The girl had already coaxed the coals of last night's fire into a flame and was reheating some of last night's venison. Dinner had been tasty, but the prince's taste buds craved some variety.

As luck would have it, Balder was also a morning person. The sound of dried leaves shuffling on the ground announced his presence before the former soldier stepped from the trees and into the grassy area where the group had set up camp. His hair was slicked back and wet. His beard looked washed and combed. Over his shoulder, he carried a long stick. Several fish were skewered on the whittled point.

"I'm thrilled he brought fish, but I fear that man is insane," said Ronvost.

"Why is that? Because he befriended a rogue dragon?" asked

Landis.

"Well, that…and because that stream we passed was over a mile back. Balder must have been up well before dawn to bathe and catch our breakfast. No sane person would see that time of day."

Landis chuckled. He was in complete agreement with his dragon on that sentiment. The days spent without the comfort of his bed and the plushness of the pillows back home were grinding down his fortitude, and each day, he was having more trouble finding a reason to wake up.

"Hey, Meara, has Dabwey given any inclination about our destination?"

"Are you so keen on avoiding my terrible cooking that you want to set out already? You just opened your eyes."

Landis eyed the fish on Balder's spear as the big man approached and cracked a smile. He was pretty sure Meara had just attempted to make a joke at her own expense.

"By all means, I will enjoy some breakfast. It shall taste that much better if I am not expected to prepare it."

"I will do the honors," said Meara. "Might I suggest eating with your eyes closed? It will guarantee the fish will be even more flavorful."

Landis grinned. Her reaction to his teasing last night had not meant that the girl possessed no sense of humor.

Balder handed his catch over to Meara and untied several water skins from his belt. When Balder handed one to Landis, he was surprised to find the skin was his own. Not only had the big man gone fishing, he had thought to fill each of their water skins. This was the kind of efficiency Landis had expected of all soldiers trained in Skalve. Landis resigned himself to the idea that soldiers like these were now a rarity.

After setting the fish over a flame, Meara addressed the group. "We have two options, and I'd like to hear your opinions on each of them. We can set out to find other dragons, or we can trek to the land of the gods."

Landis contained the laugh bubbling up in his throat. There was no way this tribal girl was going to dictate his next move. He knew exactly where he needed to go.

"Ronvost and I are not beholden to your whims. We will be departing for Skalve after we have eaten the delicious breakfast before us. I need to share all we've discovered with my parents so they can ensure the survival of my people."

Ronvost broke into Landis's mind. "There might be more options than those set before us, but I assure you, prince, there is no way we will be returning to Skalve."

Landis was so surprised by the blue dragon's words that he replied aloud. "What? We have to go back. That is my home."

Meara chimed in. "I see your dragon shares my sentiments. Have you not yet accepted that Skalve is no longer a place where you are welcome?"

"I would be perfectly welcome if I returned with Ronvost."

Meara's eyes opened wide, and she stared at Landis as if he had just disrespected Mamma Jade.

"What?" asked Landis. "I may have failed in my quest to obtain a dragon egg, but surely returning with an actual dragon would earn me forgiveness."

Meara raised an eyebrow. "Assuming you could convince Ronvost to enter a Skalven city, what do you imagine will happen once you've been welcomed back into the fold? Do you suppose you will find yourself sitting on the throne and keeping a dragon as a pet? Maybe you are thinking they will allow you to set him up in the kennels? Ronvost is a god! You are his vincule. He does not follow your wishes; it is the other way around. I know you have been bonded for less than a day, but you would be wise to base your actions on your dragon's desires."

Landis opened his mouth to argue, but Ronvost's words from the prior day replayed in his mind. He recalled the affront shown by the newly hatched creature at Landis's notion that Ronvost was the Prince's vincule. He also remembered the explanation that made it seem as if Landis would forever be at the beck and call of his dragon.

"I'm glad to see you can be trained," Ronvost said. "I accept that it will take a vincule born of high standing some time to take orders. It might help if you think of me as royalty of an even higher station. I expect it is not a pleasant feeling, but it is your reality. You will never return to Skalve unless it is to burn it."

Landis sat down heavily, disbelief consuming his features and speaking volumes to those in his company. Balder spoke at last.

"I am sure I am missing some telepathic conversations between dragons and their humans, but it seems our prince is the last to understand how profoundly his life changed the moment his dragon hatched. I understand. The months I've spent in isolation with Saldo have not been without deliberation. On some days, I've considered returning home and trying to work my way back into the good graces of the nobles. Thankfully, that has not been my intention on most days. As I've said before, my time in Nahola has taught me much."

Landis listened, but found he didn't have the ambition to respond or even to look at Balder as the man spoke. He was working too hard to reconcile the simultaneous loss of his home, his family, and his culture. He began to understand how Meara might have felt after washing up on the beach days ago. Landis chanced a glance at the girl and found her staring inquisitively at Balder.

"What did you discover while staying in the village?" Meara

asked.

"It wasn't an individual finding that changed my opinion of my own people. Staying in the village, I found I needed to provide for myself in a way I never knew while living at home. Saldo was able to hunt for us both, but one cannot subsist on meat alone. At first, I pilfered from the gardens previously planted and tended by Nahola's people. As the fruits of their labor dwindled, I needed to learn how to forage and grow my own plants. I learned from the unfinished work left in the village. I found animal hides in various stages of tanning and garments partially sewn. As you can see by the threadbare trousers I still favor, I never found much skill with stitching."

Landis allowed himself a small smile. He tried to picture himself in the situation Balder was detailing. He knew he would not have even thought to attempt any of the primitive survival skills employed by the native villagers. Landis would have survived on meat provided by the dragon until his desire for a properly cooked meal drove him home.

"I have bonded a dragon, and I'm still not sure I would have succeeded in surviving as you did, Balder. I would have attempted a return to Skalve within days. What gave you the desire to stay out here, alone?"

"I gained respect for the Nahola's treatment of their land. I appreciated the way the tribe did not waste any of the things the land provided. The contrast to my way of life was stark, and I found I was ashamed of how much I had taken for granted. I wanted to learn to do better; to be a better person."

In the silence that followed, Meara shared out the breakfast of fish. Even Ronvost had no words of wisdom as he scarfed down the large portion provided to him as a meal. If he was not returning to Skalve, Landis found he had no idea where he belonged. Of Meara's two options, neither aligned with his ideals nor the goals he had for himself. Landis sighed. He never set any goals on his own. His goals were those of his parents. Some were set with his personal interest in mind, but Landis saw now that most were aligned with the betterment of the kingdom, as opposed to securing Landis's future as an individual.

"Anyway," Meara said, as if no time had passed since she first made her suggestions. "Dabwey feels Salvo's existence is evidence that there would have been other hatchings. Both of you have knowledge of previous excursions in search of dragon eggs. Each of those would have resulted in a God Stone crossing a magical boundary when it was removed from the village charged with its protection. A dragon will have hatched and found a vincule or become rogue. It is unlikely that others would have found themselves in the same unique situation as Balder and Saldo."

"Shouldn't we search for those dragons?" asked Balder.

"That seems to be one of the options," said Landis. "I suspect this is the point in the conversation where Meara tells us why that is the wrong choice, though."

Meara took his words as an invitation. "Dabwey has shared that the ultimate goal is for the new hatchlings to unite with the old gods. I would think all the dragons would have a similar internal pull toward those who created them so many years ago. I think any hatched dragons will already be heading north."

Balder interrupted. "There is a giant green hole in your story. Saldo has not gone north. What makes you think other dragons have the desire?"

Meara paused for a moment, as if unsure how to continue. It was just long enough for clarity to cause Landis to voice the answer.

"Because it is Saldo who is trying to convince Dabwey to stop looking for other dragons and to, instead, go directly north."

"Yes," admitted Meara. "I'm sorry, Balder. I didn't know how to say it without making you feel as if you were holding Saldo back from her desires."

"Well, I wouldn't have felt that way at all if you hadn't just mentioned it," Balder answered.

Landis felt for the former soldier. As strange as it was to have another being forever present in his mind, it would be even more uncomfortable to be unable to communicate with Ronvost. Balder had built a relationship with the shimmering green dragon despite having no knowledge of the creature's thoughts or feelings. Another thought occurred to the prince.

"Saldo's willingness to stay with you speaks volumes. She is dedicated to the friendship she has built with you. I fear Ronvost would have simply turned me to charcoal and set off. He can be exceedingly stubborn and set in his ways for someone who has been alive for barely a day."

Balder grinned. The prince rejoiced internally that his words had provided some solace for the big man. The recent realization that the people and creatures around the fire were all Landis had for support right now drove Landis to try to be there for them in return. It did not come naturally for him, but he found he liked the result.

"North it is," Landis said. "Saldo spent months here with Balder. She deserves to get her wish."

Ronvost said, "It's not as if I would have allowed you to make a different choice."

Though the words were harsh and Landis might have found them degrading, Landis noticed a powerful emotion attached to the words. The prince was unsure if Ronvost had sent feelings with his prior words and Landis hadn't noticed, or if this was a recent development. Either way, Ronvost was happy with Landis's decision and proud of the reason for the choice.

CHAPTER 16: DABWEY

She was sure the group was acting hastily. Dabwey liked Saldo, but any god who chose to remain with a human that was not her vincule was worrisome. The green dragon flew beside Dabwey as they hunted for lunch. Maybe it was Saldo's lack of bond that caused her to act irrationally.

On top of Balder being human, he was Skalven. He descended from the very people the gods had hoped to keep their young from. Dabwey struggled to accept the members of the party in which she traveled. Aside from Meara, none was worthy of snot spewing from Smok's nose when he sneezed.

Landis was less deserving of a dragon than Balder. Not only was he Skalven, he was of their royal line. It was inconceivable to Dabwey how Ronvost had bonded the prince upon hatching. Of course, there was Ronvost. He was small and selfish, but at least he was a god who had adhered to tradition and bonded a human into servitude.

Though Dabwey had not consciously selected Meara as her vincule, the dragon was torn over the result. Meara was perfect for the task, and make no mistake; it was more a chore than the honor Dabwey had presented to Meara as an explanation for the title. Meara would follow Dabwey wherever the dragon fancied, without fully grasping the depth of her inability to stray too far for extended periods of time. Meara was devout in her allegiance to the gods and that made her an excellent choice for a vincule, but it pained Dabwey to know the girl would never experience a life of her own.

The clouds parted for a moment and Dabwey glimpsed a deer in an open field. She sent a thought to Saldo to be sure the green dragon had seen the prey as well. Saldo did not reply directly, but turned into a dive. Though Dabwey was twice the size of the deer and over three times its weight, her wings were still not strong enough to bear the carcass back to camp. Saldo had no difficulty as she took her place beside the purple dragon with the lifeless deer hanging in her talons. The goddess of balance might not understand the importance of finding more of their dragon siblings, but she was handy to have around when there were mouths to feed.

Just before banking and turning for camp, movement in the distance caught Dabwey's eye. The purple dragon felt herself drawn by it. Aware that her curiosity could put her in danger, Dabwey considered ignoring her inclination to investigate.

"Sister, continue on to the humans. If Ronvost has not yet eaten the humans, they will all be waiting for a meal," Dabwey thought to Saldo.

"Where are you going?"

"I saw something in the distance, possibly a human, and I want to fly over the area to get a better look. Don't let the meat spoil. I'll be along in a moment."

Saldo hesitated a moment, then turned back and flew toward the camp. Dabwey continued on, watching for more movement in the area by the lake ahead. She was sure she hadn't imagined the figure walking on two legs. The clouds and trees conspired to keep her quarry from sight. Dabwey flew over the lake and circled back for another look.

Moments before deciding her eyes had deceived her, the purple dragon saw a man squatting at the edge of the lake, sheltered by several birch trees. Dabwey's shadow passed before the human and he looked directly at her. In her intense search for the person she had glimpsed from afar, the dragon had lost altitude and was clearly visible to this stranger.

Dabwey beat her wings to climb higher and flew for the camp. It took about fifteen minutes for her to cover the miles she had strayed from the place where Meara waited. Even when her vincule was out of sight, Dabwey could locate her without issue. The farther she strayed from Meara, the fainter her presence was in her mind. On this flight, Dabwey had noticed Meara's thoughts had moved out of her mind's forefront. It was a fair distance, and Dabwey absently noted that this was an indication that she could at least pretend to afford Meara some privacy if need arose.

When the smoke from the campfire came into view, Dabwey was already composing her argument for going to find the human. The group would need to go west for some distance before turning north, anyway. If they turned and headed back up the coast, they would inevitably revisit areas where they would no longer be welcome.

The purple dragon landed near the fire and immediately tore a chunk of meat from the remains of the deer carcass. There was already meat on the fire and Saldo's teeth were stained red. Dabwey carried her portion and settled next to Ronvost on the outskirts of the group. The two dragons crunched and chomped until the stares from the humans became too much to ignore.

"They'll need to acclimate to the sounds dragons make while eating if this journey is to be a success," said Ronvost.

The prince did not attempt to hide his disgust. His hand went to his pocket reflexively and he looked as if he were contemplating offering the blue dragon a handkerchief to wipe his mouth. Ronvost went back to his meal, adding some additional chop-licking to emphasize that he had no intention of curbing his enthusiasm for the meat before him.

The corner of Meara's mouth turned up in response to Landis's repulsion. She might not enjoy the sound of dragons eating, but she was thoroughly amused by anything that was irksome to the prince. Dabwey maintained the grace becoming of a goddess, but she could admit she shared Meara's zest for all things that vexed the arrogant noble. She did not need to contrive to irritate him herself with Ronvost present. The blue dragon and the prince were entertaining, though not well paired.

By the time the humans' food was overcooked enough for them to consume, all three dragons were relaxing. Ronvost was catching a nap. It would be several days of rapid growth for the blue dragon before he noticed there were things to do other than eat and sleep. Flying might be an option for him in the next day or so. That had been a strong motivator for Dabwey to accept her rapid rate of maturity. She had enjoyed being fed and carried, but once she experienced flight, there had been no holding back her gains in size, strength, and emotional maturity. Just then, Ronvost belched, and the prince emitted a faint retch. Dabwey smiled. Ok, she was still working on maturity in general.

Dabwey forced herself to stop trying to find fault in Landis. Though it was an entertaining pastime, it would not further her plans to locate the mysterious human she had seen. There had not seemed to be anyone else in the area. The purple dragon was bursting with a need to return to the lake. She couldn't understand why she felt such a desire to investigate the area. Though it had been the human that caught her eye, she didn't feel as if he was the reason she was drawn to the area.

"Once you've finished your venison, we should set out," Dabwey said to Meara.

Meara licked her lips and made an effort to swallow the meat she was chewing. Dabwey let out a low grumble when she realized what her vincule was doing.

"Meara, you only need to think. You do not need to swallow your food before replying to me."

"We'll head north as soon as we break camp," Meara replied, ignoring Dabwey's comment and refraining from taking another bite of her food.

Dabwey saw Landis had taken note of Meara's pause in eating. The prince was not as self-absorbed as she had once thought. He was likely having his own conversation with Ronvost, but Dabwey couldn't imagine the blue dragon had much to contribute. Though he was only a few days younger than her, the purple dragon was not impressed with Ronvost's limited knowledge of the ancients. Or, maybe he knew the stories but lacked the forethought to share them with his vincule. Regardless, Ronvost was not instilling the importance of a vincule's duty to protect the gods into the prince. Landis still seemed more interested in repairing his relationship with the people who raised him than in bettering the situation of his current traveling companions.

Balder stood and kicked dirt over the small cook fire. He looked pointedly at Landis and Meara. The big man had taken the time to clean up while Dabwey and Saldo had been out hunting. It was a mystery why the former soldier kept his facial hair so neat. The time it must take to trim it and keep it free from matting did not seem worth the added warmth it would offer; especially at this time of year. The result of his efforts was a neat beard that added to the look of strength in the soldier's jaw. It was a sharp contrast to the blonde scruff collecting in messy patches on the prince's face. Dabwey hoped she could be there when Landis first chanced a look upon his own visage.

"It's time to get moving," Balder said.

"I dread retracing our steps," said Landis.

Dabwey took the chance to steer the group toward the lake.

"Tell them we should go west," she said to Meara.

"West. We need to go west first."

Balder and Landis looked at Meara as if she had a worm dangling from her left nostril. Balder voiced the source of their confusion.

"Last night, it was you who argued for a return north so fervently."

Dabwey had been speaking her logic into Meara's mind through the moments Landis and Balder used to reconcile Meara's previous declaration with her new directive.

"It's logical," Meara said. "We have carved a swath of land along the coast where we are no longer wanted. We would first encounter the Dinnen village where Dabwey's charm is sure to have worn off. Alaria will be looking to reclaim her lost dragon. She will see us as the enemy for absconding with the creature her people have protected for hundreds of years.

"If we manage to skirt the village, and keep from sinking into the bog, we will have the remains of Landis's troops to contend with. It is evident that they have no intention of permitting the prince to return home and make a report about the soldiers' unseemly behavior. If we turn west for a time, then make our journey north away from the coast, we will avoid both perils."

"Traveling more than a mile from the coast is just inviting death," Landis said.

Balder took up the argument. "Living alone with Saldo for these months, I can assure you there is cause for the warning about roaming too far from the salt of the ocean. The land is vast and home to an uncounted number of unchronicled creatures. There are also the bears and saber wolves that have been documented many times over by survivors of those groups unlucky enough to find themselves too far from the coast."

"I too have heard the tales, but I've always felt much of it to be conjecture brought about by the fear of the unknown. Besides, we have dragons with us. We are protected by the gods themselves. Traveling west toward dangers that are unaware of our presence will be safer than walking back into the sights of the people who are already hunting us."

Dabwey was satisfied to watch the faces of the two men lose the look of incredulity and adopt the more passive appearance of acceptance. She was further gratified when no argument came from Saldo or Ronvost. The humans packed up their meager belongings and continued the day's walk; this time heading west. Saldo and Dabwey took to the sky, while Ronvost sat perched on the prince's broad shoulder. As the purple dragon beat her wings to get height, she was amused to see Landis nearly knock Ronvost to the ground when the blue dragon spread his wings to catch his balance and smacked Landis in the head. It would not be long before Ronvost would need to fly or walk.

CHAPTER 17: MEARA

*H*er dragon was up to something. Meara expended a great deal of energy hiding her feelings on the subject from Dabwey. The purple dragon had been insistent that finding more of her siblings was paramount to her purpose, and therefore Meara's purpose. When she returned from her hunt, Dabwey had not only been content to travel north, but she had been full of suggestions on how to avoid trouble while doing so.

Meara appreciated the thought her dragon had contributed to their safety, but it was out of character for Dabwey to concede to anyone else's plans. If Meara had learned anything about her purple scaled goddess, it was that she was stubborn. Her suspicions about Dabwey's ulterior motives were confirmed a few hours into the trek.

"This looks like a good place to turn north," said Balder. "The hill will be on our left and the natural flow of the land creates a natural walkway here that should ease our travel and keep us from traipsing through brush for a time."

Dabwey pushed into Meara's mind before Balder had even stopped voicing his explanation. The dragon insisted they would need to crest the hill and continue farther west. Meara stopped walking. Landis and Balder turned to face her when they ceased to hear her footfalls. Meara was looking up into the sky, so she didn't notice when the men opted to sit on some nearby rocks while she argued with her dragon. She did hear the flap of Ronvost's wings as he clumsily left Landis's shoulder to alight on the ground.

"Why are you so insistent?" Meara asked of her dragon. "Are you able to see some threat of which you have yet to make me aware?"

There was no reply from the purple dragon, and Meara brought her attention away from the clouds. She was about to have a seat on the rocks with the men when she felt Dabwey's presence grow stronger in her mind. The dragon was returning to the group. Meara remained standing, waiting with her hands on her hips for the purple goddess to grace them with her presence.

Before the dragon even folded her wings, Meara was stomping toward her. Dabwey looked away when Meara stopped before her.

"Out with it," said aloud. "Don't just share your words with me, either. Tell them all why you're so intent on continuing west."

"You know I will speak to no one but you."

"Nonsense! You spoke to Aleria, more than once and you've told the price what you needed him to do. You can speak to whomever you choose."

"Those were special circumstances," Dabwey nearly whined into Meara's head.

"So is this. You will tell them why we need to travel west or I will tell them you have instructed me to turn north."

"Meara, it's just not proper, and neither is the tone you are taking with me. Did you forget I am a god?"

"God or not, you are up to something and we deserve to know what it is. Your hiding of things from me is giving me an ill feeling in my gut."

Dabwey looked directly into Meara's eyes. She blinked slowly and Meara saw deep thought behind the dragon's serpentine irises. When Dabwey spoke, Meara knew Landis and Balder heard her voice. They sat erect at the start of her words.

"While hunting earlier, I saw a man by a lake. He was all alone. At first, I was only curious about some movement on the horizon. When I flew closer and saw him sitting on the lakeshore, something within me told me to go to him. I felt it would be better if we all went together."

"So, why didn't you just tell us when you returned to camp?" asked the prince.

"I knew I was going. If you chose not to follow, it would only be a matter of time before you and Meara discovered the honor of being chosen as a vincule is also a curse. I was only looking to prolong the time we had before the inevitable."

"What curse?" Meara forced the words from her mouth.

"You will find," said Dabwey. "You see… It's just that —"

"Out with it!" Meara seethed.

"A dragon and a vincule cannot be separated. If too much space and time are put between them, the human will die."

Dabwey's words were followed by silent seconds that stretched to nearly a minute. Meara had been looking at Landis so she would not need to see Dabwey as the dragon spoke her truth. The prince stood slack-jawed over the implications brought about by the dragon's admission. He tentatively glanced at the blue dragon on the ground beside him.

"It is a safeguard for the dragon. It ensures a vincule's cooperation cannot be bought, and one will never betray the god he or she has been entrusted to protect. A bond is far more than the ability to speak to one another telepathically. Meara, the air you breathe, the blood in your veins, your very life is tied to me."

A laugh erupted from Balder's lips. It exploded in such a fashion that it must have started deep within him and burst forward with such force that it could not be halted. Meara stared at the former soldier, wondering what about the last few moments had been so amusing.

"To think," started Balder. "I have been feeling sorry for myself since Saldo and I came upon you all. I was wondering why I had experienced the misfortune of not having been standing in front of Saldo's stone when it hatched. It turns out I am actually the lucky one."

Meara sank to her knees. She swayed slightly before lurching to the side and retching. Her entire life had been in devotion to the gods. First, she had helped Mama Jade with the care of the temple, and then she had taken on the full task of the temple's upkeep and rituals. Meara had never permitted herself to dream of a life outside of her dedication to the God Stone. There was no one else depending on her and little chance anyone from her village would ever see her as more than a pariah once Mama Jade left this world.

Since being swept from her island and fleeing the beach with Prince Landis, Meara had begun to think she might be creating a life of her own at last. This adventure had been the start of new things for Meara and there seemed to be endless possibilities afforded to her. Moments ago, she could nurture the false notion that she was choosing to keep company with Dabwey, the prince and even Balder. It turned out that this entire journey was divined by the gods.

This should not have upset Meara as much as it did. She loved her gods and had always felt protected by the closeness she felt to them while in the temple on Innut Island. Tala, Meara's goddess of choice, had nurtured the young island girl no one wanted. Through the story carved in the walls of the cave, Meara had felt a sense of belonging. Still, at the time, she had known nothing other than her simple life, and had yet to experience any hope that it would ever be any different.

Meara pulled herself back to her feet. She dusted leaves and dirt from her clothing. Something in the back of Meara's mind told her she should take better care of the skins Aleria's people had cleaned for her. It seemed she was about to embark on a longer journey than she had expected.

"West, it is," Meara said.

She started walking. She kept a brisk pace, as if trying to put distance between herself and her dragon as she hiked through the brush and headed up the rise. Balder and Landis followed. Dabwey did not take to the sky. She lumbered behind the humans despite the effort it took when compared to the ease of flight. The prince did not permit Ronvost to ride on his shoulder and refused to carry him. If Meara had been in a different frame of mind, she might have distracted herself by imagining the things Ronvost was saying to Landis in response to the prince's coldness.

Due to the speed with which she stomped through the woods, Meara was viewing an irregularly shaped lake at the bottom of a gentle slope in only a short time. The sun was low on the horizon and it caused the tiny waves on the water's surface to sparkle in the gentle breeze. Her breath caught at the view. The area resembled a small paradise, with an open area on the shore at the wider end of the lake.

"That's where I saw the human," Dabwey said when Meara's focus landed on the open area.

For a moment, Meara had been lost in the view, but her dragon's voice in her head reminded Meara why they were standing on this rise in the first place. She took a breath and attempted to quell the tightness in her chest. She stepped forward.

Balder's hand grasped the back of her deerskin dress. She turned to give him a hard stare. She was not in the mood for conversation and only interested in completing the task required by her dragon so the group could move on. It no longer felt like an adventure, and Meara just wanted it all done and over with. Balder wasn't as ready to rush off to the lake.

"Dabwey saw a single human male on the shoreline, but that doesn't mean there aren't more people down there," he cautioned.

"She reported no buildings or structures of any kind. The man may have just been passing through. If so, at least it is a pretty place to camp tonight."

Landis broke into the conversation. "I agree with Balder. We have no impression of the dangers that might wait for us down there. It is possible that the area is vacant, but if it is not, the occupants might be a threat to us."

Meara looked into the sky. She could just make out Saldo's shimmering green scales before the dragon passed in front of the sun. She was large enough to cast a shadow over the lake.

"Well, if anyone is down there, they will have noticed the dragon in the sky. Either they will be prepared for battle, or cowering in fright if they remained here at all. I see no point in approaching with caution."

Without waiting for a reply, she struck off down the hillside toward the open patch of land that resembled a beach, but without the sand. She noticed it took several heartbeats before she heard footfalls behind her. The men, it seemed, were not as ready to hand their lives over to fate as she was. Dabwey left the ground and forcefully beat her wings to join Saldo in the sky. Meara noted this would likely increase the chances of any people below hiding, rather than preparing to defend their territory. Though Dabwey was less than half the size of Saldo, there were still two dragons circling the sky above the lake.

When Meara reached the base of the hill, she discovered the need to push through several feet of thorny bushes to gain access to the clearing beside the water. The branches caught her clothing, and she needed to take care to pull the thorns free so the skins wouldn't tear. The material wouldn't offer much protection from the sun if it had gaping holes in it.

Meara looked into the sky. She refrained from asking Dabwey to check the area for any movement. She did not feel like speaking to the creature at the moment. Anger still bubbled up at the thought of the dragon's voice in her head. Meara doubted the dragons in the sky would allow them all to walk into danger if they saw it waiting, regardless of the recent turn in the relationship between them and the humans.

Landis drew up beside her. As he did, Meara heard the sound of his sword sliding free from its scabbard. She glanced down at the blade and noted its unkempt state. Her eyes fell on the prince, and she noted that he shared the sword's disheveled look. If Meara had not known of this man's royal blood, she would have assumed him a pauper who had discovered the remains of a fallen soldier and stolen his weapon. She hoped his skill with the blade was a match for the pompous attitude the prince was prone to adopting. If not, anyone they encountered would only laugh at Landis. He looked far less than threatening.

Balder, on the other hand, was imposing. The size of the man was enough to make an assailant think twice, but he was also carrying an axe. It was the same one he used to chop wood for cooking fires, but its double blades shined in the sunlight and anyone would know this implement was not intended to be used as a tool; it was a weapon capable of rendering horrific wounds.

If she stepped out into the clearing and was beset upon by a tribe of screaming warriors, Landis and Balder would go down fighting. What would she do? She glanced at the ground and saw a palm-sized stone. Should she pick it up so she had a weapon? Meara was seconds from stepping into a situation that could be perilous. What did it say about her ability to survive on her own that she was only now contemplating a method to defend herself? Dabwey was her protection. As much as it pained Meara to concede this, she knew she was defenseless, aside from her dragon's desire to keep her safe. Pushing aside her feelings of betrayal, she stepped into the open, trusting her dragon and the men beside her to protect her.

CHAPTER 18: LANDIS

Ronvost's demands to be carried were irritating in a way similar to a whipple bug that refused to stop buzzing near one's ear. The little blue dragon's attempt at projecting a commanding voice while simultaneously hopping and half-flying to keep up with Landis painted a pathetic picture. The prince wanted to be rid of the scaled creature.

At first, Landis had been awed by the prospect of being chosen by an actual dragon of ancient lineage with powers lauded in bards' songs. The more time the prince spent with Ronvost, though, the more he realized the dragon was essentially helpless. It could not even fly to escape danger and seemed to be utterly dependent on him.

Of course, Ronvost did not see the situation that way. The little dragon continued to issue commands to the prince as if Landis should bow to the creature simply because he had hatched into existence. What had the dragon done to be treated with such reverence? Other than being born from the blood of past gods, Ronvost deserved no more respect than the buzzing whipple bug Landis associated with the dragon's voice.

Landis watched Meara pick through the brush. As he started to follow suit, doubt seeped into his thoughts. Was he much different from Ronvost? Was there really some unseen power at play that had destined Landis to be chained to this creature for life? Dabwey had spoken of bonds being judged by worth, but was it possible it was something else that determined the sturdiness of a connection between dragon and vincule?

Nausea returned as Landis recalled the words Dabwey had shared with them in the clearing. All of Landis's dreams had slipped through his fingers like a handful of sand. He'd watched them drain away as if they were tangible. He would never return home. He would never be king. He would never rule a kingdom and have the adoration of his people. Was he even still a prince?

Landis stepped up beside Meara as she prepared to walk into the clearing beside the lake. It was quiet. Landis heard no birds, and it seemed the breeze had stopped, causing the leaves of the trees to still. The land seemed to be holding its breath, waiting to see what was about to transpire.

"What are you waiting for?" asked the whipple bug in his mind. "Just go out there and face whatever threat there is. You have a sword, for Smok's sake. I don't see what the delay is. Wait, pick me up. Prince, you shall not leave me here in the bushes like a stray dog!"

Landis ignored Ronvost and followed Meara out of the thicket. Her bravery awed him. The girl had no weapon with which to keep herself from harm, yet she strode into danger at the head of their group. He and Balder, each carrying their weapons, seemed to be using the unarmed tribal girl as a shield. Meara stopped several yards into the clearing. She stood passively, waiting for something or someone to make themselves visible. Landis and Balder turned from left to right, surveying the fringes of the clearing for any sign of movement. There was none.

Meara continued forward toward an area where the lake spilled from the main body of water into a stream. There was a worn path there. Landis understood Meara meant to follow it. He summoned an iota of bravery and stepped out in front of Meara to take the lead. Either the path had been tread by many, or it had been used by a few people over a long period. The path led back into a thick copse of trees and disappeared from sight. The canopy was dense and would prevent Dabwey and Saldo from seeing anything the leaves might hide.

As if the purple and green dragons could read Landis's mind, they descended with a loud crack of wings behind him and his hair was blown forward by the wind the landing created. The path was not wide enough for either dragon to traverse without pushing over the smaller trees lining the narrow trail. Unless there was danger, the larger dragons would likely stay in the clearing. The irritating blue dragon at Landis's feet was another matter.

The prince did his best to keep from tripping over Ronvost as they pressed forward. Landis had once found the dragon's uncoordinated hopping cute, but it only seemed like weakness to him as they walked into the unknown. Meara took light steps behind him that made almost no sound, while Landis's own feet felt Balder's heavy boots through the ground. They were forced to walk single file such that Landis was the first to see the sturdy shelter built within the branches of a tree possessing a trunk that had split three ways.

Meara tried to peer around Landis's form as he noted the way the three branches of the trunk made a framework for a hut built about ten feet from the ground. Other than scaling one of the trunks, there appeared to be no way to enter the shelter. He stepped closer to the tree and walked around the nearest part of the trunk to the left. On the far side, he found a ladder constructed of cut birch logs connected by vines. Landis followed the ladder upward with his eyes and saw it ended in a flat landing outside of a doorway. There was no way he could climb up without someone who was waiting inside the structure simply pushing him off the ladder as he reached the top.

Landis scanned the trees for similar structures, but saw none. The elevated building was small. If it were empty, there might be room for eight to ten people as long as they remained standing and didn't mind pressing together. The prince stepped back in an attempt to see beyond the doorway. There was no waiting army to be seen, only darkness.

Landis decided to forgo the daunting task of climbing the ladder and commenced investigating the area on the ground first. There was no pit for a fire, and a glance into the dense branches above him assured Landis this would have been a hazard if one were attempted in this area. There was a neatly stacked woodpile, though, so someone had been using a flame to cook or keep warm nearby. At least one person was in residence and intended to be here for some time longer.

The prince examined the ground for footprints, hoping to get a count of the number of people occupying this stretch of trees. The ground was littered with pine needles and leaves and, though obviously trodden upon, the forest debris prevented footprints from being left in the dirt. There was no way to anticipate the number of people he might encounter here.

At a loss for his next task, Landis looked at Balder. The former soldier hadn't moved since they came upon the tree hut. He was standing, axe in both hands, in the middle of the relatively brush free area created by the tri-branched tree and turning to gaze into the thick trees surrounding them. Balder was more concerned with an attack from the ground than a threat from whoever might be in the structure above them.

Looking for some way to further stall the task of investigating the hut at the top of the ladder, Landis noticed the calmness in his head. Ronvost had ceased his unrelenting string of demands and was no longer hopping around at the prince's feet. Landis was overcome with panic. Had something happened to the dragon while he had been ignoring him? The prince retraced his steps down the thin path to the lakeshore, glancing from left to right for the glimmer of blue scales, but saw no sign of the little god.

When Landis stepped into the clearing, the panic subsided, but his remorse grew. Ronvost sat on his hind legs with his front feet at the water's edge. It was the creature's posture that caused Landis to feel a sense of wrongness wash over him. The feeling came from deep within the prince as he saw the effect his treatment of the little dragon had caused.

Landis sat down beside the depleted creature, immediately feeling dampness soak into the seat of his britches. He ignored the damp chill and focused on the dragon's feelings, allowing them to reenter his mind from the dark recesses where he had previously locked them away. The dragon's sadness was something Landis could taste. It was made even worse by the notion that Landis had done this to the young creature.

True, Ronvost's demands and assumption of superiority had grated on Landis to the point where he had wished the dragon had never hatched, but that couldn't compare to the regret the prince felt at that moment.

"I can hear everything you are thinking," Ronvost said softly into Landis's mind. "I tried to ignore you since you are only human and don't know any better, but I failed. It isn't supposed to be like this and I fear I'm not a very powerful god. I'm supposed to tell you what to do and you're supposed to do it. When I tell you what to do, you just ignore me. I'm not even strong enough to keep my own vincule from resisting me."

Landis smiled, recalling the night before swimming to Innut, and sitting by the fire with Commander Torrence. Landis had voiced a complaint similar to the one Ronvost had just shared. Though only a few weeks had transpired since then, Landis found he held a very different perspective than he had that night.

Landis said, "A wise man once explained to me that the behavior of those around you, even those under your command, is dependent on the behavior of he who leads. Well, that isn't exactly what he said, but it is what I now understand to be truth. I'm not blaming you for my behavior. I can still choose how I react to you and those around me, but you might want to consider how you've been treating others. Demanding aid from the people you see to be beneath you does not work well in the long run."

Ronvost turned his head toward Landis, and the prince could see confusion on the dragon's face. He wasn't surprised. He had not understood the advice Torrence was giving him that night at the fire, and he expected it would take time for Ronvost to digest the sentiment as well. The dragon did not seem put-off by Landis's words though, so he continued.

"Innately, you know that gods are paired with a vincule who will devote his life to you. You have wrongly interpreted this to mean that person will serve you without question. Has it occurred to you that the devotion of a vincule might be earned by the dragon? Isn't it possible that the reason a vincule is so dedicated to the god is because the god is deserving of respect?"

As Landis spoke his words into Ronvost's mind, he became more aware of how grand his failure to lead his troops had actually been. Like Ronvost, he had assumed his position as Crown Prince would cause his soldiers to respect him without question. Landis had done nothing to demonstrate to those under his command that he was capable of leading them, and certainly had not offered any evidence that he put value on their lives as individuals. Landis had seen the group of men and women entrusted to him as a singular object; *his* army to control as he saw fit.

In light of this, Landis resolved to be more patient with his dragon. It wouldn't be easy, and Landis was still furious that he had unwittingly been bonded to the creature, but Ronvost just needed to experience a little more of the world and human nature. It was possible for him to learn and grow, just as Landis had started to do. Landis scratched the top of the blue dragon's head and the creature let out a sound similar to the purr of a cat; if the cat had been the size of a small wolf.

Balder stepped from the trees and broke the moment between Landis and Ronvost. Landis looked over his shoulder when he heard the big man approaching. The look on the man's face told Landis there was news that he would not want to hear.

"Where is Meara?"

Balder shrugged. "She climbed the ladder and went into the hut."

"She did what?"

Landis was unable to contain his surprise. He had done all he could to avoid the task himself, knowing the scene at the top would determine his fate during this brief diversion. Balder sat down beside Landis.

"You know the ground is wet here? Anyway, she climbed the ladder while my back was turned. The next thing I know, she was sending me away. She said I should go wait on the beach and she would be safe."

"And you listened?" Landis hadn't thought he could be further surprised.

"I did," Balder replied. "She must have been in there for several minutes before dismissing me and no harm had come to her. I wasn't about to trust that ladder to my weight, so what was I supposed to do? I guess I could have stood there at the base of the tree, but I couldn't have climbed up to save her if she called for help."

"No," Landis agreed, "but you could have come to get me if she was in trouble."

"She's not in trouble, so far as I know, but I am here. I figured I should at least come to let you know she decided to climb the ladder."

Landis stood, allowing Ronvost to perch on his shoulder. The creature really was too large for this, and Landis hoped he would consider working on strengthening his wings so he could fly. Right now, the leathery appendages only served to get in the way as the dragon maintained his balance beside the prince's head.

Balder returned to the base of the tree with them. Ronvost and the men made themselves comfortable on the ground to wait for Meara to emerge from the hut above. Landis kept his ears focused on any sounds from above that might indicate Meara was in trouble, but otherwise, he trusted the words she had spoken to Balder and left her to whatever was transpiring in the branches above.

CHAPTER 19: MEARA

*W*hen Meara climbed the ladder and entered the dark confines of the tree hut, she saw no one. Before her eyes adjusted to the gloom, a soothing male voice greeted her from the far corner of the room.

"I've been wondering when you would arrive. Please, tell your friend below he can leave. You are in no danger here."

Meara had no cause to trust the voice, but had no indication that she had need of defense from this stranger. Besides, Balder would only collapse the ladder with his weight if he made any attempt to ascend it to access the hut. She stepped out onto the porch-like landing that comprised the miniscule space outside of the doorway. She peered over the edge and was greeted by Balder's concerned face turned up toward her.

"You can head back to the lake to join the others. I'll be fine here."

She knew the big man was not foolish enough to attempt the ladder and turned back to the hut without waiting for his reply. She paused just inside, waiting for her eyes to adjust to the lack of sunlight.

"Sit. We have much to discuss."

When Meara heard the soft voice, she switched her focus to the source of the sound and was able to pick out the silhouette of a hunched figure on a low stool. A second stool waited for her, barely a foot from the first. She moved forward cautiously and perched on the edge of the seat. When her hands touched the surface, she could feel the gouges of the tool used to carve it, though the carver had taken care to sand the wood smooth.

"I don't know you. What is it you want to speak about with a complete stranger?"

"You may not know me, Meara, but I have watched you throughout your entire life. I have had my eye on you since Jade found you washed up on the shores of Innut. I know you cared for the temple there and have shown reverence for the old ways and faith in the gods."

"How could you have watched me all those years without my seeing you or recognizing you now?"

"I have a gift, but let's not get ahead of ourselves. My name is Ornen. I am the last of the Ranellen tribe. The gods have provided me with the gift of far-sight. I am able to watch people from a distance."

"What happened to the rest of your people? I've never heard of the Ranellen. Can you watch anyone you wish?"

Ornen chuckled. It was a deep sound and had the same soothing quality as his voice. "The people I watch are specific; those chosen by the gods. It is not always clear when the gods will require service from them, but each person will be called to task, eventually. I was happy to see your mission was one of honor and did not result in your death."

"I assume you are referring to my title as vincule. I'm not sure I see the task as an honor, but I am still alive, so it seems it is not the worst calling for which I might have been predestined. I've only recently come to learn of the restrictions I now face since I have bonded a dragon."

"Yes," said Ornen. "Some of them are unfortunate, but there are great benefits to be had when a dragon chooses a human as well. I'm sure you will come to know them in time."

Meara considered asking the old man to explain any benefit to bonding a dragon, aside from self-defense, which seemed obvious. She needed to see a positive aspect of her predicament if she was to regain the familial feelings she had started to enjoy with Dabwey before she received her awakening regarding the down-side of dragon bonding. Instead, she waited for the old man to continue.

"My tribe, like yours, was entrusted with a God Stone. For many generations, we kept it safe and out of the hands of invaders to our lands."

"Oh no," said Meara. "I'm so sorry. How long ago was the stone taken? Have you seen dragons other than those we came with?"

"Hold up now," Ornen's voice raised slightly. "I never said the stone was taken. Also, how many dragons are here with you?"

"There are three dragons waiting at the lake-front. If the stone wasn't stolen, then what happened to it?"

Ornen hummed in thought. "You have a dragon, and the prince has become a vincule, but I haven't been watching any others that might have recently obtained a bond."

Ornen trailed off, lost in his thoughts for a moment. Meara waited for the old man to continue, but the silence weighed on her. At last, she prompted him.

"Ornen, what happened to the God Stone?"

"What happened? Nothing happened to the God Stone. It's still here and still safe. I have guarded it myself since the death of the women who tended the temple."

Meara sat up straighter. She understood why Dabwey had been drawn to this location. One of her siblings was still here. It seemed her dragon wasn't just spurred to investigate this location by curiosity. There was a fourth dragon to bring home to the gods.

"You need to come with us," Meara said. "There is a magical boundary around this place that keeps the dragon from hatching. I didn't realize it before, but I felt it as I came down the hill to the lake. It was as if each step took twice the effort it should. You need to bring the egg outside of the boundary so it can hatch."

This time, Meara didn't find Ornen's chuckle to have the same soothing effect as it did the first time she heard it. Why would the man be laughing? Even if he didn't believe her, laughter should not have been his response.

"Dear Meara, I am an old man. Dreams of riding a god through the sky are no longer within my reach."

"Nonsense. You must be fit to manage out here on your own and I'm sure you'll find you have more strength than you know once you're outside of the suppression boundary. Something about the spell, or whatever it is, keeps the natural magic within and around us from functioning properly. It has the effect of dulling your senses a little too. When Landis left the Innut boundary, his shoulder injury healed in no time. Where is your temple?"

Ornen sighed in defeat. He gestured for Meara to lead the way from within the hut. She stepped back out into the evening sun. It was less bright than it had been when she entered the hut, but the sun was still above the horizon. She looked over the edge as she climbed onto the ladder and saw Balder and the prince jump to their feet. Ronvost was sleeping in a bed of pine needles nearby.

"I should have known you two wouldn't stay by the beach. Now that you're here, though, it would be a good idea to start making camp. Maybe we could get a small fire going with some of those logs over there?"

"I can take care of that," answered Balder. "Best not to do it with the thick boughs overhead, though. Landis and I can carry the wood to the lakefront. We can make a fire there while Saldo grabs us dinner."

"That sounds like the perfect plan," Meara said as she reached the ground.

She saw Landis and Balder watching Ornen climb onto the ladder up above. She had been right to think he was in fine shape for a man his age. Likely, he was more physically capable than some men with half of the years he had lived.

"That," she said as she pointed to the top of the ladder, "is Ornen. He is the last remaining member of the Ranellen tribe and keeper of the village's God Stone. He and I are going to go to the temple and then we will meet you by the fire."

Landis scooped up Ronvost with a grunt and placed the dragon on his shoulder. The creature spread his wings to stretch and swiped the prince across the face. For his part, the prince merely closed his eyes and shook his head in resignation. The men each grabbed several logs in their arms, Balder carrying several more than Landis, and left in the direction of the lake.

Meara turned to face Ornen as he set his feet on the forest floor. When he turned to face her, she got her first true look at the old man. She knew immediately that he had seen over sixty years, but it was impossible for her to guess at his exact age. His head was shaved on the sides and his grey hair was twisted with leather into a single long braid that fell to below his shoulder blades. Meara found it interesting that Ornen allowed his beard to grow long and wild, but kept the hair on his head in such a precise manner.

Two vertical bars were tattooed high on each of his cheeks, and deep lines creased his forehead and the corners of his eyes. None of this was the feature that Meara found most interesting. Ornen might have the gift of far-sight, but he was surely blind. His eyes were milky, as if a thick film had grown over them. A quiet gasp from Meara alerted the old man to her location, and he turned slightly to meet her gaze with his unseeing eyes. It was disturbing how he appeared to see her while also looking as if he were gazing past her and into the trees.

"Yeah, it's not just my age that precludes me from being worthy of becoming a vincule."

Meara's cheeks warmed. She almost apologized and tried to explain her reaction by referencing her surprise at his tattooed face, but she didn't want to demean the man. He was likely accustomed to the reaction others had to the look of his eyes, and he would know his tattoos were not the cause of her gasp. Meara felt even worse as she realized she knew the exact feeling Ornen was experiencing. It was the same unworthy shame that she felt each time someone flinched at the sight of her mottled skin.

"Believe me, Ornen, if you could see me, you would know you are not the only one with a shocking feature."

"You forget; I have seen you. In some places, your skin would be considered beautiful. You've simply been living with the wrong people."

Meara considered the irony of Ornen's lack of sight, coupled with his enhanced vision. It must be a special kind of torture to be able to see so much that occurs in the world around you, but to be unable to see what unfolds in his immediate vicinity. As she followed Ornen through the trees, she was impressed with his skillful navigation over the rocks and beneath lower branches. It was as if he could feel their presence and was able to avoid them. It wasn't long before they stood at their destination.

The temple was nothing like the one Meara had known on Innut. It was little more than a hole dug into the side of a hill and protected by trees. Meara stooped to peer inside and could see the stone sitting on its pillar. The space was only about two feet wide and four feet high. She couldn't imagine how the stone had been kept safe this long. It could only be attributed to the disappearance of the Ranellen tribe, rendering the stories of this stone lost forever. That was a story Meara was looking forward to coaxing from the old man. What could make a tribe vanish?

Reverently, Meara removed the stone from its pedestal and led the way back to the lake with it cradled in her arms. The familiarity of the stone against her skin brought a longing for home. She was now the lone survivor of her own tribe. Maybe it wasn't such a mystery to find an entire tribe could disappear without notice.

It was getting dark when Ornen and Meara arrived at the lakeside just after Saldo returned with her kill. The dragons took their portion several yards from the fire and left the humans to cook their meal. Meara was pleased to see Ronvost accompany the others instead of staying behind and requiring the prince to feed him by hand. She hoped this was a positive step in the dragon's maturity. At this point, Dabwey had been flying several feet off the ground and performing mind tricks on Aleria back at the Dinnen village. She knew she shouldn't be comparing Landis's dragon to her own. Each creature was individual, and it made sense that they would mature at different rates. Dabwey had likely been quick to mature out of necessity, but Ronvost seemed to be content to remain a pampered child. It would make things slightly less difficult if the blue dragon could find some independence sooner rather than later.

Meara and the men chatted as they ate, with most of the banter falling to Balder and Ornen exchanging skills for surviving alone in the wilderness. Meara knew the former soldier, and the prince had noticed Ornen's eyes in the firelight, but the men had done a much better job of hiding their reactions than she had. When the conversation wound its way to the subject of the God Stone sitting at Meara's feet, she felt more comfortable chiming in.

"We can take Ornen and the stone out beyond the boundary tomorrow morning and hatch the egg. After that, we can all travel north."

"Hold up, Meara," said Balder. "I've already witnessed an unsuccessful hatching and I do not want to be there if it happens again."

"Fine," Meara said. "You can wait here, and Landis and I will go. We'll return here and then we can turn north."

Landis only looked slightly affronted at the assumption that he would accompany her, and Meara was grateful he didn't try to argue his way out of it. Balder seemed satisfied with the alteration to her original plan, but Ornen was anything but accepting of her idea.

"I already told you I have no intention of trying my luck at becoming a vincule."

"No," said Meara. "You told me you were too old to ride a dragon, and I thought we moved beyond that when you wove through the trees more nimbly than I could. Also, I told you the boundary suppresses strength. You have yet to experience all you are capable of achieving."

"Have you forgotten the biggest hurdle? I'm blind, Meara. No dragon will find me worthy of a bond."

Landis cut her off before she could reply. "I don't think worth is the same for a dragon as it is for us. We see worth as the sum of all we can do. Are we proficient with a sword, devoted in our prayers, or do we possess political connections that can better our circumstances? Those are things that make humans worth more to other humans. I think dragons measure worth by one's heart and conviction. Admittedly, I'm not sure how I qualified, but I hope it may have been based on my potential, and I have yet to evolve into the worthy individual Ronvost saw when he hatched."

"It makes sense," said Meara. "Other than the first few

weeks of its life, a dragon wouldn't need a fierce warrior and devotion to the gods is inevitable once you are bound to one, so there is no need for a vincule to have proven themselves worthy by way of prayers. If worth is not based on physical strength, I fail to see why your lack of sight would prevent you from being deemed worthy."

Meara turned to Ornen. He had no choice but to agree or condemn the God Stone to return to the dugout temple. She and Landis were already bonded and there was no way Balder would accept a bond since he had witnessed Dabwey's confession earlier in the day. He already had a unique relationship with Saldo and he seemed to appreciate the distance it afforded him, even if he was unable to communicate with her telepathically.

Ornen allowed his chin to sink to his chest, and he sat that way for a moment. When he lifted his head several heartbeats later, he nodded twice in succession.

"I have one condition," he said. "I'll take the stone beyond the boundary on my own. If the god refuses me, he will kill all in my company. I can't risk that. I'm genuinely happy for the confidence Meara has in my worth, but there is no guarantee I will return with a dragon. If it kills me, your dragons might be able to convince the new god to accompany you as Saldo does, despite the fact she is unbonded."

"I can accept that," said Meara. "We'll know in the morning."

Sleep came easily for Meara that night. Curled by the fire, surrounded by men she had only met recently, and magical beasts capable of killing her by tooth or claw, Meara felt safe.

CHAPTER 20: LANDIS

*L*andis paced by the fire. Meara's plan was ridiculous. She had sent a blind geezer out beyond the boundary alone. The silly girl sat nibbling some left over venison, looking as if she hadn't a care in the world. It was likely she'd just sent an old man off to die and there would be a day of dragon hunting ahead of them.

"Sit down, My Prince," Balder called from where he was skipping stones across the placid lake surface. "You're making my whiskers twitch."

Landis found a rock to sit on where he could keep his back to Meara. Each time he looked at her, he felt his annoyance resurface. Last night, he had been too tired to consider the possible consequences of her plan, but this morning he had seen things clearly. When he voiced his concerns to the group, they had almost ignored him; only offering nods to recognize he had spoken at all.

Balder abandoned his pastime at the shore and walked toward the prince. He sat on the ground, cross-legged, like an oversized schoolboy, and looked up at Landis. The prince could see that the former soldier was here to offer sympathy, not a reprimand.

"I know you think no one is paying heed to your thoughts. I don't believe that is the case. It's simply a matter of options. We have none."

"It should have been you walking off with that stone this

morning," said Landis. "No one here is more honorable and deserving than you."

Balder snorted and shook his head. He looked at the prince skeptically.

"You have a very high regard for a man you've only known for a few days. I have done many things throughout my life that I am not proud of. I've...well, I've hurt people and I've destroyed things."

"We all have," said Landis. "It doesn't mean your intentions aren't just. You would surely have been accepted as a vincule."

"Let's assume for a moment that I am the wonderful person you describe. Do you wish to condemn a person of that nature to a life of servitude?"

"We all serve someone," replied the prince. "It starts with our parents, then it's our tutors, and that is followed by our sergeants. In the grand scheme of things, we all serve the king and queen."

Balder snorted again. "For some of us, the latter is truer than for others. I suspect you've been serving the king and queen directly since your birth."

"I suppose you are correct in that regard." Landis permitted himself a chuckle.

Balder's face lost its smile. His next words had a serious connotation.

"Since Saldo came to me in that village, I've lived freely. I haven't been called to answer to anyone. I've served no one but myself. It was a lonely life, and I probably shared far too much about myself with that green dragon. Now that I know she can communicate with others of her kind, I'm afraid you will eventually hear some embarrassing tales of the former soldier you regard so well. That is beside the point, though. I have enjoyed my months to myself, with no orders to follow and no one's agenda but my own. I don't think I could go back to living for someone or some dragon's betterment."

Landis lowered his eyes to the ground. He had no notion of what it would feel like to be free to follow his own desires. There had been the smallest taste of it in the moments after Ronvost hatched and Landis had foolishly thought he could present the dragon to his parents as a means to buy his was back into their good graces. Even if that had been possible, his life would not have been his own. When his parents were gone and Landis was king, he would still be entrusted to make choices for the betterment of Skalve, not for himself. Well, he could make whatever choices he wished once he was king, but it didn't mean it would make him a very good ruler. If the populace revolted, his head might roll, making his reign very short.

The prince's thoughts were interrupted when Dabwey and Saldo landed in the clearing. Moments later, Ronvost communicated to Landis that Ornen was returning to camp. Before Landis could ask if there was a dragon with the old man, the sound of leaves crunching came from the edge of the forest and everyone froze in anticipation.

Ornen stepped lightly into the clearing and walked with confidence, directly to the fire pit. He sat on a rock, facing the tree-line, without even offering a greeting. A heartbeat later, a small yellow creature stepped cautiously into the clearing. It so closely matched the color of the flowering bush behind it that the dragon was difficult to see. Once in the open, it sprinted toward Ornen and buried itself in the folds of the old man's furs and skins, disappearing from sight.

The dragons were the first to move. Saldo was fastest to cover the distance and begin nosing the old man's clothing, trying to uncover the new dragon and force it into the open. Each time she pulled back material to reveal scales, or an eye on one attempt, the baby dragon readjusted so it was once again buried.

"For some reason, he's scared and looks to the ancient human to protect him," Ronvost shared with Landis. "Dabwey, naturally, does not agree. She thinks he's just cold and seeking the human's body heat."

"What do you think?" Landis asked.

"I'm not sure. I keep trying to talk to him, but he hasn't answered yet."

"Are you sure it's a him?" asked Landis.

"Yes, that much I can smell," Ronvost answered. "Wait, he's talking."

Landis had walked closer to try to catch sight of the tiny new god while conversing with Ronvost. He stepped up next to Ornen in time to witness his blue dragon taking things into his own claws. Ronvost found the bottom of Ornen's tunic and stuck his head up and under the garment. It was less than a second before Ronvost jumped backward, shaking his head.

"The little urchin bit me!" Ronvost cried.

Landis did his best to hide the laughter pushing its way up his throat. He managed to maintain a passive look on the outside, but Ronvost's prompt grumble let Landis know he hadn't succeeded in hiding his internal amusement from his dragon.

Meara sat beside Ornen, but ignored the old man. Landis suspected she was hoping the newest god would get curious and come out to smell her. There was no way the prince was going to stand by and wait for that to happen. It might take hours, if it ever happened at all.

"So, Ornen, what is his name?" Landis asked.

The smile that broke on the old man's face pulled at the prince's heart. Without a doubt, Meara had been right to send the geezer off with the egg. He was already smitten with his new bond.

"His name is Einok. It seems I am now vincule to the god of thought and aspiration."

"What does that entail?" Landis asked. "It actually sounds like he can read minds or something, and I'm not sure I'm comfortable with any creature that is capable of something like that."

"I did not ask," replied Ornen. "Truthfully, I've been enjoying the sights. I haven't considered much else."

Landis was unsure if the old man was making a joke or simply tuning a phrase. Surely, the blind man was not being literal. To satisfy his curiosity, and because he had always been impulsive, Landis waved his hand in front of Ornen's face. When the old man grabbed Landis's wrist, the prince let out a squeak. The corner of Ornen's mouth turned up.

Meara's eyes grew wide. "You can see!"

"Sorry about that," said Landis. "Well, not sorry that you can see. I regret the hand waving. That was improper."

"It's alright," Ornen said. "I'm still marveling over it. When Einok hatched, he ran for me. I heard the leaves, but I couldn't see him running at me. The little guy climbed up my leg and dove into my shirt. I'm sure my stomach has claw marks on it, but I don't care. The moment his skin touched mine, my sight returned. Well, not *my* sight. It's more like Einok is seeing through my eyes and sharing the images with me. He is not enamored with being out in the open. Even when he leaves my shirt, he hides."

"But…he's yellow," Meara said.

It was a statement, though Landis understood she meant it as a question. How could a yellow dragon hide? Or, maybe the better question is why would the gods create a creature with the desire to hide but make them a color that was least conducive to doing so?

Ornen reached into his shirt to pry the tiny new god out and placed him in his lap. Now that Landis had a good view of him, he saw Einok was not yellow, but tan. That made him slightly less conspicuous than if he had been yellow, but it still wasn't the best hue for remaining hidden unless the dragon planned to stay on Ornen's animal skin britches forever. He was difficult to see while sitting in the old man's lap.

Ornen stood on the rock he had been using as a seat. The sudden movement caused the baby god to fall a few inches to the stone surface, landing at Ornen's feet. Landis watched Einok's scales change from tan to dark gray, replicating the color of the stone.

"He's a shadow dragon," Ronvost whispered.

"What does that mean, exactly? He can change colors?" Landis asked.

"It's more complex than that," Ronvost answered with awe in his mental voice. "A shadow dragon can blend with its surroundings. It enables him to chronicle events while remaining unseen."

"Are you telling me Einok is a spy?"

"Of sorts. It's fitting, really. His vincule lacks the ability to see, yet possesses an extra-sensory sight. The ability to watch others without detection is another type of vision. As the god of aspiration, he would have an interest in what others are planning. His ability to remain in the shadows gives him access to peoples' thoughts because he can bear witness to what they do or say to others when they think no one is watching."

"I think you're getting carried away," Landis said. "I'm not sure this craven should impress you so much, but I admit I can see the possibilities that might result from his talent."

"He's not actually a coward," said Ronvost. "It is simply his disposition to remain hidden."

Saldo held out a long talon to the shadow dragon. He sniffed a few times before leaping onto Saldo's front leg and scrambling to where it met her body. On his way, his scale color evolved until he matched Saldo's shimmering green color precisely. When Einok stopped moving, Landis was only able to perceive his form because he already knew where the little dragon was. Saldo did not seem happy to have the creature attached to her, but she was gentle as she shook herself until the little dragon slid back down her leg.

Einok connected with the ground and scrambled to stand close to Dabwey's leg. The newest god in the group was nearly invisible, though Dabwey appeared to have sprouted a growth on her appendage.

"He's adorable!" Meara said. "I apologize to the rest of you, but this is the cutest dragon I've ever met."

Dabwey fluttered her eyes in Meara's direction and Landis smiled.

"I'm sorry, Dabwey," Meara said aloud. "That might have worked when you were newly hatched, but now that you're bigger than a bear, it's more difficult for you to pull it off. Your looks are tending more toward the terrifying side lately."

Dabwey side-stepped just enough to dislodge Einok from her leg. Ronvost approached the little creature. Landis waited to see Einok adopt the shimmering blue color of Ronvost's scales, but was disappointed in the end. Instead of drawing close to the blue dragon, the shadow dragon opened his mouth and spit a small flame in Ronvost's direction. Landis's dragon jumped back and Landis drew his sword. He placed the point of his steel in front of Einok's snout.

Ornen stepped between the prince's sword and the shadow dragon. He raised his hands in surrender.

"Easy, Landis. He's newly hatched. He just needs to learn who his friends are."

Ronvost spoke into Landis's mind. "Why does the new god like everyone but me?"

"Probably because he thought you were trying to eat him when you chased him up Ornen's shirt," replied Landis.

"Point taken," conceded Ronvost.

Ronvost placed his head low to the ground, a short distance from the shadow dragon. The blue dragon's rear legs hopped to the left and right a little, but his front legs and head remained low. Einok tilted his head in curiosity and then mimicked Ronvost's behavior.

Meara's hand went to her chest. Landis knew the girl's heart had just melted. Even Landis found he couldn't take his eyes off the two young male dragons as they playfully introduced themselves to each other. Suddenly, Ronvost broke for the trees. The blue dragon ran most of the way but interspersed his sprint with some actual time in the air. He beat his wings and managed to rise off the ground for a few seconds at a time. Einok stayed close enough to the blue dragon to nip at his tail a few times before both young gods disappeared into the cover provided by the trees.

Landis met Meara's eyes and saw understanding in her eyes. The prince shifted his gaze to Ornen, but the old man was still staring at the place where the two dragons had dissolved into the forest.

"Well," said Landis. "I fear we have our work cut out for us; at least for a little while.

CHAPTER 21: RONVOST

Several weeks passed before the group left Ornen's sanctuary and started the journey north. After some deliberation, the humans agreed that traveling with two dragons that were unable to fly would be difficult, and they remained in place until Ronvost and Einok could take to the sky. Einok, more lithely built than the other dragons, started hopping and flapping almost immediately. He achieved dependable flight before Ronvost was able to remain in the air for more than a few minutes.

It wasn't laziness on the part of the blue dragon that kept him from soaring among the clouds. The god of justice and equality was anything but equal to the other dragons in build. Ronvost had grown as rapidly as Dabwey, but where she had grown taller, Ronvost had grown wider. The prince had even tried to cut back on the blue dragon's food consumption out of fear the beast was getting fat. As days passed, though, it became apparent that Ronvost was sculpted from muscle. The strength the dragon possessed made him wide and terrifying to gaze upon, but it also made him heavy.

It had been nearly a week after Einok joined Saldo and Dabwey in the sky, that the other dragons deemed Ronvost's wings strong enough to carry him on hunts. It had been humiliating for the blue dragon to watch Einok frolic among the clouds while he waited on the ground with the humans. What Ronvost was gaining in size and strength, the shadow dragon possessed in speed. The two scaled males had chased each other through the forest for only a day or two before Ronvost gave up. Between Einok's ability to blend with his surroundings and his agile speed, the blue dragon was outmatched.

Now, weeks after Ronvost had proven he was capable of flying long distances, there was balance. Ronvost still couldn't catch Einok, but he was useful in ways the other dragons were not. The blue dragon was now larger than Saldo, with teeth and claws the length of human forearms. The shadow dragon, though swift, was smaller than Ronvost's head. Throughout the journey north, Ronvost had been the primary deterrent against predators in the forest. Though the humans spoke of gruesome creatures that prowled through the trees and the nighttime woods were full of snarls and screeches each night, no such creatures approached the group.

The peaceful journey had reached its conclusion. The four dragons and four humans stood at the top of a rise, too big to be called a hill, but too small to be called a mountain. The elevation allowed them to see into a densely populated area below. The City of Broen stood between them and the old gods in the north.

Meara wanted to wait to see if Einok would gain the strength to carry Ornen, and then fly over Broen to avoid confrontation. The prince was intent on drawing the attention of the Skalven people. Landis argued that they could walk right through the middle of the city without cause for danger by virtue of having four dragons among them. Ronvost believed the prince was more interested in spite. Privy to the prince's thoughts, Ronvost was aware Landis had been contemplating his parents' reaction to him being chosen as a vincule. In Ronvost's opinion, the prince was being ridiculous. The Skalven people did not even know what a vincule was.

As a god, Ronvost was born with knowledge from gods of the past. This was meant to be a survival tool for a newly hatched dragon. Though Ronvost did not share every memory with all gods who came before him, he knew enough to foresee the inevitable reaction of the Skalve when they took in the sight of four gods approaching the city. The trumpets would sound, soldiers would muster, and blood would spill. The only question would be if any of the blood would belong to a dragon, or if it would only be the humans who would suffer.

Ronvost tried to summon some sympathy for the people living far below, but failed. Though Balder had hailed from this kingdom and found peace with the land, Landis was also Skalven. The blue dragon was unsettled by his vincule's reluctance to relinquish many of the preconceptions he was raised with. Balder now shunned the materialistic and destructive ways of his ancestors. Why was Ronvost bonded to a Skalve that couldn't understand the wrongness of the culture he was born from? Even more troubling, Ronvost had an inkling that Landis might not be exactly who he thought himself to be.

Balder's voice pulled Ronvost from his own musings. "Meara, you and Landis could fly to the far side of the kingdom. If you remain low enough for the guards on the wall to spot you, the alarm they raise could draw most of the soldiers to follow the two dragons. Ornen and I can travel by foot on the opposite side of the kingdom, with Saldo and Einok high above. Once we are on the northern edge of Broen, Saldo can notify Dabwey and you and the prince can meet back up with us."

"It's a good plan," said Meara. "Of course, it hinges on you and Saldo remaining undetected. I hardly think there is a way to navigate any part of the Skalven kingdom without notice. There are patrols throughout the entire land."

"It is less likely that two men on foot will be noticed than our full party; especially if all eyes are looking at the dragons off in the other direction," argued Ornen.

"We should attack the palace," Ronvost said into the mind of his vincule.

Landis threw a look of surprise toward the blue dragon, but shared Ronvost's words with the others. Arguing commenced between the humans, but Ronvost noticed Saldo had narrowed her eyes at him.

"You may have grown in strength, young one, but I believe your thoughts are folly. Size will not be enough of an advantage if all the tiny humans attack you at once. Being the largest of us, you will be a prime target. Are you truly willing to place yourself before the collective steel of the Skalve?"

Without thinking, Ronvost answered, "We're gods. We would crush them."

"Or," Saldo said patiently, "they could fight back with such fury that we learn why our ancestors abandoned this land to the Skalven people so many years ago. We really don't know what those humans are capable of with regard to defense."

Ronvost considered Saldo's words. He found it difficult to imagine the humans would be able to ward off one dragon, let alone four. He had been confident of victory moments earlier, but the green dragon's words had stirred caution in Ronvost's mind.

"Tell us of your defenses," he said to Landis.

Landis held up a hand to cease the words flying back and forth between the others in the group. Once they were all looking at him in anticipation, he described the Skalven army as he remembered it.

"We never drilled for attack by air. It has been some time, but I see no reason the army would have resumed maneuvers long forgotten. There are still dragon bows on the ramparts surrounding the palace grounds, but many are in disrepair. Even as a boy, playing among the forgotten equipment of my grandfather's time, the bows were unstrung and more statue than weapon. I don't expect our dragons will be felled by dragon bolts. The soldiers are equipped with smaller crossbows, though. The bolts will not travel as far as those meant to down gods, but they could still tear through a wing."

"Also, the smaller bolts will have difficulty piercing dragon scales, but they could prove deadly to a rider," added Balder.

Landis continued. "At the time of my departure, I took almost every soldier the kingdom could afford to relinquish. I had thought it to be every fighting man and woman aside from my parents' personal guard, but I am no longer sure of my own observations. Since that day, I have learned much of what I knew to be truth was merely an illusion."

"So, all you know is that we would not face mounted crossbows, and you have no real estimate of the enemy's numbers," summarized Ronvost.

The blue dragon noticed a flinch from his vincule when he spoke of the Skalven as the enemy. There was every possibility that the prince would be unable to raise a sword against his former people. If that occurred at the wrong time, Landis might prove to be this group's biggest liability. That would be unfortunate. Ronvost did not think he would be able to scorch his own vincule's flesh if it came down to it. He would need to ask Saldo to monitor the prince. The bond between Landis and the blue dragon grew stronger every day, but the survival of the gods was paramount to any single relationship between dragon and bonded rider. Landis and he had not yet even attempted flight together.

In the end, the plan for traversing the Kingdom of Skalve combined several ideas. The humans would begin a northeasterly march through Skalve, trying to stay as far from the city as possible without adding too much additional time to the hike. The dragons would attack the ramparts, trying not to harm anyone living outside of the palace walls, several hours after the humans started on their journey. After causing enough chaos for the Skalven soldiers to light braziers and call the patrols back to the city and away from the humans' path, the four gods would fly to the northwest, hoping many of the troops gave chase.

The humans picked their way down the slope, navigating rocks taller than them and climbing over fallen trees. It took longer than Ronvost expected for the humans to disappear from sight. He tried to gauge the time they needed to reach the outskirts of the kingdom, but it simply wasn't possible. The blue dragon tried to embody patience, but his tail swished incessantly, betraying his state of mind.

When Einok started pouncing on Ronvost's tail, practicing his hunting skills, the blue dragon could no longer wait. Dabwey attempted to hold him back.

"I doubt they've crossed into the forbidden lands yet. If we attack too soon, the distraction won't last long enough for them to traverse Skalve. They'll be trapped by returning patrols."

"There is no way an attack on the city perpetrated by the god they fear will see them returning to business as usual any time soon. I doubt they will send any new patrols for days after we make our presence known."

Dabwey had spoken into all of their minds, and Ronvost had replied in kind. The other two dragons would need to decide if they planned to attack now or wait anyhow. Einok did not seem to care either way, but Saldo had stepped closer, showing interest.

"I don't care when we go, I just want to watch them burn," Saldo said.

"Saldo," Dabwey warned. "We're not supposed to try to kill

the humans."

"I said nothing about trying to do anything. I can't be blamed if the flames I relinquish take on a life of their own."

"Maybe we should use our shadow?" Dabwey asked. "We can send Einok to determine the progress made by the humans. He is fast enough to check on them and return before an hour passes."

Einok chose that moment to switch his attention from Ronvost to Dabwey's tail. She stepped back reflexively and nearly squished the shadow dragon. Einok ran between her legs and shot out the other side. He flattened himself to the ground and his scales adopted a mottled green and brown color that blended with his surroundings. Of the four dragons, Einok was the only one who had armor that did not shimmer in its natural state. With his scales reflecting no light, the little dragon was invisible.

"He's more likely to get himself stepped on than to be of use until he is a little more mature," Ronvost said.

Dabwey's laughter tinkled. "You are one to talk. I'm just glad you can finally fly."

Ronvost was done discussing the matter. He beat his wings twice to lift into the air. It took a great deal of energy for him to initiate flight, but once he was aloft, he maneuvered with ease. Saldo burst into the air behind Ronvost and he turned his attention to the target below. He could already hear the blast of trumpets as his gargantuan shadow preceded him across the outskirts of the kingdom.

The blue dragon covered the few miles to the palace in minutes. He lined up with the manned wall on the southern side of the palace grounds and swooped low to lay down a swath of fire from his open jaws. As he breezed by, he watched soldiers jump out of the way and take cover. Some, seeming to have lost all sense, jumped from the wall instead of contending with the scorching flames. Those humans might survive, but they would certainly not be fit for duty any time soon.

When Ronvost banked and turned back toward the palace for another strike, he saw Dabwey had followed him and Saldo. She was burning the Skalven soldiers from the northern ramparts. A crossbow bolt, several inches in diameter and over five feet long, sailed just over the purple dragon's head and she veered away from the wall. At least one of the old dragon bows was still functioning. If there were more, or if the soldiers managed to reload the one that was recently fired, the loss of a god was possible.

"That was too close," Ronvost called to the other dragons. "We must depart."

Saldo, having burned both the eastern wall and part of the palace garden just inside of it, seemed reluctant. Ronvost could feel her indecision and changed the direction of his flight to face the west to emphasize his point. Saldo and Dabwey acquiesced and followed behind him.

It was only then that Ronvost realized there was a god missing. He stretched his mind and tried to locate Einok. The shadow dragon spoke a moment later.

"I feel your mind searching for me. You will not be able to locate me. It is not just my scales that help me hide."

"Enough with the games. Where are you? We're supposed to be flying west."

"It might behoove you to stay within sight of the palace walls," Einok replied. "The humans are not pursuing you."

CHAPTER 22: MEARA

As they passed into Skalve, Meara could already feel tension in the bond between her and Dabwey. It didn't seem possible that the distance was already becoming too great. There was only about a mile between her and her dragon. It had been several hours, though. It was possible that the combination of distance and time were contriving to create the discomfort in Meara's chest.

The sun disappeared for a moment, causing Meara to look up. Ronvost was in the sky. Her heart skipped a beat when she saw Saldo and then Dabwey just behind the two larger dragons. It was too early. She and the men had barely set foot in Skalve. It would be over two hours before they made it to the northern border. The dragons' attack would only take minutes. Trumpet blasts sounded in the distance and then sounded again, closer than was comfortable, when a nearby patrol relayed the blast to cover more territory.

"Find a place to hide. That patrol sounds like it's going to cut its way right through us on its way back to the palace," Balder said.

Thankfully, there was plenty of cover and the patrol of six soldiers was in too much of a hurry to see anything while the hooves of their horses pounded the ground. As soon as they passed, Landis stood from behind the rock he was crouched behind and motioned for the group to get moving again.

They maneuvered through the woods with as much speed

179

as possible. It was difficult, especially for Ornen. Though the old man was afforded sight by his bond with Einok, distance between the dragon and his vincule saw the magical aid fade. Balder helped carve a clear path by bending branches out of the way to lessen the chance Ornen would be caught by one, and Landis grabbed the old man's shoulder a few times to keep him on his feet.

Ten minutes into their near sprint, an idea took form in Meara's mind. She would send Landis and Balder ahead to safety. If patrols caught either of them, they would be charged with treason. That would carry a much stiffer punishment than a tribal girl and her elderly grandfather accidentally stumbling into Skalven territory.

Meara ceased her plotting when Ornen started laughing. The old man gained speed and dexterity as he maneuvered through the dense forest. Meara thought she caught sight of something scampering alongside of her for a second, but when she turned her focus on the spot, there was nothing there. A smile spread over her lips. *I believe the shadow dragon has joined us.*

When the group broke through the tree line and into the barren swath of land surrounding the city of Broen, Meara's notion was confirmed. Einok hovered in the air at eye-level as if encouraging the group to run faster. Instead, the party slowed to a near-walk when they caught sight of the commotion above the city. Flames engulfed sections of the raised ramparts and smoke billowed into the air. Meara could see the silhouette of three dragons as they flew off to the west, in the sky beyond the city.

She and the men were out of time. Even if the majority of the Skalven army pursued the dragons, patrols would surely be sent to scout the northern border for signs of incursion by other gods. Ornen grabbed her arm and tugged her further onto the dusty plain.

"Einok is going to try to intercept any scouting parties that come too close to our position, but first he's going to go check to see how many soldiers remain in Skalve," Ornen puffed out as he ran.

The old man's stamina amazed Meara. She was finding it difficult to draw breath. Her lungs burned; especially now that they were kicking up dust as they moved over the dry, treeless land. Balder seemed to be having the most trouble keeping up the wild pace. Like Ronvost, Balder's best attributes were his size and strength. Those characteristics were counterproductive when survival called for speed and agility.

Ornen seemed to be able to read Meara's thoughts. "Einok is fast. He'll check on the city and be back to help us before we know it. We'll make it to the border."

With the shadow dragon gone, Ornen was sightless again. Meara could tell because the old man was no longer focused on the trees two hundred yards ahead of them. He ran with his eyes closed and seemed to be focused inward instead of on the environment. Meara considered speaking to him to help guide his sense of direction, but he seemed to do well on his own. There were no obstacles to avoid, but Ornen's ability to maintain his trajectory still surprised Meara.

Balder hit his knees just before entering their forested destination. Landis and Meara grabbed Balder under his arms and dragged him out of the dust and into the shade and cover of the bushes. The smoke continued to rise into the sky just a few miles from where the four of them sat, breathing hard. Landis was the first to recover enough for words.

"I forgot how barren the land has become. If many more trees had been removed for fuel and building material, the plain might have been too wide for us to make it across without being seen."

"There were trees here at one time?" asked Meara.

"Indeed," replied Balder. "When I was a boy, the forest met the walls of the city. This dusty wasteland is evidence of the wrongness perpetrated on the land by the Skalve."

Landis was quiet, but Meara thought she saw a war raging behind his eyes. Though the prince did not defend the ways of the Skalven people, Meara could tell he was not yet ready to condemn it, either.

"Einok tells me a patrol has struck out in our direction. They are making haste across the plain and he is unable to stop them. We need to keep going," Ornen warned.

Meara could see dust rising in the distance. She could imagine horses' hooves hitting the dusty ground and causing the reddish cloud that rose into the air. Meara wasn't ready to start running again, but one look at Balder told her she was more prepared for the pending sprint than he was. The former soldier dragged himself to his feet and started moving north without waiting for words of encouragement. His determination proved to be all the prodding she needed to get her own feet moving again.

Ornen wasn't having as much trouble as he should have finding his way over the roots protruding from the ground, so Meara knew the shadow dragon must be close again. If the little dragon had told Ornen he wasn't able to distract the charging patrol, there must have been more soldiers riding out than they had expected. Landis slowed until Meara was beside him.

"It's about a half mile to the border. If the soldiers see us, they will continue to pursue us. Patrols are under strict orders to bring interlopers to justice, even if they turn tail and run," the prince said. "Given the recent attack on the city, I expect justice will not include a trial."

Meara stopped running. They would not be able to outrun men on horseback. The men slowed and turned to see why she had stopped. Einok zipped out of the bushes and stopped beside her. Meara smiled at the inspiration for her sudden stop.

"Listen," Meara said. "The soldiers are riding hard through the dirt, but they will need to slow when they reach the edge of the plain. They couldn't have seen us because we were only able to see them due to the dust they were throwing into the air. Instead of moving quickly, we need to start moving quietly. If we're lucky, the patrol will come nowhere near us. Even if we are unlucky, we will hear their horses moving through the trees before they hear us picking our way on foot. At that point, we'll need to hide."

"Meara's right," Ornen said. "There is little chance the patrol will enter the exact place where we went into the trees. If they enter before crossing the tracks we undoubtedly left, the soldiers won't even know to look for us. In case they do see our tracks, we should probably change our course a little so that we are angling away from them as we continue north."

Einok proved invaluable in helping the humans move through the trees unnoticed. Through Ornen, the shadow dragon guided Meara and the others in a winding but northerly direction that avoided patrols. It helped that the soldiers appeared to be riding in a predictable grid pattern. Though they were covering more ground than Meara and the men, Einok ensured that the soldiers never stumbled on their quarry.

The few times the soldiers were close enough for Meara to hear any conversation among them, she was reassured that no evidence of their party had been detected. As the need for course corrections lessened, Meara had to fight the urge to pick up her pace again. She was tired of feeling hunted and the desire to put distance between herself and the patrols was strong.

———————————————————

Meara enjoyed the reward for her diligence when the group sat on the far side of a stream a mile outside of Skalven territory over an hour later. There would be no enemy patrols here, and they were enjoying a restful moment after each drinking their fill of water and refilling their skins. Moments ago, Meara had wanted nothing more than to sit down and rest, but waiting proved equally difficult.

Dabwey, Ronvost and Saldo were too far from the group for direct communication. Einok had left to go inform them they made it across the border and guide the dragons back to the location. It would take some time. Until the dragons returned, Meara and the others were nursing sore feet and regaining strength.

A branch broke somewhere on the far side of the stream. Meara squinted into the trees, trying to see the cause of the sound. Dabwey felt nearer, but Meara was sure the dragon was still over a mile away. There was no sign of glimmering scales on the other side of the running water, but Meara chanced a look at Landis and Ornen to see if either of them might have sensed their dragons. The men, including Balder, were staring into the trees.

With no further warning, a saber cat, roughly the height of a deer at the shoulders, leaped from the trees, landed, and then cleared the stream in a second jump. It turned its long canines in Meara's direction. Meara placed her feet beneath her and stood with her hands in front of her. She bent low, as if bowing to the creature.

"Whatever you do," Meara said to the others. "do not run. You will turn this attack into a game for the cat. We won't stand a chance."

Speaking in a low, even voice, Landis said, "Ronvost reports he is minutes away. Try not to become lunch before he gets here."

"I'm coming, Meara," Dabwey's voice said distantly in her

mind.

Meara took a cautious step toward the saber cat, remaining in her low stance. The cat stepped back and crouched. Though the creature outweighed Meara by more than a hundred pounds, it was still a product of the forest. It stared at Meara with its green eyes, measuring the level of threat she might pose. Meara took another step forward, but this time the cat held its ground. It appeared Meara had been deemed little risk to the animal.

A crack reverberated through the air, followed by a gust of wind and the shaking of the ground beneath Meara's feet. She had closed her eyes involuntarily at the loud sound, but when she opened them again, Ronvost stood before Meara, swinging his head back and forth. The tail of the saber cat stuck out from under Ronvost's front foot.

Nervous laughter came from the prince. "Well, I guess we have no need to wonder what we will be eating for lunch."

"We're too close to the border to risk a fire," said Ornen. "Unless you want to eat raw meat, that cat is a meal for the gods."

As Ornen spoke, Einok scrambled over to Ronvost's foot and gave the blue dragon's toe a quick bite. Ronvost lifted his foot reflexively and Einok tore a rear leg from the flattened saber cat. The shadow dragon struggled to drag his portion into the brush.

"Greedy little thing," Dabwey said into Meara's mind.

Meara hummed in agreement. Dabwey grabbed the saber cat by the head and Ronvost clamped his front teeth on the other end of the cat. There was a terrible ripping sound before the dragons walked off in opposite directions with their share of the meal.

"Where is Saldo?" Balder asked.

It was a moment before Landis answered. "Ronvost said

she will not be returning."

Balder's words became panicked. "What do you mean 'not returning'? Is she dead?"

The pause was longer than Balder liked, and he stepped toward Landis with his fists balled. Meara put herself between Balder and the prince.

"Hold on," Meara scolded Balder. "It's not his fault. He's getting the information from his dragon. Give him a second to get the story."

Balder stopped moving forward, but the tension did not leave his body.

"Ronvost told the dragons to retreat when a giant crossbow bolt nearly struck Dabwey. They were in the sky and flying west when Einok, spying from the ground, sent word that none of the soldiers were pursuing. Saldo flew back to the palace."

"I don't understand," Balder said. "Why would she turn back?"

"The distraction hadn't burned enough time. According to Einok's reports, you had only just reached the dust plane. Saldo went back to keep the soldiers from reforming border patrols before you could cross the open plane."

"Was she shot down?" Balder asked.

Ornen was the one to answer. "Einok hasn't shared that information with anyone yet. Give me a moment."

The group waited in restless silence. Meara couldn't bear the tormented look on Balder's face.

After a minute, Ornen relayed Einok's report. "Einok was not a witness to how Saldo was captured, but she lives. They have her caged below ground. He offered to unlock her cage, but after some discussion, they agreed the soldiers would kill her before allowing her to escape. She was only alive because she allowed them to take her easily. Einok said there is much talk among the Skalve of how a captive dragon will cause the

186

old gods to return."

CHAPTER 23: LANDIS

Landis's legs lost strength, and he crumpled to his knees. His parents had exactly what they wanted. They were now able to bait the gods into returning to Skalve. It had been Landis's desire to provide that very thing to Skalve. He would have been a hero. The idea turned his stomach. Landis was sickened when he thought of how he had planned to bring Ronvost to the king and queen in exchange for their praise and forgiveness. His own selfishness astounded him.

"They are going to use her," Landis said. "Somehow, they will send word north of Saldo's capture and hope the old gods come to reclaim her. I really don't understand how they can believe they would be able to defend against the wrath they will bring down upon Skalve."

"I am wondering the same thing," said Ornen. "Other than a single shot from a dragon bow, the soldiers on the ramparts had difficulty defending the palace from three dragons. How would they expect to defend against more?"

"None of us were alive when the old gods roamed this land," said Landis. "It was so long ago, there may be none left to seek vengeance for the capture of a new dragon."

"We know they left the God Stones hidden within this land and provided protection for them. I wish we knew what outcome the old gods were expecting when they did that."

Landis smiled. "I see you've taken to referring to them as the old gods. Didn't you once correct me on that point?"

"Yes, but the term makes more sense now that new gods have hatched. The gods I grew up worshipping are now the older generation. It has me wondering if Smok, Tala and others of their era are truly gone. I assumed gods were immortal, but perhaps I was wrong. Maybe the gods hatching now were intended to replace those of ancient times. Your people might be attempting to lure creatures who have been dead for centuries."

"I have memories," Ronvost spoke into the prince's mind. "All of them are from the time the gods roamed this land. I know nothing of their fate after traveling north."

"That assumes they actually went north," Landis replied to his dragon.

"What do we truly know for sure?" Landis asked aloud. "Until a few months ago, none of us really believed the tales of the old gods."

Meara and Ornen sent glares in the prince's direction.

"Ok," he conceded. "None of us had seen proof of the tales regarding the gods."

Landis could see his tribal friends were still not happy with his choice of phrasing, but he had no intention of further altering his words. Ornen was unwilling to let the prince continue, however.

"There are more of you," said the old man.

"More of who? More Skalven people than...tribe people?"

Landis caught himself before using the word primitive, but the look on Meara's face told him she had caught his delay in finding the right words.

"No. Well, yes. That is a truth, but that is not what I meant," Ornen said. "I meant there are more people who have discovered the true nature of the God Stones."

"I know you've shared that you were able to watch my life, as well as Meara's, but how many other people have you been watching?"

"All of them, I think," replied Ornen. "I'm still not sure, but I suspect every life I've seen unfold is the life of a person destined to become a vincule."

"Why are you only sharing this now?" asked Meara.

"All I understood before was that each of the people was important. I now suspect they were of import because they were fated to bond a dragon. Even since I've been in your company, I've watched two more new gods hatch into this world."

"Why didn't you tell us?" asked Meara.

"You never asked. If I told you of all the things I witness minute to minute, I fear I'd be insufferable company. That is my curse to bear alone."

"Well," said Landis. "Might we trouble you for a synopsis of all you've seen in relation to the gods so far?"

"I suppose you deserve one, now that we find ourselves heading north along with many others we have yet to meet. Would you prefer to wait until we make camp tonight? I suspect you'll want to put distance between us and the border if you'd like to enjoy a cook fire."

"Since we're moving at a more leisurely pace, perhaps you could regale us as we travel?" Landis asked.

Balder did not permit Ornen to reply. "That's it? We're just going to walk away and leave Saldo behind?"

"Nothing has been decided," said Landis. "Whether we continue traveling north, or turn around to attempt Saldo's rescue, we need some distance between us and the border. Once we have a safe place to camp, we can begin making decisions."

Dabwey and Ronvost took to the air, remaining just above the treetops to avoid the possibility of being sighted by any border patrolmen with keen eyesight. They would report back once they found a suitable destination for the group to make their camp. Meara started walking north and Landis fell in behind her. He noticed Balder was looking back toward the palace, but knew the former soldier was not touched enough in the head to go after Saldo alone. He knew Balder had, indeed, followed behind them when he prodded Ornen to start talking and Ornen became a walking storyteller.

"There were many children over the years. I was granted access to their lives shortly after each was born. It was as if I were always dreaming, even as I went through my daily rituals. In the recesses of my mind, I was always a spectator in another's life. The dreams came one at a time and I had no control over which one I walked through.

"I saw Meara when she was discovered on the shore of Innut Island and again, many times, as she was tormented throughout her youth over her mottled skin. I saw Landis as well, though his upbringing was very different from Meara's. His nursemaids ensured he wanted for nothing. If ever a time came that a child did not wish to play with the young prince, the child's parents were compensated and the parents ensured the child enjoyed a fine day in the prince's company."

"My parents paid people to make their children play with me?"

Landis had not meant to say the words aloud, but now that they were out of his mouth, he turned to look at Ornen, stopping to wait for a reply. Ornen nodded in affirmation. Landis shook his head in disbelief, but turned to continue walking. Ornen picked up his story again as he picked his way along the game trail the group was following.

"Unlike Meara, whose skin could not be hidden, the prince had only a single blemish on his milky skin. When he was a babe, the king and queen called in several healers and mystics to try to remove the skin blemish. Some tried by potion, others by prayer, but the mark remained."

Landis's hand went to his chest involuntarily. He had not known his birthmark had been such a concern to his parents. He tried to remember them speaking about it when he was a child, but only came up with a memory of his mother yelling at one of his nurses when the kindly woman had permitted the prince to play in the garden shirtless on a particularly hot day. The queen had scolded the nurse for allowing Landis such impropriety in public, but it could have been her shame over Landis's marked skin.

Balder broke his silence to ask, "Did you ever see visions of me?"

"I cannot say I did," replied Ornen. "Having met you and seen your relationship with Saldo, I have no doubt she would have chosen you as a vincule. Though, if my dreams foretell of those fated for the honor, then all I can offer is to tell you your bond with Saldo was not meant to be."

The group covered several miles, during which Ornen enlightened them on the details of lives that belonged to other people destined to become vincules. Some did not live long enough to see their fate realized. Accidents and disease claimed a few, and two had their lives taken by their own families.

In one case, the mother believed her child's skin was marked by evil. She brought her babe to the tribal leader for advice and the old woman had told the mother she must drown the child, lest she have evil follow her and her other children until death.

The second instance was not as heartbreaking, but no less morbid. The Duke of Livane, a small kingdom west of Skalve, discovered his only son had plotted to murder him and take his lands for himself. The duke ended the machinations by ending his son's life. He did not draw his own steel on his child, but had his body guard carry out the deed and leave the young man on the side of the road so others might conclude he had been killed by thieves.

Landis found it interesting that many of the visions were of people with Skalven ancestry. The Duke of Livane was second cousin to his mother, and there were other children born to royals in kingdoms outside of Skalve. He had expected the vincule would come from the people native to this land, but several of them were raised in Skalve or the many other kingdoms that were cultivated by those who had once been among the Skalven population.

There was one thing every life followed by Ornen had in common. Each person bore strange marks on his or her skin. Most were not as all-encompassing as Meara's. Ornen admitted that the tribal girl was the only fated vincule to be marked from head to toe. Some only had white streaks in their hair, growing from places where their scalps were bleached, and others had birthmarks like Landis that covered large swaths of the skin. The skin markings had to mean something, but Ornen insisted he had no idea what their significance might be.

By the time the group reached the location Ronvost had picked for a camp, Landis felt he had only a slightly better understanding of the world than he had grasped before Ornen's story. There were somewhere between fifteen and twenty other bonded dragons out there and it was likely they were all heading north. Like Landis and his friends, they were all migrating in the direction the old gods were fabled to have journeyed long ago. None of them even had a name for their destination.

"So, is it possible for us to figure out if there are any other dragons in the area using your gift?" Meara asked.

Ornen sat down heavily in the soft moss. Landis felt the volume of the groan the old man emitted was excessive, but he understood the sentiment.

"Unfortunately, once a person becomes vincule, I no longer

receive dreams of them. If we were to encounter a vincule on our travels, I would recognize them, but I have no knowledge of their actions or movements since they hatched their fated dragons. I don't even know the names of the gods who have hatched. You know that bright flash of light when the stone cracks?"

Landis nodded. He had been hoping the brightness of the light was an indication of how special his bond was with Ronvost, or at least foretold of the future strength of the hatching dragon, but it seemed the bright light was common to all births involving gods.

"Well," said Ornen, "that light is when my connection is severed."

As disparaging as the news was with regard to locating other vincules, Landis was relieved to know Ornen was no longer able to watch his life unfold with no regard for his privacy. It was creepy enough to know the man had been privy to many private moments in the prince's life, and he didn't want to constantly wonder if Ornen was watching him now that Landis was aware it was happening.

"Ok," said Meara. "So we've gained hours of knowledge about other vincules, but none of the information makes it any easier to decide our next steps. Do we continue north, or do we return to the palace and attempt to free Saldo?"

Meara cocked her head to the side, listening to her dragon. Landis made a note to mention to her that she was in the habit of making the gesture. One day, that movement could be an issue. It made it obvious she was listening for something, even if no one would suspect it was a dragon voice.

"There is a third option. Dabwey wants to find the fated vincules that still haven't bonded with a dragon. She wants to know if there are other dragons out there like Saldo, or if there is a possibility there are God Stones that remain hidden."

A laugh escaped Landis. "It's more likely the stones intended for those people were stolen by Skalven soldiers and the hatching dragons fried everyone in the vicinity upon emerging. I am curious to know if dragon rogues will head north, even if they aren't bonded. Saldo seemed happy to stay with Balder and would probably still be back in the village with him if we hadn't stumbled upon them."

Landis stiffened. He let his gaze wander to Balder and saw his words had hurt the man. The moment they spilled from his mouth, he knew he shouldn't have said them. Instead of apologizing, he doubled down.

"I'm in favor of trying to free Saldo," said the prince.

"I appreciate that," said Balder. "She's earned our help."

CHAPTER 24: MEARA

*D*abwey's diatribe was ceaseless. Meara had stopped listening. She was still trying to figure out how the lengthy discussion around the fire on the prior night resulted in her and Dabwey setting off on their own. Dabwey had been the only one to insist that locating people Ornen was still dreaming about had any bearing on, well…anything. Meara knew it was a fool's errand, but she couldn't separate herself from Dabwey and Dabwey was a god, so she would get her way.

Landis, Balder, and Ornen were going to rescue Saldo. Meara was on a much less exciting mission to locate people who were supposed to bond dragons, but hadn't. Ornen had supplied her with two names, and general descriptions that included where they lived. Only one of the people she needed to locate lived in the vicinity. This made Meara's secondary task paramount. She needed to learn to ride Dabwey.

"Do you suppose that might be the case?" Dabwey asked.

It was the first question the purple dragon had sent Meara's direction since they had started walking that morning. Well, Meara was walking. Dabwey flew ahead, landed, and then waited for Meara to catch up. Meara searched her mind in an attempt to uncover what Dabwey had been ranting about most recently, but came up short.

"What might be the case?" Meara asked.

"I knew you were ignoring me! I was talking about the

possibility that Trina might have been intended as Saldo's vincule."

"Why would you think that?"

"Trina was a soldier in the Skalven army until she was thrown from her horse during maneuvers. Her early retirement enabled her to move out into the countryside and start a farm. If that hadn't happened, maybe she would have been on the mission with Balder to retrieve the Nahola God Stone."

"I think," Meara said, "there is a lot of speculation in your story. It doesn't make a difference anyhow. We just need to find Trina and figure out if there is any chance she might still bond a dragon. There's no need to invent a story for her."

"Sorry. I was unaware we intended to have no fun on this journey. I shall resume my mundane task of waiting in silence for my vincule to catch up. By the way, whenever you get here, I'm at Trina's farm."

"How do you know you have arrived at the correct place?"

"Let's just say the writing is on the wall," Dabwey said.

Meara's head filled with her dragon's tinkling laughter. Meara knew she was close, but the brush was thick here and she could only see a few feet in front of her.

Seconds later, Meara stepped out of the dense forest and onto an outcrop. Unprepared for the drop-off of the ground, Meara slipped and nearly toppled over the cliff. Dabwey grabbed the back of Meara's tunic with her teeth and pulled her back to safety.

"Why didn't you warn me? Better yet, why didn't you tell me I was walking right past you?"

"I was busy being silent. You'll need to specify when you'd like me to speak again after asking me to stop talking."

"I never asked you to stop — oh, what does it matter… Let's see this farm."

Meara picked her way back to the edge of the rock. When

197

she peered over the side, she saw acres of land below enclosed by a wooden wall hewn from the trees that must have once grown in the area.

"Nothing screams Skalve like removing every tree for miles to build a giant wall," murmured Meara. "I see why you felt we found Trina. It seems she modeled her farm after the city where she was born. Wait here until I enter her compound, and then come fly in and make your presence known. It is unlikely she will have any weapon that would prove itself a deterrent to a dragon."

It took Meara almost an hour to climb down off the cliff and walk through the open gate of Trina's farm. Dabwey landed beside her moments after Meara entered the property. A chicken squawked at the sight of the purple dragon and set off a chain reaction. Other chickens clucked, which drew the attention of two hogs penned up on Meara's right. The hogs started to grunt and paw at the ground, and this unsettled the animals in the nearby barn. Meara heard at least one horse and a mule before a woman's voice turned Meara's attention to the house on her right.

On the wooden porch of a cabin built from logs, an exceptionally tall woman with golden hair in a thick braid stood in men's trousers and a tunic. She appeared not to be afraid of the god standing in her pasture, but she was unquestionably peeved by the ruckus Dabwey's presence caused among her animals.

"What in all the worlds is going on out here? Who are you and what makes you think you can be here?"

"Aren't you going to ask me about her?" Meara pointed up and over her shoulder at Dabwey.

"I'm not a fool. I can see you have brought one of the old gods here. Since you are content to send my animals into a panic, and have yet to torch my home, I am guessing you are not here to cause me harm. Frankly, I'm not sure it would make a difference if you were. What defense do I have against a god?"

"I see you know of the old gods. My name is Meara. Are you Trina, formerly of the Skalven army?"

"I do, and I am. It's nice to meet you, Meara. Would you consider asking the god to leave so the animals might settle? You are then welcome to come in for tea."

Trina was an interesting woman. A former Skalven soldier, solidly built, dressed like a man and living in the middle of nowhere, had invited Meara to tea. Dabwey must have been equally amused. Meara's head filled with the tinkling she loved to hear as the dragon took flight to find a place to roost nearby.

Meara had just crossed the threshold when Trina began speaking. "I've always been lucky. I was fated to be killed by a dragon, but I fell from a horse instead. Most felt bad for me, but I'd rather be alive."

Meara sat at the small table when Trina gestured for her to take a seat. The muscular woman placed a dainty teakettle on the fire. The sight was more incongruous than Trina's words.

"I'm sorry," said Meara. "I fear you may have skipped some parts of your story."

Meara thought she could fill in the blanks on her own, but she didn't want to appear as if she knew more than she should. She was also very aware of Dabwey's thoughts. The dragon was feeling self-satisfied and was gloating internally. Meara focused on a patch of dark skin over Trina's left eye. It could be some sort of scar, but it was the same shade of brown as Landis's large birthmark.

"I assume you're here to ask about the dragon my patrol encountered. Ever since Lieutenant Thomas succumbed to his wounds, I've been the closest thing to an eyewitness anyone can speak with. When Thomas rode back to Skalve, he had a terrible gut wound and a wonderful story to tell. I was still convalescing in the medical barracks, so I spent a lot of time with him in the days before he finally died. His wound had festered and everyone thought him delirious. I might have been the only person who believed his tale; at the time, anyway."

"Things have changed?" Meara asked.

"Yes, ever since the sightings of the old gods have started, I've been getting visits. The king sent his personal envoy to interview me about all I learned from the lieutenant."

"There have been sightings?"

"Don't get me wrong," said Trina. "I expect I'm the first person to have one of them actually land in my fields, but others have seen them in the sky, flying in the distance. I suppose I'll be getting a few more visits after this."

"This isn't good," Dabwey said. "This woman is going to run straight to Skalve for another shot at fame as soon as we leave."

"I agree. You'll likely need to do something about that."

"What did Lieutenant Thomas say to you?" Meara asked Trina.

"Our company was tasked with recovering a priceless dragon egg from the primitive village of Nahola. I was tossed from my horse the day before we were to set off, which saved my life if you believe all Lieutenant Thomas told me. I'm guessing you're no stranger to tragedy, so you're probably familiar with the idea that all things happen for a reason."

Meara was trying to be patient with Trina's ignorance. She had let the part about Nahola being a primitive village pass, but she couldn't stop herself from asking what the woman meant by her assumption Meara had experienced tragedy.

"You know… your skin. Were you in a fire or something? I bet that hurt. It's amazing you survived. Is that what you're doing? Traveling around looking for survival stories to spur faith in the old religion?"

"Sure," Meara seethed. "I'm sorry I asked. It's obvious you have me figured out. It's probably time for me to get going."

"Going? The water hasn't even boiled yet and I haven't told Lieutenant Thomas's story. I'm sorry if I offended you. I don't get many visitors out here and it's not like I had a ma to teach me manners."

"Dabwey, get down here and do something about this woman."

Meara showed herself out and kept walking. She kept her back to Trina until Dabwey landed behind her and Trina screamed. Meara whirled in time to see Dabwey open her jaws.

"Stop! Don't roast her!"

"What made you change your mind?" Dabwey asked. "You said to take care of her."

"Close your mouth. That isn't what I meant. Just do your mind thing. Convince her she doesn't need to tell anyone about our visit. I know it won't last forever, but it will give us time to leave the area."

"Are you sure you don't want me to just make her forget the whole thing permanently?"

"You can do that?" Meara asked. "Yes. Do it. That would be perfect."

"We'll need to make a hasty exit. After I remove our memory from her mind, we can't be seen by her."

"That makes sense. I'll start running now."

Meara watched Trina straighten and clutch her head in her hands. She turned and started running. Dabwey's wings beat behind her as the dragon took to the air. Moments later, Meara was clutched from behind and lifted off the ground. Dabwey's talons gripped her tightly in a manner similar to the way Saldo had carried her when Meara had first met the green dragon. Meara turned her head to watch Trina writhe on the ground as the woman's form became tinier with every bit of altitude her dragon gained.

"She'll be fine," Dabwey said.

"I'm glad. I am not so sure I'll be fine, though. Hanging in your claws can't be good for my spine. I hate to say this, but I think we're going to need to try flying together before we can cover any more ground."

"I'm ready, but then again, I'm the one with the wings. It won't be me plummeting to the ground if it doesn't go well."

"You're overwhelming me with your confidence," replied Meara. "Set me down on that plateau up ahead."

They had only been airborne for a few minutes, but they were now several miles west of Trina's farm. Meara was hundreds of miles from the ocean she had known back home and the landscape was beautiful, but foreign. Walking through forests hadn't afforded Meara an opportunity to see the contrast before this. Hanging in Dabwey's talons, Meara had noticed the drastic changes in elevation this far west. The land was still densely packed with trees and brush in most areas, but gentle hills had started to reach heights that would better be described as mountains. There were fewer trees atop these land formations, and Meara felt as if she could see the entire world from these heights. She knew that was inaccurate, but she could see a winding river in the distance. That would be where the next person Ornen was watching would be found.

"We can be there before nightfall if we fly," said Dabwey.

"We're closer than I thought," replied Meara.

"Not really. Everything looks closer when you have a view such as this. It will take more than a day for you to walk there. Start a small fire. I'll find us some food and you can burn yours to your liking. Once we've eaten, we will fly to the river."

Dabwey dropped from the plateau to hunt in the grassy valley below. Meara stared at the river in the distance for a moment longer. Along that river, there was a tribal village she had never heard of. She hadn't even known the land stretched this far, let alone that there were people living out here. She wondered how the tribe defended its population against the monsters that lived this far out in the wild.

Meara turned to gather some stones to contain a small fire. She reached for her water skin and found there to be little water left. She now had a more pressing reason to fly instead of walk. She was happy Dabwey could hunt for her, but she might die from thirst if she had to walk to a water source.

CHAPTER 25: EINOK

*I*t was not difficult for Einok to gain entrance to the city of Broen. Though the walls were high and thick, they were never intended to be impassible by every creature that came across them. There were cracks large enough for snakes and mice to wiggle through to the other side, as well as one crumbling area where a small stone had dislodged and left a hole big enough for a lizard-like dragon to squeeze through.

Trees grew in close proximity to the wall, and Einok could have climbed one of them to gain access, or the dragon could have simply waited for nightfall and flown over the rock wall. If the shadow dragon had been seen, any hope of freeing Saldo would have been smothered. The soldiers had their eyes on the sky, watching for an attack from the gods. Einok craftily entered the city only a half a foot from the ground. His scales turned from gray to green when he found himself in a grassy area behind an outbuilding.

The black and white cat Einok had followed through the breach in the wall sat in the doorway of the building, swishing its tail. Einok was unsure if the feline intended to hunt him or if it was waiting to see if the dragon would continue to pursue it. Though the shadow dragon could always eat, the cat's usefulness had expired for now. It earned the right to live by unintentionally showing Einok safe passage through the wall.

A woman approached the barn from Einok's left, and the shadow dragon headed in the opposite direction. He skirted the

204

city wall until he was in a part of the city that required his scales to take on a dark brown color to blend with the environment. He slipped through the smelly trenches alongside the dirt and mud laden roads. He was going to need to find a stream to swim through later, but for now, the smell helped Einok blend in with the local population.

The streets gradually became less cluttered with carts and foot traffic as Einok approached the palace. There was another wall there. This one was in much better condition than the one surrounding the city. Einok needed to make a decision. He was unsure if he should climb the wall or find a way to enter the palace through the main gate.

The top of the wall was crowded with masons and other laborers working to repair the ramparts burned by the other dragons. Even if he remained unseen by soldiers, there were too many eyes on the battlements for Einok to get through without notice. He could only see three soldiers at the gate, and decided that would be the better approach. Two guards, one at either side of the gate, denied entrance to seemingly everyone. The third soldier was sitting in a small building set atop the wall. He would be the guard responsible for closing the gate if needed.

Hooves beat the ground and three soldiers in royal livery approached the opening. Einok dove beneath the last horse in line, matching its stride as he ran below it. When the horses thundered by the guards, kicking up dust as they went, Einok darted out from under the horse and into a flowering bush on his left. Immediately, his scales became mottled with yellow and green to help him disappear as he remained motionless.

After a minute, the shadow dragon concluded no one had seen him enter with the swift moving soldiers on horseback. He rested a moment and searched for Saldo with his eyes closed. He could feel her nearby, but couldn't begin to guess how he would find her.

"I feel you, little spy," Saldo called to Einok. "I am below ground. It's dark and damp. I can hear dripping and it smells terrible."

With his own scales still emitting a terrible stench, Einok was fairly certain he knew why Saldo's prison smelled the way it did. It seemed the Skalven sent their waste below ground and allowed it to be washed away. Einok had seen the evidence of this in the poorer part of the city, which also happened to be at a lower elevation than the market and the palace. All Einok needed to do was find an entry point. He could leave the palace grounds and follow the filthy gutter water to the place where it spilled into the streets, but he might wait a long time before an opportunity to run through the gates presented itself again.

Einok scanned his surroundings from the safety of his bush. For the second time in less than an hour, a cat unwittingly came to the shadow dragon's aid. This one was an enormous orange tabby, and he sat, tail swishing, with his eyes looking into a raised metal grate. The cat could easily have entered the area it surveyed. There was an open portion, almost large enough for a small human. As Einok watched, a rat stuck its head through the opening and sniffed the air.

The cat moved like lightning, swiping the rat with its paw. The feline's claws caught enough of the rat's skin and fur to send the rodent flying from its hole. The rat hit the ground and tried to run, but the cat had already pounced. It tossed the furry brown creature in the air and pounced on it again, holding the squirming form beneath its paws.

Einok was stunned by the feline's cruelty. He understood the thrill of the hunt, but the orange fur ball was just playing with the rat. It was cruel to torture one's food before dispatching it. The shadow dragon had contemplated eating the black and white cat from earlier, but this one's actions assured him he had been smart to leave the first feline alone.

The hole was only a few yards away, and Einok cleared the distance and descended into darkness without being spotted by any human or drawing the attention of the cruel orange feline. The reek that greeted Einok told him he had discovered a likely entrance to the pit where Saldo was being kept. He splashed through mud and other muck toward where he felt the green dragon's presence strongest. It was only a short distance before Einok entered a wider chamber and found Saldo crouched in a corner. The ceiling was not quite high enough for her to sit upright without bending her neck to keep her head bowed.

"I admit I am glad for the company, young shadow, but you can't possibly think I can leave by the same means you entered."

"Of course not. I'm just here to gather information for the humans. Why have you not broken free from your confines?"

"I did try," Saldo said. "There is an iron bar across the lid of this cesspool. I suspect that is the case, anyway. It is possible they've managed to roll a large boulder on top of me. Regardless, I cannot lift the cover away and there is not enough room in this hole for me to gain momentum and burst through with added force provided by speed."

"I see," said Einok. "Is it safe to assume you are fed somehow? Have you been provided water?"

"It rained last night, and I received more water than I could drink. With regard to food, I'm sure you've heard the squeaking?"

"I'm not sure it's wise to eat the rats. There is a plethora of felines that might take offense to your theft of their prey. I have decided I do not trust cats."

"I wish a cat would deign to find its way to my pit. I could use some variety in my meals," Saldo said.

"If one does decide to visit, you'll understand if I refrain from confronting it. I know I'm bigger than them, but I fear I do not possess the same evil nature they do. I don't think a feline would have trouble taking my life if it should catch me."

Einok concentrated on his bond. His vincule was unique and the shadow dragon liked that about Ornen. The man was older than one would expect of a guardian, but he possessed a bounty of knowledge that made him even more attractive to Einok. As a shadow dragon, Einok placed information high on the list of things of value. The man's far sight was interesting as well. It was exciting to know Dabwey and her vincule were tracking down other gods using Ornen's descriptions. Well, Einok hoped that was the case. It would be upsetting to learn the dragons destined for the people in Ornen's visions had gone rogue or might even have been slain. At last, Einok felt Ornen was near enough for communication.

"I'm in Saldo's pit," he told his vincule. "There is something heavy keeping her from breaking through the cover. It's going to be up to the prince to find a way to get the Skalvens to open the door."

"How is he supposed to do that? We're stuck outside the palace gates. It was easy enough to walk into the city, but getting inside the palace walls is another matter entirely."

"Does anyone know for sure that the prince has been excommunicated by his parents? I know Landis has bemoaned his inability to return home and we agree it isn't in his best interest, but does Skalven royalty know anything about his bond, or does he simply fear repercussions from returning without the dragon egg he was sent to retrieve."

"I don't currently have an answer to your question," Ornen answered. "Unfortunately, I fear we have no other option than to discover that truth the hard way."

CHAPTER 26: DABWEY

The first flight went about as well as it could. It took Meara some time to figure out how to climb onto Dabwey's back. First, the girl had Dabwey stand near a large rock. Meara climbed onto the rock and tried to pull herself up onto her dragon's back. Meara proved to not have the arm strength for such a feat, even after she thought to have Dabwey curl her tail overhead for Meara to grab and use as a hand-hold.

"It's probably not the best way for a rider to mount anyhow," Dabwey consoled Meara. "It isn't like there will always be a random rock nearby when we need to take flight."

"I don't understand why this is so difficult. Can't you just grab me with your teeth and toss me over your head or something?"

"I could," said Dabwey, "but there is no guarantee you won't be severely injured in the process. That does not sound like a stunt you would want to try unless it was an emergency and there were no other options. Hey, how is your balance?"

"That's one skill in which I excel," Meara said. "Why?"

"If I put my leg out, do you think you could run up it? If you fall, you'll likely be badly bruised, but I don't think the risk is high enough to preclude an attempt."

Dabwey was encouraged to see her vincule back up a few yards and stop, waiting for the promised leg. The purple dragon rocked back on her haunches so her front legs were extended in front of her. The stretch in her shoulder muscles felt nice, but she had little time to enjoy it before Meara was charging toward her. The woman had not exaggerated her ability to balance. She ran up Dabwey's leg as if it were just a steep slope. Once Meara reached her shoulder, the girl grabbed hold of one of the spiky scales that protruded from Dabwey's spine for balance and seated herself directly behind it.

"You've even got a little handle here!" Meara said excitedly.

"Glad to hear it," Dabwey replied. "Now, is there any way for you to lock your feet in?"

"You mean like the stirrups on a horse's saddle? Why would I need to do that? It's not like I need my legs to steer you. You're a dragon, not a horse. I hardly think I should try to stand once we're in the air."

"No. I don't mean a place to rest your feet or help you stand, or even to help guide me. I truly mean a place to lock your feet in. It might be a better way to keep you from falling than just by holding the handle you found."

"You do know the handle I referenced is really just a bunch of scales that form a kind of horn between your shoulders, right? You have them down the length of your back. I'm sitting between two of them, so I shouldn't slide forward or backward, but I'm not really finding anywhere to put my feet so I don't fall to the side. Can't you hold me in place with magic or something?"

"There is no such magic. You will need to grip my sides as best you can to maintain your balance."

"I uh…" Meara began.

Dabwey did not give her vincule a chance to protest. She beat her wings twice and lifted into the air. It took a little extra effort now that she had a human on her back, but Meara was light and the purple dragon gained altitude quickly. She was satisfied when she felt Meara's legs pull tight against her and Dabwey leveled out, headed toward the river they had seen in the distance.

"How are you fairing back there?" Dabwey asked.

Meara didn't respond. Dabwey would have been concerned if not for the sense of exhilaration she felt flowing from her vincule. Still, she did need to be sure Meara was concentrating on keeping her seat.

"Meara, are you well?"

"Yes," Meara answered. "I'm amazing. This is… this is absolutely incredible!"

"I'm glad you are enjoying yourself, but it really is imperative that you focus on staying on my back. It would only take a gust of wind, or a change in our course, for you to be ripped from my scales. I'm not ready to lose you just because you're tired of walking."

"You can help ensure I stay safe by not changing direction without warning me."

"I can try," Dabwey replied. "If there is sudden danger, there might not be time, though. Be sure you are aware of our surroundings at all times. Just because we're up in the clouds does not mean we are completely safe."

"Only because you insist," said Meara. "I honestly can't imagine what could be a threat to us all the way up here."

Dabwey decided not to remind Meara that dragons who did not bond a vincule upon hatching would become rogues. She also did not mention the feeling she noticed shortly after taking flight that someone was watching them. Since they were currently on their way to speak to a man who had never bonded his intended dragon, there was every possibility there was a rogue in the area. The man's name was Kaleen, and according to Ornen, he had a twin.

Kaleen and his brother Drake were members of a tribal community, but Ornen had not known the name of the tribe. Meara hadn't even known humans lived this far west, so she had no information to contribute about the people who might live in this area. Landis had been aware of what he called 'primitive civilizations' west of Skalve, but knew no details of their people.

Dabwey saw something in her periphery. She turned her head toward it to get a better look. She couldn't tell what the dark shape was, but she had an idea, and it was approaching fast. She left her thoughts of Kaleen for later and turned her body into a steep dive. For a split second, she had forgotten she bore a rider, but when she felt Meara's small frame lift from her back, she panicked and leveled back out.

"Forgive me, Meara, but something is in the sky with us. You're going to need to hold on tight."

Dabwey did not wait for an answer as she entered into a slightly less steep dive, then turned and gained altitude again. It had the desired effect. She was now able to see what was approaching. It was a dragon, and it was a lot bigger than she was. Dabwey considered trying to flee, but the dark mass was approaching too fast. She wouldn't outrun it and with Meara on her back, Dabwey was afraid to attempt to outmaneuver the beast.

Hoping the dragon was not intent on attacking her, Dabwey decided to land. It would give Meara a better chance of survival. If the new dragon picked a fight in the air, Meara would fall to her death. The purple dragon dove, feeling Meara lift from her back again. She could also feel the girl's terror, but there was nothing Dabwey could do to help that now.

Dabwey leveled off as she neared the ground and unfurled her wings. Meara pitched forward, not expecting to come to such an abrupt halt.

"For the sake of Smok and all the gods, Dabwey! You nearly impaled me on your shoulder spike!"

"I see I didn't. I'm sorry, but there's no time to discuss it.

Dismount."

Dabwey extended her leg so her vincule could get to the ground, but Meara remained seated.

"You don't have time to collect yourself, Meara! Dismount, now!"

A crack sounded behind them as the mystery dragon extended its wings and landed. Meara was spurred into motion. She did not so much run down Dabwey's leg as much as she slid. The girl was on the ground in seconds. The earth shook as the new dragon stepped toward them. Dabwey turned to meet the creature while Meara ensconced herself between her rear leg and her tail.

The approaching dragon was charcoal gray. It lowered its head and swung it like a serpent. As it did, Dabwey saw something unexpected. There was a rider on the gray dragon's back. The man was dark-skinned, with ornate and purposeful scarring on his bare chest. The design resembled that of a scallop shell and was made up of hundreds of tear-shaped patches of light skin. The man fit the description Ornen had supplied for Kaleen.

Meara must have recognized him, too. She stepped out from hiding and addressed the dragon rider.

"You are Kaleen, are you not? I've come a great distance to find you."

"Don't you mean *we* traveled a great distance to find him?" Dabwey asked.

"Forgive me," Meara said to the rider. "My dragon, Dabwey, has corrected me. *We* came a great distance to find you."

"Leeta finds you amusing. She likes the way you've shown deference to your god."

"I am pleased to meet you, Leeta," Dabwey said to the gray dragon. "As my vincule has stated, I am Dabwey, goddess of truth."

"Tell me your truth then, my purple friend. Why is it you seek Kaleen?"

"A vincule named Ornen possesses foresight and dreams of other vincules until the time at which they bond their dragon. He stills dreams of Kaleen and so we came to discover if there might be a God Stone nearby waiting to be revealed. I admit I am confused. If you have given Kaleen the honor of becoming your vincule, then why has Ornen continued to dream of him?"

"The answer to your question might be provided by explaining exactly who I am. You already know my name to be Leeta, but I should add that I am the goddess of illusion. My rider is not the man you seek."

Dabwey took a moment to relay what she had learned to Meara. The girl was quick to respond.

"Goddess of illusion? That does not sound like a very honorable characteristic to preside over."

"Do I need to remind you that Smok is the god of smoke and flame? Those don't sound like very friendly elements for a god to control, either."

"Your dragon tells mine that you are not Kaleen," Meara said to the rider. "Are you Drake, then?"

"I am," replied the rider.

He bowed his head, but it seemed to be more of a curt 'hello' than a respectful action. Drake swung his left leg so that it met his right and stood on his dragon's back. He walked to her rear legs, where her body was nearer to the ground by almost a foot. Leeta lifted her tail and curled it so that it pointed to the front of her body in a gentle slope. Her rider walked down her tail as if he were a child walking along a log at the side of a trail.

"We might need to try that," Dabwey said to Meara.

"Can you hold your tail like that with my added weight?"

"I refuse to answer that," Dabwey replied. "You should know our tails are one of the strongest parts of our body."

"Right. I must have missed that class in dragon riding school."

Meara stepped forward to speak to the gray dragon's rider. Dabwey trusted her vincule to appropriately explain to Drake why they were here. The purple dragon turned her attention to the enormous gray creature instead.

"Your size is impressive, Leeta. How long ago did you hatch?"

"It's been over a year since my stone hatched. You are the first of my kind I have met. My initial wonderment is over your armor. Your scales are so…sparkly. I saw you glistening in the sun miles before you neared our encampment."

Dabwey had known she did not blend into the forest like Saldo, and even Ronvost's iridescent scales were hard to see in the sky, but she was disappointed to find her own beautiful scales made her a liability.

"I imagine you are not difficult to see in the sky either on a cloudless day," said Dabwey.

"I find I have little to fear from ground creatures when my form is capable of blocking out the sun entirely," Leeta retorted.

"Well, I've chanced upon several dragons over the last few weeks, and I find we all serve a different purpose."

"I can't imagine how those scales of yours could serve any purpose but to attract unwanted attention."

Leeta turned and walked off into the trees. Even with her bulk, Dabwey found the creature disappeared once she was only a few feet into the relative darkness. The purple dragon followed the gray god into the murky woods. The humans trailed after her.

The short walk ended at the mouth of a cave. Dabwey

noted the carvings that spilled from within as if the artist had run out of canvas inside and simply continued where space was to be found. There was no light in the cave. Dabwey stopped for just a moment to let her eyes adjust once she was a few feet inside the cavernous space. Her keen sight picked up the depiction of a dragon smashing small huts with its tail. It was difficult to see in the dark, but Dabwey thought she saw tiny humans running for their lives.

"I see you're impressed," Leeta said. "This entire temple, including the ceiling, is carved with the stories of the gods. I find the pictures to be eerily similar to the memories I was imprinted with. The man who carved them was a true artist."

"I never saw my own temple," said Dabwey. "I did see one dedicated to the safety of a dragon named Ronvost, though. There were carvings in that one, but they were nowhere near as intricate or plentiful."

Meara's voice echoed from behind Dabwey. "Where is Tala?"

The purple dragon's vincule had directed her question toward Drake as she ran her fingers along the grooves of the artwork. Leeta snorted.

"Of course, the bright purple dragon would have a rider devoted to the matronly goddess, Tala. Drake is mostly ignorant of the many gods depicted here. Inform your vincule she can find her god's likeness on the ceiling toward the rear wall."

Dabwey relayed the message to Meara, and the girl spun and headed in that direction. She stopped at the back wall and looked up.

"It's too dark. I can't even see it," said Meara.

Drake approached, holding one of the torches from the entrance of the cave. He held it out in front of Leeta. The gray dragon let out a gentle cough and the torch ignited. Drake handed the torch to Meara so she could examine the carvings.

"As I seem to be hosting a dinner party this evening, I suppose I will need to find some food. I'll return shortly," Leeta said. "Please rest a while, but I beg you to wait for my return before you begin swapping stories. I admit, I am very curious to know more about you and the other dragons you've found."

CHAPTER 27: MEARA

*T*ala's image was identical to the one inside the Innut temple. Memories of her island home flooded Meara's mind as she marveled over how even the flowers at Tala's feet were the same as those in the temple she had frequented throughout her life. She wondered what Mamma Jade would have thought of all of this.

The old woman had dedicated her life to the care of the Dragon Egg within the Innut temple, and the temple itself. She had been saddened by the depleting number of people who joined her in the temple as the years passed. She'd felt the gods were being forgotten and Meara couldn't help but wonder if that was what made it easier for the Skalve to pillage temples up and down the coast. If the only deterrent was a little old lady, how could a company of soldiers be stopped?

The only thing that had allowed Dabwey's egg to survive as long as it had was its island location. Even then, it had taken a rogue wave and a heavy dose of luck that Meara had been washing the stone in the ocean at the perfect time. Maybe none of it was luck? She turned her gaze to watch the return of the enormous gray dragon. The gods were powerful and mysterious.

Leeda dropped the carcass of an animal Meara was unfamiliar with near the fire. Drake carved off the hind leg from the horse-like creature. She had thought that was what the animal was, but it was larger and shaggy, like a forest cat. When

Dabwey grabbed the creature's head, Meara saw it had tusks like a boar.

With information to be exchanged, there was no way Leeta and Dabwey were going to chomp their meal outside of the cave. The sloppy sounds of tearing flesh echoed in the chamber, and Meara had to force herself to focus on cooking her own meal over the fire. Drake had pulled the skin from the leg, but left the hoof attached. He used the creature's foot as a handle each time he lifted the meat from the fire to turn it. Meara could not tell if the dragons were engaged in conversation, so she spoke loud enough to include them in case they weren't.

"How is it that you bonded a dragon instead of your brother?"

Drake removed the meat from the fire and tore some pieces off for himself before proffering the animal leg to Meara.

"I'm sure Kaleen would have you think I stole Leeta from him, but that isn't exactly what happened. We were inseparable. Everything he did, I did with him."

Meara noticed Dabwey had turned her ears toward Drake's voice. If the dragons had been sharing their own conversation, it had ceased. The dark-skinned rider continued.

"As boys, we stumbled upon this cave. It sits several miles from our village, and it seemed to have been long forgotten. We used it as a fort when we were young, pretending the dragons in the carvings were real and we made plans to defend our village from the monsters in the pictures. As we grew older, and spent more time hunting with the elder members of our tribe, we connected the superstitions they held with the images in the cave. We came to realize the monsters we'd pretended to hunt as boys were actually the gods worshiped by our ancestors."

Drake chuckled and looked at his dragon. Leeta snorted and Drake held his hands up good-naturedly, as if warding off an attack.

"Ok, ok! Leeta insists that I acknowledge the failures of my tribe to teach the young about the gods and instill proper reverence. She wants you to know she was mortified when she learned I didn't know who any of the gods carved into this cave were."

Meara considered telling Drake how most of her own tribe had let the gods fall to memory. Only older members like Mamma Jade spoke of the gods with frequency. Meara might have been the only person on the island without gray in her hair who believed the gods were real. She decided against it when she felt Leeta's stare fall on her.

"Anyway, there was this big stone on a pillar when we first found the cave," Drake continued. "By the time we understood it represented the eventual rebirth of the gods, it had been sitting outside of the cave for nearly ten years. On one of trips to the cave, Kaleen brought a girl with us. I did what all good brothers do, and I waited outside of the cave when Kaleen brought her in to show her the carvings.

"They were in there for some time when I stumbled upon where we had left the big rock from the pillar. There were carvings on it, but it was so covered in dirt at that point that I decided to take it back to the river and wash it off. My brother was clearly enjoying himself in the cave, and I expected I'd be back before he even knew I had left. Leeta later explained what I didn't know then. The river was outside of some magical boundary that surrounded this cave."

Understanding dawned, and Meara began to imagine how the events of Leeta's hatching unfolded. She couldn't begin to fathom the actions that were meant to unfold in order for Kaleen to take his place as vincule, but it hadn't happened that way. It seemed Drake was just as worthy as his brother, though, for he had been honored with the title of vincule.

"What happened when you returned to your brother with a baby dragon?" Meara asked.

"I didn't return; not at first. We had spent so many years playing games of imagination where we hunted and destroyed beasts like Leeta. There was no way I could present her to my brother, especially when she was so newly hatched."

Drake paused, and the corner of his mouth turned up. Meara noted that this seemed to be his reaction when his dragon spoke to him.

"Leeta would like you to understand she was fully capable of roasting my brother from the moment she came to be. It might be more accurate if I said I was protecting my brother from her by not seeking him out at that moment."

"You are extremely lucky. Many people who accidentally hatch a dragon are found unworthy. The god roasts them with fire," Meara said.

"So I've been informed." Drake locked eyes with Leeta.

"Leeta stayed out of sight, living on the edge of the village for several weeks. Once our bond was strong enough for us to be farther apart, she came to live here in the cave. I spent as much time here as I could, but my brother couldn't understand why I seemed to be begging off from time with him. I brought him out here, but we never even entered the cave. I started telling him the story, but he reacted poorly.

"The secret cave had belonged to both of us. Aside from the day he shared it with Awabee, who he married, by the way; we had only come here together. He was hurt and felt I had stolen something for myself that should have belonged to both of us. I can only imagine how he will feel if he discovers the role of vincule was meant for him!"

"Have you seen him since then?" asked Meara.

"I've seen him, but we only speak when we must. Our tribe thinks we fell out over Awbee. I believe even Awabee thinks I harbored a crush that destroyed me when she joined her life with that of my brother. She is a follower of the old gods, but she hasn't been out to the temple since that day. I'm sure if she was not trying to maintain her distance from me, she would have been out here often.

"Kaleen never shared my secret. Even when tribe members claimed to have seen one of the old gods in the skies, he did not affirm those sightings with his own truths."

Dabwey pushed into her mind. "Leeta has shared that Drake is from a tribe of warriors. Though there are fewer people this far west, those that choose to live out here do not live in harmony. Also, the beasts that roam the area are deadly. All men and women out here are raised to be proficient with a bow and are capable of defending themselves while alone in the forest. These are fierce people, Meara. Do you suppose we might convince Drake and his brother to join us on our journey?"

"I'm not so sure about that. I can't imagine Kaleen would simply leave his wife behind. That's if he could even be convinced to forgive Drake."

"So," Drake said. "You have my story. Now it is your turn to explain why you have traveled so far."

"It's become Dabwey's mission to locate as many of her siblings as possible. The dragons traveling with us have all felt a pull to the north to join the old gods and find purpose. Dabwey thought some of the rogues might need guidance and any God Stones that remain unhatched should be found. It doesn't seem that way, though. Is there a reason Leeta has not taken you north?"

"Oh, she has tried. From the time she hatched, she has spoken of a call she hears in her mind. Up to this point, I've convinced her it's nonsense, but your arrival has solidified her claim. I fear I will never hear the end of it."

"Well," said Meara. "I'm glad you have not yet left for the north. A rogue dragon named Saldo has been taken captive by the Skalve. They hold her in hopes of drawing the old gods back to the land. The Skalven people believe the old gods are controlling the weather and resources from afar. They think it is the gods' interference, causing the land the Skalve call home to become uninhabitable."

"That's amusing in the most terrible way. The people who cut down every tree in sight for miles around their home wonder why things seem out of balance and the land can no longer sustain them?" Drake marveled.

"No, actually. They aren't wondering at all. They blame the gods. If they'd taken any time to wonder over their situation, I don't think they would be wasting energy trying to lure the old gods to their death."

"Leeta and I have flown toward Skalve a time or two. I can't imagine what those people eat. They appear to alternate between farming dust and cultivating mud, depending on the season. A simple trip to forage would take the better part of a day, with the nearest tree being over a mile from the city wall," Drake laughed.

"There are some trees and shrubs in Skalve," Meara said. "From what I've heard, they are used for decoration, and sometimes shade. The prince tells me there are many trees just outside of the palace walls to help afford privacy to those dwelling there."

"Prince? How in Smok's name did a tribal girl befriend a Skalven prince?" Drake asked.

"I've told you of him already. Landis is the Crown Prince of Skalve."

Meara wondered if she should mention the stop she and Dabwey had made to see Trina before being discovered by Leeta. Trina was also meant to be a vincule, and she was

Skalven. It wasn't as if the gods belonged solely to tribal people. She decided against it since Trina's destiny had ended up altered, anyway.

Dabwey spoke to Meara, "Leeta is ready to go. She has an interest in helping to save a fellow dragon. Also, though it pains me a bit, I must add that she would like to 'roast some Skalven hide'. Those were her words, not mine. She thinks Kaleen would go with us, even if it's only as far as the palace. Leeta agrees that he would likely want to return to his mate."

"It is interesting to have the Skalven prince among us," Meara said aloud. "It speaks volumes of his character that he was chosen as a vincule. On top of Landis, we have another Skalven soldier we call a companion. Balder was discovered on the beach of the village his company destroyed. Saldo is technically a rogue. She ate all the soldiers in her vicinity when she hatched. Though Balder was not meant to bond her, they have formed a friendship."

"It's a sight to see," said Meara. "They are very close. Balder was crushed when he heard Saldo was taken prisoner. I think Leeta would find a kinship with the green dragon as well. They have a similar taste for…adventure."

"So, Saldo enjoys destroying things, does she?" Drake asked with a twinkle in his eye. "Well, then let's go get her!"

"I'd still like to meet your brother. I think we should see if he would join us. When we assault the palace, it would be nice to have more than one skilled archer."

"As I said, I am ready for the challenge. Leeta here is not interested in including my brother on this excursion."

The gray dragon snorted. If Meara had not been privy to Leeta's true feelings on the matter, she would have thought the dragon was only emphasizing Drake's point. Meara tried to spot the origin of the lie. Dabwey, as the goddess of truth, wouldn't lie, but it was possible Leeta had lied to Dabwey. The gray dragon was the goddess of illusion, but Leeta had nothing to gain from lying about wanting to include Drake's brother.

"Drake, you may be vincule to the goddess of illusion, but *you* are a terrible liar," said Meara.

"I'm upset by your accusation, Meara."

"Save it. Dabwey already discussed the matter with Leeta. Your dragon is the one requesting we bring Kaleen along."

"The dragons can communicate with each other?"

"In much the same way you and I are talking right now, but better. They don't make a sound when they speak."

CHAPTER 28: LANDIS

*T*here was no way the guards were going to believe he was who he said he was. Landis was waiting as patiently as possible for the soldier sent to the palace to find someone to verify the prince's identity. When Landis left his home, there wasn't a soldier who would fail to know his or her prince on sight. It seemed some of the new recruits were not as astute. It was also possible Landis looked very different when he wasn't in his gleaming armor and finery. Maybe it was not the prince the soldiers recognized as much as the prince's clothing.

Landis was pleased to see the messenger returning with one of his father's personal guards. A serious man named Markus, whom Landis had known as long as he could remember. The gray-haired soldier kept his matching beard neat, and he held himself with dignity as he covered the ground in long strides. The pathetic man sent to retrieve Markus was made to look all the more pitiful as he scurried in the royal guardsman's wake.

Markus was sizing Landis up before he even stopped walking. The prince could feel the soldier eying his filthy and torn tunic. Landis had sensibly removed the skins he had taken to wearing over the long shirt when it was determined he would be entering the palace. This mission was going to be difficult enough without his parents thinking he had gone feral.

Though dirty, Landis knew his pants were in good order and his boots looked impeccable. Every soldier knew that caring for your feet, and therefore your boots, was paramount to survival. After another moment of scrutiny while Markus stood before Landis, the guard settled to one knee.

"Your Highness, I am amazed to see you returned to us. Other than the dirt, you look well."

"I did suffer a hole through my shoulder by the hand of some driftwood on the beach near Innut, but I am well now. Please, rise. There is no need for formalities. I am simply...happy to be home."

"You'll find your quarters as you left them. Take a moment to freshen up and then come to the receiving hall. Your father waits for you."

Landis let Ronvost know he had gained entry to the palace. He wasted no time before going to his rooms to change. As promised by Markus, the prince's chambers were exactly as he had left them. He stripped off his filthy clothing and used the washbowl and a towel to scrub his face, neck, and hands. He donned new britches and a blue tunic with gold embroidery. He re-laced his boots and took a few precious seconds to admire himself in the mirror. His tunic shimmered in a manner not unlike Ronvost's scales.

It felt strange when Landis entered the receiving room. Normally, he would just walk in when he needed to speak to his parents, but today they kept him outside the double doors until he was formally announced. When he entered at last, he found his mother and father sitting in their high-backed chairs on the dais, watching him expectantly as he walked the length of the unnaturally long room to arrive before them. Though Landis had only ever done so during special ceremonies, he felt it was appropriate for him to take a knee before his parents.

"You may rise," said King Palden. "Queen Brynn and I are most interested to hear how you fared on your journey."

The overwhelming use of formality was disorienting. Landis

had truly missed his parents and had hoped to use a reciprocal emotion from them when bargaining to free Saldo. A stranger would be hard pressed to name the two people on the dais as Landis's acquaintances, let alone his parents, based on the reception he was afforded.

"I assume your interest lies with my acquisition of the dragon egg?" Landis asked.

Neither of his parents spoke, but Landis noticed his mother had straightened even more in her chair when he mentioned the fabled treasure.

"I was able to gain possession of the dragon egg, only to learn that it is not possible for it to leave the sacred temple where it is kept," Landis said.

"Speak plainly. What prevented you from retrieving the egg?" asked Landis's father.

"Nothing, father. I did have the egg in my hands. The island was hit by an enormous wave and I washed up on the shore of the mainland."

"You lost a priceless dragon egg in the ocean?" The Queen sat up so straight in her chair, she nearly stood.

Landis had rehearsed his speech, but nothing was going as planned. He had forgotten how easily flustered he was when his parents became involved.

"As I said, it's impossible to remove the dragon egg from its protective barrier. Once I crossed out of that zone, the egg hatched."

That was definitely not something Landis had planned to say to his parents. He had intended to keep all talk of dragons out of his story. He was going to simply tell them the egg disintegrated and was no more. This time, his mother did actually rise from her chair.

"It's true," she gasped. "There has been talk of a dragon in our midst. You stole the egg, and it hatched into an actual dragon. That explains everything."

Landis did not know how to respond. What he wanted to do was ask his mother how the ramparts had burned. He was tempted to ask her to take him to the dragon she currently had in her dungeon. He maintained his composure. It was possible that his mother didn't know the palace had a dragon in residence. On the other hand, nothing happened in this kingdom without his father's knowledge. Landis turned his gaze to King Palden.

The man has his eyes narrowed on Landis. He hadn't moved, but he was definitely considering his next words carefully.

"Landis, what color was the dragon that hatched from the egg?" asked the king.

"Green," said Landis, without hesitation.

"How is it you survived this encounter?"

"I don't know. It hatched, and it flew off. I guess I wasn't worth eating."

The prince's attempt at levity fell flat. Landis saw his father look over at the head of his personal guard. The soldier next to Markus, a new man Landis didn't recognize, gave a nod so difficult to perceive that he may only have been swallowing.

"A few weeks ago, a soldier rode into camp alone. The man's name was Lieutenant Gabriel Thomas. He had been part of a company of soldiers sent out to claim a dragon egg from the primitives living in a village called Nahola. The green dragon that hatched from that egg killed and ate every soldier present. Lieutenant Thomas was gutted, but crawled to his horse. The horse carried him back here. He did not live long, but he told some fantastic stories while he lay dying.

"Most took his words to be those of a man hallucinating from pain. My healers did not. They had read of similar things in old scrolls kept in our libraries. I called in the scribes and had them dig up any written word about the gods from the time of our ancestors. A single scribe traveled with the Larsen family when they came to this land. Krieg Larsen possessed a chronicle of his entire journey by the time they started building Skalve, and the Larsen family has ensured those scrolls remained safe.

"I have read all available accounts of dragon contact. Several of them refer to dragon births and include details about what to expect when a dragon emerges from its stone. There is no way you could have stood before that egg when it hatched and be standing before me to tell of the tale. You are lying to your king."

Landis's mother had retreated to her chair again as she listened to her husband. The look of disbelief painted over her usually emotionless face was the proof Landis needed to be sure she was unaware of the dragon King Palden held captive. It was possible she had been sequestered and remained ignorant of the damage to the ramparts and the dragons that inflicted it as well.

King Palden turned to his guard. "Lock him up, Connell."

The guard Landis did not know came forward. Markus didn't move. The look on his face said he would need further convincing if he were to move against the prince. Connell did not need Markus's help, though. Three other soldiers stepped forward with him to take Landis into custody.

"Mother!" said Landis. "Are you going to let this happen?"

Landis's words had the effect of releasing the queen, who had slumped into her chair, from her own thoughts. She summoned her strong façade and faced her husband.

"I will not have you locking our son up like a common criminal. Explain yourself, Palden."

"Our son... I knew this would come back to haunt me. That boy is no more my son than the hounds I use for hunting."

Queen Brynn's skin went white, but her face only showed rage. Landis was sure the woman could tear the king to bloody shreds at that moment. His mother's fury almost kept Landis from contacting Ronvost, but the prince was able to push the news of his impending capture out to his dragon.

"You promised," Brynn said to Palden. "You swore you would raise him as your own. I didn't ask to be raped by that primitive, and you were never able to give me a son. You swore you would treat him as if he was your own!"

Suddenly, Landis lost interest in Connell's brandished sword. He felt so defeated by his mother's words that he offered no resistance as Connell and his men took him under the arms and steered him away from his parents. *No, they are not my parents. The queen is my mother, but I do not know my father.* His mother's sobs followed him as he was dragged through the long room to the double doors. *Why is she crying? She just admitted her only interest was in the ability to provide an heir.*

"I always loved you, Landis! It is true, I tried to give you and your sister up, but your father needed an heir. I am so glad I got to be your mother."

Landis glanced over his shoulder to witness the queen sliding to her knees before her throne, defeated and pitiful. *You're going to need to decide, mother. Did you always love me, or did you want to give me up? You can't even get the lies you tell yourself straight.*

The royal guard escorted him to a cell below the palace. Landis noticed Markus had decided to follow King Palden's order and was among Connell's faction. Ronvost's words blossomed in his mind.

"You have a sister?"

"That is what you chose to focus on?" Landis asked. "I just found out I am the bastard child of some unknown tribesman. My claim to the throne is false; a farce contrived by the people who raised me."

"The queen is still your mother," said Ronvost.

Landis sighed. "Clearly, she knows little about what happens outside of the palace walls. I am fairly certain she was not even aware you attacked the city. How could she have been raped when she never even ventures outside? None of it makes any sense."

"Maybe," said Ronvost, "the rape is the reason she no longer goes outside?"

Landis sat down on the cot in the center of his cell. A single royal guardsman remained by the stairway. The cell was clean, though the subterranean nature of the location left a musty smell. Landis had played down here as a child, and he knew the only way in or out was up the stone stairs that remained guarded. Even if Landis could convince the guard to come close enough, there was no guarantee the man possessed a cell key for Landis to attempt to steal.

"I've informed the others of your troubles," said Ronvost. "Neither Balder nor Einok have any suggestions. Saldo wants me to let you know she sympathizes."

"Lovely. I suppose there is no news from Dabwey?"

"Not yet. She is still too far away."

The guard moved away from the stairway and walked toward the cell. When the torchlight caught his features, Landis saw the guard was Markus. The soldier did not speak at first. He stood for a moment, with his head lowered and hands on the bars of Landis's cell.

"That must have been hard to hear," said Markus.

"Which part?" asked Landis. "I now know I am the queen's bastard, I have a sister I've never met, and my father would rather have no heir than continue to claim me as his son."

"Yes," said Markus. "All of that is true. There is more to the story, though. I have been with your family since the beginning. Would you like to hear the truth of your birth?"

"Why not," Landis said. "It can't be worse than what I've heard, and it seems I suddenly have some time on my hands."

"The most important thing for you to know is that your mother wasn't raped. Over the years, I think it has helped her to reshape the story in her mind. The rape story was your father's idea, but I think your mother started to believe it as much as the soldiers and advisors close to the king and queen were meant to. Your mother was very much in love with your father. When the king had the tribesman killed, your mother was only able to deal with her grief by pretending your father had wronged her in the worst way possible."

"Great, so my mother is an adulterer and completely insane on top of that," said Landis.

"I think she would have gone crazy if she hadn't lied to herself to cope with her pain. In many ways, your mother is more a victim than you are."

"That's funny. I'm the one in a cage and very likely to lose my life. I wonder what story my fath — the king will contrive to explain my untimely death."

"I don't intend to let that happen," said Markus. "I will get you out of this cell."

"To what end? How would I leave the palace grounds and where would you expect me to go if I could?"

"I'm sure you could make a life. When I saw you at the gate today, it didn't go unnoticed that you'd found a way to survive without all the palace finery. You could also go live with your sister. She was once a soldier, but now she tends a farm to the west of Skalve. She can be a little ornery, but I'm sure she'd take you in once you tell her you are her twin."

"You know my sister?" Landis asked.

"Well enough to know she'd trounce you for sitting here and accepting the fate you've been handed. She didn't have anyone to care for her when she was growing up, and she is more than capable on her own. As her twin, I should think you could find that strength within yourself as well."

CHAPTER 29: MEARA

Kaleen was not what Meara expected. The description relayed through Dabwey had been that of a warrior. Though the man before her had the same strong build as Drake, Meara found him softer in his mannerisms. When she and Drake had entered the village, they had found Kaleen sitting on a stump outside of his hut with a child barely old enough to walk. It turned out the boy was not even one of Kaleen's. His own two children sat inside with their mother, darning clothing.

Kaleen had promptly set the boy to toddle off when he saw Drake approaching. Without a word, Kaleen had risen to his feet and entered his hut. This had forced Meara to present herself as a visitor at the door. Drake refused to accompany her inside. Meara sat down with the family of four and waited.

"My name is Awabee. Welcome to our home. Who are you and why do you come seeking my husband?"

Meara ignored Kaleen's silence. She was unsure if it was a tribal custom for the woman to control family matters, but that was the way this particular family was run.

"My name is Meara. I am of the Innut tribe on the coast. I seek your husband's aid in a bid to liberate a friend."

"This friend; who holds him captive?" Awabee asked.

"*She* is a captive of Blackwell Palace and under lock and key by order of the Skalven king."

Awabee laughed. It was not the gentle laughter of a dainty

woman. The sound burst from Kaleen's wife as if it were shot from a crossbow. Kaleen's lips twitched, but he showed no other response.

"Dear child," Awabee said through the remains of her laughter. "Why would I send my husband off to a confrontation with those people? Aside from an occasional scouting party that roves too far west, we have no quarrel with those people."

"The Skalves seek to extend their land. They have exhausted their resources and I expect you will soon experience more regular incursions by their scouts," said Meara.

"That is not my immediate concern. My son and daughter may well be into their adult years before that problem rises in importance on my list of fears."

Meara needed a different tactic. Her eyes ran over the small children sitting peacefully among them. Awabee might portray a hard exterior, but she was still a mother. Meara could use that.

"A small Skalven scouting party massacred my village. They killed the children in the same sweep of a sword as they did the men. I am the only survivor. My village lived in peace one moment, and was gone the next."

Meara saw fear enter Awabee's eyes. Meara's words had brought the Skalven threat to the present. Meara pressed on.

"The Skalves are a threat to tribal life. They do not care about nature or the bounties she offers. They spread and consume the land like a plague. I need your husband to help end their scourge."

"That is very different from asking him to rescue a friend. I fear you request a fool's errand of him, though. The city of Broen is protected by armies. What difference could one man make in your suicidal mission?" Awabee asked.

Awabee's question was an honest one. Meara could tell the woman wished to have the Skalven population removed from the land, but couldn't see a realistic way for that to happen.

"What is your relationship with the gods?" Meara asked.

"I hold Tala dear to my heart," said Awabee. "She has blessed me with my children and I thank her for the very air I breathe."

Though this was a common response among tribal people when speaking of the gods, Meara felt the woman before her was pure in her faith as she spoke of Tala.

"I too, give thanks to the Goddess of Air and Breath. I cared for the temple in my village and feel as if the gods had a hand in molding me into the person I am."

Awabee narrowed her eyes. "If you are as devoted to the gods as you say, why have you left your temple unguarded? You said you are the last of your tribe."

"I learned, only recently, that it is not the temple I was entrusted to care for. It was the contents of the temple that needed guarding."

"You speak of the God Stones. Many a fool has devoted his or her life to tending to a rock."

"I have spoken at length with Drake, and I suspect you know the God Stones are not mere rocks."

Awabee straightened. "So it is not only the one? The gods have returned?"

Meara nodded. She permitted a knowing smile to spread across her lips. This was the reaction she needed from this woman. She needed Awabee to see there was a chance for victory.

"Out of respect for my husband, I've never ventured to see the gray god that defends our village with Drake upon its back. I have seen the dragon in the sky overhead, though. I had thought it was a gift to guard us from the Skalven incursions, but maybe there is an even greater purpose for which the gift was intended."

"It is a she, and her name is Leeta. I know your husband

237

and his brother have had a strained relationship since the dragon hatched, but Leeta is willing to take the brothers into battle together."

Kaleen could hold his tongue no longer. "How is that possible? The gods take a single rider."

Meara turned to Kaleen. His puckered tribal markings matched those of his brother. Meara's eyes were drawn to the white scars. Her tribe had not used skin markings of any kind, but she knew some tribes burned the skin as a rite of passage when members turned sixteen.

"You and your brother shared the discovery and care of the temple cave. Though you may not have been aware of the cave's purpose when you were young, the God Stone was there with you. The dragon that hatched from it feels a kinship with both of you. I am sure of it. She sees you as one, maybe because you look so similar, down to the markings on your chest."

Kaleen ran his hand over the white lumps earned on the day he transitioned to manhood. His eyes became unfocussed as if he were remembering those moments.

"We chose the shell because there are two halves. Like Drake and I, it is only whole when you bring together both sides."

Meara turned back to Awabee. "Would you like to meet some gods?"

The woman looked at her husband. Meara could see how badly the woman wanted to go, but respected her desire to refrain from overstepping some boundary Kaleen must have set over a year ago. Meara detected a slight nod from Kaleen, and Awabee was on her feet before Meara felt her next heartbeat.

Meara led the couple outside, and Drake rose from where he had been waiting. He averted his gaze, looking at the ground.

"Brother," Kaleen said.

"Brother," Drake said with relief.

No further words were exchanged between the two men, but they walked side-by-side as they disappeared into the nearby tree-line. Awabee had left the children to their sewing. She may have trusted in the gods, but not enough to trust them around her children. Meara could understand that. Dragons had a lot of pointy parts.

Awabee was tentative as she approached the two dragons relaxing near the river. She shied from Leeta when the giant dragon greeted the woman with a brief snort. Drake grabbed his brother's arm to keep him from grabbing Awabee and pulling her out of harm's way. He had to do it a second time when the woman's hands went to her head, squeezing her palms to her temple. A moment later, she dropped her hands and stood still with wide eyes.

"It's ok," Meara said to the brothers. "One of the dragons is speaking to her."

"They can do that?" Drake asked.

"Yes, if they feel like it. At one point, when I was unconscious, Dabwey spoke to Landis the entire time. Once I woke, she stopped speaking to him."

"But we are both here and conscious," said Drake. "Why would they need to speak to her?"

"I don't know," said Meara. "They are gods. I've found they like to make the rules up as they go."

Awabee turned to wave her husband over to join her. Meara heard the tinkle of Dabwey's laughter in her mind.

"Sorry," said Dabwey. "I couldn't help myself."

"What did you say to her?" Meara asked.

"I thanked her for sharing her husband with us…and then I may have said a few things about her being a devout worshiper of the old gods."

"What could you possibly have said about that?"

239

"Well, after listening to the conversation you had with Awabee in the tent, I felt like she needed a pat on the back for still showing reverence to the old gods. I told her Tala had heard her prayers and that she would be rewarded in the afterlife for all things she did in the name of the old gods."

"You said what?" Meara tried to yell mentally and felt she pulled it off. "Is that even true? Is there an afterlife? Have you spoken to Tala?"

"If Tala can hear people's prayers, I'm sure she is grateful for them," Dabwey said. "I am a dragon dedicated to truth. I simply told Awabee what I believe to be true."

Meara rolled her eyes and shook her head. She wasn't sure how to express the sentiment, but she knew Dabwey could feel her emotions. By physically completing the action, Dabwey would receive the message even if she wasn't looking Meara's way.

Meara and Drake stepped forward to join Kaleen and Awabee as the couple marveled over the dragons. Leeta nosed Kaleen's hand from her scales when he tried to pet her, and Drake explained that she really wasn't the type of animal you pet. Dabwey did permit the couple to touch her scales, but only because it was more of an examination than an act of stroking her as if she were a dog.

A moment later, Drake ran up Leeta's tail and stood upon her back. As if they were boys again, Kaleen immediately attempted the same stunt so he would not be outdone. Leeta twitched her tail when Kaleen was about half-way up and dumped him onto the hard ground. Meara ran towards the brother to check on him and found him sitting up and laughing as she reached his side.

"Sorry, brother!" Drake called down. "We couldn't let you make it on your first try!"

It was Awabee's turn to shake her head. "Men. They don't

speak for over a year, then pick right back up again as if they are twelve again. Why don't we give them some time to bond? I'd like to bring Dabwey back to the village with us, if she doesn't mind."

"I can ask," said Meara. "What would you have her do?"

"She wouldn't have to do anything. I just think it's time our people got a fresh lesson from the gods."

The answer sounded ominous to Meara, but Dabwey was excited to be of help. She was willing to do whatever she could to help the tribal people stick to the ways that respected nature.

Dabwey's purple scales seemed to have an extra shimmer when she landed in the center of the village after Awabee called the entire village out of their huts. She said nothing at first. She allowed the people to murmur and gawk for several minutes. When the noise died down, she began with the story of the God Stones.

Whether a person believed the story or not, all tribal people know the story. Awabee was onto something with having Dabwey present, though. The story takes on a different meaning when you are staring at a god with gleaming scales as you listen. Meara felt closer to the land, and her traditions than she had felt even in Mama Jade's hut, as the old woman had told the story to Meara for the first time.The tale kept the villagers enraptured until the end.

Leeta flew over the village. The timing could not have been better if it was planned. The dragon swooped low, and Meara saw Drake and Kaleen on her back. The brothers were standing, arms outstretched, similar to how some of the young boys on Innut would ride waves on wooden boards. When the gray dragon disappeared from sight, Awabee spoke again.

"It is our faith in the gods and our respect for the land that separates us from those who would do us harm. We can never fall prey to their materialistic and wasteful ways. Nature provides for us and we take only what we need to survive. Love and happiness come from those we share our lives with, not from things we build and accumulate."

To Meara, it seemed like Awabee's words should have summoned a rally cry, but they had the opposite effect. Everyone in the village fell to their knees, heads bowed before Dabwey. The purple dragon, for her part, lowered her head and swung it back and forth. Meara could feel how much her dragon was enjoying the positive attention. She stood tall and permitted villagers to come forward and kneel at her feet. Some reached out and touched or even kissed her toes.

"Meara, you would be amazed how much that tickles! I'm trying so hard not to kick them inadvertently when their tiny lips touch my skin. You might want to make them stop. I have pretty amazing reflexes, and I don't want to hurt anyone."

Meara stepped forward, trying to emanate purpose and strength. Dabwey extended her leg and Meara climbed it gracefully. She placed herself between the spike on the dragon's shoulder and the one adjacent to it. Dabwey carefully spread her wings wide and the villagers retreated. The purple dragon beat the appendages and lifted into the air. She climbed above the treetops and flew back to the riverbank.

CHAPTER 30: BALDER

Balder paced in the forest on the side of the dust plane opposite Blackwell Palace. The sky had cleared of smoke and patrols had resumed regularity. It was easy to hide in the dense brush, even while accompanied by a giant blue dragon. Balder had never been assigned to a patrol when he was a soldier, but now that he'd seen how ineffectual they were, he was disgusted on behalf of those who were.

The men riding the grid made enough noise to be heard from yards away and the forest was so thick, the riders couldn't see more than a few feet beyond their location. As long as Balder and Ronvost remained still, they could watch patrols pass by within twenty feet without raising any suspicion.

"This is maddening," Balder said for the third time in twice as many minutes. "At least when Ornen was here, we were getting information from Einok. I feel as if we've just been left here to degrade into the soil. We're useless. We don't even know if the plan worked."

Balder sat on a rock for less than a minute and then he was up again and cutting a path in the flora. He stopped again when he realized the path might tip a patrol off to their presence.

"Aren't you going crazy not knowing if the prince is ok? Do you think you should fly in there and see if you can see what is going on? You just need to watch out for the dragon bows. I still think they have more than one working. Do you think Landis will be able to convince — "

There was a jolt of pain in Balder's head. It only lasted a moment, but it caused his legs to feel weak and he sat down.

"You must cease your prattle, human. It's enough to drive a god to madness!"

"Ronvost?"

Balder eyed the dragon suspiciously. On the surface, Ronvost hadn't moved. He was a giant blue statue of patience.

"Stop staring at me. You have not earned the privilege."

"The prince wasn't kidding when he said you leaned toward the arrogant side."

"Name calling will only get you roasted alive," Ronvost said. "I might excuse my vincule for the indiscretion, but I owe you nothing."

"You're right," said Balder. "You are a god and you deserve respect. Forgive me. I am on edge and concerned for my friends. Why have you deigned to speak to me?"

"I feel we will need to communicate if we are to work in concert when we are summoned. Also, I am concerned your constant questions will prevent us from hearing the approach of the next patrol."

Balder knew the dragon was correct, but it still stung to be told he was too loud. If anyone should know how important it was to be silent, it should be a man of the military. He'd never experienced worry like this before today. He'd had no one to worry about. It startled him to know how easily he could be incapacitated by the emotion.

"There now," said Ronvost. "Now that you've calmed yourself sufficiently, I will tell you what Einok and Landis have relayed from within the palace."

"You've been talking to them the entire time?"

Balder's voice had gone up an octave. He took several breaths. He knew Ronvost was already finding his nervous behavior irritating, and he needed to remain in control if he hoped to hear any information.

"Einok remains with Saldo. She is well, though she sits in a pool of excrement. She is forced to eat rats and only has rainwater to drink. One would think a culture that tosses about the word 'chivalry' would have better manners with regard to the treatment of captives."

"It sounds smelly," said Balder. "Please pass on my happiness at hearing she is as well as can be, given her surroundings."

A moment passed where Ronvost was quiet. Balder knew he was talking to someone and forced himself to keep from asking after Landis. He hadn't known the man long, but he was the Crown Prince of Skalve, and had held Balder's respect before the men had even met. Balder still respected Landis, but for different reasons. Over the last few weeks, Balder had seen how the prince adapted to life without excess and privilege. He found the prince's newly discovered humility and ability to adapt inspiring. Balder felt like Landis and he were equals and had started thinking of him more as a friend than as his prince.

"I'm not sure how you will react to my next bit of news," Ronvost said.

"I want to know everything you have been told," said Balder.

Balder was quiet as Ronvost described the revelation Landis had endured. The former soldier tried to imagine how the prince was feeling. *Was he actually still the prince? If he wasn't, then the king had no heir.* Balder's own confusion had him pushing the implications of Landis's parentage out of his mind in favor of wondering over who the queen's lover had been. *The man had been tribal. How had the queen met him?*

The information about Landis's sister hit Balder hardest. Balder had replaced a female soldier named Trina on that mission. She had sustained an injury during training. He didn't know the woman well, but he had heard she had a foul mouth and a big heart. Balder's new company had teased him at first, making comparisons between him and Trina. If there was any truth to the jokes, Trina had bigger biceps than Balder and was better with a sword.

"Tell Landis I knew of his sister and he might be glad they didn't grow up in competition with each other. She was a formidable woman."

Ronvost laughed. The dragon agreed that a young Landis getting beat up by his sister would have been entertaining to see. The next sound from Ronvost was not one of amusement. The dragon grumbled in a way that was decidedly unhappy.

"What's wrong?" Balder asked.

"Landis wants me to fly into the courtyard and grab him in my talons."

"Sounds to me like that means they have a plan," said Balder. "I don't see what's so bad about that.

"It's the part that comes just before grabbing Landis that I am unhappy with."

"Are you afraid of taking a bolt from the dragon bow?"

"I am a god. I fear nothing. I do, however, feel insulted. The plan requires me to bring you to the palace when I go."

"I get to ride dragon back?" Balder asked.

"There is no other way to get you across the plane quickly."

"I'm in," said Balder. "What do I need to do?"

Ronvost released a rumbling sound that could only be interpreted as a sigh.

"We will fly in low and fast. The hope is that there will not be time to load any bolts into the dragon bows. If the strings remain in the taut position, they lose force because the rope stretches. I will ignite anything I can on my way past the ramparts. As the soldiers cower from my flames, you will jump from my back."

"What happens once I am on the ramparts?"

"It will be your job to disable any dragon bows you can. You will be on your own at first, so you will probably do better with stealth while you can use it. Also, I will no longer be able to speak to you. We are not bonded and I must be within sight of any other I wish to communicate with."

"You really weren't kidding when you said I would be on my own. What happens next? How do we free Saldo?"

"Ornen is outside of the palace gate. The advantage held by men of Ornen's age is that few pay him any attention. He will make a dash through the gate when all the soldiers' eyes are drawn by Landis's fantastic escape. It is his job to remove whatever object is keeping Saldo from breaking free from her prison. Once Saldo is free, she will retrieve you from the roof, and then we all do our best to run or hide."

Balder was not a military strategist, but even he knew the list of events Ronvost had just shared was not a plan. Maybe it could be considered the outline of a plan, but there were many holes that needed filling. Balder expected he would be discovered and killed before Saldo was ever freed from her prison, but even if all went as Ronvost had described, what did 'run or hide' mean? It did not sound like there was any strategy for a managed retreat.

The former soldier opened his mouth to explain this, but found Ronvost hunching down low to the ground as if he might be getting ready to take a nap. Balder stood there, eyes narrowed at the dragon, trying to decide if the god was in some sort of pain. He certainly looked uncomfortable.

"I've never carried a human before," Ronvost said. "Climb up into that tree and then lower yourself from that branch onto my back."

"I'm sure there is a way for me to climb your scales or something. I can't imagine there would be a tree available each time your vincule needed to mount you."

"Logically, I agree," said Ronvost. "Unfortunately, we don't have time to figure that out right now and the tree will afford you enough height to reach my back easily. Now, climb the tree. We only have about ten minutes before I need to be there to grab Landis from the palace courtyard."

Balder hadn't climbed a tree since he had been in short pants. He stood at the base of the pine tree, plotting his route. There was a lower branch at about chest height that he knew he could access. From there, the next branches he would be able to reach were on the opposite side of the tree. To get to the branch reaching out over Ronvost's back, Balder would need to get back around the tree's trunk.

"It might be faster if we just figured out how to climb you," said Balder. "There really isn't an easy way up this tree."

"Climb, human, or I will leave you behind."

Balder flung his arms over the lowest branch and heaved himself up until he could lean his body over it and spin so he was lying face down on the branch. He sat up and got to his feet, placing his hands on the tree's trunk for balance. Next, the soldier jumped to a branch on the other side of the tree. From there, he was able to use the next three branches in a manner similar to using a ladder, but then the trunk was directly between him and his destination.

Balder wrapped his arms around the trunk, feeling his fingers sink into the sticky sap seeping from the bark. He squeezed the tree in a tight hug and propelled his legs in the general direction they needed to be. He managed to curl a leg around the branch he wanted and wiggle his upper body so that it was above the branch. He sat there for a moment, amazed his stunt had worked.

A snort from Ronvost sent Balder back into motion. He climbed to his feet with his back against the trunk. After a single deep breath, he pushed off and walked along the branch with his arms out for balance. He half fell onto Ronvost's back and sat himself in front of a large, bony plate that protruded from the dragon's spine.

"What am I supposed to hold on to?" Balder asked. "It's not like you have a mane like a horse."

"Grab some scales or something. I promise not to roll upside down," Ronvost replied.

The dragon beat his enormous wings and fought to gain altitude. Putting something of Ronvost's size into the air was not a graceful procedure. Two minutes into the flight, Balder was sure the take-off had been the easy part. Flying, hundreds of feet above the ground, with his chest and face pressed into Ronvost's neck was something he swore, repeatedly, to never do again if he survived.

"Open your eyes, human. We are nearly there."

Balder's eyes began to tear as soon as he peeled his face away from Ronvost's back. Fighting the wind, Balder watched the remains of the ramparts grow closer. He saw the destruction left by the initial attack by the dragons, and places where masons were already working to rebuild the damage. He also saw many soldiers working to spin dragon bows to face Ronvost. Thankfully, it took time. There was a single bow facing the general direction of the dragon's approach. Two men struggled to crank back the rope holding the bolt. A third soldier ran to aid them. Ronvost opened his mouth and fire engulfed the bow; soldiers and all.

"Time to jump," Ronvost said.

The dragon rolled to the side and Balder slipped from his back. Thanks to Ronvost's warning, he was able to get his feet under him as he landed and rolled to prevent himself from breaking a leg. Balder came to rest behind a barrel filled with arrows. He felt like he was in one piece, but his body was so flooded with adrenalin, he wasn't sure he should trust the notion. After a visual inspection, he found he was uninjured.

Balder peered around the barrel in time to see Ronvost's tail disappear as he dove toward the courtyard. The former soldier picked up a nearby torch in one hand and drew his axe in the other. It had been many months since he'd used his blade. Saldo had been the only defense he had needed. He lit the torch from the fire left in Ronvost's wake and started toward the nearest dragon bow.

CHAPTER 31: ORNEN

As soon as the soldiers guarding the gate looked up to see what was causing the commotion on the ramparts, Ornen dashed through the gate and ducked behind an ornate bush cut to resemble a horse's head. There was one on either side of the path, as if they were sentries. The true guards lowered the gate into place as soon as they saw Ronvost's wings blot out the sky above the palace grounds. With the gate closed, the guards turned their attention to the blue dragon.

Ornen used the distraction to make his way to what looked like the cover of an old well, but much larger. The circle of steel had a diameter of nearly twelve feet. Though there were four handles, spaced evenly about the circumference, they were of no help to Ornen. It likely took men of incredible strength to slide the cover even a few feet.

"We have a problem," Ornen thought to Einok. "There is no heavy object atop the pit."

"That's wonderful! I fail to see the problem."

"The problem is that the lid is the heavy object. I don't know how thick it is, but it is solid steel."

"I can come give you a hand. It will just be a moment."

"Don't bother," said Ornen. "We'd need twelve of us to move this thing. There is something better you could do, though."

"There is no going back now. What do you need?" asked Einok.

"I need Ronvost. I'll tie a rope to one of the handles, but only he is strong enough to lift the cover off of the pit."

"He's a little busy right now," Einok replied a moment later.

"If Saldo is to be freed, then Ronvost is going to need to find a way. I'll let you know when I have the rope tied off. All he needs to do is swoop in and grab it in his talons."

"He said he'll try to make it work, but it needs to be soon. He's about to grab Balder and retreat into the woods. He um…"

"What else did he say, Einok?" Ornen coaxed his dragon.

"He said it isn't his fault if the old man isn't strong enough to open the lid."

"Einok, you tell that overgrown blue lizard he needs to get down here or Saldo isn't going anywhere. I'm sure Balder will understand."

A stern voice came from behind Ornen. "You there! Old man! You have no business here!"

Ornen swung around in time to see a soldier drawing his sword. The man did not look as if he intended to take time to hold a conversation. With all the chaos in the vicinity of the palace, this soldier had no reason to ask questions. Ornen backed away. He carried no weapon. The soldier did not care if the old man was armed or not. The sword came up into the air; its bearer ready to slice down into Ornen's skull.

It never happened. The soldier fell forward onto his face. Ornen watched the sword clatter to the ground and then shifted his eyes to his attacker to be sure the man was not going to get up. An arrow protruded from the back of the soldier's head. Ornen looked around for a bowman, but saw no one else in the area. A shadow traveled over Ornen at a high rate of speed, causing the old man to look up.

A giant black dragon was in the sky. Standing on the dragon's back were two men Ornen recognized from his dreams. Ornen wasn't sure how Kaleen had bonded his dragon and continued to walk through his dreams, but he hoped he would get the chance to ask. Ornen watched Kaleen and his brother fire arrows in succession, never missing a target. The old man was mesmerized momentarily by their accuracy while remaining balanced on the dragon's back. He broke eye contact and reached out to Einok again.

"Meara has sent a new dragon here. See if Dabwey has also arrived. Send her to help lift this cover if you can reach her."

"On it," said Einok.

Ornen searched for something to attach to the handles of the cover to make it easier for the dragon to grab. Hooked to a cart by leather straps and only twenty yards away, stood a draft horse. Ornen made his way to the animal. He set about unbuckling the intricate harness.

"Ornen, Dabwey is ready when you are. Let me know when to send her down. She and the others are burning their way through every soldier they see to give you more time," said Einok.

"I'm working on it."

"Work faster. Ronvost took a bolt through his leg. He's ok for now, but he needs to fly north. He's taking Balder and Landis with him."

It was all falling apart. *What made me think I could handle this part on my own? I really am just a silly old man.* He tried to shake the doubt from his mind as he dragged the straps from the horse. The animal continued to munch grain from a bucket as if the palace wasn't in turmoil around her. Ornen found the harness too heavy to carry, so he commenced dragging the leather belts back to the cover of the pit. Smoke was in the air, as more than the ramparts were set ablaze. It made it difficult to breathe.

Something hit Ornen from behind. It was as if a hurled rock had caught him in his right shoulder. The arm on that side stopped responding to Ornen's commands. The old man looked down to check his fingers and saw the metal point of an arrow protruding from his chest. He had been shot.

Ornen squatted down reflexively and heard a second arrow sail just past his head. He continued to drag the harness with his left arm, reduced to crawling toward the iron disk keeping Saldo contained. The sun disappeared for a moment as the gray dragon passed overhead. A scream, followed by a crash, sounded from behind Ornen. He glanced behind him and saw an archer bent over the side of the horse cart. His inverted, lifeless eyes stared at Ornen. Two arrows protruded from the man's chest, which formed the highest point of his arched body. The man's feet were somewhere in the wagon.

Ornen wished the twins had taken him down moments earlier. The arrow in his own body was slowing his progress considerably. There was a loud crack of wings, and Ornen glanced back again. The giant gray dragon slowed about ten feet from the ground. Before it launched back up into the sky, one of the twins jumped to the ground and rolled to protect his body. Ornen slumped over the harness.

When the bowmen arrived at Ornen's side, the old man tried to lift the harness and hand it off, but his strength was sapped. There was no need, anyway. The newly arrived rider knew what to do. He grabbed the leather straps and hauled them to the pit. He buckled them through handles on opposing sides of the iron lid and ran back to Ornen.

"Tell your dragon to call for Dabwey," the man said.

Ornen did not understand. He didn't have the strength to talk to anyone right now.

"Wake up!" the man yelled. "Tell your dragon to call for Dabwey."

Ornen turned his thoughts to Einok. It was difficult to focus, but he found their connection within his mind and told

Einok to call for Dabwey. Ornen could no longer hold up his head. He let it sink into the grass. The green sprigs tickled when they went into his right ear, but he was unable to do anything about it. The old man had a good view of the pit as the tribal rider held the harness up so it would be easy to grab. A purple streak passed in front of Ornen's vision and then green scales burst from the ground.

The roar of anger from Saldo when she burst from captivity shook the ground. Ornen shut his eyes at last; his task was complete. Einok was not ready to let the old man give up, though. As the shadow dragon climbed from the pit, he called to his vincule.

"Not yet, you silly old man! Stay awake! You may have done well, but that doesn't mean you are done."

Einok arrived at Ornen's side and bit off the end of the arrow's shaft. The rider who had carried the harness and hooked it to the cover of the pit joined Einok next to Ornen. Ornen could faintly hear their words as his mind struggled to stay present.

"You must be the shadow dragon, Einok. Leave the rest of the shaft where it is. You might cause him to lose blood even faster. My name is Kaleen. My twin, Leeta's rider, is called Drake."

CHAPTER 32: MEARA

Dabwey did not complain, but Meara could feel the effort it took for the dragon to lift the steel cover from the pit. As soon as the leather straps pulled tight, Dabwey's momentum slowed, and the dragon remained low to the ground.

"Ok," Meara told her. "You're clear, drop it!"

The purple dragon launched higher, now free of her burden. She dipped her wings to dodge a bolt from the single remaining dragon bow. Meara squeezed her legs and clung to Dabwey's shoulder spike.

"Everyone is clear. Head for the meeting point."

Meara absorbed the now familiar feeling of the dragon eye roll equivalent, and Dabwey grumbled audibly.

"We could do that, or we could finish the job we came here to do," said Dabwey.

"There is no way we can take on the remaining Skalven forces on our own. Don't be ridiculous. Head north."

"As much as I would love to wipe the remains of the Skalve from the land, that is not what I mean. Unlike other gods, I am not foolish enough to think that is possible at this time."

Dabwey dipped her left wing to turn so Meara had a visual of the problem she was referencing. To Meara's horror, Saldo was not fleeing north with the others. The green dragon was on the ground in the courtyard, smashing statues with her tail and breathing flames at anything that moved.

"She's going to get herself killed," Meara said. "All this for her, and she's going to sacrifice herself, anyway."

"Don't forget the prince," Dabwey said. "We rescued him as well."

"You know what I meant. Anyway, what do we do? If we go down there, we're only going to get ourselves killed as well. Can you convince her to follow us?"

"Do you actually think I have not attempted to call to her? She is so full of rage right now that she either doesn't hear me, or she ignores me. I think I have an idea, though."

Moments later, the sky darkened with Leeta's presence. When the gray dragon slowed beside Dabwey, Meara saw there had been a change to her riders. Drake was still present, but Balder now joined him.

"Ok, three dragons are better than two, but do you really expect we can take on every last Skalve?"

"Unlikely," said Dabwey. "I figured if anyone could convince Saldo to leave, it would be Balder. Since he can't communicate with her telepathically, we'll need her to see he is not willing to leave until she does."

"While I do follow your logic, what makes you think we won't all get ourselves killed pulling this stunt? Ornen is proof that it only takes a single lucky shot to stop one of us in our tracks," warned Meara.

Drake yelled from Leeta's back.

"I see the doubt in your eyes, Meara. Balder is prepared to do whatever it takes to save Saldo. As for me, I rode all the way here to help you save a green dragon, and she is still not safe."

Meara gave a curt nod and Leeta dove a heartbeat later. The gray dragon made sure to swoop down in front of Saldo before Balder leaped to the ground. The former soldier rolled and gained his feet with agility Meara had not known he possessed. His axe was drawn, and he was tearing through the Skalven hoard, as they launched spears and sent arrows into Saldo's hide.

Dabwey dove and spread a streak of flame through the Skalven forces closest to Saldo. As they flew by, Meara could tell the green dragon had seen Balder in the melee. She faced him as she fought, trusting her tail to hold off any attackers that made their way to her back.

"Meara," Dabwey said. "Yell to Balder. Saldo said he should climb onto her back so she can protect him."

Meara tried, but her voice could not pierce the sounds of battle. Drake added his voice to Meara's pointless screaming. Suddenly Dabwey pitched forward toward the center of the throng. Meara panicked, looking around to check her dragon for a protruding bolt from a dragon bow. Dabwey had not taken a hit. The purple dragon thrust her feet forward moments before colliding with the throng of Skalven soldiers and plucked Balder from the mass of bodies. She banked hard and came back around. As she flew over Saldo, she dropped Balder onto the green dragon's back. Saldo propelled herself into the sky carrying Balder, who was disoriented and facing backward.

Leeta and Dabwey followed Saldo north. Meara was afforded a comical view of Balder trying to spin himself around so he was facing Saldo's front. The former soldier had displayed no fear when he had rejoined the fight by hitching a ride with Letta, but all he had needed to do was sit down and hang on. Maneuvering on dragonback was something Meara had never attempted, nor did she have plans to do so as long as she could put it off.

Eventually, Balder managed to get himself righted by turning himself with his arms and legs while on his stomach. Meara permitted herself a giggle when she envisioned a carving on the wall of some forthcoming temple for future generations to ponder, depicting the scene that unfolded before her. As the three dragons drew abreast, Meara watched Balder speaking animatedly to Saldo. She could not hear the man's words, but she imagined Saldo might be wishing she had not agreed to the plan to rescue the former soldier. The green dragon had a soft spot for Balder, but Meara was unsure if it stretched to the point of having her ears talked off.

"Do not worry about that," Dabwey thought to Meara. "When I met Saldo, she told me Balder had an endearing propensity for chatter. She might pretend it irritates her, but she enjoys it."

Meara laughed aloud. Balder might not be Saldo's vincule, but they behaved as if they were an old married couple. It was sweet, but it saddened Meara that Balder couldn't hear Saldo's thoughts. Though having Dabwey ever present in her mind had been worrisome at first, she could no longer imagine wanting to be completely alone.

The dragons landed in the designated area to the north. Ronvost sat licking the wound caused by the dragon bow bolt. It looked as if the blue dragon had torn the shaft from his own body and likely caused more damage to his leg in the process. Ornen was laid out next to the fire. His reddish skin was as pale as the inside of a clamshell. Einok was curled beside him, with his scales colored to match Ornen's skin.

As soon as Meara's feet were on the ground, Landis approached. Without thinking, Meara threw her arms around the prince. The adrenalin had receded and her emotions were in turmoil. Tears fell from her eyes. She stepped back, surprised at her reaction to seeing him. Meara wiped the wetness from her cheeks.

"I'm sorry, Landis. I thought maybe I wouldn't be seeing you again. When we made the plan, I figured your parents would keep you safe, regardless of how they felt about your request that they release Saldo."

"It turns out King Palden felt no such compunction, and rightly so, I suppose. That is a story for later, though. We need to get Ornen to a healer. He has lost a lot of blood and has not been conscious for some time. He sweats, but shivers, and I fear we have little time if anything is to be done for him."

"Where can we go?" Meara asked.

"Kaleen feels we should attempt to fly him to a village called Galnen. He said there is a gifted healer there."

"He would know," said Meara. "That is the village where the brothers spent their entire lives. If Kaleen said to fly there, we should."

There was a rustling sound in the brush to Meara's left. It took her eyes time to make out the broken pattern among the leaves. When she did, Einok stepped onto the brown dirt so he became visible. She had not seen the dragon leave Ornen's side. Meara looked from Einok to Ronvost, then glanced at Ornen and looked back at the prince.

"How will we get everyone there? Ornen needs to fly. It makes sense to put him on Ronvost's back. With your additional weight, I'm not sure how your dragon will fare. He has lost a lot of blood and his wound is still bleeding."

"We could put Ornen on Leeta's back," Landis said.

"Maybe. The twins could ensure he does not fall. Can Ronvost carry you?"

Landis paused for a moment. Meara waited while the prince checked in with his dragon. She concluded they were arguing when Landis didn't reply to her question after a few seconds. Eventually, he informed Meara that Ronvost thought the wound looked much worse than it actually was.

Precious time was used to contrive a method for lifting Ornen onto Leeta's back. Eventually, Dabwey lifted the injured man as gently as she could in her talons, to the waiting arms of Drake and Kaleen. Drake sat with his back to his dragon's neck and Ornen's head and shoulders in his lap. Kaleen placed Ornen's legs where they hung on either side of Leeta, hoping it might help to balance the old man. Kaleen sat himself facing his brother and holding on to Ornen's knees as best he could.

"Leeta is fast. We'll go on ahead and get the old man there safely," said Drake.

The gray dragon was in the air before her vincule received a reply. Einok streaked after her.

"It's amazing," Meara said aloud. "Our two fastest dragons are our largest and our smallest. One creates speed from strength and the other through dexterity. Einok reminds me of a bird at times. I wonder if his bones are hollow."

"They're not," replied Dabwey. "He's just small. His wings beat ten to fifteen times for every one beat of my own as we fly. The poor guy will be exhausted and hungry when he reaches Galnen."

Balder had never dismounted from Saldo. He was clearly enjoying his new method of transportation, as well as the closeness it afforded him to the green dragon. Meara and Landis mounted as quickly as they could. Ronvost hid it well, but Dabwey saw the blue dragon falter when he lifted off from the ground.

"He's hurt worse than he let on," Dabwey said. "I feel as if I should fly behind him to be sure he is alright during our journey, but I need to lead us to the village. You should turn often to check on him."

"You didn't even have to ask," Meara replied. "I will be doing just that."

It had taken hours to travel from Galnen to Blackwell Palace earlier in the day. Dabwey had pushed herself to her limit in an attempt to keep pace with the gray dragon and Meara suspected Leeta had been holding back. It would take even longer on this return trip due to Ronvost's injury.

Meara's concerns for Ronvost were unfounded until they finally flew over the plateau where she and Dabwey had first attempted flight. As it was her first time in the air, she remembered the location vividly. That was why she was able to compare the rate at which the river grew closer today with the rate they had approached it the day of her first flight. As uncomfortable as she had been on Dabwey's back that day, their speed had been considerably faster than it was now.

"Hey, Landis, how are you two doing back there?" Meara called.

"We are well, but Ronvost has said he is hungry and hopes there is food waiting."

Dabwey thought, "Ronvost lies to his vincule. He's flagging. I'm not sure he is going to make it."

"If that blue buffoon falls from the sky, he's too big to be caught by you or Saldo," Meara replied. "Do you think you can convince him to rest?"

"Probably," Dabwey said. "If I do, I fear we will not be flying again. If we land, he will probably die. I can smell the blood still leaking from his leg."

"If he falls, we lose him and Landis," Meara said.

"I do not know the strength of their bond, but if Ronvost dies, we likely lose Landis anyway. Death is the ultimate in distances between god and vincule."

Dabwey's words caused some of the resentment to resurface from weeks ago when Dabwey had admitted that vincule were cursed to live a life chained to that of their dragon. A vincule would die if separated from his or her dragon by too much space or time. If Dabwey died, Meara would die too.

Anger burned beneath Meara's flesh. She had not chosen to be a vincule. Why should she be sentenced to this life without being given the choice? As quickly as it surfaced, Meara tamped down her resentment. Dabwey had not chosen this life for her either. The gods bonded by instinct at birth. Dabwey had not even known Meara at the time.

Landis cried out from behind Meara. When she turned, she saw Ronvost's left wing fold in and the blue dragon pitched toward the earth below. Meara watched, helpless. Ronvost's right wing bent and he dove toward the ground. Landis gripped the dragon's back with his arms and his legs. There was no sound for a moment, then a giant crack sent a pulse through the air.

Ronvost leveled out and started to rise. When the blue dragon became level with Meara's line of sight, she saw gray scales below him. Landis transferred from Ronvost's back to sit behind Meara and Leeta dove for the river, carrying the bulky blue dragon.

CHAPTER 33: LANDIS

*L*andis was shaking, and he thought his heart might leap out of his chest. He wrapped his arm around Meara as he sat behind her atop Dabwey and buried his face in her back for a moment. As he regained his composure, a wave of embarrassment dawned within him. He loosened his grip on Meara and took a few deep breaths.

"Boy, Ronvost is going to be pretty affronted by that one. A big, bad dragon having to be carried the rest of the way by the only dragon larger than him… I'll never let him hear the end of it."

There was no response from Meara, so Landis knew she wasn't buying his act. Saldo flew in close. Balder was gesticulating wildly with his hands, but Landis didn't hear his words until the green dragon was within feet of Dabwey.

"We nearly lost you! I had my eyes closed. I didn't want to see the mess when you hit the ground," Balder said. "I'm so grateful for that gray beast."

"As am I," Landis yelled back.

"You should both be thanking Dabwey," Meara said. "For the second time today, she called Leeta in to rescue one of you men."

Balder and Landis were quick to agree and give their thanks to the purple god for having the forethought to contact the gray dragon when she was needed. Landis spent several quiet moments making a list of all the people he needed to thank for

264

today. It upset him to think the man he had called father was not related to him at all, but the real pain came from the realization that the king might truly hate him. Landis was the son of his wife's lover. Likely the only reason Landis hadn't been killed at birth was because his life afforded his father an heir and a way for the Larsen name to live on.

Dabwey landed in a clearing near the river. Landis thought it might be a tributary of the grand Serpent River that flowed near the coast, but he did not know the name of the fast moving body of water near the Galnen village. Not for the first time, Landis discovered how little his people actually knew about the land they called home. The Skalve had the land they occupied, and then there was the rest of the land, unknown and waiting to become Skalven land. It was a ridiculously self-centered view, considering how much more land was outside of the Skalven territory.

Landis, Meara and Balder walked the short distance to the village and found it buzzing with activity. Women ran in and out of a large hut near the fire pit at the village center. Children were grinding poultices on stone from herbs set out on the ground before them. It seemed everyone was set to a task. Kaleen walked toward the trio with purpose.

"Ornen is being cared for by our healer, Danya, in that hut there."

The tribesman pointed to the larger hut that seemed to be the center of the villagers' activities.

"His prognosis is uncertain, but I think I saw hope in the eyes of the healer."

"Where is Ronvost?" Landis asked.

"As you might imagine, caring for a dragon within the village is difficult. The blue dragon is at the temple where he can be watched by the gods. Most of the men have gone to aid Drake with his care. The activity you see here is not just to aid

Ornen. The poultices and potions the healer has set us to mix are for the dragon as well."

"Will Ronvost be alright?" Landis asked.

"We have been waiting for your arrival to make that determination. Though Leeta can speak to Ronvost, he has not answered her. Only the dragon's vincule is able to feel Ronvost's emotions. We were hoping you could tell us if it is weakness, unconsciousness, or something else, causing the blue dragon to refrain from speaking to Leeta."

"Then let's go!" Landis said. "Lead the way."

Kaleen worked his way through the brush to a more worn path, with Landis in tow and Balder following behind the prince. Landis saw nothing but green and brown as he moved as fast as he could without tripping. He would not be able to find his way back to the village on his own after his near dash for the temple.

The cave was lit with torches on poles so the men inside could see what they were doing. In the large chamber at the back, Ronvost's crumpled body seemed smaller than it should. His leg had been wrapped, and it was not bleeding through the cloth. Landis was happy to see that until he considered it could be because the dragon's heart no longer pumped blood through his body. Now that he was close to the blue dragon, Landis searched his mind for Ronvost. He felt nothing. Drake caught sight of Landis as the prince's eyes widened in horror and strode to meet him.

"Sit. You need to be calm to feel him since he is not actively trying to communicate with you. Come, relax a moment," the tribesman said.

Reluctantly, Landis sat down on the earthen floor. He placed his head in his hands and closed his eyes. After several deep breaths, Landis looked into his mind again, trying to locate the corner Ronvost usually inhabited. He was there, but like his physical form, Ronvost's presence in Landis's awareness seemed diminished.

"I'm here," Landis thought to his dragon. "You are safe and these people are caring for you."

Ronvost did not reply. Landis could feel the pain the blue dragon experienced as well as the exhaustion. Landis looked up to find Drake waiting expectantly.

"He lives. He is in an enormous amount of pain and has no more strength."

Drake smiled. "That is good. We will keep his wound clean while he sleeps. We shall boil bones and drip the liquid into his mouth until he wakes and can feed on his own. Kaleen will send his wife with blankets and we can sleep here tonight."

Landis nodded. The strength seemed to leave his body even as some relief was afforded to his mind. He and the blue dragon did not agree on much, but Landis felt like a part of him would die if he lost the dragon. Actually, understanding crept into Landis's thoughts. There is every chance Landis would die if he lost Ronvost. In his rush to check on the god, Landis had forgotten what it meant to be a vincule. His life was tied to Ronvost's. His concern for Ronvost was sincere, but he now remembered to add concern for himself into the mix.

Landis looked around the cave for the first time. The carvings he had seen in the Dinnen temple were the work of young children compared to the artistry covering the walls and ceiling of this cave. Landis did not pretend to know the old gods, but he recognized Smok from the horror stories of his childhood. The carving on the wall to Landis's left showed the mighty dragon cutting down his ancestors as if they were mere insects. The picture told the story exactly as Landis had heard it, but seeing it here, Landis did not feel the same fearful sensation stirred by the story told to him in his youth.

At that time, Landis had been a young prince, destined to

take the throne and help his people thrive, despite the scourge of the old gods. What was he now? *I'm a half-breed created by two opposing sides of a war born centuries ago. I am of two people, and this actually leaves me with no people to call my own.* Landis felt a stirring in the recesses of his mind. It seemed far off, but Ronvost's voice pushed into his mind for just a moment.

"Your people are the other vincules."

The blue dragon had a point. Their numbers were small, but the vincules were people he shared much with. More importantly, though, Ronvost had spoken to him. Landis did not reply, but sent relief and warmth toward his dragon's consciousness.

A woman entered the chamber carrying blankets woven in bright colors. She saw Landis, still sitting on the floor, and approached him. She placed the blankets beside him and observed the blue dragon sleeping on the far side of the room.

"My name is Awabee. Kaleen sent me with blankets so you and Drake could remain here through the night."

"Thank you," Landis said. "Ronvost has spoken to me. It's a good sign, but I really don't want to leave him. I cannot thank you all enough for everything your people are doing for him."

"He is a god," said Awabee. "It is our duty to serve them in any way we can. I can't imagine denying one aid at a time when he most needs it."

"Still," Landis said. "You have my appreciation as well."

"It is strange," the woman said, "having them all here in the village. You grow up thinking of the gods as beings watching from afar. You wonder sometimes if your parents invented the stories just to give you the impression you are being watched and should take care to live well, even when you think you are alone. You grow older and have children of your own. You pass the stories of the gods on to them, hoping they believe. Then one day, a god shows up in your village, and then another.

Soon, you are surrounded by creatures who are alive, present, and vulnerable. It's overwhelming."

"Have you always been faithful?" Landis asked.

"More than most, but still less than I should have been. Honestly, Meara is the first person I've spoken to who is not crippled with age that may have dedicated her life appropriately."

"I hope you don't beat yourself up too badly over it," said Landis. "I speak from experience when I say the gods do not favor us because of the devotion we've shown to them in the past."

Awabee looked Landis over for a moment. Her eyes lingered on his pale face for just a moment before a laugh escaped her lips.

"I suppose you are correct, Prince Landis of the Skalve."

"Please don't call me that," said Landis.

"I meant no disrespect. I only mean to say it should have been obvious to me that you did not spend your life in service to the gods; yet here you are. You were chosen as a vincule, the highest honor that can be bestowed upon a human by a dragon."

It was Landis's turn to laugh. He let out a sigh, pressed his lips together, and nodded in agreement.

"An honor and a curse, unfortunately. My life will never be my own."

"Are our lives ever truly our own?" Awabee asked. "We can choose to whom or to what we answer, but we still must choose something."

"Who have you chosen to serve?" Landis asked.

"I used to think I only served my family, but since the arrival of the gods, I've thought on it. I can serve my family, my people, and even myself, by serving the land as the gods intended." Awabee smiled. "I've even started telling the stories

269

of the gods to my people around the fire at night. I don't want them to forget what sets us apart from your people."

The expression on Landis's face must have shown his emotion. Awabee's hand went to her mouth and her eyes grew wide. Landis confronted all he had learned about the destruction his own people wrought on the land and the effect it had on their ability to survive. He contrasted this with all he had learned about tribal life during the time he had spent with Meara and Ornen.

"Forgive me," Landis said. "Old habits die hard. I really do not consider myself to be of the Skalven people any longer and I sometimes forget I do not need to feel disrespected on their behalf. I have learned much since I left Blackwell Palace. I fear the greatest sin of the Skalven people is not what they do to the land, but their refusal to believe their ways might not be the best way."

Awabee allowed her hand to fall from her face as Landis spoke. She relaxed visibly and her smile returned.

"Your words offer proof of why I said what I did. You look Skalven, but you think like you were raised by a tribe."

"Speaking of tribes," said Landis. "How do your people fare with Ornen's care?"

"When he woke, his first words were to ask us why we were bothering to bring an old man back to life. He then started laughing. At first I thought he might have sustained a head injury, but the more he spoke, the more I realized he just didn't want to be a bother to anyone. He is a selfless man, and I'm glad we were able to pull him from the clutches of death."

"Oh, that is wonderful news. I'm sure Einok is thrilled swell."

"Who is Einok? I have not met him yet. I thought all the men were down here at the temple."

Landis started laughing. The shadow dragon was likely

inside the hut with his vincule, watching over the old man. There were tears streaming from Landis's eyes as he imagined the poor woman who might first notice Einok's presence.

"I do not understand what you find funny," Awabee said.

Landis smiled. Remembering Awabe's description of the gods as unseen beings that watched children when they thought they were alone, he considered how he might tell the woman about Einok.

CHAPTER 34: EINOK

Ornen was too weak to sit up, but that did not stop him from talking. Every woman who entered the hut was graced with his voice throughout their visit. Einok had tried to get the old man to rest, but Ornen insisted he was simply making up for lost conversations. He claimed he'd missed out on far too many by living on his own for so long.

Einok admired his scale color match for his hide. Ornen's blankets pooled at his side in a swirl of color. When the shadow dragon curled up next to his vincule, his scales had taken on the same spiraling rainbow as the wool fiber. The tribeswomen came and went without noticing the little dragon's presence. Einok dutifully relayed all he heard discussed about Ornen's condition and treatment plan to Dabwey so she could share the news with Meara.

When Meara had first arrived at the village, she had pushed into the hut and tried to sit by Ornen's side, but the women of the tribe had complained she was in the way and banished her. From what Einok had heard, Meara was set to grinding poultices by the fire with the children. If not for his worry over his vincule, Einok would have taken the opportunity to tease Dabwey over the station her chosen one had been afforded.

Meara truly was not needed in this hut. Though she had claimed some knowledge of the healing arts, Einok knew she compared pitifully to the women of this village. Yes, they used traditional salves and disinfectants on Ornen's wound, but there was something else at play. Einok saw several women enter the tent, place a hand on Ornen's head and just stand there for several minutes. When the women removed their hands, they slumped and needed to be ushered from the tent, exhausted.

Danya was the name given to the woman the villagers referred to as the healer, though to Einok's eyes, it seemed all the women in the village had some kind of restorative power. The tribeswomen followed Danya's directives and spoke of her often with each other. The healer had only visited the hut twice and each time, her magic was not as subtle as that of the other women. When Danya stood beside Ornen, Einok's scales tingled, and he thought the wrinkled woman had winked at him when she first examined Ornen. Whatever magic this woman controlled, it was not wielded from an external source, as much as it emanated from within her.

When morning dawned, Ornen was able to sip some bone broth while propped up in his bed. The rich smell from the bowl made Einok's stomach rumble. To his delight, the two women feeding Ornen the broth only giggled and commented on how Ornen's excessive talking must have made him hungry. Einok took the rumble as his cue to search for food of his own. When the two women turned to leave, and before another could enter, the shadow dragon scurried out of the hut by squeezing between the floor and one of the thatched walls.

"Dabwey, are you and Saldo by the river?" Einok reached out.

"The green dragon and I are hunting. How is your vincule?"

"He is well enough that I have ventured from the hut. Would you deign to share your spoils upon your return?"

"I can't promise Saldo will share, but I shall bring you my cast-offs if you wish, little one."

"That would be appreciated. I'm starving, and it will take time for me to hunt down enough insects and rodents to satisfy my need. Do you know how Ronvost fares?"

"Leeta checked in early this morning, before the light crested the horizon. The blue dragon spoke to his vincule, but that is all I know. Go to the temple and look in on him. I will meet you back on the shore of the river with your meal."

Einok changed direction and headed toward the temple. He had never been there, but he followed Leeta's presence. The gray dragon was so large that her essence surrounded the area. Einok had only to move toward the point where it was strongest. He found the giant god sitting outside of the temple, swishing her tail like a mountain cat.

"Will they not let you inside?" Einok asked.

"I go where I please, little shadow," Leeta said. "If there is a need for me, Drake will let me know. Ronvost is well. His arrogance has returned with some of his strength. I find the atmosphere more pleasant out here."

Einok climbed up the outside of the cave entrance. His scales morphed to match the gray, rocky surface. He skittered along the interior wall until he reached the part of the temple that opened up into an expansive cavern. There, he opted to travel along the ceiling. The many carvings provided ease for his movements. His sharp claws found purchase with every step he took. Einok stopped above Ronvost to observe the activities below.

Landis stood staring into Ronvost's open eyes. The dragon refused to look away. Though Einok was not privy to the conversation between the blue dragon and his vincule, he knew they were arguing. A strong warrior dragged a leg from a hind quarter of some large mammal in front of Ronvost's maw. The dragon snatched it from the ground, nearly taking the human with the meat shank. The warrior fell backward onto his rear and scuttled away. Landis threw up his arms and turned away from his dragon.

"I take it he still insists he is fine?" Drake asked as he approached the prince.

"Indeed. He said he is ready to take to the sky at a moment's notice, but I have yet to see him even attempt to stand," Landis said.

"In your dragon's defense, once he is in the air, he has less need of his leg. He only needs the strength to keep it tucked up to his body," said Drake. "His appetite is back. If he keeps eating the way he is now, he'll be healed in no time, anyway."

"The food helps," said Landis, "but I suspect the magic your people have imparted to him deserves much of the credit. Do all your people have healing ability?"

"We do," said Drake. "Sickness has been little threat to our tribe, for we all possess a predisposition for restorative magic. Danya has always been the strongest. She has supplemented her magic with knowledge of the healing arts passed down to her from her own parents and grandparents. They are long gone, but Danya has shared her knowledge with many women in the tribe. She has no children, so she has spread her knowledge openly among any who wish to learn."

"If Ronvost is so keen on convincing me he is healed, I beg of your people to stop bringing him food. Let the blue brute fend for himself if he is feeling so strong," said Landis.

"That is a good idea, actually. It will either put your mind at ease or humble your dragon. I shall let the others know that they should stop bringing kills to Ronvost."

Einok chose not to stay long enough to find out how the plan unfolded. He had his own ideas about Ronvost's reaction to the cessation of a steady stream of food, and he did not think it would be pleasant. Instead, Einok exited the temple and went to the river bank.

Dabwey arrived a moment later and dumped the remains of a rib cage onto the rocky ground. Einok happily set to picking

275

the vestiges of the meat from the bones. He watched Leeta take to the sky and momentarily block out the sun. It was a good bet Ronvost had been told he would no longer be served meals since he had deemed himself healed. Saldo landed and went to drink from the river while Dabwey picked grizzle from between her teeth with a talon.

All three dragons looked up to the sky several minutes later when Leeta pushed her thoughts to all of them at once.

"Get word to the humans. A sizable force approaches from the west."

"The west?" Einok asked. "Why would the soldiers from Broen travel all the way to the far side of the village and approach from that direction?"

"The Skalve are not the only invaders to this land. These humans carry the banners of King Matthew Blake. His people hold much of the land to our west. I have already notified Drake."

Einok did not communicate the threat to Ornen. Dabwey stomped off in the direction of the village. She would already be filling Meara in on the approach of Blake's forces. The sound of boots running through dried leaves came from the woods further upstream and Balder burst into view.

"The village is going to fall under attack! Saldo, my giant green beauty, would you honor me by carrying an old soldier into battle?"

Saldo swung her head back and forth. She was trying to communicate with Balder, but the human was too frenzied to grasp her meaning. Saldo looked at Einok for help. Einok was not sure what Saldo expected of him. If Saldo wasn't willing to speak into Balder's mind, there was no reason for him to do so.

"Oh, would you just open a link to him already?" Einok said to Saldo. "If battle is coming, it can only benefit you to be able to communicate directly with a human."

Saldo snorted, but turned back to Balder. The former soldier's hands flew to his head and his fingers whitened as he pressed them to his temple. A moment later, Balder passively regarded Saldo as he listened to her words. The shadow dragon trusted Saldo to explain the foolishness of flying off into battle alone and skittered into the woods to head back to the village.

Upon his return, Einok found the village was no longer occupied solely by women. Many of the men had returned from the temple to prepare for the coming assault. The little dragon darted from tree to shrub to rock, blending his scales with his surroundings until he reached the back of the large hut where his vincule rested. Einok wiggled under the thatching and slipped under the covers at the foot of Ornen's bed.

The old man was trying desperately to get information from his attendants about what had caused the village to stir into action. Einok filled the old man in. He hadn't wanted to upset Ornen, but the sounds of the roused villagers had agitated him enough already.

"Tell Meara I can fight. I won't be left here in a straw hut to die," Ornen said aloud.

The two women tending to the old man acted as if they had not heard Ornen. It was plain to Einok that the villagers felt the best place for Ornen was exactly where he did not want to be. They were going to leave him where he was and hope the invading force did not reach the center of the village.

"Tell them to move you to the temple," Einok coached his vincule.

Ornen took a breath and managed to make his demand sound more like a polite request. This time, the women placed their heads together to share words even the shadow dragon could not hear. A moment later, they both left the shelter.

"Well, that did not have the desired effect, my friend. It was a fine idea, though. I was told Ronvost is convalescing there. I think I'd be well protected."

"Much like you, the blue dragon has made incredible gains in healing. He might not be at the temple anyway," said Einok.

Ornen's minders returned with two long poles; an animal skin stretched between them. Einok, head poking out of the covers, watched as they spread it out on the floor next to Ornen's bed. Two large males entered the hut and Einok understood what the humans intended to do. He drew his head under the covers in anticipation of the rage his vincule would undoubtedly spit forth. Ornen did not disappoint.

"You must be joking! I am not an invalid! I do not require these men to carry me. They should be preparing for the impending fight."

"They have much to do, indeed," said one of Ornen's two caretakers. "Let's not hold them up. Get on the stretcher and let them transport you to the temple without further argument."

"This might be the only way you get where you want to go," Einok said to Ornen.

The words hit their mark. Ornen threw off his covers and made his way to the stretcher as best he could without falling to the floor. Ornen's body had repaired itself thanks to the magic imbued into his skin over the past few days, but his strength had yet to return.

Einok used the attention drawn by Ornen's unsteady movements as a distraction and slipped off the bed unnoticed. As soon as the old man was settled onto the animal skin, the men used the poles to lift it from the ground and carried Ornen from the hut.

CHAPTER 35: LANDIS

*D*rake prepared to address the small group of warriors from Leeta's back. Landis, like the other men gathered outside of the temple, stood before the gray dragon waiting for orders. Ronvost seemed completely healed, but hadn't had time to demonstrate the truth of the claim before the announcement of raiders approaching from the west. With an untested dragon, Landis found himself grounded and dreading the words Drake had to share.

"It is best if we meet King Blake's host before he reaches the outskirts of the village. The army approaches tribal land as I speak. There is no way for our warriors to travel to the location with the required speed. Instead, I will take the small group of dragons our village has been blessed to host. I know this is not what you wanted to hear. Each of you is a dedicated member of the tribe, and I know you desire to take part in the defense of our land and our way of life. I am sorry to take that honor from you on this day, but they come in large numbers. If we allow them to approach, our own gods might destroy our land as they simultaneously help defend it."

Drake did not stay to listen to the dissenting comments. Leeta took to the sky and Landis watched the purple dragon launch after her from the other side of the village. Within moments, a green dragon joined them in the sky. Landis knew Drake spoke true. Three dragons were enough to decimate a force of thousands. The soldiers would not have brought weapons capable of firing bolts large enough to down a god.

The roar that came from within the temple caused the ground to shake. Landis had left it up to Dabwey to communicate to Ronvost that he was to sit this fight out. Landis did not need to check in with his dragon's feelings to know the blue dragon had just received the notification. It was a good thing all the men had left the cave to hear Drake's speech because the stumbling bulk of an unsteady god crashed from the mouth of the cave a moment later. If anyone had been inside, they would have been trampled.

The hulking blue dragon stopped before Landis and lowered his face to the ground to stare the man in the eyes. The warriors in the vicinity backed away from Landis, leaving him to face the wrath of his dragon alone. Landis softened his expression and tried to project empathy.

"I'm sorry, boy. I understand your pain. We've been left out of the battle."

"Do not patronize me! You are only human. Your presence in the battle would have minimal effect. I am a god. I could end the fight before it ever begins."

Any compassion Landis had mustered drained from within him. He did not appreciate the way his dragon had just deemed him insignificant. Landis turned and walked toward the village. The urge to console Ronvost had vanished.

"Wait," the dragon's voice said softly. "That was wrong of me. I would like for you to stay. Maybe we can complain to each other about being forced to sit the battle out?"

That was as close to an apology as Landis could hope to get. He turned back toward the blue dragon and the pair was about to enter the cave when two warriors carrying Ornen on a stretcher arrived. The old man loudly insisted he could be useful in a fight, but he was ignored.

"We can add one more to our pity party, I suppose," Landis

said aloud.

Ronvost and his vincule followed the stretcher bound man into the recesses of the temple. Ornen quieted when the warriors placed him on the ground and then retreated back down through the tunnel. Ronvost curled up in the spot where he had spent his recent days, and Landis took a seat on the floor beside Ornen. The old man looked away from Landis.

"Is it shame or sadness causing you to hide your gaze from me?"

"A little of both, I think," Ornen replied. "I feel entirely useless; so much like I always imagined an old man to be."

"What do you suppose my excuse is?" Landis asked. "You're old, Ronvost is injured, but I'm fine. I'm a perfectly healthy man in my prime, yet I am not out there fighting either."

"I see your point. If you're useless, then what can be expected of someone my age, right?"

"That wasn't my meaning exactly," said Landis. "I only meant to bring to light that there are many people still here in and around the village. You should not assume you were left here because you are old."

Landis expected another rebuke, but Ornen suddenly sat up and went still. His already milky eyes hazed over even more until they were nearly white.

"Ornen, are you alright? Are you in pain?" Landis asked.

He lunged for the old man's wrist and felt for a pulse. Ornen did not appear to notice the intrusion, but Landis found the man's heart to be beating at a regular pace.

"Should I call someone?" Landis asked his dragon. "What's wrong with him?"

"I have no answer for you," Ronvost replied. "He seems frozen."

Ornen gasped suddenly. He glanced around the temple,

seeming to be unsure where he was for a moment. At last, he looked Landis in the eyes and grasped his shoulders.

"You need to get to the village. Your sister approaches."

"How did you… I didn't tell anyone I found out I have a sister," Landis said, narrowing his eyes at Ornen.

"So you know of her! I'm glad. You will have no questions. Remember, I can see those who were intended to be vincules. Like you, your sister was meant to be one. Her dream plays in the back of my mind perpetually. I witnessed the Skalven soldier called Markus arrive at your sister's home. He told her who she is. That is not why she comes, though. Something must have happened while I was distracted. I missed something important in her life. She is riding hard. She'll be here in moments."

Landis hurried to his feet and left the temple. He ran through the trees, tripping once and nearly sprawling. He arrived in the village as a call was put out that a rider approached from the east. Warriors grabbed bows and ran to greet the stranger.

"Wait!" Landis called. "Don't hurt her. She is my sister."

Moments later, a horse and rider entered the village. The horse reared when its rider yanked the reins. It took a moment for Landis to reconcile the figure on the horse with the image he had painted of the woman who would be his sister.

The rider was not the demure young lass Landis assumed would be a sister of his. At first, Landis confused the person on horseback for a man. She was nearly as tall as he was and almost as broad in the shoulders. As she slid from her horse, Landis saw the curves that marked her gender, but they did not prevent her musculature from taking center stage. *I think I'm happy I did not grow up with a sibling. She very likely would have beaten me senseless for entertainment each day of our childhood.* Landis straightened his posture and strode toward the woman. She dropped to one knee as he approached.

"Prince Landis, this may come as a surprise, but I am your sister Trina."

"It is no surprise. There is no need for this. Get up off the ground. I don't think I'm actually a prince any longer."

Trina stood, but eyed him quizzically. "Markus told me he had informed you we were siblings as well, but how could you know it was I who entered the village?"

"A story for another time," Landis said. "What I don't know is *why* you have come. It must be a matter of urgency based on the froth around your gelding's mouth."

"My farm was burned. Our own people arrived last evening and commandeered my land. They started setting up headquarters right there in my kitchen. I demanded information about the battle they planned for. They shared nothing. I told them they would have to leave, and I drew my sword on their captain; a man called Connell. They began killing my livestock in an attempt to get me to comply. When I still didn't cower before them, they set my barn alight. It has been dry on the plain. As I fled, I watched the fire spread. The roof of my house was ablaze as I crested the horizon."

"That is all very scary and very unfortunate, but why would you ride to a tribal village for help?"

"I'm not here for help, you fool. I'm here to warn you! Any plans I overheard hinted at a land grab. It was to be a joint attack on this village."

"Still, you do not know these people. Why did you come?"

"The sky is vast on the plain. The huge gray dragon is hard to miss when it takes to the sky. I last saw it come this way, with other dragons following behind. Markus told me you and your friends are dragon riders. I knew I'd find you all here."

It started to make more sense to Landis. Markus must have told Trina more than just who her brother was. The woman before him had likely spent a day or two pondering how different her life would have been if she had been raised as a princess. It must have been devastating to hear the woman who birthed her had given her up and allowed her to be raised as a pauper and that Trina had become an ordinary soldier while her brother led a lavish life as a prince. Trina would have been in a foul mood when the army arrived to take her farm. Landis decided his sister's story downplayed how recalcitrant she had been when Captain Connell arrived with his men.

"You said the army was planning a joint attack. Who was to join with the Skalve to do battle?"

"You misunderstand. They were not to join with another army. They were to attack from the east and some king in the west was to flank the village from their own lands."

Realization dawning, Landis looked around at the tribal warriors who had been left out of the battle in the west. None held weapons. None were prepared to fight. Most, like him, were nursing feelings of rejection or helplessness after being told they were not needed for combat.

Landis raised his voice so all in the vicinity could hear. "The gods have afforded us another blessing. By having us stay behind, this village is not defenseless. An army approaches from the east. King Blake's host is merely a distraction. We were all meant to ride out and meet his attack. The Skalven army is to arrive from the east and take your lands with ease. Grab your weapons! We cannot allow that to happen!"

To Landis's surprise, no one questioned him. The warriors dispersed to don the thick leathers most had only recently cast off. They grabbed bows and spears and entered the woodlands on the eastern side of the village. Unlike the Skalven army, the tribal people used the landscape as their greatest weapon. They would not meet the army on the plane, but wait for the soldiers to cross the river instead. The strategy depended on stealth and the ability of the warriors to stay hidden among the trees.

"Hey Ronvost," Landis thought to his dragon. "I have some good news. It looks like we'll be fighting after all. Is Einok in the village, or did he go with Leeta?"

"The shadow dragon is near."

"Tell Einok to go to the temple. When he arrives, he can fill Ornen in. The old man will want to know what's happening. I'll be there shortly. You and I are going to burn some more Skalven soldiers."

Landis was already making his way toward the temple. Word traveled fast throughout the tribe, and once again, everyone was preparing for battle. Warriors passed Landis, heading to take up positions in the tree line along the river. When he arrived at the temple, Ronvost was outside, swishing his tail in anticipation.

"I'll mount you, but we will not take to the sky. You are nearly as terrifying on the ground as you are in the air. I dare say you might have more of an effect if the enemy sees your size when compared to that of a human."

Ronvost huffed, but gave no argument. Instead, he permitted Landis to climb to his back and trudged off in the direction of the river. The dragon did not limp or appear to be experiencing any pain. This was reassuring. Landis did not wish to cause Ronvost discomfort, but more than that, he didn't want the big blue dragon to appear weak in any way. The god's presence needed to be a deterrent on the grandest possible scale.

Landis stopped their progress while still under the cover of the trees. From his perch atop Ronvost, he could see where the line of enemy soldiers stood on the plain, on the far side of the river.

"They are trying to decide how best to cross," thought Ronvost.

Landis laughed. "I think they might be waiting for us to ride out and meet them. Say, how did Ornen take the news?"

"He armed himself with one of the tribesman's wooden pikes. He will go down fighting if those soldiers reach the temple."

"I have no doubt. Have you any news from our dragons on the western front?"

"None, and that concerns me," replied Ronvost. "I should have been there to help end the fight quickly."

"Well, I am glad you remained here. Shall we step out onto the riverbank and give our enemy an eyeful of what they will face?"

Ronvost shifted his weight to comply, but before he made any forward progress, a shout came from farther down river. Landis swung his head toward the sound and saw Skalven soldiers entering the woods. They had crossed the water somewhere south of the village and the battle had already commenced. Some were falling before reaching the tree line, but many made it out of the open area along the river bank to face the warriors within the forest.

Landis swung his head back to the soldiers standing on the other side of the river. As he watched, he saw something in the sky. It came closer, arcing down toward his position after hitting its pinnacle, and Landis saw it was a fireball the size of Ronvost's head. The molten sphere hit the river bank and rolled toward Landis and his dragon. It set small shrubs and dead leaves ablaze as it rolled into the forest, spitting fire as it went.

"Sap," Landis said aloud. "They're launching bundles of burning tree sap. They're going to burn the entire area to ash!"

"Even if we win this battle, there will be no tribal land left for these people to call home," thought Ronvost.

"I know I said you were to remain on the ground, but I think you'll need to fly," Landis said as he slid down to the ground.

"Go. Set their arsenal on fire while it remains on that side of the river. I'm going to help fight those soldiers down river."

Landis heard the snap of his dragon's wings as he ran into the forest toward the village. It wasn't long before he encountered resistance. The fireball had ignited the dried leaves of the forest floor and it was spreading quickly. Landis had to change course several times before he found himself within earshot of the village. The smoke and trees limited his sight, but he caught the glint of armor from an enemy soldier to his left.

Landis hunched down and scouted the area with his eyes. The Skalven soldier was part of a line of men walking several paces apart, methodically blazing a trail toward the village. An arrow seemed to spring from one soldier's head, and he fell where he stood. The soldiers on either side of the dead man moved in closer to reform the line. A warrior leaped from a tree branch, driving a knife into the neck of a Skalven soldier only twenty yards from Landis.

Landis heard the sound of boots shuffling in the leaves behind him and realized the line of soldiers encircled most of the area. Somehow, Landis had slipped through the line before it fully formed and he was on the inside of their closing ring. He stood and ran toward the village. When he burst out of the trees, the first thing he saw was Trina atop her horse. She was forming the women of the village in a circle around the huts facing the trees. Every woman was armed with a bow or a spear. This was the village's last line of defense.

The first of the enemy broke through the tree line a moment later. One of the tribal women released her bowstring, and the soldier fell with an arrow through his chest. Similar acts played out around the edge of the village. The Skalven soldiers carried their swords held high as they met the villagers. Most never had the chance to use them, as they were not able to get close enough to their targets. Many of the enemy wavered in their resolve to enter the openness of the village proper as they realized their swords were useless against the tribeswomen firing arrows to kill at a distance.

Landis watched as the warriors from the woods began to take down enemy soldiers where they stood at the edge of the forest. There was no bugle call or command from a superior, but the enemy soldiers moved all at once. They charged toward the village defenders and the tribal people began to fall in great numbers.

Landis's skill with a sword was unmatched by these common soldiers. He cut down every Skalve he could reach. Likewise, a woman holding a bow was outmatched by any soldier, and it wasn't long before Landis knew the village was lost. Landis pulled his sword from where it had stuck in the breastplate of a downed Skalve and stalked toward his next target.

A roar came from the sky, and the sun disappeared from sight. Landis looked up, expecting to see Ronvost, or even Leeta if the other dragons had returned from fighting in the west. The dragon swooping down from the sky was bright red. On its back was a rider with mottled skin. At first, Landis thought it was Meara, but as the dragon neared the ground, he saw the rider was a man. The rider locked his golden eyes with Landis as the dragon grabbed two Skalven soldiers from the throng and carried them into the sky. The red god crested the treetops, then dropped the soldiers to their death and turned around for another pass.

CHAPTER 36: MEARA

*M*eara held tight to Dabwey's back as the purple dragon came around for another pass at King Blake's host. Leeta had led the initial dragon attack. Saldo, and Dabwey had flanked the giant gray dragon as they swept in and each left a swath of charred bodies as they passed over Blake's army. On the return pass, more enemy soldiers burned.

When Dabwey faced the hoard of soldiers in black and gold again, she hesitated. Instead of diving at the center, she cut a diagonal path toward the right side of the enemy line. Leeta went up the middle again. Saldo was only just completing her turn to make another pass. Dabwey closed her jaws and cut off the stream of fire. As the dragon banked, Meara turned her head to see the approaches the other dragons chose.

"Let's run our next pass from here to the host's right flank," Meara said to Dabwey.

As the dragon dipped her head to dive, Meara saw Leeta's flight falter. The dragon roared, and Dabwey pulled up reflexively to allow for time to assess the situation. She and Meara watched as Leeta turned and flew away from the army, landing about a half mile farther west.

Meara searched the ground with her eyes, focusing on the rear portion of King Blake's host. There was a cluster of soldiers in the center that drew her attention. Dabwey, sensing the area of Meara's focus, flew toward the rear of the army to afford the pair a better view. Ten soldiers were frantically reloading a giant crossbow. The weapon was mounted on the back of a small cart.

Bow teams drilled endlessly to master the skills needed to re-load and fire a dragonbow with speed and efficiency. The company of soldiers working the weapon at the rear of Blake's army was unpracticed, but enough time had passed so that they were nearly ready to fire again.

"Warn Saldo," Meara told Dabwey. "We need to go check on Leeta and Drake."

Dabwey flew west while Meera searched the ground for the downed dragon. She was frustrated by how difficult it proved to find an enormous scaled beast. Leeta must have seen them in the sky and spoken to Dabwey because the purple dragon changed course and Meara made out Leeta's shape in a copse of trees. Dabwey landed several yards from the area and Meara slid to the ground. She searched the sky, but saw no glint of green. Saldo had continued the assault on her own.

"Did you expect less of her?" Dabwey asked.

Meara ran into the trees. She found Drake on the ground, his leg twisted into an unnatural position. Leeta was chewing at the wooden shaft protruding from her right side.

"Leave it!" Meara said. "If we learned anything from Ronvost's wound, it's that pulling it out will probably cause you to lose a lot of blood."

"She can't fly with it embedded in her side," Drake grunted. "The shaft gets in the way of her wing."

Meara dropped to her knees beside the tribal warrior. She wanted to bend his leg back, even if it was just so she no longer needed to contemplate the wretched look of it, but she knew better.

"You might not have a choice," Drake said. "It's not ideal,

but the look on your face tells me you and I have reached the same conclusion."

"I might do more damage when I straighten it," said Meara.

"You'll have to if you intend to splint it. I'll need a splint if I'm to mount Leeta and return to the village."

"You just told me she can't fly." Meara said.

"She can't fly with the shaft sticking from her side. Patch up my leg as best you can and get it stabilized. I'll mount Leeta, she'll rip out the bolt, and we'll fly for the village."

Meara found two relatively straight branches and broke them from a tree. She broke off each protruding branch from the main shafts. She removed her belt from where it held her tunic at her waist, and Drake removed his own.

"Oh gods," Meara said. "I'm sorry, but this is going to hurt."

She grabbed Drake's leg just below his knee with one hand, and his ankle with her other hand. Meara drew in a deep breath and counted to three in her head. She closed her eyes and pulled with all her strength to straighten the leg. The scream that came from Drake's mouth rattled Meara's bones. She opened her eyes, expecting the warrior to be unconscious, or possibly dead, if the awful scream had been an indicator of his wellbeing. He was sweating and his brow was furrowed in pain, but he was awake.

Meara used the two belts to strap the tree branches on either side of Drake's leg. Leeta lowered her head and gently nudged Drake. The warrior grabbed the horn on the front of her snout and used it to haul himself up onto her head. Leeta raised her head until Drake slid down the back of her neck. The man yelled again and his legs bounced along her scales. He used his arms to slow his descent to her back and seated himself.

Leeta grabbed the shaft of the bolt protruding from her side and wrenched it out. She spit the projectile to the ground and launched into the air. Blood streamed from her side as she made for the village. Meara returned to Dabwey. The purple dragon extended a leg so Meara could mount, but before that could happen, the noise of hooves pounding the ground came from the direction Leeta had just flown. Meara turned to see a line of mounted soldiers, clad in black and gold, charging toward her.

Meara lunged for Dabwey's leg and scrambled to her back. The dragon beat her wings and took flight before she could even seat herself. As they gained height, Meara saw King Blake's foot soldiers following those who were mounted. They were being harried by three dragons and the smallest was Saldo. Dabwey fell in line with the other dragons and commenced to dive at the retreating soldiers. King Blake's army had dropped all semblance of formation and the soldiers were running for their lives.

"These are old gods, Meara. I feel many summers on them," Dabwey thought.

Meara watched the two brown dragons, each many times larger than Saldo, work as a team to force the soldiers closer together. Saldo then swept in to burn the lot of them. The two new arrivals had riders, but neither had attempted to speak to Meara, though that may have been due to the whipping wind and the intensity with which they focused on the fleeing enemy.

One brown dragon had a female rider that spurred great interest from Meara. In her sleeveless skins, it was obvious she had the same skin pattern Meara had been shunned for throughout her life. This was the first time she had ever seen someone who looked like her. The male rider was light-skinned with the same blond hair as the female, but he bore no obvious marring of his complexion.

"I think these three have things under control," said Meara. "We should make our way to the village to be sure Drake and

Leeta made it back."

Dabwey cut an arc through the sky and turned them back toward Galnen. Meara had Dabwey set down at the site where King Blake's host had initially gathered. The smell of scorched skin permeated the air, forcing Meara to cover her mouth and nose. She examined the cart carrying the weapon that took down Leeta. As she suspected, it was a dragon bow, like the ones from the ramparts at castle Blackwell. Meara gasped. It wasn't *like* those dragon bows. It *was* one of those dragon bows.

"Look at the carving on the base," Meara said. "That's the Larsen family crest. We need to get back now! King Blake was only the distraction. The real attack is coming from the east!"

Minutes after taking to the air, Meara saw her fears confirmed. It looked as if half the tribal lands were on fire.

"You were correct, Meara. The village was attacked by Skalve."

"I gathered that. I can see the smoke too, you know."

"No, I have reached Einok through a mental connection. He sits at the temple with Ornen. Balder has joined them there. They fear the village is already lost."

"Go straight to the temple. Maybe we can still be helpful there," Meara replied.

Dabwey navigated the smoke-filled air to land near the temple. It was impossible to get any closer due to fire. It burned in patches, as if torches were thrown into separate areas of the tribal lands surrounding the village. Meara dismounted and kept as low as she could to avoid the smoke that filled the air. There were no flames in this area, but breathing was difficult. She had expected to hear sounds of fighting, but it was eerily quiet.

A burning swath of forest caused Meara and Dabwey to move off of the path they traveled and instead approach the mouth of the cave head-on. The temple entrance came into view just as a contingent of soldiers was stepping inside.

"These are the greedy ones," said Meara. "Instead of fighting, they are here to loot the temple. They are in for a surprise when they discover it has been empty of treasure for years, and run into Balder instead."

"I do wonder what Drake and Kaleen did with the treasures that must have been here," mused Dabwey.

"Seriously?" Meara asked. "I thought you said the fascination dragons have with gold is a myth."

"It is," Dabwey said. "Our fascination with human behavior is another story entirely."

"I think we should just follow them in," said Meara. "Just remember, Ornen and Balder are in there. No fire."

Dabwey strode toward the entrance and Meara followed. Meara heard the clang of swords and switched to a sprint. Halfway through the tunnel, she easily reached around the first soldier she encountered and cut his throat. This caused the Skalve in front of that man to turn. One of them screamed when he caught sight of Dabwey's swaying head above Meara. He turned to run and collided with the man behind him.

Meara ducked and Dabwey lashed out with the talons on her right paw. She caught two soldiers in the motion, pinning them against the rock wall of the cave. Meara heard bones crunch. When Dabwey pulled her front leg back to take another swipe, her talon stuck in the shoulder of one of the dead men. She shook him off in a motion similar to one Meara would have used to get a spider web off of her hand after accidentally touching it.

"That was…unpleasant," Dabwey thought. "Burning them is much cleaner."

"No fire," Meara repeated.

Meara dodged a sword strike. The clang of the metal hitting rock echoed through the cave. She kicked at the soldier's legs while he was off balance and he pitched forward to land in front of Dabwey. She stepped on him.

"You didn't like them stuck to your talons, but you're ok with squishing them between your toes?" Meara asked.

"No. That was even more unpleasant," Dabwey sighed.

The dragon lunged forward with her long neck and grabbed the next soldier. She shook him by thrashing her head and then released him into the wall of the cave and his body fell to the floor. He did not move.

Meara made it to the wide opening at the end of the tunnel and found Balder fighting off two soldiers at once, with a sword in one hand and his axe in the other. Einok was threading through the legs of two other Skalve while they tried fruitlessly to bring their swords down on him. Meara jabbed her knife into the throat of the nearest man and Einok was left with only one soldier to entertain.

Ornen let out a growl as he jabbed his spear forward and tripped a Skalve. The soldier fell forward and landed on top of the old man. Meara rushed forward to drag the writhing figure off of Ornen. The soldier twisted as Meara tugged, and he stared up at her. Their gazes met for an instant before Ornen sat up and drove the point of his spear into the soldier's right eye. The man's struggles ceased.

Meara spun, glancing around and checking for more Skalve. There were none still fighting. The soldier that had been trying to pummel Einok had been put down by Dabwey. She sat picking her teeth with a talon, and only the man's lower half was left on the floor.

"Now *that* is disgusting. You actually ate him? Armor and all?" Meara asked.

"He had no helm, and his breastplate was surprisingly thin. I'm sure it will pass right through me," Dabwey said.

Her dragon's tinkling laughter filled her mind and Meara wondered if Dabwey might be going a little insane from all the bloodshed of late. To Meara, the purple dragon had always seemed to be the most docile of all the new gods, but her conviction on that point was wavering.

Meara sat down beside Ornen. She let her head hang between her bent knees and drew a few deep breaths to slow her heart rate. The fighting seemed to be over, at least in the area of the temple. Also, the group was safe from the fires while they remained in the cave. She was desperate to check on the village, but knew she should take the opportunity for some rest.

"Has anyone heard from Drake or Leeta? The dragon took a bolt before the two brown dragons saved us from Blake's army."

"What brown dragons?" Balder asked. "Where is Saldo?"

"King Blake had a dragon bow from the ramparts of Blackwell Palace mounted to a cart. Leeta was injured badly and when she went down, Drake broke his leg. They flew back here for healing before I realized the entire attack from the west was a distraction organized by the Skalve. Saldo was joined by two enormous dragons as she chased back Blake's troops and Dabwey and I flew here to help defend against the Skalven attack."

"So you don't know where Saldo is?" asked Balder.

"No, but she is with two dragons, each twice her size. I am sure she is safe," said Meara.

"Einok would like you to know the two brown dragons must be old gods. If they are so large, they must have hatched a long time ago."

"Yes," Meara said. "Dabwey relayed a similar thought when we first saw them. It was the riders that intrigued me, though. The woman looked like me."

"Maybe you are sisters," said Balder. "You were adopted after being found on a beach, after all."

Dabwey snorted in Balder's general direction. The former

soldier held up his hands and took an involuntary step backward.

"No, I don't mean our features were similar," said Meara. "She had the same marked skin as me. I need to know where she is from. I don't think she is my sister, but I imagine I must be from the same people."

CHAPTER 37: LANDIS

The red dragon set down beside the fire pit at the village center. It swung its neck like a snake, looking for its next target. The dragon had used no fire. Instead, it had used tooth and claw to dismember and chew through the enemy. Some Skalve, like the first two, were carried into the air and dropped. Each time the dragon did this, the villagers would continue their fight with the soldiers still on the ground.

The tribal warriors in the forest, led by Kaleen, harried and herded the Skalven raiders from the cover of the foliage and into the open area of the village throughout the assault. This had resulted in a seemingly unending stream of enemy combatants entering the village. The red dragon and its rider were the only reason there were still villagers to stand and gawk at the enormity of the god before them.

Landis surveyed the people gathered and awaiting an explanation. With the threat from the Skalve gone, all anyone was interested in was the identity of their saviors. The red dragon stood with its wings tucked, scales shimmering under the light from the dancing flames in the fire pit, but the rider had yet to speak. Trina came to stand beside Landis. Her horse had been killed when a Skalven soldier slashed its neck. Trina hadn't said anything about it, but Landis knew she was hurting. He contemplated putting a hand on her shoulder or squeezing her hand and holding it. This was his sister, after all, but he had only met her hours ago.

Ronvost pushed against Landis's mind. He hadn't heard from the blue dragon since he sent him off, riderless, to destroy the fire-throwing weapons of the Skalve. Anxiously, Landis opened himself to hear what the dragon had to say.

"We are safe. Leeta and I are tended by strangers from a lost time."

"A lost time? One of them is here. Is he truly friendly?"

"They are old gods, Landis. Trust their words. I must rest. We will see each other soon."

The sky, already dark with smoke, darkened further as the village was bathed in shadow. Dual cracks, sounding one after the other, rang out and two brown dragons with mounted riders landed outside of the circle of villagers. The humans opened a path for the gods to join the slightly larger red dragon at the center. The ground moved under Landis's feet as the beasts covered the distance in a few steps. All three riders surveyed the crowd from their places on their dragons' backs.

"My name is Frazeer. I represent an ancient tribe called the Vincule. We are dedicated to the preservation of the gods," said the red dragon's rider.

A few of the tribal people fell to their knees. Slowly, others began to follow the lead of those already showing deference. Landis looked at Trina and shrugged. They joined the others and kneeled on the ground.

"Please rise. The people of the Galnen tribe have risked and lost much in defense of our people already. You need not bow to us. It is us who owe you a debt of gratitude."

The villagers lifted their heads to view the rider as he spoke, but none returned to his or her feet. The rider searched the crowd with his gaze.

"Where is the woman called Awabee?" he asked.

There was movement near the large hut of the healer. Awabee kneeled there with Kaleen and their children. The little girl was nudging her mother in encouragement. Awabee pulled herself to her feet, but did not move forward.

"A special blessing from the gods is gifted to you, Awabee. You have held the teachings of the old ways close to your heart and ensured the people of this tribe remember them. It has not gone unnoticed."

Awabee lowered her head and returned to her knees. Her shoulders shook and Landis thought she might be crying. Kaleen placed a hand on his wife's shoulder.

"We came here to rescue our clansmen and carry them off to our sanctuary. The land of the Galnen has been ravaged, and I fear you will only face worse at the hands of the wasteful invaders. The dedication shown to the gods by this tribe has earned its people an invitation to join us when we depart. We shall remain on your land until our wounded dragons have healed. At that time, you must choose."

The murmuring started before the dragons and riders even took to the air. Talk only paused for a moment to allow the tribes people to watch in awe when the dragons took flight, then continued animatedly. Kaleen sprinted over to Landis.

"What did that mean? Who were those people?"

Landis held his hands before him to force some space between him and Kaleen. He had not processed Frazeer's words and certainly had no additional information to add. He was raised as a Skalve. Landis did not even know the true stories of the old gods, let alone possess insight into the cause for their return or details about their proclaimed sanctuary.

"I need to find Meara," Landis said. "She needs to know about this."

"I'll come with you. I have not seen Drake since he left for battle in the west."

"Drake will not be found with Meara and Dabwey. Ronvost told me Leeta was injured in battle and is under the care of our new…friends."

"Did Ronvost mention Drake?"

"No. He faded into sleep before saying anything but for me to trust these new arrivals."

"Then I am definitely coming with you," Kaleen said. "Ronvost may have communicated with one of the other dragons. Meara might know more than we do."

"Bring Awabee. She is the reason the tribe received an invitation, after all."

"I'm coming too," said Trina. "I just met my brother for the first time. I have no intention of letting him disappear from my sight."

"Fine," said Landis. "They took Ornen to the temple before the attack. We'll probably find Meara there."

The foursome picked their way through the charred remains of the forest that surrounded the village. With some areas still burning, it proved easier to retreat to the river bank with plans to cut back into the trees from there. When they reached the river, however, they took a moment to stare out onto the plain. Just beyond where Landis remembered seeing the Skalven army mass, there was a new encampment. The shapes of massive dragons dominated this one. They were too far for Landis to discern their number or color variations, but there were more gods out on the plain than Landis had already met.

"There's something I never thought I'd see," Trina said. "Even when I first saw the big gray one in the sky near the farm, I never thought I'd be close to it. I certainly didn't expect dragons to be more than predators hunting and eating everything that moved. Each time the sky darkened with the dragon's shadow, I hid inside just in case."

"The gray dragon is called Leeta," said Kaleen. "My brother is her vincule."

"Vincule was the name of the tribe Frazeer mentioned.

Aren't you and your brother Galnen?" asked Trina.

"A vincule is a human who is chosen by a dragon at birth to protect the new god. The pair is able to communicate through telepathy. If the dragon grows large enough, the vincule is often invited to ride upon it. I assume the use of the word vincule stemmed from the tribe name spoken about by Frazeer. If all dragon riders were once from that tribe, it would make sense."

The group turned from the magnificent spectacle in the distance and reentered the forest. Much of the area around the temple was still smoldering as they picked their way forward. When they arrived at the cave entrance, it was evident that the flames had consumed everything right up to that point. Inside the cave mouth, there was nothing but dirt and rock, so the temple had been spared from the fire.

Landis was welcomed into the chamber at the end of the tunnel by a knife pressed to his neck. The wielder stood behind him, but he could tell from the angle of the blade that the would-be assassin was shorter than he was.

"Hello to you too, Meara. I'm happy to find you here protecting the old man," said Landis.

Balder stepped forward from the shadows to rebuke the comment.

"Ornen is not as old as one might think, and he did a fine job protecting himself."

"Ornen is here as well?" Landis asked. He allowed a grin to split his expression.

"Ever the arse, this one," Balder replied through his laughter. "Who is your new friend?"

Balder nodded to Trina. Landis shook his head and stepped up to the former soldier, placing a hand on the big man's shoulder.

"Don't go getting any ideas. Allow me to introduce my sister, Trina."

Balder moved forward and took Trina's hand. To Landis's surprise, the woman allowed the big man to do so. Trina blushed as Balder raised her hand to his lips and kissed it.

"It is a pleasure to meet one such as yourself," said Balder. "May I say that you have lovely shoulder muscles?"

Trina giggled and Landis shook his head. Balder had been teased relentlessly by his unit for his inability to measure up to Trina's strength and abilities as a soldier. Landis should have known Balder would end up finding her attractive.

"Come," said Meara. "Let's all sit. There are stories to be exchanged. I'm guessing it will take some time and we should be comfortable at least, though I have no food to offer."

"After today's events, I have no appetite," Kaleen said. "Have you had word of my brother?"

Ornen answered, "Einok is among the old gods. He sent word about your brother earlier. Drake sustained a terrible injury to his leg and Meara was concerned there might be permanent damage to the limb. Einok refuted the claim. He told me Drake was visited by a healer god and was told he will be fine within a day or two."

The tension in Kaleen's face faded. With all of his family members accounted for, the man no longer looked feral. Ornen continued sharing what he had learned from Einok.

"Saldo has befriended the two brown dragons that helped rescue Leeta and Dabwey. Those gods are called Molt and Balta. They hatched from the same egg and are considered to be some of the rarest creatures ever to walk the land. They are identical in every way, including their refusal to bond with a human. As you might imagine, it is one of the things that has Saldo so smitten with them. It's also a good omen for Balder. According to Meara, the brown dragons both had riders, even though they are unbonded.

"Ronvost sleeps. He sustained no fresh injuries when he

flew to attack the Skalve and their fire launchers, but he was still weak from his prior injury. He collapsed from exhaustion around the time the old gods arrived."

Awabee straightened at the mention of old gods. She had been quiet and seemingly lost in thought since she was recognized publicly for her dedication to the gods.

"I am a believer, yet I find all of this difficult to grasp. All the stories say the gods retreated to the north to save themselves from the invading humans. What I saw today makes it obvious to me that the stories cannot be entirely correct. It only took one god to fight off an army and defend a village. If all of the gods had stayed in this land, they could have rid themselves of the Skalve and all other invaders with ease. There was no need to run."

"Maybe that was the issue," said Meara. "It is possible the gods left so they would not destroy an entire race of people. It could have been an act of mercy, not cowardice."

"That is not a question we will be able to answer among ourselves," said Ornen. "Only the gods can tell us why they left."

"Ornen is correct," said Kaleen. "What we can, and must decide, is if we are going to accept the gods' invitation to travel with them back to their paradise. If they've truly created a haven in the north, we should consider leaving this land."

"This land is the home of our people," said Awabee. "Abandoning it to be destroyed by the invaders is not something I can do happily. I wonder if my future is here, continuing to teach others the way of the old gods. I cannot just give up."

Trina countered by saying, "It seems your gods have given up on this land. Why should it be up to you to try to continue a cause they have forsaken?"

"I'm not sure 'forsaken' is the correct word," said Landis.

"They are here now, and they saved the village."

"They only came to save the hatchlings," Balder weighed in. "If the Skalve had attacked the Galnen and there had been no baby gods in peril, I don't think they would be here at all."

Dabwey snorted and blew a tiny cloud of steam in Balder's direction. The big man took a step away from the purple dragon.

"Of course," he said. "I am very grateful the gods chose to save our scaled friends."

Meara spoke next. "I am happy about that as well, Balder. I'm sure Saldo appreciates their arrival as much as us, and I know Leeta and Ronvost are happy to receive the care of the gods. As for joining them in the north, that was the intention Dabwey and I had from the start. There is nothing left for me here. My village was destroyed and all my people were lost. Quite frankly, I wasn't very happy among most of them even before I discovered the God Stones were actual dragon eggs, and the woman who raised me was swept away by a wave. I will be leaving with the gods."

"By that reasoning, I will be joining you," said Landis. "I am of two different people. One has trouble accepting me, and the other is one I do not wish to be accepted by. I would enjoy a new start among people I have things in common with."

"I have something else to consider," said Balder. "The dragons are welcome with their vincules and the Galnen have been extended a formal invitation, but I am not even sure I am welcome in the north. I am neither a devoted Galnen tribesman, nor a bonded vincule."

"You could stay here with me," said Trina. "I am in a similar situation as you are. It will be hard to part from my brother now that I know I have kin, but I don't think I would be welcome in the north either, for the same reasons you've pointed out for yourself. Landis has a giant blue ride back here any time he wants to see me. If I was meant to have my brother in my life, he will keep in touch. Drake could accompany him to visit with Kaleen if his family stays here, too."

"I'm sorry," said Awabee. "It's just not that easy for me to decide. I envy those of you who have a reason for the choices you've made. I really just don't know what to do."

Ornen spoke at last. "We need to speak to the gods. They said we needed to decide before they left, but they never said we couldn't ask questions. I'm listening to all of you speak and I'm hearing many assumptions. The only thing we know for sure is that the gods will leave soon, and they have said the invaders will destroy this land."

CHAPTER 38: MEARA

They rested on the far bank of the river. Dabwey had acted as a pack mule and ferried Ornen across. The old man was able to walk now, but fording a river was still beyond his capabilities. They had struck out for the old gods' encampment as soon as the sun broke the horizon. Aside from Awabee, each of the group members had a notion of whether they planned to depart when the gods left the area. Still, they all wished to ask questions about the dragon paradise and the reason the gods would not stay and fight.

When Meara stood, she saw movement in the dirt patch to her right. She was careful not to step on Einok as she started walking. The shadow dragon offered one slow blink of his eyes to show his appreciation. He darted into the grass and his scales melted to green. Meara tracked the dragon for a few seconds but lost sight of him. A moment later he appeared on Ornen's shoulder and burrowed down by the old man's neck and into his shirt.

"Meara has the right idea," said Ornen. "It is time we were off."

The bedraggled group started across the plain. Tired of walking, Dabwey took to the sky. Meara watched the purple dragon drop in altitude a moment later to enter the area the old gods had claimed as their own. As Meara approached the encampment at the head of her diminutive troop, she saw a figure leaning on a crutch a distance from the dragon camp's perimeter.

Drake waved his hand high in greeting. When Kaleen noticed, he broke into a run. Hobbled by his injured leg, Drake just continued to wave. Awabee stepped up beside Meara and the two women watched the brothers embrace when Kaleen reached Drake.

"I fear my mind may be decided before we ever offer our questions to the gods. It is as if there were never a rift between them. I can't expect the two of them to part again, can I?"

"As Trina said, there is always the ability to travel. What seems like a great distance on foot can be traversed quickly when one is on the back of a dragon," said Meara.

"Then let's pose our questions to the gods. This indecisiveness that has settled over me is making me anxious," said Awabee.

The women waited for Ornen, helped along by Balder and Landis, to catch up and then the group continued the advance together with Trina a step behind. Drake welcomed them all into the camp when they arrived. Meara saw the two brown dragons at the center of the area. They swung their necks and bobbed their heads as if in animated conversation, though Meara heard no sound from them.

"They are quite the jesters," Drake said. "The one on the left is Molt. He hatched minutes before Balta, and he likes to pretend that makes him superior. All it really does is provide entertainment for the other dragons. They argue like an old married couple."

Drake gave a pointed look at Kaleen. Kaleen, in turn, winked at Awabee. The tribal woman shook her head.

"What of the red dragon?" Landis asked. "The one ridden by Frazeer?"

"Toro is the oldest of the gathered gods," said Drake. "The others look to him for leadership. From what I've determined, he descends directly from Smok, and has a temper to match. He doesn't revel with the others, and even now he has taken refuge, alone atop that distant plateau."

Meara noticed, with some amusement, that Drake pointed to the same location where she had first attempted flight with Dabwey. *Maybe I do have some nice memories of this land.* Meara's chest tightened as she recalled some of the memories from her village she would be happy to leave behind. Another thought occurred to her. It was possible the gods knew who her parents were or how she came to be abandoned on an island beach. She added the question to her mental list.

"Walk straight through to the far side of the camp," Dabwey called into Meara's mind. "I'm with Leeta and Ronvost. They are awake and both of them are happily eating. It would be nice if everyone could gather here so they can take part in the conversation to come."

Meara relayed the request to the others and then walked toward the opposite side of the camp. Landis doubled his stride and soon disappeared from sight in his rush to check on Ronvost. There was no fire burning at the center of the encampment, but it seemed to be a place to congregate. There were more gods gathered than Meara had expected. She tripped and looked up to meet a golden-eyed stare. The canvas tent next to her moved, and she realized it was the body of a dragon when its scales shifted color. The last scales to change were those on the tail that had caused her to stumble. The now black dragon stared at her.

"Excuse me," Meara said. "I didn't see you there."

The shadow dragon turned away from Meara. Apparently accepting her apology, his scales melted back to match the color of the tent. Einok was tiny and slow to grow. In contrast, this dragon was Meara's height at its shoulders. If its rate of growth was similar to that of Einok, Meara imagined the dragon was far older than its small size showed. *What secrets would a shadow dragon of that many summers possess?*

A deep blue dragon, much less vibrant than Ronvost's color, blocked Meara's path to Dabwey. It didn't actively prevent her from moving forward. It was simply very long and sprawled in her path. Its eyes were heavily lidded. It looked old and tired. If Drake had not told her otherwise, Meara would have concluded that this was the eldest among the dragons camped on the plane. She turned to motion to the others that she intended to go around the beast.

"That's Blue," Dabwey said. She is the healer. "As you've guessed, you will need to go around her. She's exhausted and won't be getting up for some time."

Meara passed Dabwey's words on to the others. As she passed by the dragon's head, she paused.

"I appreciate what you've done for my companions," said Meara.

The dragon offered a sluggish blink. It was the only indication Blue had heard Meara speak. Awabee bowed low to the enormous healer as she passed. Balder gave a quick salute, and Ornen dipped his head to show his appreciation. Trina smiled warily; looking like she thought the dragon might rise and decide to eat her at any moment.

When Meara was at last reunited with Dabwey, she found the purple god engaged in the head bobbing antics of dragon conversation with a dark yellow being. Like all the dragons Meara had encountered, this one had gold eyes which made looking at the god's face unnerving. In shadow, it appeared the dragon had no eyes at all because the color was so close to that of the beast's scales. When the light made the dragon's scales shimmer, its eyes appeared shrouded in darkness. Meara decided she liked the dragon better when it appeared to have no eyes. The darkened gold orbs seemed to be able to look right through her.

"Moira is a historian," Dabwey said. "It is to her, you shall pose your questions. Why don't you get comfortable?"

Never taking her eyes from Moira's darkened gaze, Meara sat on the ground near Dabwey's feet and crossed her legs. Trina mimicked her motion, but remained as far from the present dragons as possible. Landis sat near Ronvost already, and Balder helped Ornen to the ground before taking a place at the old man's side. Meara glimpsed Einok as the shadow dragon slithered from Ornen's shirt tail and into the man's lap. A pang of longing overcame Meara for just a second as she realized how similar the act was to the way Dabwey had behaved with her when she was just a hatchling. There would never be another time when Dabwey would sit in Meara's lap.

Kaleen and Awabee helped Drake to sit near Leeta and then joined him. Awabee straightened and looked as if she was about to speak, but the crack of wings cut her off. Saldo alighted behind Balder. The former soldier turned and nodded his head to her in greeting. Whether Saldo had chosen to maintain her line of telepathic communication with him or not, it was plain to Meara that they both still preferred to speak without words when possible.

"Thank you for speaking with us," Awabee said to Moira. "We have some questions for you before making our choice about following you to the north."

Awabee would have continued with the first question as planned, but Moira chose that moment to establish a communication link with the human visitors. It was not as painful as when the newer gods engaged in telepathy, but Meara still felt a pressure from within her forehead before the historian spoke.

"Greetings to you all. I am Moira and I am responsible for chronicling the history of the gods. With this in mind, I would be more comfortable telling you our story than standing before you as if this were an interrogation. Would you be inclined to indulge me?"

Meara knew Awabee had some very specific questions for the gods. The tribal woman felt a weight imposed upon her by the need to decide if she would lead her village to join the gods or remain here to continue preaching their ways to all who might listen. Meara gave the woman a look that implored her to be patient.

"I think I speak for all of us when I say we would enjoy hearing the truthful story of the old gods from the one responsible for keeping the words," Awabee said.

Meara sat back and released a breath she hadn't known she was holding. Surprisingly, Meara saw Trina lean forward. She had not realized Landis's sister held such curiosity about the god's history. Moira saw it, too. The dragon's dark eyes appeared to soften when she took in Trina's anticipation.

"Contradictory stories of our origins are prolific in this land," said Landis. "The whole truth, as told by those who were there from the beginning, would be refreshing."

Meara was impressed Landis was so open to the truth. It was his ancestors who landed on the shores of this land to begin the conflict with the gods all those years ago. Meara hung her head. Landis had also recently discovered he had ancestors whose way of life was completely disrupted when the Skalve landed on those shores. She smiled to herself good-naturedly. It seemed Landis should be very interested in reconciling the truth between the two sides of the story, after all.

"The gods created humans many years before any of your own kind thought to record their story," Moira said. "Your purpose was not your own, and you only knew the will of your makers. Over time, many of the gods formed an attachment to you and even singled out a favorite human to share a special bond. This practice morphed from a novelty to a tradition until the tribal people of this land were mostly left to their own devices, aside from those chosen few who were selected to have their life bound to that of a god."

Meara felt pressure in her chest and she turned her head to catch Dabwey's eyes. She smiled at the purple dragon as a means of silently thanking her for choosing her as worthy. Some of that feeling dissipated as Moira continued.

"The practice became so common that the gods evolved to make that choice involuntarily at the time of hatching. The human closest to the egg at the time of hatching became vincule to the dragon. I know what you are wondering," said Moira. "It was only later that the need for qualifying a vincule's worth became necessary.

"When the invaders came from across the great salt expanse, the gods defended their creations with fervor. These other humans had been culled from the god's original creations and left to travel far on their own. During that time, they nurtured the poor qualities the gods had found displeasing. The favored humans of this land were loving toward others and considerate of the natural world. They implored the gods to have mercy and permit the newcomers to stay and share the land.

"For a short time, the gods shared the lands with their favored humans, as well as the others. They tried to facilitate the invaders' re-assimilation into the peaceful society, but it did not take long to see that the belief system and temperament of the returning humans was too different from the traits the gods desired them to possess. The gods left, but not before setting up a contingency for the future. It was their hope that the tribal people would be able to guide the invaders to a better way of life over time. The gods themselves had no patience for such efforts, but they were willing to revisit the land if the tribes they left behind succeeded."

Dabwey pushed into Meara's mind. "I know you were disappointed when Moira talked of vincule selection being more automatic than based on worth, but I just found out I am nothing more than a contingency plan. Your revered God Stones were just a last ditch effort for an experiment to find a way to help itself succeed."

"We left the stones protected among the tribes," Moira continued. "I don't think any of us expected they would be more than a reminder to the tribes of our past involvement in the making of this land, as you know it. We moved on. We started again. This time, we found a more permanent way to cull the undesirable humans from our tribes. We only returned when we heard the God Stones here were hatching, and even then, there were those of us who felt we should continue to keep our distance. Our majority felt it would be wrong to leave newly hatched gods among the wretched humans who take all they want. The dragons you see here are the gods who were sent to transport the newly hatched to our sanctuary, where there are no humans to destroy what we have built."

Meara had watched her friends straighten as Moira spoke the last part of her story. She felt anger kindling beneath her skin and imagined there were those sitting with her for whom that feeling was even more poignant. It took only seconds for Meara to confirm her suspicions. Balder shot to his feet and started pacing. Moira tilted her head and stopped telling her story.

"I'm sorry," said Balder. "I might be the only one for whom this story is causing rage, but I need you to stop so I can be sure I am not misinterpreting your words. I am hearing that the gods created humans but didn't like some of them. Instead of helping the more troublesome of their pets, they left it up to the well behaved humans to try to fix the others. In the meantime, the gods created another civilization in the north where the bad humans were killed and the good humans passively served the gods as they were intended to do. You are here now to carry your baby gods north to live where your new humans serve them unquestioningly. Is that correct?"

"Well, yes. For the most part," said Moira. "What you didn't let me say was that we did not expect to find any humans here with desirable qualities. We thought the invaders would have overpowered and driven out any worthy of becoming vincule."

"So, again, you will run north and leave so many here to suffer war and death instead of helping to right the wrongs you created?"

"We felt it made more sense to invite you to a place that is already paradise than try to fix a land that is too far gone," said Moira. "I do need to ask a question, though. Why do you harbor the notion that our new home is in the north? I already told you we left this land."

"All stories we have heard are in agreement that the old gods went north when they left this land," said Landis.

"We left the land entirely," said Moira. "We did not travel north or in any other direction. We started from scratch in a place that cannot be reached by the humans here. It is untouched by any of our past mistakes and we have been very careful to keep it that way. It is one of the reasons making the journey here was not condoned by all of my kind."

CHAPTER 39: BALDER

alder's face was hot and sweat dampened his tunic as he struggled to come to terms with the reality of his origins as a species. His people had been formed from the castoffs. They were the bad seeds and unworthy of the gods just because their ancestors had not possessed the qualities that were deemed preferable in the gods' creations.

He sat back down heavily. The former soldier drew in a breath and squeezed it out slowly between pressed lips. Getting worked up was unnecessary. He was angry and displeased with gods that never truly belonged to him anyhow. He was being forced into nothing. There was no reason for him to go to the dragon paradise. He could remain here. His muscles did not relax, and he did not feel any more peace of mind than he had before reprimanding himself. He had loved the prospect of living a peaceful life with Saldo, similar to the way they had been living before finding Landis and Meara.

Looking at Meara, Balder saw concern on her face, but nothing to indicate feelings similar to the outrage he was experiencing. She was from a primitive clan. She probably didn't understand that Moira had all but admitted the gods had made humans to be servants. The girl was probably happy to do their bidding. At least Landis had suitably pinched features on his face. The man was raised as royalty. He knew not to simply bow before these creatures and accept them as his masters. Balder started to formulate the correct words to rally his fellow humans to throw off the chains of their oppressors when the seldom used mental tether to Saldo grew taught.

"When we lived together in the ruins of that village, did you consider yourself my servant? Did you bend to my will because you feared repercussions?"

"No," said Balder. "It was different back then. You didn't know I was created to serve you."

"Ronvost did not know that either, yet he has always treated Landis as if he were his personal servant. Like humans, all dragons have different personalities."

Balder laughed uncomfortably. "Yes. You are much more vicious than most. Even after the others begged off of the attack on Blackwell Palace, you continued the onslaught. You were so intent on destruction that you managed to get yourself captured."

"Have you considered that I am simply more protective than the other dragons? The Skalve posed a threat, and I felt it would be better for them to be gone."

"That sounds a lot like Moira's description of how the gods felt about my ancestors. They didn't like them, so they tossed them out," said Balder.

"And maybe they did that out of love for those they wished to protect, not out of hatred for those that became a menace," said Saldo.

Balder's shoulders lowered, and he unclenched his jaw as he reluctantly accepted Saldo's words. He was forced to admit that the actions of the gods seemed harsh, but they may have been done with good intentions.

"It bothers me to think of myself as a servant. I don't like the idea of living to attend to someone else and having no life of my own," said Balder.

"We all serve someone," said Saldo. "This is the same argument made by people who accept the role of vincule. If I were to choose you to be my vincule, would you decline because you don't want to serve me?"

"It's not the same," said Balder. "I know you and I feel like we are friends of a sort. At least, I feel like our relationship is mutually beneficial."

"I feel you may have reaped more rewards from my presence in your life than I have from knowing you," Saldo said.

Balder was about to allow his anger to redouble when he realized Saldo was making a joke. The subtle way her lips curled was a dragon smile. Balder released a boisterous laugh.

"It's a moot point," he said. "We missed out on our chance at a genuine bond."

"Still, if we could form a bond, would you want to do so?" Saldo pressed.

"I don't see why you're suddenly hung up on this, but yes. I wouldn't mind sharing a life with you. I already feel like I worry about you and want to do what I can to help you stay safe."

Brightness flashed from Saldo, and Balder shut his eyes. He heard the gasps from the others as the light attempted to burn their eyes as well. The tether Saldo had planted in Balder's mind seemed to swell until it felt as if it had embedded itself within Balder's head. He opened his eyes and stared at Saldo in disbelief.

"Interesting," said Moira. "It seems one of our new gods is unwilling to leave her favorite servant behind."

Balder bowed his head. He had clarity on the relationship between the gods and their chosen humans, but he still wasn't willing to admit it aloud. Balder also knew the vincule among them needed no clarification on why a dragon might wish to protect some while ignoring others. It was more like protecting your family than a pet. Considering Moira was a historian, she might have chosen her words better when telling her story.

Kaleen was not bonded, but he had ridden on Leeta's back and Balder assumed Leeta had spoken to him. Trina and Awabee had no relationship with a dragon. He watched the two women closely for any outward indication of their feelings. Awabee spoke first.

"I have spent my life in service to the gods. More recently, I have worked to have other people mind them in their daily lives as well. What kind of hypocrite would I be if I rebuked a personal invitation, directly from those gods, to do so in tranquility? I will leave this land and encourage others from our tribe to do the same. I will tell them they have the choice to stay here and serve the gods from afar or to leave this land and serve them in a land of peace."

Balder switched his gaze to Trina and saw she had tears streaming down her face. She was silent in her apparent misery. She noticed his stare and wiped her cheeks with the back of her hand. He moved closer to the woman. He wanted to ask her what was wrong, but there were so many obvious answers that knew he was considering the wrong question.

"What is it you would like to know from Moira?" Balder prodded her.

Trina lifted her gaze to meet Balder's eyes. She seemed to be drawing strength from him as he watched her expression change from doubt to conviction. She stood and faced Moira.

"I was not invited to your paradise. I have yet to know if I am judged worthy by your kind. Is there even a reason for me to trouble myself over a decision to stay here or to leave this land?"

Moira lowered her long neck so her head almost reached the ground. She then raised it to look Trina in the eyes. The dragon could have spoken solely to Trina, but Moira chose to voice her words to all the present humans.

"I am so very sorry. I had thought you understood and I

should have been sure before beginning my story. Trina, you are Landis's twin and you were both fathered by a tribesman who was devoted to our ways. Chosen by a dragon or not, you are welcome in our paradise."

Trina smiled with relief. Balder felt it flowing from her. His heart was full knowing Moira's words had brought her peace, even if she did not decide to take the gods up on their offer. For the first time in many months, Balder found he had no concerns. He felt a lightness he hadn't known since it was only Saldo and him fending off the elements. He turned to the green dragon and smiled mischievously. As was common between the pair, there were no words needed. Saldo extended her foreleg and Balder mounted with a running start. He seated himself at the base of Saldo's neck and she launched into the sky.

The sun shimmered over the dragon's green scales. The air was crisp, but Balder welcomed the chill, even as his eyes teared. Though it was not his first time on dragon back, it was the first time he had shared a flight with Saldo just for the sake of enjoyment. The feeling in his stomach as she dipped and swirled was exhilarating.

"I hope you don't think this means you can order me around," the dragon said.

"I wouldn't dream of such things, My Lady. Besides, I think we've spent enough time together to know that each will do for the other, in turn. When was it that you decided to make me your vincule? How did you know it would work?"

"I've wished for you to be my bond since we met Dabwey and Meara. I didn't press the issue because it seemed we had missed our opportunity. When I found myself captured by the Skalve due to my persistent nature, I thought I might try to find out if there was a way."

"So you questioned the old gods?" Balder asked.

"No," said Saldo. "I never had the chance. When Moira

told her story, I realized how much the traditions regarding the vincule had changed. I also found it interesting that they were traditions and not laws. I figured choosing a vincule might be possible at any time in a dragon's life and humans had only become accustomed to that choice being made at the onset of a new god's life."

"So, it was another experiment?" Balder asked.

"In a way."

"What if your glowing light had been stronger as an adult and you succeeded in incinerating me?"

"I assure you, I would have mourned your loss for a few hours. After that I would have flown for Blackwell Palace and tried to finish the job."

Balder chuckled, but silenced the sound almost immediately. It was very likely Saldo was not making a joke. The green dragon did not have the same proclivity for lighthearted witticisms as Einok.

"You know me so well," Saldo said. "I think I'm going to enjoy being bonded to you."

Balder stiffened. He hadn't said anything to her.

"Don't tell me you forgot that conversation in the woods the day Dabwey shared the truth of a vincule and his dragon? Once bonded, we are never alone. Your thoughts are no longer safe from me."

Balder made a mental note to speak to Meara and Landis. He needed to ask them if they had mastered blocking their dragons from their thoughts.

"Good luck," said Saldo.

CHAPTER 40: MEARA

*T*hat evening, sixty-two humans stood in the center of Galnen. The smell of charred wood that lingered in the air gave the impression of a recent bonfire now that dark was falling to cover the destruction left by the battle the day before. There was a small fire burning in the oversized pit, casting just enough light to illuminate the area in the center of the innermost huts.

The few villagers who had chosen to stay behind peered from the doorways of homes or hugged loved ones who would be making the trip to the dragon paradise. Awabee had explained to her people that the dragons did not come from a place to the north, but from somewhere so distant that it was unreachable. She ensured the villagers understood that once this choice was made; there would be no opportunity to change it.

The conversation Meara found most amusing was one between Landis and Trina. The siblings had spent several heated minutes deciding if leaving this land meant they were abandoning their mother. Trina had argued that she'd never known the queen as anything more than a bejeweled figurehead that posed on the balcony of Blackwell Palace each time the king made a proclamation. Queen Brynn had abandoned Trina to the slums, and the soldier felt she owed her mother nothing.

Landis had been conflicted. He was still riddled with anger over the betrayal caused by the secrets his mother had kept, but he had been raised in the palace and had been privy to her daily routine. Landis understood now that Brynn was a prisoner in her own marriage. Had she been permitted to follow her heart, she would have lived out her days with both of her children in a tribal village with the man she loved. Trina had eventually won the argument by pointing out that Landis's empathy did not equate to him owing the queen anything. She made her own choices, beginning before Landis and Trina were born and it was not up to Landis to try to right her wrongs.

Meara searched the faces gathered around her for Danya. Awabee had tried to convince the healer to travel with the gods, but Danya was committed to remaining with the tribal people who stayed behind. Meara had sent Dabwey to speak with Danya. Though Meara understood the woman's argument, Meara maintained that someone with such powerful gifts from the gods deserved paradise more than most. It seemed the purple dragon had been unsuccessful in changing Danya's mind, though. Meara saw no sign of the healer in the crowd.

The crack of wings announced the arrival of the first dragon. Meara watched as Toro's red scales caught the light of the fire from the pit. She scanned the sky, curious to see which other dragons would attend this occasion. At first, Meara thought the darkness hid the other gods from view, but after the crowd quieted and no other dragons appeared, she decided the others must have departed already.

Her eyes tracked to Frazeer, and she waited for the vincule to speak. His eyes met hers. His gaze looked almost apologetic, and Meara felt her knees wobble for a heartbeat.

"Are you alright?" Balder asked from beside her, catching her arm.

"Yes," said Meara. "I just felt dizzy for a moment."

Frazeer had not taken his eyes off of her. The man definitely wore an apologetic look on his face. He seemed to be pleading with her from across the sea of people.

"Truthfully," Meara said. "I'm suddenly uncomfortable about this whole thing. Doesn't it look like Frazeer is about to deliver bad news?"

"He does look a bit like he just ate his wife's cooking and doesn't want to tell her it tasted terrible. This could get interesting," said Balder.

"All those years ago, it was another dragon and another vincule standing before a different village. At that time, Tala extended an invitation to all members of the tribe to journey to another land and start over."

Meara's heart swelled when the name of the surrogate mother she had claimed as a child was spoken aloud. The temple carving of the ancient dragon entered Meara's mind, and she wondered if the god still lived in paradise.

"I am honored to offer a similar opportunity to all of you. Our new land is now well established and those here will be joining a thriving community of humans dedicated to the gods. You will know peace," said Frazeer.

The tribe's people began to mummer to each other. For the most part, Meara felt the sentiment was positive, though she caught a few concerned comments. She really wished the dragons and vincules would stop using the word 'serve' when referring to the gods. Everyone understood that was the purpose, but it was still difficult to think of oneself as a servant.

Frazeer continued. "As we did then, a contingency will be left in this land to be enacted in the event the people here can heal themselves enough to be worthy of the gods' presence. Those who remain will be gifted twelve new God Stones. The humans will be entrusted with their protection and the understanding that the stones are to remain behind the wards we provide."

Meara concentrated on Frazeer's words. This was news. She had thought the gods had completely forsaken this land, but leaving God Stones behind meant they thought there was at least an inkling of hope for their failed experiment.

"The keepers of those stones will need to start new populations. If the populations succeed and grow, a vincule child will be sent to be raised among you. That child will be the catalyst for the stones to hatch and we will return again to see what has become of this land. I will admit, the result was disappointing this time. I sent my own daughter as the catalyst and it is why I was chosen to sit here before you."

Frazeer's eyes had found Meara's again. Her skin crawled as realization dawned and she understood why the vincule had seemed apologetic earlier. Frazeer had known his words would hurt her. Landis jostled her from behind.

"I knew it! When he swooped into the village yesterday, I thought he was you at first. The similarity between you and Frazeer was shocking," Landis said.

Meara had known it too. The dragon rider that shared her skin markings had fascinated her. Given more time to think about it, she might have come to the conclusion on her own, but the decision about returning to paradise with the gods had taken over her thought instead. This was her family. This was the tribe she hailed from. Frazeer was the reason she had been left on the beach for Mamma Jade to stumble upon outside of the temple.

Meara barely registered the glowing disc that seemed to materialize from nowhere. Its blueish glow reflected in Frazeer's eyes. The man continued to stare at her as he gave directions to the gathered crowd on passing through the portal into paradise. The sorrow on his face did little to ease the ache and confusion welling within Meara. He had abandoned his own daughter.

Meara sank to her knees. She had never belonged here. Somehow, that made the torment of her childhood less painful.

The other children must have felt her otherworldliness on a subconscious level. Frazeer had put a lot of trust in Meara. She might not have grown into the person she was. There had been the chance she would not have felt the need to care for the God Stone and the temple.

Just as a prickle of pride shined within Meara, she considered all that transpired to put her where she stood. The temple's keeper was the one who discovered Meara. Meara had spent so much time in the temple because she had been friendless. A rogue wave had forced Meara out of the magical boundary with the God Stone. Landis, another vincule, had been there to save her from the wave. With the coincidences piling up in her mind, Meara's emotions moved toward anger. She glared at the man atop Toro. She took a step toward the red dragon, but a welcome voice entered her mind.

"Breathe," said Dabwey. "You're focusing on the negative. I have never known you to brush away all the good as you are doing now."

Meara inhaled and blew the air out slowly through her nose. She was able to take in some of her surroundings again. Most of the tribe members had passed through the portal.

"Better, but I'm still seething," said Meara.

"I can see the regret and sorrow he has. He chose his own child, so no other would need to make that sacrifice. He is a good man, Meara."

"He sacrificed me. He sacrificed my opportunity to grow up with a family who loved me."

"Knowing you as I do, you would have taken that responsibility on for yourself if you had been old enough to make the choice."

"But I didn't get to make that choice," said Meara. "I was forgotten; discarded."

"I doubt that," said Dabwey. "Look at him. I bet he

thought of you every day."

Meara watched the last of the tribe pass through the shimmering disc. Trina and Drake helped Ornen to the portal. Einok skittered between the legs of all three of them. The shadow dragon couldn't contain his excitement.

"Dabwey, how do you feel about going to paradise?"

The purple dragon did not respond immediately. Einok and the three humans passed through the portal. Leeta's hulking form blocked the light from the opening as she followed behind her vincule. Landis turned to look back at Meara just before passing through the portal. He smiled and then followed Ronvost's shimmering scales out of sight.

"I don't want my opinion to color your own thoughts on your choice, but you asked, so I will be honest. This is very important to me. This land is no place for a god. Though there are those among your kind who still revere the land and hold to our ways, most humans would prefer to see us dead. To them, we are a threat. That is not the relationship the gods intended to have with humans. To stay here and ensure my own safety would mean the destruction of any human who stands to hurt me. I do not wish to spend my days killing. I want to live happily with the vincule I've come to love."

"Well, when you put it that way," said Meara.

She took a step toward the portal with Dabwey beside her. Awabee and Kaleen ushered their two children before them as they walked past Toro. Meara heard the little girl's squeal of excitement for just a moment as she was moving from one land to the other. A smile curved Meara's mouth. There was a lot of good that had come from her strategic placement in this land as a catalyst.

"We should do this together," Meara said to Dabwey.

The purple dragon extended her leg and Meara climbed to her back. Dabwey stopped next to Toro on the way to the portal. The red dragon was at least four times Dabwey's size and Meara had to look up into her father's face. She studied him for a moment and she felt her features soften. The resemblance was undeniable.

"We have a lot to speak about," Meara said. "I forgive you and I understand why you left me here, but I do not have to be happy about it."

In a voice barely more than a whisper, Frazeer said, "You are more amazing than I ever could have imagined. We shall talk soon and then often after that."

Meara turned her head toward the blue light and Dabwey moved forward. As they passed through the portal, the skin on Meara's arms twitched and her body grew warm. She closed her eyes against the brightness that greeted her on the other side. The sun warmed her face and there was a scent of a recent rainstorm in the air.

"It's beautiful," Dabwey said.

Meara opened her eyes to a dream. The many shades of green in the grasses and trees were punctuated with pinks, yellows, and blues of flowers Meara did not recognize. She and Dabwey had stepped out onto a rolling plain. Meara turned toward a rumbling sound to see a waterfall cascading from a hilltop about a mile away. Beyond that, the land rose even higher into mountains bare of trees and white with snow. Meara exhaled, finally remembering to breathe.

"Welcome home, Meara." Frazeer said from behind her.

"This is incredible," she said. "Where did all the people go?"

"Head to the right and keep walking. There is a village just inside the trees you see over there. I can't wait to introduce you to your mother."

ACKNOWLEDGMENTS

Thank you, as always, to my supportive family. My husband for giving up his time with me so I can write and edit, my parents for listening to me prattle on about whatever I am currently writing, and my Aunt Jo Ann for being my biggest fan and faithfully reading all of my books as soon as they release.

Thank you to my Period 1, Period 3 and Period 4 from the TZHS class of 2030 for doing chapter critiques for me instead of playing board games that last week of the school year. Special thanks to Audrey K., Olivia Y., and Giuliana H. for such thoughtful reviews and detailed recommendations.

Thank you to my Alphas, Betas, and Arcs. This was the first time I had multiple people reading different parts of the book at the same time. It made my head spin, but I think we got it done.
Thank you to Davida De La Harpe Golden for doing a full read and pulling it all together.

ABOUT THE AUTHOR

Jennifer Abrahamsen is a full-time mathematics educator in Blauvelt, New York. She holds a degree in mathematics, a post-graduate degree in Computer Science, and a second post-graduate degree in literacy. Abrahamsen's dream is to live in a realm where all of her students find wonder and excitement when seeing the intricate mathematical patterns found all around them. Until that realm is discovered, she lives in Port Jervis, New York with her husband, Phil.

When Abrahamsen is not grading papers or planning lessons, she enjoys reading, writing, crochet, embroidery, genealogy, creating chainmaille jewelry, dog obedience training and spending time with her husband, Doberman/Springer Spaniel mix named Bernie, Golden Retriever/Boxer mix named Elske, and cat Stormy.

The Elven Roots Trilogy

Book 1
Finding the Past

Book 2
Preserving the Present

Book 3
Forging the Future

www.ingramcontent.com/pod-product-compliance
Lightning Source LLC
Chambersburg PA
CBHW021532250626
47154CB00006BA/2083